Claire Reichert

Burial in Beirut

This is Orin's book - a novel, but much of their personal life & experiences are told in it. It is really about Kate & Orin

Burial in Beirut

Orin Parker

Writer's Showcase presented by *Writer's Digest*
San Jose New York Lincoln Shanghai

Burial in Beirut

All Rights Reserved © 2000 by Orin D. Parker

No part of this book may be reproduced or transmitted in any form or by any means, graphic, electronic, or mechanical, including photocopying, recording, taping, or by any information storage or retrieval system, without the permission in writing from the publisher.

Published by Writer's Showcase presented by *Writer's Digest* an imprint of iUniverse.com, Inc.

For information address:
iUniverse.com, Inc.
620 North 48th Street
Suite 201
Lincoln, NE 68504-3467
www.iuniverse.com

ISBN: 0-595-00698-1

Printed in the United States of America

To my wife Rita and our five children
whose hometowns are
Baghdad and Beirut

To Clairelyn —
Appreciate your long friendship — I'm lucky to be one of the "Rooms-05". Hope we'll see more of you in future. Friends and family are the real riches of life —

Love always

Orrin (+ Rita)

Burial in Beirut

"There are no graves here.
These mountains and plains are a cradle and a steppingstone.
Whenever you pass by the field where you have laid
your ancestors look well thereupon
and you shall see yourselves and your children
dancing hand in hand."

—Khalil Gibran

Prologue

May, 1975

The morning sun wakens Baghdad, then Damascus. Climbing the steep slopes of the Lebanon mountains, it reaches into the dew-coated fields of the Bekaa Valley. The rays are coaxed over the coastal range, lighting the sleepy villages that slow the freeway's downward rush. No longer a hot desert fireball, the sun sends a gentle diffusion of light through the haphazard mix of business and residential neighborhoods. The earliest rays carefully, almost individually illuminate the confusing patchwork of avenues, streets and hillsides that connect, and divide, the pulsating metropolis. Beirut, Mecca of materialism, the Arab's Paris, Geneva and New York.

As the pre-dawn glow settles on empty streets, soft awaking sounds give way to the hum of the morning's machinery. For Beirut is first and foremost a business city. No one knows this more than the bent old man rising from his simple cot and quietly donning pants and sandals. He crosses the room, focusing for a moment on two small grandsons sleeping on a pallet in the corner. Then quickly he splashes his face with water from a basin and pulls his ragged, faded shirt across bony shoulders.

Unfolding a round of thin mountain bread, he spreads it with thick creamy lebneh, dribbles olive oil across it, sprinkles on tangy spices and tightly rolls it. Mornings are hurry time.

Glad to find a seat on the rickety bus winding its way from the slums of Beirut's "belt of misery" to the marketing center called the Bourj, he eats the sandwich, wondering how he will pay for the boys' schooling next year.

He steps down carefully as the bus lurches to a halt near the Souq Tawil, the Long Market, with its pungent odor of spices, coffees and fresh-baked bread. Hurrying to his cart in the alley, he unlocks the chain and pushes it quickly to the French Market, where he can pick from the less attractive vegetables and fruits kept behind the beautifully symmetrical displays. Stacking tomatos, carrots, onions, leeks, cucumbers, and eggplant, he then arranges bananas, oranges, lemons, apricots, mangoes, peaches and carefully places strawberries at the top. Counting out the lira and piastres to pay for his supply, he then retrieves his box of staples from under the cart and inventories them: small jars of coffee, plastic bags of sugar, pepper and cinnamon and three tins of cooking oil. These, and the small items like matches and paring knives, had caused his customers to call him "Abu Kulshy", Father of Everything.

Pushing the heavy-laden cart, he breathes deeply, inhaling the jasmine scent as he passes the flower market, and ABC, the city's only department store. He turns from the wide avenues of the business area and urges the wheels up the narrow street to Ras Beirut. The coastal promontory where American missionaries a century ago founded a university, Ras Beirut now bubbles with prosperity and international business development. Its discourse is in all languages, its sights in all form of dress and custom.

Straining to maneuver his cart up the hill along the edge of the traffic, Abu Kulshy arrives in the wealthy Hamra neighborhood with its high-rise apartments housing ground-floor shops. Turning onto Sadat Street with cars parked on both sides, he calls to the maids and housewives already on the balconies with baskets tied to long ropes, ready to buy. "Fawakia wa hudrawaat", he calls. "Fruits and vegetables."

Suddenly he feels a rush of air. Then the ear-bursting explosion. Metal car parts flying in every direction. The cart is upended. Tomatoes, mangoes and eggplant fall in a casserole soon covered by a shower of sharp shards of glass from the windows above. Abruptly, the rain of glass and shrapnel ends. It is quiet. His legs pinned under the cart, the old man opens his eyes. A large triangle of plate glass from the window above teeters, catching a gleam of sun. Then it falls, spearing him through the heart. Abu Kulshy's last thought was a worry about his daughter's two young boys.

Shrieks of terror and grief, cries of the wounded and those rushing to the scene fill the length of the street. But the "Father of Everything" is silenced.

Just blocks away, the troubled city awakens, unaware, and begins its new day.

Chapter 1

> "My Lebanon is a temple in which my soul finds haven when she wearies of this civilization that runs on grating wheels."
>
> Khalil Gibran

Marking the Ras Beirut promontory is a lighthouse, its unneeded light still rotating over the small apartment buildings nearby. This area, named Manara for the towering black and white striped structure, is a neighborhood of both foreign and Lebanese families. All friends, the Muslim, Christian and Druze families know and care for each other. The city's news is instantly shared and, more important to Beirutis, the rumors also, which often foretell coming events, sometimes with accuracy and usually with humor.

David Draper stirred and stretched his lean frame in the large bed, pushing the sheet away to enjoy the gentle breeze wafting through the window and out the open veranda door. Had he heard that loud thudding sound or had he dreamed it? The bombings downtown were spreading. He turned to embrace the still-sleeping Lora, but hesitated. It would be a busy exciting day. Better let her sleep. Closing the bathroom door so the whir of his shaver wouldn't disturb her sleep, he quickly shaved and showered, hoping the click and roar of the Butagas water-heater wouldn't awaken her. Quietly he donned socks, loafers and the ever-faithful blue button-down shirt and khaki trousers.

The apartment had never looked lovelier. Bright field flowers and sprays of mimosa were everywhere. Both Lora and David had brought armloads thinking the other might forget. One of Lora's classic arrangements with yellow carnations graced the carved wood octagonal table under the window which framed the blue sky and sparkling sea.

About to leave, he saw Lora down the hallway. "How'd you sleep? Something woke me early." He kissed her, his hand lingering to caress her unbrushed but shiny brown hair. "I'll go pick up some croissants and check the mail."

"Croissants. It's hard to think of anything I'd like more, except maybe another kiss. I'll wake Rob and Dannie. They have a Saturday makeup day at school because of the troubles last week. Don't be gone long." The Troubles. Ominous events were now dominating every aspect of Beirut life. But they can't spoil this happy morning.

Dave usually found some reason to be out early. He enjoyed the feel of Beirut as it opened up the new day. It was only ten minutes to the Post Office. Happily threading his way down steps and then up to Hamra Street, he strode over and around the ever-present breaks in the city's sidewalks and curbs. Thinking about Rich coming home for the summer, he failed to notice the gathering of people at the Sadat Street intersection.

Dodging traffic, he greeted shopkeepers as they hustled to open shutters and display their wares. He eagerly accepted a glass of freshly-squeezed grapefruit juice from his favorite vendor but the tense conversations around him didn't penetrate thoughts centered on Rich's homecoming. The aroma of Hamra's endless varieties of oven-fresh breads with their sharp or sweet spices and the meaty smells from shops preparing the breakfast sandwiches so loved by the Lebanese. A strong temptation, but not today. Breakfast and important plans were waiting at home.

The Post Office was just opening. He ignored the Institute's box, looking instead for Mohammed. Even simple things in Beirut were best accomplished with a personal contact. For the past year the mail service in Beirut, never good, had been a disaster. The letter bombs sent by Israeli agents to Palestinian leaders and offices in Beirut had almost ground to a halt the whole postal process. Now, outbreaks of fighting were preventing postal workers from reporting to work. Mohammed handed him an Ohio University catalog and a packet of Institute newsletters. Nothing he needed or even wanted at this point.

"You heard about the bombing, Mr. David?"

"Yes, but they say its all over now." David smiled.

"Inshallah." God Willing. Mohammed shrugged. These foreigners don't really care, even when its a neighbor.

Sensing an unfriendly tone, David wondered if Mohammed was blaming Americans for the troubles.

Turning onto Sadat Street to pick up the croissants, he rounded the corner and stepped on broken glass. People were scurrying everywhere. Smith's Grocery was a blasted smoking hole with its wares and shelves heaped in disarray through the blackened space. Mrs. Smith, the resourceful Lebanese matriarch whose British husband had died years before, stood amid a gooey sludge and broken bottles reassuring neighbors and insisting that the store would reopen soon. Her oldest son was already working to make that happen.

"Mrs. Smith! I didn't realize. So close and we didn't even hear it. Mohammed at the Post Office asked me about it but I thought he was talking of the bombings in Ashrafiyah."

"No, Mr. Draper, it's here too. We hoped we were safe."

"Oh, Lora will be…we're both so sorry. I hope you have insurance." Her blank look told him probably not. She should change the name of the store, use her Lebanese family name. But everyone knew that her store was totally Lebanese. Anyway, foreign businesses were not being targeted.

Every window of the street's six and seven-story apartments must have broken. He picked his way warily over a six-inch layer of broken glass that had rained down, stopping to commiserate with tenants and business people he knew. Told that Abu Kulshy was killed, David offered help. Maybe he could give some money to the old man's family.

At the end of Sadat and to the right was the bake shop that made the best croissants in Beirut, or possibly the world. The smell of the buttery crusts almost made him forget what he'd seen. The old woman serving him kept repeating "Beirut haram". There was no better summation of the morning: Beirut's awful.

Opening the apartment door, David met an excited Lora. "Oh, David, Smith's was bombed last night. I hope no one was hurt. Everyone heard the blast except us."

"I just saw it, Lora. It was just an hour ago. It must have wakened me. The whole street got it. Broken glass a foot thick. Mrs. Smith was there and so was Farouk, already cleaning up and vowing to open tomorrow. Oh, and Abu Kulshy was killed. You know, the vegetable man?

"Oh, no! Such a gentle man. What's happening to Beirut? I love this place. We've had problems, but now…?"

"It'll be alright, Lora. We've got Rich coming. I wanted him to forget his Law School for the summer but this is not what I had in mind. Well, like Scarlett O'Hara says 'We'll think about it tomorrow.'"

Lora took the croissants. "I'll bring breakfast."

The round table on the veranda was set with a flowered cloth. Faint wafts of jasmine flavored the morning breeze. Spearing a sparkling slice of orange from the plate before him, Dave tried to force the morning's events into the back of his mind. Lora brought a plate of his favorite scrambled eggs, with bits of cheese and green onions and set the basket of gold-crusted croissants before him, accepting the smiling response in his glance.

Lora's caftan-like robe, bought at Woodie's in Washington a decade ago, always looked glamorous to David, its rich silk-like material patterned in some Persian design. The swish of her robe with its hint of the full firm body beneath and the shine of morning in her hair and eyes brought him to his feet. Ignoring the breakfast, he kissed her in a close comfortable embrace that recalled so much to both of them. Their eyes met for a moment of remembered pleasure. Then, both with the same thought: "I hope the plane's on time."

"We should leave by ten. Maybe we can be back before Rob and Dannie are home from school." She sat in the tall butterfly chair which always transformed its occupant into a queen. Lora liked to seat her plainest guest in the chair and claimed that it did something to any woman's confidence to be so seated. She liked the chair and sat somewhat imperiously, her chin held high.

When they'd found the large airy apartment with its uninspiring decor, Lora had decided to make it an informal summery place. It was an easy decision since neither the Drapers nor the Institute could afford the kind of impressive furnishings that graced the luxury homes of their friends. They'd stored their own furniture in the U.S. David wanted to teach his family that "things" weren't important.

Previous directors of the office had left a motley collection of furniture. After a month of painting, draping, slip-covering and adding warm green rugs, the living area was transformed into a large airy white and yellow summer house. Glass-doored walls opened to the large balconies and a profusion of green plants. In the dining room A mirrored Victorian armoire, painted white against pale-blue walls, was framed by towering philodendrons. Lebanese village chests, painted ivory with amber rubbed into the crudely-carved designs accented the living area. The sunshine colors of fabric and paint had covered over the worn condition of the furniture and eliminated the pretension of quality. Even in status-conscious Beirut, guests liked the summer-house feeling of the Drapers' home.

"Will Rich be cross about the party, I wonder? He'll be tired, I know."

"He'll be okay. He knows its something we have to do. Good for him, a chance to meet people. Everything okay? You got that waiter to come and serve drinks?"

"Yes, Phillippe, and he'll help Angela in the kitchen before for a couple of hours. I'm completely organized." and she stifled a yawn. "But I'm worried about Angela. The whole wall of her kitchen is gone now." The fighting in Ain Romaneh, where Angela lived, had been constant since the "bus massacre" in mid-April. A contingent of Palestinian commandos had been stopped in the main square by Christian militiamen. Over twenty had been shot on the spot.

"They've swept their problems under the rug for too long, Lora. The establishment 'warlords' and their religious parties don't know how to share power anymore. Palestinians and all the other Arabs, and Israel too, all fighting their battles in Beirut." He didn't want to share his worry that they were headed into another civil war. Lebanon in 1975 was not prepared for crisis.

The doorbell rang and Inga Moore swept in, blond hair falling loosely about her shoulders and radiant in a crisp green cotton dress which changed her blue eyes to aqua. "Morning. Don't get up, please. I'm just begging some eggs from Angela until mine are delivered. Have to finish a quiche for lunch and go with Allen to Ain Romaneh." Her distinctive German accent and low cello-like voice matched the charm of her wide smile. She and Lora had been instant friends from the moment the Moores had taken the apartment below.

"Ain Romaneh? Angela says they were fighting again last night. Apparently there's been shelling again from the Palestinians in the camp. You sure you ought to go?" David wondered at Allen's willingness to take Inga with him.

"No, really, its alright. Allen's been invited to come. An interview with Pierre Gemayel. He's asked for an investigation of the bus massacre. Says none of his men were involved, that it was a plot against the Phalange. It's a beautiful day. We may drive on up to Broumana to see the children. They're having Sports Day." The Moores' two daughters were at the Quaker school in the mountain town of Broumana. "Allen has to get something filed for the Sunday News Special. What he really wants is a story on the Kata'ib, you know 'Lebanon's Private Militias', but Sheikh Pierre doesn't want anyone to know what an army he has. But you two aren't thinking about Lebanon at all, are you? You're getting the whole family together again. Everything okay for tonight? Need extra ice? Sabah can get it for you." Angela appeared with the eggs. "Thanks for the eggs. See you tonight." Out as quickly as she entered.

David finished the worry that was on his mind. "I wish the Palestinians were less arrogant about their so-called rights in Lebanon. It will be interesting to find out what Gemayel tells Allen. This country can't handle these fights. No effective Army and no respect for government. And now the Palestinians are making trouble.

# # # # # # # #

In Athens, a taxi maneuvers through the traffic crush at Ellenikon Airport and brakes suddenly as it angles into the curb. The door opens and a shapely leg emerges as the driver rushes around to help his passenger. She shoulders a carry-on and reaches back in to retrieve a small square suitcase. As she hurries in she glances at a young man standing at the side of the wide doorway. After she enters, the man gives an unobtrusive wave to a tall dark figure in jeans and a black shirt standing in the taxi pickup area. Shapely, with shiny blonde hair, she wears the blue form-fitting El Al uniform with style. She moves confidently to the unmarked Israeli Airline office door located behind the luggage carousel and next to a small cubicle used to handle baggage problems. Stopping before the door, she steps to the side, looks around, and then leaves the black plastic suitcase with the assortment of unclaimed bags, placing it back against the wall behind an over-large leather case. Then, looking at her watch, she turns, walks past the Israeli security man sitting on the edge of the unused carousel. Ignoring his casual "shalom", she hurries to the Ladies Room at the other end of the baggage area. Edging past a woman applying makeup, she chooses the end stall, closes the door and quickly removes a black plastic bag from her carry-on. She peels off the blonde wig and removes the black shoes. These, with her skirt and jacket, are stuffed into the bag, along with the earrings and her El Al identity card, passport and a wallet containing credit cards, few dollars, drachmae and Israeli shekels. Carefully she removes a pair of taupe walking shoes and matching handbag, then removes a beige and black suit which she quickly dons, adding large gold earrings that glow against her black hair. Using a hand mirror, she applies a darker shade of lipstick and adds more blue to the eye shadow. Finally she combs the dark wavy hair to fall around her ears. Emptying the black carry-on bag of its other contents she deftly turns it inside out to become a piece of beige luggage trimmed with brown cowhide. Replacing her belongings in the bag, she checks her purse for passport, ticket, wallet, Greek and Lebanese money and then, with a final look in the hand mirror, she stands and shoulders the bag, clutching the loose plastic bag so that it is partially hidden by her shoulder carry-on. Listening first, she exits the stall to find no one in the Ladies Room as she leaves. She walks slowly to the check-in area for Middle East Airlines. Stopping to sit on a bench as if checking her bag for the ticket, she places the plastic bag on the adjoining seat. As she does so, the man who observed her arrival approaches and sits two seats away. She rises, takes the carry-on and stands in the check-in line for the flight to Beirut. The young mustached man stands and dons a brown corduroy jacket. Looking carefully around to see if he is being observed, he stoops to pick up his sports bag, also taking the black plastic bag. He walks slowly down the concourse past the TWA waiting area to the Men's Room. Inside, he waits for the only occupant to collect his bags and leave. He carefully removes the bulging liner from the waste-basket and shoves the black bag into the bottom, then replaces the garbage liner on top. He returns to the MEA waiting area where he has checked in earlier. He won't be able to sit with his sister, who will fly first class to make sure they won't be seen together. There must be no slip-up now. Ibrahim would stay behind and make the telephone call for the Front. He and Muna would be in the air before the bomb explodes.

########

David called the taxi, then checked that the bedroom was ready for Rich doubling up with Robbie. Lora gave instructions to Angela about the party and they hurried to meet the taxi below.

Settling comfortably into the almost-new Chevy, they were glad Salman was their driver. He'd helped them understand the intricacies of Beirut family lines and religious identifications. Himself a Druze, Salman's insights often laid bare the complicated mechanisms of the Lebanese personality. A puppy Robbie had been given had ravaged the apartment for a week and then been given to Salman for his family in the village. This had somehow cemented a bond between them, the Drapers always asking after the dog and Salman always describing his growth and behavior in heroic terms.

"Airport again, sir?"

"Yes, but this time it's special, Salman. It's family. Our oldest son. You've met him but may not remember."

"I remember. The tall smiley one. He finish university?

"No, just here for the summer. Salman, what's happening? Can they work this out?"

"No, Mr. Draper, our big men are all foreigners. Gemayel is a Frenchman, Chamoun is an American, Solh is a Syrian, Saeb Salam is probably an Egyptian this week and our Jumblatt must be Hindu again. And Arafat. He's Palestinian, the worst of all. We don't have any real Lebanese leaders.

"Not even the President?"

"Franjieh? He's a Zghortawi. How you say? He's Mafia.

They want him to bring out the Army to stop the shooting from the camps, but he won't. He's afraid we'll find out how weak the Army is, so he'll keep them in hiding."

Not getting a response, Salman turned on the radio to the music of the Lebanese songstress, Fairouz. Suddenly, the song was interrupted for a news bulletin. David translated for Lora but asked Salman to clarify.

"Yes, Mr. David, it looks like the Front has done it again. Bomb at Athens Airport. Two Israeli flight crew and a so-called security man killed. Very bad. We'll get an Israeli air raid from this for sure."

David and Lora muttered their concern. Always some new terrorism around the corner. They sped along the rugged coastline on the "Corniche", the shore highway that led South from downtown hotels past the American University. Passing the Riviera-like suburb of Raouche, perched on the cafe-crowned cliffs of the shoreline, Salman's taxi dodged traffic along the stretches of public beach where Israelis had made a bold commando landing a year earlier to kill off Palestinian leadership. The road climbed again to an area studded with Arab embassies and bordered on the sea-side by beach clubs: St. Tropez, San Simone, San Michel, Riviera, Acapulco.

The taxi turned left onto the airport road at the edge of the city and honked its way through the heavy Saturday traffic leading up to the mountain villages that are the real homes of all Beirutis. Uphill to the roundabout, they passed the garish Kuwait Embassy with its row of yo-yos along the roof that Robbie had identified as hamburgers. Speeding down past the refugee camp, a village of crude shacks nestled under a pleasant canopy of plane trees, they reached the long straightaway that ends at Beirut's International Airport building.

Salman would park and wait with them, the taxi having been hired for the trip. Reasonable taxi rates had early on convinced David that taxis were the only way to go in Beirut. He'd told the children when they'd left the states and sold their cars that they had learned to walk once and now they'd learn again. Watching others driving in the tiny clogged streets with their clutter of parked cars, congestion and reckless drivers had convinced him.

The arrival area was crowded with family gatherings enjoying their togetherness and the anticipation of welcoming loved ones. Dave and Lora enjoyed this reunion spirit. But it was next to impossible to be identified by your passenger through this milling crowd, so they went upstairs to check the Arrivals Board. The MEA flight from Athens was the only flight listed. Must have gotten away before the bombing. So the London flight must have arrived early. Lora pushed out to the balcony where she could look down on the busses as they disgorged their passengers.

David nudged her shoulder to tell her he was behind her and they breathed in the acrid exhaust of the busy airport, trying to locate the plane from London. Anxiously checking two unloading busses they saw the familiar tall figure of Rich jumping out the rear-door of the second, his bags, camera and racket bobbing around him like the wares of a street peddler. Stopping to look, he stretched to full height, making eye contact first with Lora and then with Dave. His wide smile made it a private moment all their own.

"Where's the VIP lounge?" he shouted. Always a laugh, usually built out of sarcasm. With a wave he disappeared under the balcony and into the Arrivals maze and its always-changing procedures. David sought Lora's hand as they hurried through the crowd into the crush of the lobby below where they could watch the progress through passport control and the battle for baggage. Finally, he headed for Customs. They hurried to the exit, counting on the way Beirut customs police always expedited foreigners through the line. But apparently the Athens passengers were coming through first. A beautiful young Arab woman wearing very dark glasses was waved through, attracting Lora's admiring gaze. "Oh, Dave, I've always wanted a beige and black suit just like that."

Then spying Rich's tall form in the line, Lora's eyes began to sparkle with the tears to come. David felt the quickening tug of the heart that always marked homecomings, whether his own or any of the family's. Rich had been gone for three years. They'd only seen him once briefly in London. When he burst through the crowd of welcomers, Dave and Lora clutched him in a long embrace.

Salman appeared to take charge of the luggage, sensitively holding his own greetings. As they walked up the incline, Dave noted the changes in his son. A new firmness and assurance, a relaxation in his stance and movements, a gracefulness and "give" in his manner that marked him, somehow, a gentleman in spite of the jeans, tennis shirt, nylon jacket and tousled medium-length hair. Maybe the more valid part of the picture was that suitbag that he so guardedly carried and carefully lay flat on the luggage in the trunk.

Meeting Salman, Rich gave him all his attention. "The London Times said there were bombings all over Beirut. Anything in our area?"

"Oh, a couple of blocks away last night."

"Salman, let's open up that trunk again. I might get blown up around here. I'm too young to die. Haven't even found me a bird yet." He saw that Salman didn't understand and explained he'd spent two years in England before Law School. "Birds are girls in London."

Laughter and light banter filled the cab as they rode back, catching up on news of family and of friends in London where Rich had rented a Morris-mini and met friends from his mission service there. Lora mentioned the party scheduled for that night, "We couldn't help it. You've met Dr. Knoll. This was the only time he could give us."

"Sure, maybe I'll meet a beautiful girl."

"It'll be a good group", David offered. He didn't like big parties. You usually had to invite the people that your guest knows rather than the ones you know, the important people rather than the enjoyable people. And then you add in all the people who've invited you and there's no room left to have just plain friends or people you want to be with. But tonight all those categories made a guest list of pleasant and provocative people.

"Dannielle and Robbie are having to make up school because of last week's troubles, but they'll be home soon after we get there, so tell us your news, Rich." Lora hung on every word of Rich's stream-of-consciousness reports as Salman hurried the taxi through the coast road traffic to the apartment.

After happy greetings from neighbors who happened to be outside, they climbed to the third floor where the heavy teak door, its Jerusalem tile plaque lettered with "Ahlan wa Sahlan" or "welcome" in Arabic and

"The Drapers" in English. The door was pulled open by a wide-smiling Angela, clucking words of welcome to Richard whom she'd met on his only visit three years previous. Rich enveloped her in a big embrace, lifting her off the floor. Her laughing chatter was mixed with tearful sobs as she joined her emotions with those of the family. Lora's eyes teared up again and David wished he could be as genuine and free in expressing affection as was his son. Angela, with two grown sons of her own that were in Beirut's war zone, expressed that special Arab regard for sons in her lavish attention to Rich. Fourteen-year-old Robbie couldn't quite cope with Angela's coddling, but Rich both wanted and rewarded it.

They moved into the bright living-room while Dave, always the organizer, took the bags to the bedroom.

"The place looks great, Mom." Rich strode across to view the Mediterranean, bordered in lacy green by the top branches of the giant tree dominating the garden of the house below. "Beirut's a fun city. I'm tired of law. Going to have a great time this summer"

"Well, Beirut's certainly a place to forget the law, Rich. I just hope the place doesn't fall apart." Dave stood by Rich looking at the sea view. Lora reached for her son's arm and pulled him over to the sofa. His lanky frame dwarfed its ample dimensions. His feet stretched under the brass tray-table with its bowl of clustered marigolds.

"Don't listen to your father's pessimism. It's going to be a great summer." Lora was determined.

"Is he here yet?" The sentence started in the hall and ended as Dannielle's eyes provided the answer. She swept around to her brother who didn't quite match her speed as he struggled up to give her a big hug and a pat on the rear. "Danny, you have grown up. Dad, just how many boyfriends do you have to deal with these days? I've got a friend…in fact, several friends you'll have to meet." She pulled back to look in his eyes, needing to confirm his approval.

Rob had stood in the doorway, still carrying an armload of books. Not really shy but quiet, patient, sensitive. He waited until everyone else was finished. "Hi, welcome home. I bet you're tired."

"Not too tired to take you on, brother," Rich teased as he grabbed him in a bear hug. Rob wasn't sure whether he was pleased or belittled by the gesture. "Was it a good flight? Did you have a 747 from the States?" Rich told him the technical details of their flight and listened to his account of a ski trip to the Cedars the month before.

The conversation deteriorated into the mini-comments and interruptions that characterized Draper family communication. At the same pace and high-decibel sound level, they moved in to eat the light lunch of stuffed cabbage, salad and fresh crusty bread that Angela brought to the table, family-filled for the first time in three years. Lora was queen again, even without the high wicker chair on the balcony.

Chapter 2

> "Beauty is not a need but an ecstasy. It is not a mouth thirsting nor an empty hand stretched forth, but rather a heart inflamed and a soul enchanted."
>
> Khalil Gibran, "The Prophet"

Mathew Knoll arrived early as David had requested. The consummate academic was dressed in a baggy suit of a fabric too heavy for Beirut. A nattily-attired Rich welcomed him, hoping to seek Dr. Knoll's advice on international law as a specialization. David was fetching Allen Moore who'd asked for time with Knoll.

Mathew Knoll headed the Middle East Center at Stanford and had published several books dealing with Egypt under Nassir. He had studied and taught in Egypt and Tunisia and had spent three years on the staff of AUB immediately after Lebanon's '58 crisis. The book he had written on Lebanon then had predicted the breakdown that was now being faced. In a 1969 study for the Foreign Policy Council on the "Black September" ousting of Palestinian leadership from Jordan, Knoll had predicted that Lebanon would end up with the same Palestinian dilemma.

Dr. Knoll had served ten years on the Institute Board and was now Vice-Chairman. He and David had overseen a dramatic increase in American academic exchanges with Arab universities and organized systems to assist graduate students pursue their studies in the U.S. He'd made many high-level visits in the Arab world with David, helping build the Institute's solid reputation.

When Dave knocked at the Moores downstairs, Allen and Inga both answered with drinks in hand. "We are serving drinks, you know." Dave chided. The Drapers didn't drink but served alcohol at "official" parties.

"You don't mind, do you, Dave? I'd opened this wine and we both felt like wine instead of anything stronger." Inga liked wines and was very particular, so she frequently brought her own.

Climbing the stairs, they entered to meet Dr. Knoll and wave to Lora. Allen started his interview and Inga drew Rich aside. He smiled at the attention of the glamorous Inga. "You're studying Law, aren't you, Richard? What is your specialty?"

"Well, I've been thinking about divorce law", he kidded. "Think of all the interesting women I'd get to meet." His knowing smile made her wonder if he really was only 23, and an ex-missionary, too. He was certainly handsome, assured.

"You do and I just may get a divorce myself." She was taken with his crystal blue eyes. "I'm sure you want to hear what these wise men are going to say about Lebanon, Rich, and I must find your mother. If she's like me, she needs help just at this point. Something always goes wrong ten minutes before a cocktail party. That's Inga's Party Principle." Her flowered gown, split up the side, looked ravishing as she whirled away. Rich wondered if she was really forty. On the veranda Allen's voice seemed impatient.

"So what are the Palestinians' intentions in Lebanon?"

"You can't speak of 'the Palestinians' any more than you can speak of 'the Arabs', Mr. Moore. In fact Palestinians are the Arab World in microcosm. Disunited, some leftist, some rightist, some rich, some poor, some Moslem, some Christian, some independent, some rigidly controlled, some revolutionary, dedicated, disciplined and others completely self-serving. What you want to ask is what are PLO intentions in Lebanon? The Front and other groups can make trouble but they won't have much to do with Palestinian policy or power and I include military power."

The gray-haired scholar was lecturing and Allen didn't want a speech. "Well, what are the PLO's intentions here, then?"

"I'm sure you news people have read their statements: they have their back to the wall. They want a home in Lebanon until they can have their own land back and they want to use that home as a military base. I suspect this is why Mr. Gemayel and Mr. Chamoun want them out. They're willing to give Palestinians a home but not an attack base.

All this was not what Allen sought but it helped him decide that Dr. Knoll would not be the 90-second interview for his evening relay. Not really interested, he tried again: "Do you think the PLO will fight to stay in Lebanon?"

"Yes, the PLO and the other groups, too. What do they have to lose? They're not up against the Jordan Legion here. Right now the Palestinians are the best-trained, best-equipped, and best-motivated military force in Lebanon, I would guess."

"Gemayel's Kata'ib militia would dispute that. If you're right, Dr. Knoll, there's going to be serious trouble. I spent an hour with Pierre Gemayel today. He certainly means business." Allen was disengaging so Rich asked him "What about Lebanon's own problem, the Moslem demands and the "Belt of Misery? Isn't it a battle of the Haves and the Have-Nots?"

"Yeah, Rich, it is. Five percent of the Lebanese control ninety percent of the wealth. Only wage earners pay income tax. The Palestinians aren't the main problem here." Allen had just done a piece surveying Beirut's social problems.

Dr. Knoll agreed. "The Palestinians aren't the main problem. But they may be the reason why the main problem can't be solved."

"Won't the U.S. try to help," Rich asked.

"Afraid not. Charles Malik told me last night that the tragedy of Lebanon this time is that it has no big-power friends. No France, no America to count on as in '58. He thought only Syria might be depended on to help. I was amazed that Syria seemed that acceptable to him. He was thoroughly discouraged."

"Of course he's also thoroughly discredited. He's passe', not a part of the establishment now. Malik's philosophizing is old hat." Allen had no use for what Lebanon's world diplomat might be saying.

"Yes, I know. Everyone sees him as bought by the Americans. But of all the crumbling old politicians that constitute Lebanon's leadership today, he alone speaks the language of statesmanship."

That view, differing so much with Allen's view of Malik, broke up the interview. David came to bring Mathew Knoll to start greeting guests. But Knoll pulled him back away from the door, looking serious.

"David, I've heard of secret arms shipments of the militias. Where are they coming from?"

"Don't know for sure. My secretary saw a middle-of-night shipment at the Palestinian camp near her apartment. Her husband says it included mortars and rockets."

"I was told at the university that Christian forces are receiving major weapons down at the port area in open daylight. They claim their forces could take over the country now. Maybe you should be thinking of leaving."

"No, Mathew, this is Lebanon. They'll work it out. But I know someone who's been selling arms. In fact, he's coming tonight. He's the husband of one of our church members here. He gets his permits from the State Department. Why did Nixon and Kissinger start selling weapons to anyone who'll pay?"

"Balance of payments, David. They want the business and there are countries like Saudi Arabia and Iran that will pay very high prices. Apparently the factions here will, too."

The guests were beginning to arrive but David wanted Knoll to make protests in Washington. "The U.S. shouldn't sell arms here, Mathew. They're not selling to a government. They're helping equip political militias, terrorists, both sides. When you get to Washington, go see Dr.

Kissinger. Talk to Senator Percy." The discussion ended in a flurry of guests at the door.

The gregarious Knoll, raised in Beirut by Missionary-teacher parents, needed no introduction to most of those invited, certainly not to the first contingent that now filled the entry foyer. His best friends in Beirut, the old-guard contingent at the American University, had all arrived at the same time, maybe because they were all so alike in their habits and schedules and thinking. Theirs was an inbred society; conservative, intellectual, simple but purposeful, devoted to the real Lebanon of tribal families rooted in mountain villages. Their chief concerns centered on the ravages of modernization in this land where many of their parents had also served.

Newcomers, unable to break into their closed circle, had pronounced them clique-ish, and they were. Some American business types had dubbed the university "Incest U." The Drapers were not part of their almost ritualized academic-social life, but Dave and Lora had a deep appreciation of and regard for their quiet dedication to the students, their understanding of Middle East mysteries and the purposeful gentility of their lives.

With as much fervor and affection as they could summon, they smothered Knoll with remembered acquaintances and inquiries about mutual friends. Being academics, they also set about correcting his recently published insights.

"So you came to see us before the battle begins." The young Dean of Arts and Sciences embraced his former professor. The Dean's wife, also a professor and intent on discussing the situation, chided her husband "What do you mean 'battle'? For that you need an Army. Using them in Sidon last month was a mistake. It exposed how weak they are." Plainly dressed but attractive, she gave Dr. Knoll a daughterly hug.

"But Lebanon has never tried to defend its southern border."

"Yes, we have Palestinians to defend the south. Of course, its because the Palestinians are there that the border must be defended. Will Dr. Kissinger try to help Lebanon, Dr. Knoll?"

"I'm afraid Lebanon doesn't have anything the big powers need."

"We're worried this time, Mathew." The Dean moved on so others could come in.

Richard dutifully stood to meet the guests but soon tired of the routine. He joined Inga who was talking to a Lebanese couple that had bypassed the university group, hoping to meet Dr. Knoll later.

"Rich, come and meet the Khouris. They're from East Beirut, and you need to hear the other side of this controversy." They shook hands. Hearing he was studying at Berkley, Mr. Khouri asked if he knew his nephew. He didn't. Inga steered into political waters again: "The Khouris don't classify Lebanon as an Arab country."

"Well, I don't say it so much but most of our people say they are Phoenician. We have strong ties to the Lebanese immigration. Lebanon has a 'diaspora' too, you know. We could stage an 'Aliyah' like Israel." He was much too earnest for the captive Richard. "They all blame us for the so-called 'bus massacre' but it was a plot by the Syrians to weaken our demands."

Trying to lighten the conversation, Inga smiled and kidded: "You Lebanese with your conspiracy theories!"

"Well, the journalists always distort things. They say that President Franjieh personally killed 21 people in church."

"I thought that was true."

"Well, he may have killed 21, but not in church. I just don't see why you have to malign the President of the Republic."

Rich gulped and made his excuses. No one looked very interesting so he might as well continue his lessons on Lebanon." An aging AUB professor he'd met earlier had settled in a chair near the fireplace. "Is it true, sir, that the last census in Lebanon was in 1936? The man's hand shook as he took a long drink.

"Yes, that's right. You see, the French insisted at Versailles, after the First World War, that there be a Christian country in the area. So Lebanon's boundaries were drawn to provide a Christian majority and the government was set up to represent the different religious groups."

"But how do they know the Christians are still a majority?"

"Oh, they haven't been a majority for a very long time, son. They know it. Muslims are at least 60% of the population. The Maronite Christian community is probably not much larger than the Palestinian population today. It's changed a lot in twenty years."

"Why doesn't the Parliament just vote for a new census?"

"Oh, the Parliament took leave of its 'census' a long time ago." The old man chuckled at his wit and reached for the now empty glass. Rich signaled Phillippe, the waiter who was dancing through the crowd with his loaded tray. With a new drink in hand, the professor was prepared to continue. Looking around, Rich wondered: Is this as good as it gets?

"When I came to Lebanon it was the Arab world's Statue of Liberty. Now it's their brothel. Arab leaders aren't supporting the Moslems here because they don't want Lebanon to stop being governed by the Christians."

"Why do you say that?"

"Because the concubine must be a non-believer."

Rich politely excused himself. This was a long way from Law School at Berkley.

David edged Dr. Knoll away from his friends to meet the steady flow of Lebanese government, business and education leaders rapidly filling the apartment. The decibel count reached the point where the background music Rich had selected was inaudible.

A number of Lora's "miscellaneous" guests arrived, personal friends, members of their church and neighbors. Dave and Lora had each developed friendships which cut across class, religion and nationality lines; he through work mostly and Lora through an amazing network of involvements that were her special delight and her family's frustration.

An Omani graduate student, a Druze merchant and his lovely but illiterate wife, an aging Iraqi exile with his Greek-American ,wife, a Maronite secretary at the Japanese Embassy, two Jesuits the Drapers met in Baghdad, and a Stanford sophomore in jeans were greeted in quick succession. Others came from the Embassy. The social editor of Beirut's Daily Star arrived and was taking photos.

The Drapers' long-time friends and neighbors, the Hakims, entered. Fuad's eye-creasing smile and commanding voice welcomed Dr. Knoll to Beirut and informed him that he was wrong about the situation in the South. He'd read Knoll's interview with Beirut's leading publisher. Knoll had met Fuad before but was unprepared for this challenge. "Well, of course I'm seeing all this from ten thousand miles away."

Fuad's arm instinctively embraced Knoll's shoulder and he drew his wife close to meet the professor. "It doesn't matter. It's a small thing. We Palestinians must learn to be satisfied with what we can get. You, Dr. Knoll, have always been an honest friend of justice for our people. This is my wife, Nadia. She took a class from you at UCLA."

"No. She would have been only five or six when I taught there." They laughed as she held his hand.

"I think my English was only five, anyway. What can we do for you in Lebanon, Dr. Knoll? We must have you over for lunch. We're just across on the other side of the manara, the lighthouse. Fuad won't rest until he briefs you about the South."

Fuad interrupted: "Yes, but I'm going to make the lunch date secretly from Nadia. If I don't she'll be inviting everyone here to join us and I want you to myself. Dave, you can come." They moved on.

Lora signaled Rich and asked him to check on the drinks. They always hired Phillippe, a quick slender man of sixty whose past must have included ballet lessons from the way he pirouetted, dodged and side-stepped through a crowded party without even a jar to his heavy-laden tray of glasses.

Rich turned to leave but his glance froze on he doorway scene. A striking black-dressed matron swept in. Behind her, framed in the doorway, a girl was poised, waiting to enter. Simply dressed in light-blue silk, her posture proud but relaxed as if she were waiting to perform, she stood perfectly still and for Rich, so did time. His eyes wouldn't leave this radiant loveliness. After what seemed like a full minute, she moved forward to meet Lora. His heart pounded as her eyes met his and momentarily recognized the intensity of his gaze.

"Dear Lora. It is so good to see you again."

"Fawzia, is this beautiful girl your daughter?" Where had she seen her? Was she the one in the beige suit at the airport?

"No, Lora my dear, this is Muna, my niece. She just arrived from London. She promised to come on Monday but she made me wait. Young people have their own priorities. But I have persuaded her to live with me. I insisted she come with me today." Rich nudged Lora. Introduce me, his eyes signaled.

"Richard, I want you to meet my dear friend, Fawzia Masmoudi. And this is her niece, Muna."

He leaned down, extending his hand to the aunt first. "So handsome," she murmured. "Such a tall young man." Her handshake was soft, creamy and damp. He could feel rings on every finger. Turning to take Muna's hand, he felt the smooth firmness and warmth as the girl's palm throbbed against his own. He felt the electricity as he held it tightly, looking at eyes which now pulled away from his.

"You must tell him, Fawzia, about your work on the Jerusalem problem, to bring all three religions together there so that it won't just be a Jewish or Moslem city but a city for all faiths."

"Yes," Rich said, "Yes, I'd like to hear about that." Mrs. Masmoudi began to explain in her soft cultured voice. But he wasn't hearing and realized that he was still clutching Muna's hand. As he released it, she was pushed forward by others and her shoulder brushed against him.

More electricity. "Thanks for making my day. I like my parents' friends but I was beginning to feel a bit out of things."

"You mean the 'generation gap'?" She still hadn't smiled.

"Well, not just age, though I think you and I are almost the only under-thirties here. Everything is so serious. I can see it will take time to realize I'm back where everything's an insoluble problem and disaster is just around the corner." Why was he getting into politics? This wasn't what he wanted to say.

"You'll have to learn not to think about it. Like the Lebanese. We don't want to be a problem to the Americans." There was a defiant glint in her eyes. Eyes that he'd earlier decided were dark brown were now blue…or black, even. But beautiful.

"Let me guide you through this traffic jam to the veranda where we can talk. We might establish a record, the only people here not talking about the crisis."

"Thank you but I should stay with my aunt, I think." Her pronunciation of "aunt" reminded him of her London background. It also seemed, somehow, a sort of put-down. So Rich watched her drift on into the crowd. He tried to find Phillippe as Lora had asked earlier but was unable to match the waiter's quick gyrations. Instead he watched Muna, the soft curve of her near-black hair around the shoulders, the ivory flawlessness of her face, the regal squaring of the shoulders.

Lora noted her son's lingering examination of the girl and smiled. Was she the one at the airport? But no, Fawzia said she flew in from London, not Athens. Sighing, she wished the party was over. She wanted so much to spend the evening with her son and the family.

Seeing his tall son above the party chaos, Dave also noted Rich's intense interest in this striking guest. He was beginning to feel trapped by the party but continued to circulate and play host. Large parties were work. You could never count on joining a good conversation, or even finishing a sentence. He deplored trivial, repetitious cocktail chatter at most parties. Lora would frequently find him alone examining a shelf of books or gazing over a veranda railing. But at his own party, of course, he could not be bored. Again he looked at the tall figure of his son, socializing but with eyes darting over the crowd to find the Palestinian girl who had come with Madame Masmoudi. Once, close enough to hear Rich as he approached the girl and her aunt, he overheard what seemed like a cool exchange.

"I'd like to talk with you. Maybe you could tell me about your aunt's ideas on Jerusalem?" Rich's eyes were almost pleading.

"I know very little of her ideas. Here, you must ask her to tell you," and she left him to a flood of enthusiastic cooing about peace, brotherhood and religious tolerance that marked Madame Masmoudi's description of her hopes for the three religions sharing of the holy city. Rich's look was a mixture of confusion and anger as he watched her disappear into the leafy green of the balcony.

Making the rounds to urge guests in to the buffet, Dave noticed the impatience of Rich as he tried to break away from Fawzia Masmoudi. Lora was presiding over the food and Dave whispered over her shoulder "I thought Rich's summer project was going to be the research job at the Embassy. Now I'm not so sure. He's been trying to talk to that girl all night."

"I've been watching him too. He's smitten. It's understandable. She's lovely. But Nadia just told me she's with the Fedayeen, the Rejection Front. I can't believe it."

"Well, she must have had some kind of training in defensive tactics, the way she's stood off Rich's offensive this evening."

"No, seriously. Nadia said she and her brother were involved in the Rome airport bombing last year. She claims the girl's wanted by Interpol. Probably just a rumor."

Rich had finally broken away from the Jerusalem crusade of Madame Masmoudi and edged his way through the crowd of chatting, eating guests to where Muna sat alone. Her eyes were fixed on the blue-white waves breaking against the rocky shore below. "May I join you now? I've made the Jerusalem pilgrimage with your aunt." She smiled. He realized it was the first time he'd seen her face break from its serious sad cast. Her smile was full and genuine, breathtaking. He sat beside her, racking his brain for something humorous that would hold the quizzical upturn of her lips and brows. "Look, I just want to get to know you."

"Why are Americans so direct?"

"Because we like to know where we stand."

"As an American?"

"Look, I plead guilty to being an American. But I'm a lot of other things too, including an ex-Londoner. Why can't we talk about Hyde Park, Victoria, the tube, the Royal Shakespeare, what?"

"Very well. Let's see if your London is my London. How long were you there?"

"Two wonderful years. And you, were you studying there?"

"I went there with my parents after the '67 war. Yes, I was a student. Language, GCE, then ballet." That was her stance in the doorway, Rich thought, a prima ballerina. "What were you doing in London, attending university?" Her speech was so British but her eyes so eastern.

"Serving as a missionary, converting the heathen Englishmen."

"But they're Christian. Aren't you Christian?"

"Is anybody, really? In my church we try to help people who haven't found answers to their questions or a way to make religion fit their real lives. Lots of blokes like that in London."

"Have you found answers to your questions?..."

"Almost all of them. I'm working on one right now."

"and a way to make your religion fit your life?"

"Oh, yes, indeed. I was the first one I helped. See, in our Church almost every young man spends two years as a missionary. It's great for showing you what's important, what you really need and what you can do without. You even learn to cook sometimes."

"So what is important?"

"Love." She had looked straight at him and now couldn't avert the response of his deep-gazing eyes that stirred her more deeply than if he were looking at all of her. She felt his intense seriousness in pronouncing the one word. She tried hard to break that one word's hold on her mind.

"And, what is it that you really need?"

"Love." Again the strange impact of the word and its implications. It was as if he'd said "you".

"And what can you do without?"

"Right now, all these people and this noise, everybody but you. I have to know more about you, you know. As fellow Londoners we must stick together in this uncivilized place where crude Americans and Arabs plot to change the important institutions of civilization such as High Tea and dressing for dinner. Are your parents still in London?"

"Both are gone now, my father just a year ago." Why did it wrench her so to tell this to a stranger? She mentioned it to other acquaintances without this feeling.

Rich paused, groping for the best way to show the sudden sympathy he felt. "I'm truly sorry. I hope you're reconciled to it." What a stupid comment to make!

"Yes, death becomes more common as life goes on."

Hurrying to change the subject, Rich asked about her ballet and as she described the course, the demanding Russian master and the other dancers, he pictured her in every ballet he'd seen—which was two. Rejecting the dying swan image, he settled on Juliet, then cringed as the final scene played in his memory.

Suddenly, she was laughing, recounting pranks the students had played on the haughty ballet teacher. For a moment she seemed to bridge the distance that her earlier aloofness had paced off between them. He dared to take her hand and wondered why he didn't just kiss her as he'd wanted to do since they'd first made that physical hand contact on meeting. He could wait.

Now her hand sought him, resting lightly on his large hand that capped crossed knees. Electricity. "I did so love London. We had a quaint flat near Marble Arch where father practiced with an old friend in his clinic, until he became ill." Her face clouded. Rich held her hand in both of his and they listened to the buzz of the party. "You're staring, you know."

"I know. I'm trying to solve the mystery of Muna. What's the most important thing in your life?"

"Palestine." It was a whisper, emitted almost as if in pain. The word came as a shock, an intrusion. He wanted to believe he hadn't heard it, to push it back down her throat. He'd lived with the Palestine problem all his life, but it had never affected him. Now it was a threat. Why not ballet, Islam, Women's Lib? His expression signalled the dismay he couldn't put into words.

"Palestine. I know a lot more about it than you'd think, Muna. I was raised in the Middle East and our home was always filled with discussion of The Problem. I've written research papers on it, the British mandate, the Balfour Declaration. We'll have some long discussions."

"There's really nothing to be discussed."

"Why? Because I'm an American? Muna, I've already pleaded guilty. Now I throw myself on the mercy of the court. Educate me. But don't push me out and away."

"You don't understand. It's full-time with me. I don't have any other life now."

"But that's not right. What can you possibly do that has to take all of your time? I want to see you, Muna. You've probably given your share already."

"This isn't a two-year mission., Richard. We know we're not accomplishing much but…oh, its complex. You couldn't possibly understand."

"The word is 'accept' not 'understand'. I understand, all right. Let me help. At least to try to keep you healthy and in good shape for the battle. I prescribe some early morning tennis, lots of long walks in the afternoons and maybe some dancing in the evening. Monday morning we start, okay?"

"I haven't played tennis since London. Look, I shouldn't even be here today. I can't make any promises."

"I can. I promise to see you again. Monday." Rich looked up to see Madame Masmoudi's imposing figure waiting on them, eyes twinkling.

"I've been watching you two and you haven't seen anything but each other for the last half hour. Muna, we must caution this young Draper man about how conservative we are in Beirut. I believe I should have been here chaperoning this tete a tete."

Rich stood, offering his seat, "A purely political discussion, Mrs. Masmoudi. That and tennis. I'm insisting that the least Muna can do for a newly-arrived tourist is to show him where he can play tennis on Monday morning."

"Of course, Muna. You played very well in London. She needs some diversion, some exercise to give her an appetite."

"But I really don't know of any courts. Honestly, you'll have to call me tomorrow. I don't know my schedule."

"She will come, I promise."

Lora came up, placing her arm around Mme. Masmoudi's waist. "And a promise from Fawzia is as good as done. What have you been promising my son, Fawzia?" They moved off together, through the now-deserted dining room into the large living area with its scattering of guests mostly seated now, and into the foyer. "You don't have to leave. I'd hoped you'd join us for a post-mortem with Dr. Knoll. It's my favorite time at a party, when the crowd subsides and you can put your feet up with friends and decide whether or not the world will hold together another day."

"No, Lora, I must visit my cousin Miriam while I'm in your area. She phoned me about the bomb this morning. It was only one street away. And you know where we live. We can't be out too late. The troubles are not over, my dear, and we must all be very careful. I hope you'll tell the children. Now, young man, where is it that you plan to play tennis with my niece?"

"Well, the place I know is right down the hill here. But if there's a court near your place…"

Muna interrupted. "No, it would be better over here, I think. I'll still have to call you to confirm this. Thanks for…understanding, if not accepting. It was a nice evening here in your lovely home." Her eyes surveyed again the light colorful rooms. "Tell your mother I think she's very beautiful. If I can't come on Monday, I'll ring you."

"Ring me anyway. We'll talk. You talk, I'll listen." His smiling eyes went with her down each step. Then, remembering Middle East custom, he hurried to accompany them down the two flights and up the small street to their car. Nothing more was said, but Rich's frequent eye-messages brought smiles again to her face. She drove the aging black Mercedes that was her aunt's. As she adjusted the rear view mirror, their eyes met again. Why was she sad? He watched until the car left the narrow alleyway.

His mind filled with Muna, Rich bounded back up the steps and joined the goodbyes being said. He thought all the guests were gone, but in the living room several were seated with Dr. Knoll, still discussing the political situation. Didn't it ever stop? He circled around through the dining room and found Lora in the kitchen helping put things away and paying the elfin Phillippe. Rob and Dannie were there too, heaping their plates with snacks to take to their rooms. Neither liked parties until they were almost over. Then they'd come and be introduced.

His mother was going to be busy for awhile, so Rich went back with Dannie. He wanted to tell someone about Muna and Dannie was ecstatic that this big handsome brother actually wanted to talk to his high-school sister. She stretched out on her bed while he recounted every detail of his evening. He was always breezy and irreverent about people. Rob, bored but willing to listen, consumed most of the food.

Mathew Knoll, grateful for a chance to relax in a comfortable armchair, watched his hostess as she a tray of pastries and supervised the passing of coffee. "A good party is an achievement, Lora. You know, these cocktail receptions don't wear well on me anymore. I've completely lost the ability to discuss insubstantial things. Simply can't stomach the silly talk you usually get when people are drinking in large groups. But I don't think I heard anything tonight that wasn't sensible or provocative or both."

"That's because no one dares to be other than sensible around Mathew Knoll" Inga sat by the scholar. "Shall I tell you some insubstantial things I heard? Three categories: Maid Trouble, High Prices and Scandals."

"Well, of course, I'll take category three. Here, sit with us, Lora. Make these lazy academics get their own sugar. Now, what about the scandals? Anything really juicy?"

"Not really. We did have a bona-fide lady commando with us tonight, though. So beautiful, sophisticated. Dazzling, really…and so young! And Allen told me that at least three of our guests were armed. One was the Ambassador's bodyguard but two were just packing a rod. How's that for intrigue? You can go back to the university with exciting tales to tell of Beirut."

"He doesn't leave until next week, Inga. He may have much more excitement to report than just that." Fuad sat close by.

"Oh, no you don't, Fuad." Lora interrupted, "We're not going to end this evening in the dumps. We're going to be positive, optimistic."

"And unrealistic." This from Allen, leaving with Inga.

Fuad, preoccupied with the crisis and wanting to continue talking, was pulled away by Nadia to say goodnight. There was some discussion about AUB finances but no one was prepared to freshen the conversation and Dr. Knoll left with the university contingent. Dave didn't try to keep them. He wanted to have some family time. What was the story with Rich and this girl? Was there anything to this story about her being a Rejection Front terrorist?

Guests finally gone, the family sprawled over the floor and furniture like a pride of lions. They were all talked out. So the evening ended almost as abruptly as the party had, with bits of conversation and comment tossed between bedrooms, bathrooms and hall like slow-moving frisbees, some caught and returned, some sailing off unnoticed.

When the others had bedded down, Dave found Rich in pajama bottoms standing on the bedroom veranda. The door was open to Robbie's room. As Rich described his meeting with Muna, Dave's eyes surveyed Rob's room with its sports trophies, posters, scout badges and adventure books. The day's discarded clothes trailing from dresser to closet to bed where young Rob was already asleep. All of this was Rich just a few years ago. Thus the explicit feelings Rich was describing were somehow alien. How can a father respond to his son's breaking away? How could he be happy about Rich and this mysterious young woman?

"She makes me come alive all over, Dad." He looked at his father's smiling response and laughed. "No, not just that. I noticed something for the first time. I really have some feeling here." His large hand spread across the width of his chest. His eyes were now far away, seeking this someone else who had entered his life. David smiled, put his arm around his tall son, and murmured a good-night. Going back to the living room to turn out the lights, he stood watching the moonlit waves wash the shoreline. Pensive, wary, he was not ready to share with Lora his deep apprehsion about Rich's evening.

Chapter 3

> "Love gives naught but itself and takes naught but from itself."
> Khalil Gibran "The Prophet"

When Rich strode out of the building in his tennis whites the vibrant summer sun had already warmed the rain-washed earth. Breathing deeply the clean sea breezes, he turned down the lighthouse lane, noting how many growing things managed to take hold in the cracked streets and walls. Purple oleander, soft white jasmine, bright yellow daisies, scraggly trees and bushes, all fought the city's overlay of buildings and pavement.

The flowers were winning this April battle. The litter, so much a part of Beirut's walkways, seemed to enhance the greenery and its bright blossoms. The worn and crumbling evidences of man's handiwork couldn't compete with the beauty and toughness of nature. A few old houses with arched windows and ornate balconies were almost hidden by luxurious new buildings. The connecting vacant lots were unkempt and littered. He'd heard his mother tell friends in the states that "Beirut is the nicest—and untidiest—place we've ever lived."

Rounding the corner, Rich broke into a run on the steep incline where Bliss Street wound down to the beach road or Corniche. Where do you live? At the far end of Bliss. Good name for a novel. His mind jumped from one thought to another, fending off how he'd handle the morning with Muna. In her call yesterday she'd said yes, she'd come, her brother would bring her. Is she that conservative? Anyway, she's worth it. Can a girl that slinky play good tennis? She'd probably clobber him. How was he going to keep his eye on the ball? He slowed at the sign marking the club entrance. "Renaissance Tennis Club". Only the Arabs would call a tennis club and socialist political party by the same name.

About to turn into the gate, he noticed a Fiat parked further down the street. Two men in dark clothes leaned against it. Looking under the hood was a third man wearing the kaffiyah the way Palestinian fedayeen had come to affect, its edges pulled around so only a small area of face was visible. As he stopped, they saw him and opened the car door. Muna climbed out, a light coat thrown over her shoulders, racket in hand, her face searching for him in a way brought a lump to his throat. She moved toward him and he to her. Behind her, one of the men trailed.

"Tennis, anyone?" After he'd said it, he felt foolish. "Hello, Muna. I'm glad you could come." He stepped forward. "Your brother? Hi, I'm Rick Draper. He extended his hand. A strong grip. Silence.

Her face was strained. "My brother, Munir. Munir Atallah. We're twins, you know." Still the brother didn't speak. She introduced the other man, swarthy with a drooping full moustache and an unfriendly manner. Again a strong hand-grip. Munir broke the silence, his face still dark with disapproval. "My friend Ibrahim."

"Glad to know you. Rick Draper." He often introduced himself as Rick instead of Rich as the family called him. Didn't know why. It never stuck, anyway. "Do you two play tennis? We could have a foursome." It would be just his luck if they got tennis things out of the boot and joined the game. No response. They didn't look like they played anything.

"Not any longer." It was clear Munir had relegated tennis to the unimportant, childish. He looked very like Muna, his features fine with dark pentrating eyes, almost obsidian black. His moustache was trimmed but heavy, his hair black but not shiny. He was lean and wiry. The word that fit him best was intense. Clearly, he didn't like Muna's tennis date. Was it because he didn't want her dating or was it because he was American?

Rich's mind was spinning, trying to put it all together while drinking in Muna's nearness. "Look, Muna, I can bring you home if your brother has something else in the schedule?"

"No, we'll be here." It wasn't an offer. It was a decision.

"Well, I'm sure I'll be knocked out by nine."

"And I'll be exhausted much earlier." She looked lovely. And anxious to get to the courts. Not as much as Rich was.

"Well, we'll see you later then." They turned. He held the gate, smelling a lemony perfume as she brushed past him, and followed down the steep stairs where she finally hunched off the coat to reveal a white-clad figure so symmetrically perfect that Rich couldn't help but comment. "Wow, Muna, what you do for tennis!" The brief tennis dress was like a ballet costume. What a stunning ballerina she'd be. Paying for a court assignment, his eyes were glued to where she stood, lifting her arms to tie back her hair. She looked ready to come leaping across the stage into his arms.

They went to the court, he taking the side facing the sun. They volleyed. She was good, perhaps even very good. Rich got off to a bad start, perhaps because he hadn't played on clay courts since England, possibly because he found it difficult to follow the ball after it left her immediate vicinity. He didn't suggest a game.

She did, though. Soon he was puffing to keep up and aware that he'd have a tough time maintaining a lead. It was important to do so, at least this first time. So he "girded up his loins" as a missionary companion used to say, and zeroed in on his game. After a 6-3 set, they found a table under the clump of trees that shaded the tiny clubhouse and asked for the tall glasses of fresh orange juice that are so available everywhere in Beirut.

"Aaah! I've never played tennis with a ballerina before. That was some dance, Muna. Are you as bushed as I am?"

She laughed. "'Tennis, anyone?' That was so funny. If you only knew Munir and Ibrahim. The perfect comment for the moment. I hope they've seen that you did want to play tennis, at least." She looked up to the road. Rich turned, surprised to see the two and their head-wrapped friend leaning on the wall above, smoking.

"You mean they're waiting for you? I thought they'd come back. Is it really that conservative in Beirut nowadays? You lived in London. Surely you had dates there..."

"Oh, it isn't that. It's...well, they don't think any social life is necessary in our work. Munir didn't want me to come, but Fawzia insisted. She can be very strong sometimes."

"What about you? Didn't you insist" "No. No, I didn't insist. I've given up trying to be part of Beirut life, trying to be all things to all men."

"Why don't you try to be all things to one man for awhile?"

"Oh, Rich, I like you but it's very complicated, very deep and complicated. You'll be here and then go back to your law studies. For us here life is going to be very complicated."

"I know your brother doesn't like me, or maybe doesn't like anyone. What about Ibrahim? Is it him? Is he the one?"

"The one? What do you mean?"

"The one the family has chosen for you."

"Oh, Richard, you've been reading about the Arabs again. No. He's not the one. He's...he's actually the other. In terms of what I want, maybe you could some day be the one. But everyone here wants the other, the war. Don't you see, you're the peaceful settlement and it's not to be. You're....what do Americans say? The copout?"

Rich looked away. "What can I say? Tennis, anyone?" He tried to smile. But it was a shared silence, their thinking much more alike than was apparent. What could he do to hold onto this exquisite but elusive person? Would she at least try to see him again?

"Rich, I really don't feel like another game. I enjoyed it, but I have work. My aunt tells me you have work too, at the American Embassy. I thought you were here on vacation."

"I don't have to be there until ten today. It's my first day. No, got to earn some money. Law school tuition is very high. This is just a research job, probably trying to project how wealthy Lebanon be if everyone paid their taxes, eh?'"

"Or how much wealthier they'd be without the Palestinians?"

"From what I hear, Palestinians created a lot of the wealth that's here now. Well, how about tomorrow? We'll both be in better shape, and we'll outlaw politics. Or is it only me that's tired of insoluble problems?"

"It's your government that makes it insoluble, Rich." She regretted immediately that she'd said it, but it was better that she discourage this impossible new enjoyment she felt with him.

"Guilty as charged. Punishment: a grueling game of tennis."

"I'll call you."

"I'll sit by the phone till you do." They climbed the stairs and joined the somber trio. This time, Rich walked her to the car. He saw the machine-gun on the back seat and noted the bulge that hid Ibrahim's gun holster. Offering a hand to the short driver with the fedai' headdress and shouldered weapon, he said "Sabah il khair". Rich's Arabic was not good, but he'd learned most of the repetitive greetings that lubricated conversation in the Arab world. Surprised, the driver responded "Sabah 'inour" and Rich added the customary "Ahlan wa sahlan".

Muna meanwhile was talking with Munir who seemed to assent to something. She turned with a smile that bore the look of triumph. "I'll come tomorrow. Same time? Thanks." She entered the back seat of the car, her brother picking up the machine gun and sitting beside her. Rich's wave goodbye went unanswered. Walking slowly home, he decided he had little to be encouraged about. Very little to contradict what Fuad Hakim had told him about her fedayeen connection. He hoped it wasn't true. He had to find out. Rounding the corner by the lighthouse, he wondered if he could find out more at the job his Dad had arranged for him with a friend at the Embassy.

########

But the next morning she didn't come. Impatiently, he checked his watch, then to see if there was somehow a back entrance to the Club. The attendant hadn't seen her. After an hour's wait, tossing up balls and breaking their fall with his racquet, he walked back up the hill to the apartment, his senses turned off to that same spring beauty that had put wings to his spirit the day before. Halfway through breakfast, her call came.

She was sorry. Unavoidable. Munir was called away. He wanted to ask what her brother's absence had to do with it. Instead, not believing it would do any good, he proposed lunch at Raouche and was amazed when she immediately accepted. He didn't know a good place to eat but said he'd come and pick her up. No, she would meet him. A restaurant called Nasr, overlooking Pigeon Rock. Two-thirty. The family was disappointed. They'd planned to take Rich to the beach and suggested he call her back and ask her to join them. But he wanted more time alone with her. Or would Munir come too?

In grey slacks and blue shirt, his light hair reflecting copper flashes as the sea-breeze curled it around his face, Rich's tall, impatient stance was easy for Muna to recognize. He noticed the car first, her aunt's ancient Mercedes. But he didn't recognize her at first. Large very-dark glasses and some kind of scarf arrangement imprisoned that beautiful hair. She came to him alone. "Hey. Hi. You're alone today."

His arm lightly circled her shoulder as he passed her through the doorway. Her answering smile, without the support of her masked eyes, didn't say enough. They were shown to one of the tiny tables on a narrow balcony that hangs on the sea-cliff with its spectacular view. The two rock islands hugging the coast were called "Pigeon Rock" for some reason he'd heard but was certainly not interested in today.

The waiter addressed himself to her, assuming this foreigner wouldn't know what to order. Rich interrupted, ordering by name all the preliminary delicacies that make up a proper Lebanese "mezze". Saying they would like to see the fish before ordering the entree, he asked for mineral water and outglared the waiter as he left.

"Now, is this Muna Atallah…or some famous international beauty that looks like her?" He reached over and removed her glasses. "You looked like an Italian movie star behind those shades. Hmm. You still do." She looked out over the sparkling blue of the sea, relaxed in a way he hadn't seen before. His comments darted and skimmed across her consciousness like the seagulls circling and dipping around the rock cliffs.

"Looks too blue and pure from here. I've read that it's so polluted they may not be able to save it. You know, I've never lived here, just visited the family. This is the only place my Dad's worked where I really wanted to live, too. Maybe I'll specialize in maritime law. I was sure your eyes were brown the other night. Today they're blue." She looked at him, steadily returning his probing gaze with a frank open response he couldn't interpret. "Hey, turn on the lights down there." A smile softened her face. "See that gull? Now I know why the Brits call girls 'birds.'"

The waiter brought the food and she scooped the eggplant pate' that the Lebanese call Mutabbel on a piece of thin local bread and offered it to him. It was the most intimate gesture she'd made and it sent a spark through him. Slowly picking at the array of finger foods, they reminisced about favorite places in London; streets and parks, theatres, the tube. "Our dance company always ate spaghetti after performances at a little upstairs place off Shaftsbury."

"Yeah, the best food was certainly not English. That steak and kidney pie never quite made it with me." They agreed that Italian, Chinese and Middle Eastern cafes were best, particularly if you were eating on a budget. The waiter asked about the entree but they decided the spread of "mezze" was all they could handle.

Rich paid the check and persuaded her to walk along the sea. He decided her green slacks and candy-stripe blouse were sleek and stylish. As she donned the large black sunglasses, it struck him. The shades and head scarf were a disguise. She didn't want anyone to recognize her with him. Or maybe even just to recognize her. Was she really wanted by Interpol? No one at the Embassy knew.

People turned to watch them as they wound down the curving Corniche sidewalk. They stopped to watch the Lebanese Army half-heartedly practicing landing from rubber boats at Bain Militaire, the officers' Beach Club. Strolling on past the American University, they sat facing the sea on a bench across from the Embassy where Rich had spent his second day.

She'd been right about his job. It did involve Palestinians: an in-depth survey of the factions taking control in the South. His desk was stacked with press summaries, news clippings and hundreds of Embassy cables, declassified by simply clipping off the top and bottom "Secret" labels so he could work with them. He was going to know all about Lebanese politics and more than he wanted to know about Palestinian involvement.

Except for this one Palestinian. He was learning about the Front but still knew nothing about her involvement. This Front member at my side is now an important part of my life. How important was she in the Front? All his instincts told him to worry. Were the reports of her role in the Rome airport bombing and the hijacking attempt true?

Both silent, they watched the waves break on the seawall. Rich asked what Munir had studied in London. "Architecture. Father had always wanted him to be a doctor, take over his surgery in Jerusalem. But after the war, the '67 war, we went across the Jordan to friends in Amman and then to London. Father wanted Munir to choose something individualistic, so he wouldn't be dependent on other people. Strange, isn't it? Now he's dropped his studies and is only concerned with others. Never anything for himself, always the movement." Rich sensed that she was speaking of herself as well.

"Father and Mother were never happy in London. Munir and I didn't realize how difficult it was for them. Mother was very ill. She died in the winter. 1970. You see, I had a little sister, Alia, who died in the war. She was in hospital to have her tonsils removed. Father performed the operation. They brought her home but the Israeli attack brought many wounded and

Father stayed where he was needed. She hemorrhaged and Mother didn't know what to do. She sent Munir for Father but he was held by the Israelis. We couldn't even bury Alia. Our neighbors did."

"Father escaped to the Jordan forces and sent for us, so we found ourselves down at the river, climbing across the girders of the broken bridge. I didn't want to leave. Mother wanted to go back, too. She loved the sun and the dryness of Palestine. But the Israelis wouldn't allow anyone to return. After almost a month in an awful camp in the Jordan valley, a friend of Father's took us to live with him in Amman. There were many Doctors who came over from the West Bank and there was no work; so Father wrote to his colleague in Britain and we left for London."

"I'll never forget the camp. We couldn't have stayed on for years like the others have. It was the only time I saw my father unshaven, shabby, dirty. He was proud and gentle, certain to the last that we would return. America would make Israel give back the land, like Eisenhower had in 1956. He would sit evenings in our London flat listening to those comforting BBC analysts tell how the Americans were finally going to settle the conflict."

"The last year he couldn't work so he tried to write. But he told me one afternoon...we always had tea together at four before I went to the theater...that one shouldn't write unless what he wrote could help others. He sensed I was becomong active with Munir though I didn't ever discuss politics with him. Whenever Munir commented on the situation, it resulted in a quarrel. He worried about Munir. He wanted us to be loyal, but he told us to be sure we were helping people, not using or misleading them."

"I would like to have met him."

"You know, some of your missionaries did. I remember now. I came home one day and he talked for hours about the two young men from America who'd spent the morning with him. Father was Muslim. Mother a Christian. I suppose we're in a sense both, if anything. Wouldn't that have been strange if you'd been one of the two?"

"I'd have remembered him. No, I didn't ever visit in the Marble Arch area."

"I've told you my whole life's story and I don't know anything about you except that you're reading Law, you play tennis and you're doing some secret work at the American Embassy."

"What makes you say it's secret?"

"Isn't everything secret in that place?" She glanced back across the busy divided highway that separated them from the unimposing apartment building that had served many years as U.S. Embassy in Lebanon.

"Let's walk some more and I'll tell you about my life. Maybe I'm a refugee, too. I haven't lived in the U.S. anymore than you've lived in Palestine. So will you stop holding me personally responsible for everything the U.S. does or doesn't do about the Arab-Israeli dispute? I've always been on your side."

"I'll try, Richard." She removed her dark glasses and looked at him. "If a war comes, you'll be on the other side."

"War? The U.S. isn't going to fight in the Middle East. Listen, the Vietnam disaster is America's last 'duty' war."

"No, Richard, not the last. When Israel needs you, the U.S. will fight for them." The tenseness, the bitterness was there again, the distance. They got up, walking back in silence.

Both noticed the figures coming toward them on the wide walkway. Munir and Ibrahim, their car parked with the gun-toting guard or whatever. Taking in the scene, Rich realized how monitored and watched his whole relationship with Muna was. It made him angry. They exchanged cool greetings, handshakes and Munir mumbled that they'd seen them as they were driving by. He wondered if Muna was going directly to the meeting and shouldn't she join them now so she wouldn't be late. She checked her watch, displayed agitation at having forgotten the time and agreed, turning to explain that she was already late.

"I'll call you then, tonight?" Rich asked.

Munir answered: "Tomorrow would be better. How do you like your job?" Somehow the tone was taunting.

"Routine. Boring. Not very much change from Law School."

"Maybe you can educate them about the Palestinians, how important it is that we help Lebanon protect its southern border."

For a moment, Rich wondered if somehow Munir knew what his Embassy project was. "I'm sure they know much more than I do. Most of the Embassy people I've met are pro-Palestine, you know. The problem is back in Washington."

"We think the problem is that America has the wrong motives. It wants the oil, and it wants to protect its capitalist markets. It will do anything to divide the Arabs and keep them weak." It was the first time Ibrahim had indicated his thinking.

"Maybe. I don't think it's just that. We're a large and complicated country. Have you ever lived in the U.S.?"

"Yes, I studied at New York U. for a year. Then I went to England. I couldn't stand New York."

"I don't blame you. You should have seen more of the country, not just New York. You'd understand us better."

"We understand it. We study it, everything Dr. Kissinger does. We study the U.S. because it is the enemy. Israel and the U.S. They are not separated."

Munir cut in, apparently not wanting a confrontation. "But we know there are Americans who think right. Your father seems to be a friend of Palestine."

"Well, he's agonized over the problem all my life. I can't remember when we weren't involved in it. In the States he's always giving lectures about the Arab-Israeli dispute."

"Tell me, why do Americans persist in calling it the Arab-Israeli dispute? It's a problem of Palestine."

"Aren't Palestinians Arab?"

"Yes, but the Arabs aren't Palestine." This from Muna.

"Then why don't you organize a government-in-exile, like the Algerians did? If you want to consider Palestine as a nation, you should act like one."

"Your friend here, Muna, wants us to think like the Americans," Ibrahim interrupted, "Americans always have simple solutions. But they never work."

"Anyway, I'm with you. I want what you want. I'm not your enemy. I know the Koran says the friend of my enemy is my enemy but I don't support our Israel policy."

Ibrahim continued, "You don't understand. The problem is bigger than Palestine. There has to be a revolution so the people can control the means of production. Until that happens we're all pawns on the capitalist chessboard."

"We can't solve these problems today, eh, Rich? We'll see you again. Keep the Embassy in line, alright?" Munir's face relaxed in a near-smile. But he noticed that there was more than friendship in the way Rich held his sister's hand. They said goodbyes, English and Arabic. Rich walked home, somehow feeling good.

He was glad to find the apartment empty, the family still at the somewhat scruffy San Michel beach-house they shared with two other families. He took a long, leisurely shower, the soft warm stream of water caressing him as he hoped she might some day. Drying his lean, lightly-muscled body, he decided he looked pretty good, as good as he felt. He dressed slowly, almost dozing in his reveries and then, reluctantly, took the briefcase of press reports he'd brought from the Embassy. Caldwell had said he could arrange his own hours and could take published materials to work at home. It was clear, though, he'd have to work a fairly heavy schedule in order to get through the stacks of information before mid-July when his Washington seminar began.

Just as he was beginning to doze over the dialectics of a Naif Hawatmeh statement, the phone rang and the family stormed in from the beach. He held the phone, cupping his other ear. "Are you there?"

Hearing her voice, coupled with the amused reaction he always had to this British telephone greeting, brought a laugh. "No, I'm still down on the Corniche, but if you'll hold, I'll go get me." A pause. She couldn't figure out his convoluted humor. "I thought I was to call you…and not until tomorrow. But you've made my afternoon. I was already calling you, but not by phone. The noise you hear is the family, hot and hungry from the beach, not the Mongols overrunning Baghdad. What's up?"

"I called because I…my aunt wants…" She left the sentence in mid-air and began again. "I wanted to tell you I enjoyed today, but I don't think we can get together. I…my aunt has some things we must get done and I may go to the mountains with some friends. I, well, I thought I should call you."

"Hey, wait a minute, don't plan so far ahead. If we can't get together tomorrow okay, but things will work out for later. You have to go to the mountains?"

"Yes, Richard. There are things we have to do. It's not like your life. It's probably better if we…" Again, she broke off. He could hear her talking, even arguing, with someone, her hand probably over the mouthpiece. He waited. "Richard? I'll telephone you when I can." Her voice was tense, strained. "Richard, Munir….he wants to speak with you." Rich's heart sank. This was going to be the 'Don't bother my sister' routine.

Instead, Munir's voice came on strong and friendly. "Marhaba, Richard. I just wanted to ask a favor, for my aunt. You see, she bought an Arabic-English dictionary for the son of her friend. He works in the American Embassy. She wonders if you would take it to him. It's a gift."

"She could just leave it for him at the front desk. But, sure, I could take it to him." *Strange, but I guess you wouldn't expect that Munir could take it there.*

"What time do you go in the morning? You walk, don't you?"

"Yes, about eight. I'm supposed to be there at eight-thirty." *How did he know I walk to work?*

"Okay, I'll meet you by the AUB gate. You know, across from the beach? I'll be there at eight-fifteen sharp."

Sharp? Oh, well. "Fine, Munir. I'll see you. Is Muna still there?" A long pause. Then the phone was dead. Well, it didn't sound like Munir was a problem. Maybe her aunt was insisting she go to their summer house. Most Beirutis did move up to the mountains in the heat of summer. Rich went back to reading and marking his reports. Lora fixed a light supper. Dannie and Rob went to an early movie and Rich settled down with his parents for what seemed to be a dull and sleepy evening since both Lora and Dave were tired from the surf and sun. Soon after the moviegoers returned, they drifted off to their rooms, Dannie for some homework, the others to read and start the pre-bed routine that is so simple for some and so complex and lengthy for others.

David called them all together for family prayers at about ten-thirty, a custom they had always followed. The children seemed to appreciate it even more as they grew up. Many of Dave's friends seemed uneasy and embarrassed by religion, unable to reach their children in a spiritual context. Dave and Lora were so sure of their own beliefs, so open and independent in expressing them, that each child had developed an individual faith, nurtured but not controlled by family influence.

David and Lora worried about their children't morality, but believed people are intrinsically good and must use their own free agency to work out their destiny. They knew parents could never force a moral or ethical code on children and they only hoped they were providing the basis for a value system that would fit their children's needs. Gibran, the Lebanese philosopher-poet, was right: "Your children are not your children. They come through you but not from you, and though they are with you yet they belong not to you. You may give them love but not your thoughts, for they have their own thoughts. You may house their bodies but not their souls, for their souls dwell in the house of tomorrow, which you cannot visit, not even in your dreams. You may strive to be like them, but seek not to make them like you." Dave always felt a sadness for friends who were not parents. It was far the most exciting and satisfying of life's adventures for him. Certainly the most trying.

Chapter 4

> "And think not that you can direct the course of love, for love, if it finds you worthy, directs your course."
>
> Khalil Gibran, "The Prophet"

A long flight of walled steps leading down to the sea along the AUB campus. Taking them two at a time, Rich stopped and checked his watch. He wanted to keep Munir waiting a little. Overhanging jasmine scented the path leading past the walls of International College. As he rounded the corner of AUB Faculty Apartments to the line of palm trees bordering the sea road, he saw the car, the kaffiyah-wrapped driver and Munir on the sidewalk waiting. No sign of Ibrahim.

"Morning, Munir. Beautiful day, isn't it?"

"It is, yes. This is the gift." Rich took the heavy book, neatly gift-wrapped with a blue-linen envelope taped to it. "Maybe it will fit into your briefcase. You take it to the desk of George Hamoud. He works as a translator. On the fifth floor. If he isn't there, please leave it on his desk. Do you want to write the name? George Hamoud." Rich assured him he could remember. "You will deliver it first thing? Righto. Goodbye then."

"Ma'a Salameh," Rich went on, looking baack to note that they hadn't left yet. Whistling, he strode quickly down the shaded walk, jumping the ever-present breaks in the paving and the occasional trash that was always visible, even in the nicest sections of the city. Passing the army road-block that screened cars and pedestrians approaching the American Embassy since a rocket was exploded in a parked car the summer before, he answered with a wave the smile of a soldier eating a breakfast sandwich.

On the sea side of the road, he noted a figure walking that looked familiar and then realized it was Ibrahim. Probably didn't want to meet the American enemy again, he thought, as Ibrahim reached the place where the Corniche walk abruptly ended. He turned back, probably to join Munir, not looking at Rich.

In the Embassy, he walked up the wide marble stairs, presented the pass they'd given him to the Lebanese receptionist. The Marine guard checked his name, recognized they'd met the day before and asked to see his briefcase. Rich opened it, explaining he was allowed to take work home. "What's the package?"

"A dictionary. A gift." No reply. Rich climbed the stairs to his cubbyhole on the third floor. His desk was covered with additional stacks of reports. Taking the dictionary out, he noted it felt heavy. He'd better deliver it before he started work. Taking the stairs two at a time he reached the fifth floor and asked in an office where George Hamoud sat. He found his way down the corridor that led to the metal-screened partition guarding the communications section. Also the CIA, he'd been told. At the right, just before the barrier, was a small hallway. As directed, he found Hamoud's small office but with no one in it. In the neighboring cubbyhole an older woman said Hamoud was on leave this week, in Damascus. He placed the gift on some papers in the box marked "Incoming", murmured his thanks as he passed the woman's open door again and hurried back downstairs to his work.

After an hour of concentrated work, Rich found himself thinking of the package he'd carried upstairs. Something about it was strange. It had seemed heavier than when Munir had given it to him. How could that be? Dictionaries are always heavy. He went back to his work, but something vaguely stirred his memory. Suddenly it came to him. The gift-wrapped book had been heavier on one end. He'd had to shift it in his hand as he went up the stairs. How could a book be heavier at one end?

Oh, no! Of course, it had to be. It figured. He froze, a deeply-rooted dread choking and pressuring his chest. He stood, grabbed his jacket and went up the stairs three at a time. Walking swiftly down the corridor, he tried to appear businesslike as he turned into the small hallway under the gaze of two Embassy officers talking outside the barred secret area. Opening the door to Hamoud's small office, he stepped to the desk, lifted the parcel, confirming immediately now that it wasn't, couldn't possibly be only a book. Flashing through his brain were pictures he'd seen of hollowed-out volumes with intricate bomb mechanisms inside. His pulse beat rapidly as he removed his jacket, picked up the "gift" and covered it in his hand. He must get it out of the Embassy quickly. He hurried down the stairs.

Rich's mind was racing, trying to fathom Munir's thinking, the group's intentions. Was Muna in on this? Did they want to kill George Hamoud? Or had they known he'd be in Damascus? They obviously wanted to bomb the Embassy, or the Communications and CIA section. How powerful could a bomb that small be? Could it possibly be just a joke, some kind of present hidden inside the book. Yeah, a joke, alright…but not on Hamoud. On Rich. He was being set up. They'd counted on the Marine guard finding the bomb. It was a test. Would he expose Muna? Either way, it would get him out of the way. But Muna must certainly be in on it. She'd been there when Munir had asked him. Did she really not care? He could be killed.

Perspiring, he descended the last flight of stairs. The Marine looked up, surprised. "Forgot something. Be right back." He managed a grin. Out of the Embassy, he turned up the road, then crossed over after the roadblock to the seaside Corniche walkway. He should turn it in to Security, but all the quick scenarios passing through his mind would endanger Muna. He couldn't do that, not until he knew.

Where could he get rid of it? He walked close to the railing. The Corniche was almost deserted. Looking over where water came up to the sea wall, he gauged the depth to be at least eight to ten feet. Looking around him, he made the sudden decision. Leaning over the rail, Rich dropped the package into the water a dozen feet below. It sank rapidly to the bottom. But the water was clear. The "gift" was easily visible.

To avoid the attention of casual strollers, he walked on, thinking hard. What should he do now? Should he go back and tell the Embassy? Who? Caldwell, his father's friend? The Security Officer, whoever that might be? He stopped. What if some kid swimming or fishing went in after the package? Hurrying back, he peered down where he'd dropped it into the deep pool. He could barely see it. Absorbing the water it had taken the color of the bottom. A wash of garbage, orange halves thrown over by the juice-seller, was being nudged by small waves onto the surface. You could always count on Beirut beach litter. If it wasn't there now, it soon would be. Not thinking about the possible explosive that lay below, he gazed down, angry and deeply hurt.

Was he that unimportant to her, that he could be used, his life endangered? After yesterday's long talks, how could she be so cold, calculating? Anger welled up in him as he thought of how easily he could be killed in this kind of caper. She must think him a naive fool, someone that could just be used and then blown up. The stirrings of a breeze calmed him somewhat, bringing some focus to his unsolved predicament. He turned to walk again. He would see her. She would look him in the eyes and answer his questions. Then he'd know. Tense and exhausted, he started to walk again, his step faltering. Where should he go? Should he report it? If he did, everybody would know he was just a naive student. Maybe it wasn't a bomb, after all. Maybe just a book, hollowed out for a bottle of liquor.

But intuition told him he'd been used by Munir and that the package had some kind of device in it. Too many other things now fell into place; Muna's strange phone call, the over-specific instructions, the elaborate wrapping, the surveillance by Ibrahim as Rich entered the Embassy. Were they still watching him? When was the bomb set to go off? Would it still explode immersed in water? The radical groups had targeted the Embassy in the past. But this must be just to get him in trouble, to frighten him away from Muna. Other scenarios raced through his mind. Were they hoping to recruit him? No, they clearly wanted him to be exposed, blamed.

Quickening his pace, he now knew where he was headed. Crossing the avenue, he turned up the side street and hurried to the long curving flight of steps he'd so happily skipped down an hour before. Taking them three at a time, he quickly walked to the Bliss Street building that housed the Institute's offices.

########

Looking up, David knew something was wrong. "Rich, what is it? Is it the family?"

"Dad, I've got to talk to you. Can I close the door?"

David got up, took his son's arm and they sat, both bewildered in different ways. Rich rose, crossed to the window, trying to sort out how or where to begin. "Big trouble, Dad." In short, quick sentences, he finished his report of the morning's events. "So I need advice, Dad. What should I do? I mean about the Embassy. I know what I'm about to do about Muna."

Dave had listened, incredulous at what Rich told him. "Are you sure she was part of this, Rich? Didn't you say it was her brother that asked you to take the package?"

"But she was right there, Dad. She turned the phone over to him to ask me. But, Dad, the problem is that package down there in the water. What if it blows up and hurts somebody? Shall I tell the Embassy, get the Beirut police or what?"

Thinking of the possibilities, the older man saw larger dimensions to the problem. Complications and sub-problems flooded Dave's thinking. Rich was right. If the package was a live bomb, the first consideration was what damage it might do. "I'm not sure but I think you've pretty well taken care of it, Rich. I know something of explosives. It's probably no more powerful than a grenade. Have you ever seen them fishing with grenades off the coast here? It's a shame, but if the explosion takes place in that much water it'll probably only hurt the fish." He grabbed his jacket from a closet hook. "Let's go take a look. We can talk along the way."

During the fast ten-minutes walking to the Corniche, David had decided what his advice would be, but didn't want to give it until he could confirm that the bomb…if, indeed it was one, wasn't a danger to passers-by; As they approached the place, Rich groaned "Oh, no, I left my jacket on the railing, see? I didn't miss it all the way up to your office. I really marked the spot."

Considering the implications if the bomb had exploded with Richard's jacket nearby bought a shudder and then a surge of gratitude. So far so good. Why hadn't someone taken the jacket?

They looked down into the now-cluttered surface. Rich had to locate the package for his father under the floating orange rinds, plastic cups and other detritus. The water was a couple of meters deep and the surface was at least twelve feet below the walkway. Dave calculated that any explosion would be straight up. Only if someone was leaning over the railing above would they be harmed. If the bomb was still operable in the sea-water, and if it really was a bomb. Dave pulled Rich back away and they walked on down the Corniche toward the Embassy, sitting on the bench where Rich and Muna had sat the day before.

"Rich, this is what I think. It's your decision, of course, but if it were me I'd want to make as sure as possible that the bomb didn't' hurt anyone. So let's consider when it was supposed to go off. I personally don't think they'd want it to kill anyone. It would just make too many problems for them because it would be traceable through you. No, I think they would set it to go off after Embassy hours, for just the propaganda value. Also, you might not report them. Or even connect the bombing with the package. They knew this George whats-his-name was going to be away and counted on it staying on his desk. Did anyone see you put it there?"

"Well, not really. A woman in the office knew I was looking for his office."

"Luckily, it's just an academic question. You sure did the right thing, son, getting that out of the Embassy. We can be thankful it didn't blow up while you had it. Anyway, my advice is not to inform the Embassy of this, at least not now. It goes without saying, this morning has been a major course for you in the uses of trust and caution, eh?"

Rich looked totally crushed. Locking eyes with his father, he wanted an answer the question that really worried him. "Am I really that naive, Dad? Do I come on as just an innocent, stupid ignorant kid that they could think they could use me like this? It's such a put-down. Especially from Muna."

"Look, Rich. I don't know how well Muna knows you now. It appears you don't know her very well. Sure, you come across as maybe an idealist. You're pretty straightforward. Sometimes people in the Middle East interpret this American approach as naive. But I don't think anyone could believe you're ignorant or innocent. You weren't taken in. I'd have done the same thing for a good friend of your Mother's. Now forget it for awhile. The best thing for you to do is to go back to the Embassy and try to get some work done. You're going to lose this job if you don't keep better office hours." He smiled, trying to reassure this young man who was becoming such a stranger.

David watched as his tall son cut across the wide boulevard and entered the Embassy building. He knew he'd been more reassuring than a realistic assessment justified. Grenade fishing took place in deep water, where the force of the explosion was dissipated downward so that it barely roiled the water surface as it killed off all sea-life in the vicinity. When a bomb explodes on the bottom of a shallow rock-rimmed inlet, the force of the explosion can only be upward. The seawall offered protection, but….He peered again at the mysterious "dictionary", trying to imagine the explosion that could come from such a small "gift".

He'd have to stick around. It was a beautiful morning for a walk on the Corniche. The work he'd gotten such a good start on this morning would have to wait. It was now eleven-thirty. The Embassy was on summer hours, closing at two. It would be a long vigil, but how to be sure it wasn't necessary? What if some fisherman decided that was a place to set his pole? Or if some kids came to play in the area? What could he do to dissuade them if they did? At least he'd better stay close by. He'd walked on the Corniche many times so he was familiar to the juice-sellers and Chiclet boys. A tall bent tree marked the spot, one of the few remaining from years ago when they'd landscaped the beautiful coast road.

Maybe he could use the time to do some good basic thinking. He liked to joke that he was way behind on his worrying. There were always new ones to add and it was difficult to get rid of the old recurring concerns. Living in the Middle East so many years had built up for him an inordinate number and variety of worries that wouldn't have plagued him in an American environment. This morning's events were just another sample. His mind reviewed their earlier crises: a coup and then a revolution in Iraq, anti-American demonstrations in Greece, fording a flooding river in Turkey and now Beirut with bombings and street warfare. Wasn't it time to go back to the States?

########

A little after two o'clock, David saw Rich hurrying out of the Embassy. Foot-sore from pacing the sidewalk and seat-sore from the concrete benches, he signaled to Rich, who looked surprised and hurried across the Corniche, dodging a taxi.

"You stayed here, didn't you? You told me not to worry. You think it's dangerous, don't you? What can we do, Dad?" They walked together to look again at the cluttered pool of water. "You're tired, Dad. Look, I had a hamburger from the snack-bar. I'll stay. You go on home. Only, what do I do if someone get's close?"

"That's a question I've been asking myself for two hours, Rich. I guess you just pray they won't. If they do, you have to move them somehow. The only fisherman today is set up down there, see, and the kids can't climb anywhere around here, so they stay down there or up by the AUB beach. I'd say we could both leave but there might be something come up you can't foresee. Maybe you should stay for an hour or so. I'll come down again. Maybe I'll bring your Mother with me. But I don't think we should tell her. She'd worry herself sick."

"Oh, I agree. But I thought you always told her everything."

"I do. This is the exception. I'll be back. I don't know any other way to make sure, Rich."

"For sure, Dad. Thanks. I couldn't get much work done. I was thinking about how I'd been had. I'm really bugged about this." Steel darts of anger accented the words.

"You know, Rich, the brother may be warning you away. This could be simply an effort to get you into trouble." Rich didn't reply and David didn't press the point. He was hot and sweaty from the jacket he'd worn to the office. In May you could never tell what clothes to wear in Beirut. Turning, he signaled a taxi.

At home, a welcome lunch of Angela's fried eggplant and yoghurt with cucumbers was on the table. She also served a tasty meat loaf to satisfy the protein hunger of the youngsters. There was always an overflow of conversation so Dave, mercifully, was able to just listen, or half-listen. After eating one of the succulent oranges that were still being brought up every morning from Damour, he felt more like a nap than anything. His daily habit was to settle comfortably with a book and soon doze off into an upright sleep that was a major source of family humor. "Dad's reading but should wake up soon." or "It's a new kind of speed reading. You don't even turn the pages." or "Opaque eyelids. All Dad;s family have them, you can read with your eyes shut." Glad to be able to contribute a laugh, Dave didn't mind the taunts.

Today, his suggestion that he'd like to take a walk on the Corniche surprised Lora and he hoped she wouldn't want to go. But she did, inviting

Danny and Robbie, who'd pushed unsuccessfully for another beach day. Dave put on some walking shoes that felt better on his tired feet.

It was about three-thirty when Dave and Lora reached the AUB beach area, with Dannie and Rob lagging behind. Abruptly there was a loud rumble. A charged column of white water rose twenty feet into the air just off the sea-wall, glinting in the sun. Strollers ducked and scattered. Dave saw Rich, only a short distance from the explosion and soaked from the shower of water. They hurried on, Dave intent on seeing if anyone had been hurt.

"That's Rich! Rich!" Lora called to him.

Dave hurried ahead to his son. "Was anyone hurt?"

"No, I'm sure not. I just came by. No one was close. Bigger than I expected, though." He was trying to dry himself.

The family came up, excited, asking is he'd seen what it was. Dave greeted Rich as if they'd not seen each other. "Just get off work, Rich? Lucky you weren't any closer." They stepped over to the railing. The water had subsided and there was nothing except bright orange-halves patterned across the wet walkway.

"Probably someone trying to get some fish with a grenade," Rich contributed, looking sideways at his father.

"Oh, Beirut, what is happening to this city?" Lora waited while the young ones went on down for a closer look. It made her nervous. David had always been overly-curious in the face of danger. Now the children were acting the same way. "Come on, let's go home. I'll warm up some lunch for you, Rich. Dad said you'd called him and had to work late." Lora was feeling increasingly worried in this Beirut that had been so relaxing before. She wanted to be home, away from this violence. The strange explosion troubled her. There was something going on that she didn't understand. Rich's involvement with Fawzia's mysterious niece was another problem. Somehow things were closing in on her and she felt threatened in a way she'd never experienced before.

Chapter 5

"And how shall you punish those whose remorse is already greater than their misdeeds?"

Khalil Gibran, "The Prophet"

The number was ringing. Using the phone in his parents' bedroom, he clenched the phone, wondering what he would say. Not hearing a second ring he realized it had been picked up but there was no response. "Muna, this is…" A barely audible gasp, a choking sound came over the wire. "Muna? The gift—-was it for me? Was it for me, Muna? Well, I fed it to the fish. You can tell Munir.…" The line went dead. He dialed again. No answer. Ringing. Finally, he hung up. Well, she knew now.

What did she know? That he was alive? Was that why she'd gasped when she heard his voice? The picture of her in his mind brought sudden anger. How could she do this? How could he have been so sure she liked him? Why did she have to be so incredibly beautiful?

Robbie's low voice, "Come on, Rich. We're all ready" brought him back to the promise he'd made to join Rob and Dannie for tennis. He changed and joined them, Rob's friend made a foursome. Rich played well but silently, driving the balls so hard Dannie called, "You're turning mean, big brother. Tennis is supposed to be a game." He felt better after the hour of exercise, but the day dragged by numbly. He had to get out, so after dinner he announced he was going for a walk. Heading for Hamra and its diversions, he soon found himself turning back down toward the shore, retracing his walk with Muna the day before. The sea was calm. A quarter-moon lit a pathway far out into the dark horizon. His anger was gone, replaced by an overwhelming despair. He hadn't planned on love. It had captured him. Why was it so tangled with problems?

He returned home and Lora called from the living room, "Rich, come in and talk awhile. You haven't told us anything about Berkley. How are your grades? Do you like Law? What about dates? Are you still seeing Kathy? Here, sit down with us."

Rich looked at his Father, who understood how tired and moody he was. "I think I ought to go to bed. Must still be jet lag.

We'll have lots of time later on." David alone understood what he left unsaid, "…now that I won't be seeing Muna any more."

Lora sighed, looking at Dave for support. "Okay, I guess your Mother will have to wait for her news. Are you hungry? There's some chocolate cake left. Let me cut you a piece."

"No, I'm fine. I'll just turn in. See you in the morning." His drooping figure receded down the hall.

"Maybe the job is a strain, probably doesn't know what they expect of him. I wish he'd had a week or two of real vacation before he started. He looks so unhappy." Lora saw from Dave's expression that he knew something she didn't. Was it about that girl Muna?

He got up and went over to sit by her. "Don't worry. Something's bothering him but let him have his own thoughts now." Kissing her cheek, he wondered if Rich could be as in love, as consumed with love as he'd been. But he was strong. He'd cope.

The next day at work Rich called the Masmoudi house twice, both times to be told by the servant that Muna wasn't at home. Arriving home at two-thirty, he found a family note urging that he take a taxi and join them at the beach. Instead he called again and talked with Muna's aunt. Madame Masmoudi said Muna had been out all morning but she'd be back at three. Could he come for a a visit? She assented, giving him the details of the address.

Changing into jeans and a green polo shirt while listening to Dannie's Neil Diamond album, he left and found a street-taxi. After two miles along the new unfinished highway cutting through the city, the driver stopped and pointed to an unrailed flight of stairs winding up the face of a steep hill.

Mrs. Masmoudi had said the house looked very strange from the street, "Like a warehouse", and she was right. Climbing the stairs, he found himself on a narrow partly-paved walkway leading along a high stuccoed wall. Except for the busy traffic below it could be a pathway in one of the mountain villages he'd visited. A black iron door and an electric buzzer embedded in the wall gave the only indication of life in the rock-strewn landscape with its smell of pine trees mixed with the jasmine growing along the wall.

His ring brought a sound of small steps and the door was opened by a little wizened woman who probably didn't deserve the label of "crone" but that word came to Rich's mind. "Masa'il Khair. Tfadhil." She showed him through a patched and cluttered garden with most of its plants in unmatched clay pots. A broad veranda had been cut to half its former size when the roadway was blasted through below. There, behind an ornate balustrade, sat Madame Masmoudi with tea things spread on the table. Muna was nowhere in sight.

"Richard, how very nice of you to come. How is your dear Mother? Come and sit with me here. I have some special mint tea that I make when your Mother comes and I hope you like these Ma'moul. They're Easter cakes filled with almonds." He shook hands, sat and took one of the rich cookies which, as he feared, were strongly flavored with rosewater. Where was Muna?

Answering his thought, Mrs. Masmoudi reached forward and teased "You're looking for Muna, aren't you? The impatience of youth. Well, I'm afraid I'm impatient too. She hasn't returned and I'm sure she hasn't had lunch yet, either. They don't care how much I worry. And I must leave for an appointment at four."

"I'll wait for her, if you don't mind." He took the cup of mint tea, another taste he wasn't really crazy about.

"Well, I guess it will be alright. Um Ali is here. I'm sure Muna would like to see you but she doesn't know about your coming, does she? She keeps me waiting without any word but she wouldn't keep you, now would she?" Rich didn't answer. He looked around, wondering why this cultured lady would want to live in such a place. Again, she divined his thinking. "It is a rather crumbling old house, isn't it? But, like so many of us in Lebanon, I live here because it's mine. I was born here when my father was an important Ottoman official. We weren't Palestinians then. Just Arabs. This house has memories, but isn't very comfortable by modern standards. Nevertheless it's valuable land and I have to protect it. You might find it interesting....some of the furniture..."

She rose and led him into the house. Its ornate oversized furniture dominated and formalized the small but high-ceilinged foyer. Dazzling yet dismal, with damask-covered walls and corinthinan columns, the interior living-dining area was crowded with gilded furniture. He was relieved when she decided it was time to leave.

"Mrs. Masmoudi, I understand your friend's son works at the Embassy. George Hamoud?"

"Hamoud? I don't believe I know anyone who works at your Embassy. Does he know me?" She brought some old family picture albums and laid them on the table. "These may amuse you. This was Beirut in the early part of the century. I must leave you now. I'm sure Muna will be here soon." She shook his hand again, gave some instructions to Um Ali who hovered nearby and then followed her to a gate on the other side of the garden. Apparently there was a back road that allowed access by car.

Um Ali returned, seating herself in a corner of the garden where she looked serenely up at him as if she'd been left as his personal servant...or guard. The albums were interesting, the captions in French and Arabic, but his attention was focused on the meeting he would have with Muna.

Two hours passed. He'd studied the albums over and over. The sun sank below the wall so that a soft indirect light filled the garden. Rich leaned back and stretched. The aging wicker of his chair sighed as if it was also tired of waiting. Um Ali had dozed but now her eyes darted to him. She struggled up from the small wooden chair, her ancient bones almost audibly creaking, and hobbled up the veranda steps. She turned and looked at Rich, then proceeded to clear away the tea things, taking with her also the two albums. He supposed this was some kind of signal that he should leave. He'd gotten "you should go now" vibes from her a number of times but he was determined to confront Muna.

As the old woman returned to the deep dusk that now suffused the veranda, he heard the sound of a car coming up the hill. It stopped. The door opened, then slammed and the low whining of its motor backing down the hill covered the sound of the gate opening. Rich saw her first and the shock of her appearance held him in his seat. Wearing loose-fitting green fatigues, she pulled from her hair a check-patterned kaffiyah. She looked like a tired and unhappy child. Walking clumsily forward in heavy boots, head down, she almost reached the veranda steps before she sensed something. She stopped, looking up at Rich who stood twice as tall as the stooped Um Ali who came quickly forward to meet her. Something flashed in her eyes as they met Rich's, making them suddenly visible in the semi-darkness. Then she looked away, slumped back to one side as if to find some support to lean on.

"Ooooh." A moan of exasperation, resignation. Quick angry comments in Arabic addressed to Um Ali brought the old woman closer with a whisper that "Sit Fawzia" was responsible. Then, tenderly, the wise old woman took the kaffiyah and, somehow knowing that she wouldn't come and sit with this young man on the veranda, brought a small chair for Muna to sit down. She didn't. Her face now strong and impassive, she looked through him as she turned to face him. "What do you want from me?" It was a statement that said "What you want I cannot give."

Rich's mind kept emptying itself of intended comments.

When he'd first seen her, his heart had pounded again like always. He felt pity rather than anger. How could he make demands? He wanted to take her in his arms and tell her he forgave her. Forgive? What was he thinking? She could have killed him with this stupid prank! "I came for an explanation. The bomb. Even a stupid American can tell when he's being used. I threw it in the Med. It exploded, but no one was killed, not even me." He paused but she didn't look up. "Do you really care so little…?" His voice thickened and he couldn't continue.

"I told you when we first met that you didn't understand, that I…." Her voice stopped.

"You're very right about that. I thought being an American was my problem and that working at the Embassy made it even worse. But no, that was the only reason I even got to first base, wasn't it? Sorry, to first wicket I suppose I should say. Well, I don't happen to believe that lives are so cheap that they can be used at the whim of you self-appointed saviors of Palestine. Who gave you the right to do these stupid things in the name of the Palestinians? Who elected you to office?" Her stance remained tall and proud but her eyes received every blow. He could see her changing expression, even in the darkness. "Well, what do you want me to do next?"

"I want you to leave, Rich." Her voice quivered. He knew at that moment that he could never leave her.

"Well, I won't." His voice was deep, emotional. Um Ali had watched the angry exchange, fussing, mumbling, not understanding but knowing that this was no way to treat a guest and that this was no way to speak to a young lady. Finally, she shuffled into the house, turning on the garden lights which gave a low illumination to the corner fountain and some of the shrubs and trees.

They stood, stubborn and immovable, neither expressing what was foremost in their minds. For Muna, he was alive, unhurt. Munir had assured her there was no possibility of the bomb going off prematurely. But there were innumerable ways in which things could have gone wrong, like in the Rome airport fiasco. Why, oh why had she allowed it?

For Rich, she was his only love. Surely she must have some feeling for him. "Muna, tell me, why did you do this? You don't have to explain why the group does these things. I think you're all crazy and doing nothing but harm for your cause but that's something else. You led me to think you liked me. You knew I love you. I'd have been just as stupid and willing to deliver the package if you'd never have agreed to see me. What do you want? You're hoping I'll become one of your agents?"

"I can't answer your questions. I don't know the answers. You should just go and try to forget about it, about me. My life is very complicated. There is no place in it for." She didn't finish, turned away, her back to him, shoulders now slumping. She wished she had the kaffiyah, a handkerchief, a tissue. Turning, she walked to the corner of the garden, hoping he'd leave. Then, she knew he was behind her. Large hands gripped her shoulders, drawing her back to him and then his arms wrapped around her, his head beside hers, the closeness she'd thought so much about this past week.

Suddenly she was shaking with sobs. He held her tightly for minutes, then turned her around and pulled her tear-streamed face to his, kissing her in a passion that stopped the flow of tears and blocked out all the fears and uncertainties. He sat close by her on the edge of the broken fountain. "It was Munir's idea, wasn't it?"

"No. But he went along with it. Oh, Rich, I did too. When I called I'd planned to ask you myself. I couldn't, so Munir made me give the phone to him. I was sick all last night and this morning. They dragged me off to the camp for training. I couldn't think of anything else all day. The camp is always depressing. They want me to inspire the girls to become fedayeen. The poor people, they live like animals. It's filthy. But the worst is the way the they think. Mothers bring in their eight and nine-year-old sons, Rich, for commando training, some of them so afraid they're crying. Now they're bringing their teen-age girls. We have to bring an end to it. I have to work with them. There's nothing else. This kind of life is impossible. We can't stop until they have their land back."

He noted that she'd said "their" land, not "our" land.

"Muna, Muna, you can't get their land back this way. You haven't even started fighting Israel. When you do, you'll have Britain and the U.S. to take on. Why don't they settle for some small piece of land on the West Bank. Make a Palestine and let them decide whether they have to have more land. How do you know what they really want? Israel is here to stay, Muna. The U.S. might be able to make them behave if your fedayeen would stop the terrorism."

"The Jews won't give up the land. You know it. Not unless we take if by force."

"I agree. But not necessarily by force of war. There's lots of other ways. The oil, for instance. Work for an oil embargo. You're sentencing the people in the camps to another twenty-five years. Doesn't Munir realize that? Doesn't Ibrahim? At least Arafat seems to be coming around."

"He's a traitor…he's giving up all the gains we made."

"So what's the answer? You all sacrifice your lives and the lives of a whole generation? I believe in individual rights. I don't think much of politics and parties, or movements like yours. What of your life, Muna? What are you going to do with it? Flush it down this, this sewer of terrorism, killing, using people? You're using people in the camps in the same way that you tried to use me."

"But if they're not part of the battle, how can we get the land back?" Her voice was now more desperate than angry.

"Will you feel any better if you get it back and put the Jews back in their camps? Is that what you want? You could get along with Israelis, divide up the land. The world wants to settle this problem. Give them a chance. Cooperate." He was tired of the whole subject, wished it would go away and leave them alone. He wanted to discuss the small personal things of love.

She didn't answer. She was drained of emotion, tired, confused. Her mind was left with only one thought. What could she do about Rich? Munir and Ibrahim were sure that, whatever the effect of their "bomb test", it would end her threatening friendship with this foolish American.

They wanted her in the movement. Her beautiful, aristocratic bearing was an asset wherever they moved, whether with the simple peasants in the camp or with the educated leadership; with the Iraqis, the Libyans, even the Japanese and Germans who sometimes worked with them. It proved to all that the movement was representative. They wouldn't use her again as they had in the London bombing or the delivery of plastic explosives to Rome and Athens. But they needed her and would not loosen the bonds that the Popular Front had woven around her.

Muna knew this and suspected that Munir's high position was also because of her worth. She wanted to help and wished vaguely that she could be a nurse or teacher. But she'd seen firsthand the hate they were teaching in the camp schools and what she'd seen of the clinic at Tel al Zaatar camp had sickened her. It was so beautiful here in the garden with Richard. She looked up at him, seeing the frowning concentration in his face. "I'm glad we've had this last talk, Richard. I know you can't forgive me. But I feel better now. You must go," Her throat caught as she said the words.

"I will. But tomorrow. When can we get together?"

"We can't, Rich. We can't tomorrow and we can't. I can't see you any more, Rich. Don't you see that? It would be trouble for me and it might be dangerous for you. I'll always remember my tall Richard who tried to convert me to the world of love." She looked away, unable to look at him any longer. "It's too late. I'm already converted to war. I was converted in London three years ago."

Rich stiffened at the chill of her words. "You can't mean that. I'm not going to stop seeing you." He pulled her around to him, his gaze probing her tear-glistening eyes. "They can't control your whole life? Talk to Munir. I'll talk with him. They can't expect…"

"But they do. And I'm committed to it. Please, Rich, don't make it more difficult."

"For who? For you? What about me? Maybe you're willing to give in to this. I'm not. I have to see you again."

"It's not possible. You don't know. The danger."

He held her to him, his hand pressing into the silky mass of hair to bring her face and lips to his. How could he possibly stop seeing her? "There has to be a way. What about the day we had lunch? You don't work at this every day."

"But, Richard, there's trouble coming, you don't know. The Phalange are trying to make the Front leave Lebanon. There will be fighting."

"When it comes then we'll deal with it. You listen to the radicals too much. Palestinians seem to be running things already."

"Oh, I wish you knew. No, I don't. You have your life."

"My life." He thought a moment. "My life isn't just mine anymore, Muna. Your life is mine, too. Now, tomorrow."

"No, not tomorrow." She turned to him, seeing that he wouldn't give up. "Maybe we can meet on Friday. Do you know the AUB campus? Well, at three I'll meet you in back of Nicely Hall. There's a small garden there. But, Rich, promise not to tell anyone. Even your family, especially your mother."

"I'll keep it quiet. But why especially my mother? Is she supposed to be a gossip?"

"No, no you must promise. It's very important. I didn't mean your mother is a gossip. Its just that women share confidences more than men, and I know your mother would let something slip to Aunt Fawzia if she knew we were seeing each other. My aunt simply cannot keep anything from Munir. I had pleaded and even coached her about not telling him that I was lunching with you last week. He had it out of her in a minute. Rich, you have to trust me in this. I know. If Munir or the Front leaders find out I'm seeing you it will be dangerous. I'll see you, but you must not tell, ever. Promise?"

He promised, feeling uneasy. Later he even wondered if he was being set up again for something. How could he feel that way one minute and know that she loved him the next? There was something in all this that bothered him deep in his subconscious somewhere. The phrase "So close to heaven and so far from God" came to his mind. Fleeting thoughts as he traversed the graveled pathway to the gate. The diminutive Um Ali was there, holding the door open for him. He knew she'd been in the shadows observing their quarrel, their embrace. Somehow she was on his side. He voiced the warm Arabic words of parting that would keep her that way, then turned for a last glimpse of Muna.

"Goodbye, Richard. Give my salaams to your mother and father." It was a cool, controlled goodbye, staged to bolster the story she would tell Fawzia of having quarreled and then parted friends with the young American. She hoped Um Ali had not seen their close embrace. She also hoped no one else had been sent to listen over the wall.

Rich walked along the path to the steep uneven steps, almost stumbling as he skipped down to the main highway below, with its stream of traffic. Finally negotiating a crossover to the other side, he walked several blocks in deep thought. Stopping, he realized he simply didn't know the way back to the apartment from where he was so he signalled a taxi to take him home.

The family was entertaining some friends, an AUB family with children about the same ages as Dannielle and Rob. Lora asked where he'd been. "There's been fighting in the mountains again, Rich and there was a bombing this morning at Martyr's Square. I was worried when you diddn't come to the beach."

Remembering Muna's fears, he lied: "Sorry, Mom. I met a grad student at AUB that I'd met last year at Berkley. We walked around, talked politics and had a shawerma at Faysal's."

"Well, I wish you'd left us a note or called. Bring your friend to the beach. We must have him for dinner sometime. Now, come and meet the Wahlmans."

He went with her, parroting the necessary social phrases. Glancing at his Dad, he sensed that David knew where he'd been. Rich smiled, his eyes confirming to David that things were alright. Later, when the company had gone, he and David remained in the living room, munching on the cookies that remained on the coffee table. David grinned at his son. "Well, you're not Sysiphus any more, pushing the rock up the hill."

"No, Dad, I'm up above the rock now, trying to hold on to it so it won't roll down and hurt someone else."

"You saw her, didn't you?"

"Yes, I saw her. Now I know." That was all he wanted to say, David sensed. Well, he had the right to his own secrets and problems. A not-yet-round moon shone on the sea as David looked out the window, wondering how to warn his son away from what he had now confirmed was the most actively anti-U.S. group of the Rejection Front. He remembered what the Arabs tell of Antar, the legendary strongman hero of early Islam. When asked how he became Antar, he answered "No one hindered me." Maybe parents can't see the difference between help and hindrance, he mused. Again he found himself thinking he should take his family back to the U.S. where life was simpler. The lovely and languishing Lebanon they had so enjoyed was becoming a place of problems, perplexities and possible peril.

Chapter 6

> "When love beckons to you, follow him, though his ways are hard and steep. And when his wings enfold you, yield to him, though the sword hidden among his pinions may wound you. And when he speaks to you, believe in him, though his voice may shatter your dreams as the north wind lays waste the garden."
>
> Khalil Gibran, "The Prophet"

The campus of American University of Beirut is built where the edge of the Ras Beirut plateau slopes softly down to the sea. Enfolded in the city's reaching arms, its campus is a garden of botanical and architectural delights. Three gigantic banyans dominate the pedestrian ways. Cars are banned and even the buzz of student activity is dulled by the overgrowth of trees and shrubs. A carefully tended hodgepodge of flora complements and enhances the beauty of graceful old sandstone buildings.

Those hardy American missionaries who built AUB had studded the stubborn rocky coastal acres they'd purchased for a song with every kind of tree they could find or bring to Lebanon. Year after year, they added new kinds of shrubs and flowers, slowly designing and improving walkways, rock walls and gardens. Beautiful…and romantic, Rich thought, as he entered the Main Gate from Bliss Street. Descending a flight of steps, he turned to note the biblical quote in English and Arabic engraved across the top of the gate-house: "That ye may have life and have it more abundantly." An apt slogan for Beirut. Abundance was what Lebanese life was all about, he mused. But that was what American life was all about, too. "The Lebanese drive to make a buck is more forgivable. Unlike us, they're equally driven to enjoy it."

With security tight he'd wondered how he'd get on campus without some special pass. Only months before AUB had been liberated from a leftist student occupation that had effectively closed the university for three and a half months. Mostly-Marxist student groups occupied campus buildings, took over faculty and security offices and posted their guards at all entrances, even at faculty apartment buildings. For weeks they controlled the buildings, destroyed and defaced property and delved into university records and files. Anti-American graffiti and threats were left in classrooms and administrative offices. Finally, the weak Lebanese government had been persuaded to send troops in a middle-of-the-night attack which caught the revolutionaries asleep and ousted them. Over a hundred were expelled from the University in January. Long involved mediation efforts had cleared the air so the academic year could proceed.

Now, the campus was guarded by Lebanese security forces and entry to the area was carefully checked. Except that it wasn't. Rich, obviously a foreigner, was simply assumed to be a student. If he'd been stopped, a claim that he had forgotten his card would have worked. There was always a way around things in Beirut.

The campus was almost deserted, precisely the reason Muna had chosen Friday. Rich didn't know, but her concern was that Front students would recognize her. The Front had been deeply involved in the takeover but the student leaders she knew personally were still being held. She'd been given a forged student card for use as a courier in the early part of the action. It was this card she now presented at the Medical Gate and then to the security man. No questions. She passed on through and headed down the wide walkway past the main buildings to Nicely Hall.

It was a beautiful day and she wanted to forget other days, both past and future. She'd never studied at AUB but loved the informal beauty of its gardens. Munir had spent a year as an architecture student, but only for political reasons. She was glad he hadn't been involved in the takeover. Pushing politics out of her senses, she succumbed to the arresting scent of jasmine as she rounded Nicely Hall. Rich's broad-shouldered back brought a surge of feeling too deep, too confusing to analyze now.

"You're early."

He turned quickly, smiled, looked around and then pulled her to him for a quick clumsy kiss. "You're early, too." Each knew why the other was early. The small circular garden was enclosed on one side by a rock wall and on the others by trees and hedges. No view of the sea, but they had no need of the sea or any view. An hour passed in small talk, his studies, her love of dance and a spirited cultural treatise on the oriental dance, which "should never be called belly-dancing". They steered away from the political, but only by abrupt changes to other subjects.

After another hour they rose from the hard concrete bench and walked slowly through the campus. The setting sun sifted through the mixture of pine and leaf-trees to cast soft patterns along the shaded macadam paths. The tiny jasmine petals were closing, withholding their heady perfume from even such obvious young lovers. The more generous oleander and specially planted beds of poppies and chrysanthemums lent their support, however, and the recurring glimpses of glistening blue Mediterranean through the greenery nurtured the "all's well" feeling that Rich so wanted for the afternoon. They'd face their problems some other time. He imagined walking with her on his campus at Berkeley. Not such a beautiful setting, always with far too many others around. But wasn't that the answer, taking her with him? It was for him.

She headed back to their secluded place and he straddled the bench, peering into those dark answering eyes. They said so much more than her voice which always seemed to have bad news.

"Rich, I can't stay any longer today. I'm sorry, but there is something else I must do. I have to be back by five-thirty."

He'd expected it, but it was all so damned frustrating. "I'd hoped we could spend the evening. Okay. You know what you're doing." Petulance in his voice, but gentleness, too.

"I can come next week."

"Next week? You mean next Friday? Seven long days?" That's what she did mean, there could only be meetings on Fridays. There was no other way. She'd understand if he didn't want to continue this way. He cut her off "Muna, I love you. I have to see you. If only on Friday, then only on Friday." He smiled, "Never on Sunday?" The joke didn't take hold. "Next Friday, then. I'll walk you to the gate. Are you taking a taxi?"

"No, I have to leave you here. I'll be going out the Medical Gate. I can get home with no difficulty." She rose. Struggling, he stumbled as he unstraddled the bench, laughing at himself. She reached to steady him and he bent to kiss her, tender and tentative at first. Then, wanting the feel of her, he kissed her intimately. She broke away and left. The day went with her.

#########

Somehow, the week passed, marked only by a new rash of Israeli border crossings. Determined to enjoy the family while they were all together, David left the office at two sharp most days and by the time Dannie and Rob walked in from school the family and assorted friends were packed for the beach, with some kind of late lunch in the picnic basket, enough to include the flow of school friends who gravitated to the Draper's cabin. Rich joined them most days, resigned to the schedule Muna had imposed and wanting to get some Mediterranean sun and surf.

One day he met a dazzling French girl named Francoise, and spent a couple of hours with her, convincing Lora that he was interested in this curvaceous girl whose English was so quaint. The myth suited his purpose so he let it build, contributing just enough comment to encourage his mother and the kids. His Dad knew otherwise. He hadn't talked again with

David, but somehow his father knew he was seeing her…and was worried about it. Rich recognized it in his Dad's searching glances but he couldn't talk. It wasn't just the secrecy. He simply didn't know the answers to questions that David would raise. He'd deal with them later.

It was easy on Friday to tell them he was spending the afternoon with his friend from the States. There really was such a friend, Steve Sloan. They'd talked one day at the Embassy, but he hadn't seen him since. He ought to get together with him and work out a better arrangement to back up his story.

########

Another beautiful Friday at the campus, but the chemistry was different. Conversation was stilted. There were periods of silence when they both tensed up, not knowing what to say. Rich felt an element of desperation, a feeling that something was slipping away from him. He wanted to persuade her to come with him to the U.S. He didn't know how he'd support a wife in Law School. He knew he could work it out. But he didn't broach the subject, knowing it would bring back the reality of her problem and open again the gulf between them. He sat across the end of the bench holding both her hands, sometimes caressing her hair and face, wanting all of her, fighting the feeling that he was losing her.

"Rich, you're getting brown. You're becoming an Arab."

"Come to the beach with me. We'll practice beach landings. I'll get some frogman gear and we can train to sabotage Israeli ships," he kidded. She accepted his humor but was too miserable about things to laugh. Her lack of response seemed to accuse him of immaturity, and suddenly he was angry. "Okay, I'm not serious enough. But don't you ever feel like just chucking it—the whole mess, I mean? Why can't you have a life of your own, smile, have fun, go back to dancing, get married and have children? Who says you have to go through life with a long face for the cause?"

"No one." But of course the whispered words weren't true.

"What good does it do?"

"No good. None at all." It was her father's argument and she had no answer now just as she hadn't then in London. But it didn't change the commitment. Commitment, with a Capital C, for chain, she mused. "I'm not good company, Rich. I have to go."

"You have to, or you want to?" Rich was still angry, mostly with himself or maybe just with the dilemma. He saw he had hurt her and tenderly reached his arm to draw her to him, his other hand lifting her head so that her grave drawn face was next to his. "Muna, we both know now that I love you. That's all that's important. I don't even want to know whether you feel the same love for me. I don't want to argue with you, to disagree with you. I want you to be happy. You have a right to that, even if you are Palestinian, even if others aren't happy. That's why we're here, Muna, to find happiness." He placed his rough cheek against the smoothness of hers, hoping the tear in his eye would blink away. His did, but hers didn't. She broke free.

"When do you go to the beach? It's San Michel, isn't it? Do you go on Wednesday? After four, walk down to the end, near Acupulco, the next Beach Club, you know? Maybe I'll be there. I'll try." Walking away, she turned and waved, tears filling those ebony eyes. "I'll really try." Quickly she left him.

Wednesday, another week, almost. He was getting nowhere. Home, Rob ready for the tennis he guessed he needed. Rob was already good, skillful enough to return almost everything Rich lobbed at him, so it was a good sweaty hour of exercise. He joined the family for a movie, Dannielle's friend included. They returned for a late supper of quiche, salad and Lora's special lemon pie. Avoiding his father, Rich went to the kitchen with his mother, offering more encouragement than help. She enjoyed their light conversation the more because it wasn't serious or weighty. It was a delight to be around this magnetic young male she'd borne twenty-four years ago, but every year she knew him a little less.

Saturday they took a long tiring trip south to Sidon and Tyre. Rob challenged him to a race around the Hippodrome. The historic ruin was large and Rich gave it all he had, his long strides quickly leaving Rob behind. But in the searing heat, he slacked off to a jog that brought him in just barely ahead of the dogged Rob. The family cheered and crowned them with makeshift laurel wreaths, one for the winner and one for second place.

Back to work on Monday and an interesting invitation. One of the younger political officers, Jim Powell, wanted him to join a meeting between the Fedayeen and the American AUB students. An AUB professor and member of an articulate group called Americans for Justice in the Middle East, thought a dialogue between radical Palestinians and Americans would be useful.

"I thought the U.S. Government wasn't talking to PLO"

"They aren't, officially, and of course this isn't PLO.

But it's okay. I'm a student, still working on my Master's thesis and I got the Head of Section's okay. Besides these aren't top leaders. Second-level, as I understand it. Embassy doesn't have info on either of them, but they're close to Habash and Hawatmeh and maybe I can do a report on what they'll say."

Rich agreed to come on Tuesday evening and to bring his friend Steve. When they were admitted to the small apartment and saying hellos at the door, he turned to see the dark piercing eyes of Munir, his facial tenseness admitting surprise, even alarm. Seated on the small couch, Ibrahim was exercising his dialectic in earnest. Hearing him say "capitalistic oppressors," Rich knew it would be a long night. But maybe he could talk with Munir alone.

Introduced around, he shook hands with Munir and Ibrahim. Then he and Steve took seats on large Kurdish floor cushions.

"Yes, we've met Draper before. Socially." The hostess was surprised, but Munir continued, "You work at the American Embassy, I believe."

"Well, yes, part-time." Looking straight into the unfriendly eyes, he continued "As a sort of messenger-boy. But I'm not very good at it. You see, I like to read the messages."

The others laughed.

"Ah, but the point is, do you deliver them?" Munir smiled.

"I never deliver messages I don't agree with."

This brought laughter and comments. "Bravo", "That's why the Embassy never knows what's going on." and "I've got a message for Dr. Kissinger you'll agree with."

The serious discussion resumed, dominated by Ibrahim's preachy pomposity and empty rhetoric. Several times Munir glanced his way. Rich held his gaze with answering hostility until Munir's impassive eyes turned away.

Ibrahim's lecture was explaining that the Vietnam War was the work of the capitalistic older generation. That kind of conflict won't occur again because the new generation is no longer capitalist in their thinking." Rich had taken about all he could of this fuzzy thinking. He stood, interrupting Ibrahim. "Excuse me. Some of us here know a lot about the war in Vietnam and how it developed. I say it's just a stupid decision. Stupidity knows no age, nor nationality, nor sex, nor color....nor even economic system. Everybody's capable of stupidity, maybe even the leadership of your own movement. As for the new generation, you're wrong if you think they are any less capitalist. The most popular major in universities is Business Administration. Not just Americans, either. Most Arab students, including Palestinians, are taking either business or engineering. Our generation is just as much interested in making a fast buck as their elders."

Ibrahim was disturbed at having his lecture interrupted. It was important to present the argument in proper order. Munir came to his rescue. "Maybe Americans, safe and pampered as they are, will never see the wisdom of social justice. But the world is moving away from American-imposed solutions to their problems."

"But I thought that's what the Palestinians wanted: an American-imposed Israeli withdrawal," Steve Sloan countered.

"We would like that, but it won't occur until Americans change their economic system. So we prepare to fight."

"Where? In Lebanon?" Jim Powell couldn't help asking this key question and was rewarded with a steely glint in Munir's eyes.

"Yes, if you want me to say it, I will. We will fight in Lebanon as we did in Jordan. Is that what the U.S. wants?" His harsh voice and direct gaze demanded an answer.

Seeing the conversation was turning emotional, the hostess spoke: "Of course not. But Americans regard all this fighting in other countries as just pure terrorism. They understand the fighting, even the terrorism, when it's directed against Israel."

"But we're fast running out of borders where we can fight Israel, haven't you noticed? Of course, what our friend has said is right," indicating Rich, "there is stupidity in our leadership. We should never have left our land. In the '47 war when the Arab troops betrayed us while we were being driven out; in the '67 war when Jordan was ordered by the U.S. to pull its troops out of the West Bank, we should have stayed and fought. We believed the Arabs would help get back the land. Now only Syria, Iraq, Libya and of course Algeria are helping. Lebanon is a question mark."

"A question-mark fast becoming an exclamation point." Rich felt sympathy for what he'd heard and a kind of gratitude that he'd seen this more human side of Munir. He'd still like to deck him sometime for the trick he pulled. Was it because of Muna?

"But what of your terrorist tactics? Aren't they just making more and more enemies?" The hostess confronted Munir.

"Yes, our enemies are growing. I'm sure you know that there is much division about the attacks. They are the work of small groups. You know the Arab story of the man who sells his donkey. The buyer is unable to make him budge. He goes back to the seller who takes a giant club and hits him brutally on the head, saying 'First, you have to get his attention.' That, in truth, is the rationale for what you call our terrorism."

"You mean if you want the attention of the American Embassy, you put a bomb in it?"

Jim Powell's innocuous question caught Munir off guard. He looked questioningly at Rich. Muna said he hadn't reported the incident of the gift. Now he wondered. "Well, that's the theory. But we're not planning to bomb your Embassy." This brought a ripple of laughter in the room. Munir again searched Rich's face.

"But in theory you might do it. And you might use anyone, whether they realize it or not, to accomplish these projects?" Jim wondered why his friend Rich was being so aggressive.

"In theory, yes." Munir's face was impassive, empty.

"Well, of course, someone did it about a year ago with the rocket set in the trunk of the car parked across the street from the Embassy. That got some attention, I remember." Another comment from Rich's friend, Steve. His nonchalant mention of this serious incident had the effect of dampening the discussion.

The hostess fired it up again, reading a list of questions for Ibrahim and Munir. The rest of the evening was a basic review of PFLP policy. Jim was getting his detailed report.

Afterward, cheese snacks were served with wine and cokes. Rich found himself alone at the table a moment with Munir. "How is your Aunt?" He pointedly left Muna out of it on the assumption she'd told her brother it had been an unfriendly break-up. Not waiting to hear about the health of Madame Fawzia, Rich made the one point he had wanted to. "What right have you to use me that way? That's what you're doing with your Palestinian brothers. You don't really know what they want. You don't ask them. You don't care. You're a dictatorship like all the others. Just as bad as what you criticize here in Lebanon. How many generations of Palestinians will have to be used this way before they get a chance to tell what they want?" No response. Rich moved away.

The venom of Rich's accusations sank deep into Munir's thoughts as he watched the tall straight-shouldered American collect his friend, wave goodbye and leave. Then he turned back to the persistent questions of the young Embassy officer he knew to be a CIA operative.

Chapter 7

"And ever has it been that love knows not its own own depth until the hour of separation."

Khalil Gibran, "The Prophet"

Rich joined the family beach trip on Monday and Tuesday. Maybe if he could get a deeper tan it would make a difference. Wednesday Rob had a softball game at school, so he went with Dannie and a friend. He'd already scouted the Acapulco Beach Club adjoining San Michel to the South. As four o'clock approached he walked down the wavering line of water dancing its samba with the sandy shore. Dodging the darting children on the crowded beach, he circled the clusters of strutting boys ogling the girls and whispering girls ogling the boys.

He saw the large distinctive oval sunglasses first. With each step forward he viewed in greater detail the form and shape of his incredibly beautiful Muna. She kicked the water as she walked, sending sparkling curtains of light that highlighted the exciting proportions of her dancer's figure. The simple one-piece black bathing suit, more a leotard really, understated all her perfections and he loved her more than he could stand. Seeing him, she gave a sudden kick that sent a spray of drops all over him as he came straight on, grabbing her hands to pull her close.

She looked guardedly around, then broke free and ran into the surf. "You want to swim?"

For an answer he dived into the waves and came up further out. She gracefully crawl-stroked, breasting the crests of the waves. "You were early again. It's only five minutes to four."

"Early? I've been here all afternoon waiting for four o'clock."

"I know. I walked down in front of your cabin fifteen minutes ago. Who are the pretty girls?"

"My sister Dannie and a friend."

"That's your story, anyway." She was close now as they treaded water. The occasional touch of their bodies sent sparks of physical pleasure through him.

"Dannie's the one with long blonde hair. She writes poetry, music. Her grades always made mine look pretty average."

"But you're an Honors student."

"Where do you hear these things?" and he reached out to poke her stomach. "My mother to your aunt, eh?"

"Yes, at the party that night. You know, my son the Honors student?"

"I'm going to be lucky to have the 'honor' of passing the bar. I'm not doing all that well. I'm on the Law Review but I'm barely keeping up with the real brains. Trouble is, I'm not motivated. Motivate me!" He grabbed at her playfully. Pulling back, she dived under a wave. Following fast, he embraced her. A private blue water-world encased their entwined bodies. He kissed her as they rose to the surface feeling the sweet need of each other, each wondering if the other felt these urges as strongly. Holding her close, his sunlit wet face intensified the hungry look in his blue eyes. "When are we going to talk about marriage?"

"Marriage! Oh, Rich, I…."

"Yes, marriage. You have to face it. I love you."

"I…Oh, can't we just swim today? I can't even face whether I can see you again." She saw the devastated expression on his face and had to look away. She was getting in deeper and deeper. It was like swimming so far out you don't think you can return. She had to stay closer to shore. As if it would help, she swam in and walked through the shallows until he joined her. They headed down the beach toward the Acapulco Club with its swarming crowds.

"I don't want to go where all those people are. Let's sit down. Muna, sometime we have to talk about the future. I...I have to leave next month."

She interrupted. "You said you wanted us to think only of the present. Not the past. Not the future. I don't know the future."

"Another month, Muna, and I can't leave you here."

"I can't talk about the future at all, Richard." She went back into the water, wading out and then swimming, long slow strokes taking her out into the smoother-surfaced sea. Rich followed, not trying to catch up to her. The surging water massaging his long moving limbs, tense with frustration. Finally, he put all his energy into a fast crawl stroke that sent him speeding past her. Out so far that the shore was a blur, he turned. Soon her more graceful strokes brought her to him, breathless and flushed.

"It's wonderful, isn't it? I'm so white. I came too late today. The best time for tanning is around noon." She chattered on, her shallow comments signalling her determination not to talk of what he wanted. The banter continuing all the way back in until they lay together on the hot sand, breathing and laughing in gasps over Rich's imitation of his Pakistani professor of Intenational Law. She picked up the sunglasses where they'd been dropped earlier but he wouldn't let her put them on. "Don't hide from me." Lying back in the slanting rays of the afternoon sun, every subject exhausted but the important one, they were silent, dozing.

"Muna. Muna Atallah, is that you?" The girl who spoke was leaning over as they both opened their eyes. Muna jumped up and embraced the friendly form in the brightly colored beach-coat.

"Amal, when did you come to Beirut?"

"Last year. I've been trying to locate you, but no one knows who your aunt is. I heard you were...well, you know, involved in politics." They switched to Arabic and Rich wondered if Muna wanted to introduce him or whether he should just lie there.

"Oh, Amal, this is Richard Draper. He's....his father was a friend of my father. I'm helping him get to know Beirut."

Amal smiled and accepted Rich's outstretched hand as he jumped to his feet. "Well, I'm a part of Beirut that you haven't gotten to know, so Muna isn't doing a very good job. Do you come to the beach often?" She's direct, he thought, affirming that yes, he came with the family quite often. "Well, we usually have a crowd of crazy types at our place, right up there, with the green and white stripes, see? Ahlan wa sahlan. Do you know what that means yet?"

"Naam. Ma'loum. Shukran."

"Afwan." She giggled, then turned to Muna. "Of course, I mean both of you to come up. Right now, I'm leaving and there's only my brother with his boring doctor friends. But look, come by any day." Then, an inspiration: "Oh, but you must come next Friday. Not this Friday, Friday a week. Okay? We've having a big blast, all the people you know. Well, anyway, the people you ought to know. I'll be here from noon on and I'll expect you. Now, Muna, we have to get together." Again they switched to Arabic and Rich saw in Muna's and Amal's glances that they were talking about him. Amal was being pressed by Muna to do something and it concerned him. Damn it, this was a frustrating day. Amal left, with a wave and "Ma'a Salameh". Muna was again his own.

"Rich, I may be able to come to her party. But I don't want you to come. I have to come alone and I've asked Amal not to tell anyone about seeing us together. Amal knows about the movement and understands." She looked at him "But do you understand?"

"Yes, I understand. I don't care whether I go to the party. But I have to see you."

"That's it. I'll come at four again, go to her party for a half-hour and then meet you down at this end of the beach. Okay? After I see who's there, maybe you can join the party. I'm sorry, Rich. I don't know why you put up with all this trouble."

"Okay, I'll tell you why, because I don't think you heard me out there in the Mediterranean Sea. I love you. I want you to marry me. I'll put up with anything you can throw my way if you'll understand those two sentences."

She sighed. "I understand English, Rich."

"Yes, but this is American English. In English "I love you" is a statement. In American "I love you" is a plan. Do you really understand?"

"I have to leave. A friend is driving me home. Next Friday?"

"Not before then? That's ten days, Muna. Can't you come to AUB on Friday? I'll be there, just in case." He'd brought her hand up to his cheek and then kissed it, his other hand brushing the side of her face in a way that made her almost shudder with yearning to be in his arms. A roistering crowd of boys passed, splashing and fighting in the surf. But Rich hardly noticed as he searched for a way to part without pain.

"Don't come Friday, I can't be there, Rich. I'll be here next week, though, at Amal's. I promise." She turned and walked rapidly away. After a moment he followed, watching her as she circled around the makeshift barrier that unsuccessfully tried to separate the two beach clubs. She disappeared in the crowd, her receding form engraved on his memory. Rich turned and walked slowly along the waterline. Back at the cabin, he told Dannie and her friend that it was time to go home. The curfew would start soon. They were reluctant but helped pack in the chairs, umbrella and other things. Locking the cabin, they left to get a share-taxi into town.

"Kind of a boring summer, isn't it?" Dannie said after her friend was dropped at Raouche.

"Yeah, boring. I almost wish it was over now," and he did wish it. Not because it was boring but because he was filled with foreboding and impatient to know how it would end.

The following week he spent afternoons at the Embassy to cut down the size of the stack of raw reports and materials that were piling up on his desk. He was learning much more than he wanted to know of Palestinian rhetoric and it was depressing. How much of all this had Muna swallowed? Was she as brainwashed as the PFLP seemed to be? Was Munir really one of the Front leaders? How was he going to pry her loose from them?

########

The family had all commented on his increasing despondency and preoccupation. David tried several times to talk, sensing that he was still infatuated with the Palestinian girl. But he never telephoned her and wasn't seeing her. Surprised that his son wasn't being more aggressive, he wondered if Rich had gotten some kind of warning from the girl's brother. He'd mentioned the coincidence of meeting him at the political discussion that night and told him of their exchange. Something, was going on that David didn't understand. The boy was becoming positively sullen. It wasn't the kind of summer they'd hoped for.

The worsening situation had cast a pall over everything in Beirut. The Israelis continued their border attacks, killing nine Lebanese children in the most recent one. The pitiably weak government of Rashid Solh had fallen and new clashes had erupted near the Tal Zaatar camp. There was a large-scale exodus of old Beirut hands, faculty families from AUB and the American school. Adding to the gloom, the usually ebullient Rich was turning distant and pensive, disappointing his Mother who had so looked forward to his breezy and jocular presence. In addition to his full-day work, he spent evenings on an article he'd delayed finishing for the Berkley Law Review. One thing was clear. That first child who had always seemed so vulnerable was now his own man, determined to make his own life.

#######

Friday finally came, accompanied by the formation of a military cabinet which was supposed to bring order out of the growing chaos. The daily bombings and outbreaks of fighting, tied to names of areas in the city Rich didn't know, might as well have been happening in another country. The neighbors, disturbed at the way the Drapers continued their beach-going, had filled Lora with worry. When Rich arrived at two-thirty announcing he was going to the beach, Lora tried to dissuade him.

"The Issawis are sure there's going to be trouble, Rich. There is strong opposition to the military government and they're calling a strike tomorrow. I don't think we can go today."

"Mother, I'm going to go. I'll be careful. If I see anything out that way, I can always turn back or skirt around it." She couldn't remember him ever being so hard in his tone with her, so curt, and she didn't quite know what to make of it. He wolfed down the sandwich she'd set before him, promising he'd be home for dinner at seven. She sat with Rich, wishing David wasn't saddled with the Illinois University group. Deciding to avoid a confrontation, Lora reflected that it would be surprising if her son weren't independent and sure of himself. She wondered aloud if she ought to walk down to the school and make sure that Dannie and Rob came on home.

"Oh, Mother, there's nothing going on. They said this morning they planned to stay to help with that program that keeps getting postponed."

"Oh yes, the 'Spring Thing'. They're going to try again next week. I guess you're right. The school wouldn't let them stay if there were problems. Maybe I'll go up and lie on the roof."

"Well, keep covered, mom. Those Israeli pilots that fly over have very good bombsights," he chuckled, rising to go. On an impulse, he reached down and gave her a hug and a kiss. He quickly changed clothes, grabbed the worn canvas bag which held his towel and trunks and was off. Down on the Corniche, he flagged a servis-taxi, paid his lira, and tried to get some sense out of the political discussion going on between the driver and a front-seat passenger in a uniform that Rich didn't recognize. There were all kinds in Beirut these days.

Arriving at the beach cottage, he found the Caldwells there. Friends over a number of years in different cities, the two families had been happy to share the considerable expense of renting a beach cabin. In fact, Caldwell had found another Embassy family to go in as well. Today, they were spreading out an impressive lunch. Declining their invitation to eat, Rich quickly changed into his trunks and accepted the handful of apricots and grapes they urged on him. Jumping over the veranda into the hot sand, he leapt like an antelope to reach the cool wetness of the waterline.

After eating the fruit, he went in for a long swim and then went back to shower off and lie in the sun for a few minutes. He didn't want to get too involved in conversation, so after politely reporting how well he liked his job—Mr. Caldwell had been a major factor in his getting it—and talking briefly about law school and the ever-present crisis, he said he was meeting someone and took off down the beach.

Walking past the wide veranda of the clubhouse he looked up the slope to the green and white awning marking Amal's cabin. His eyes scanned the veranda, picking out the familiar figure of Muna with those ridiculous Martian shades. Getting closer, he heard the rocking music. Quite a crowd. This was the kind of good times he'd expected for the summer. He walked on, wanting to make sure that Muna would see him and know he had arrived on scene.

On the shore in front of the party-filled cabin a frail little boy, probably about three, was trying to dredge enough of the wet sand to build a castle. Stooping to help, Rich excavated large piles of sand on both sides of the primitive shape the boy had formed. Then, invited by the youngster's trusting open face, he helped form tall corner battlements, showing him how to form the walls and scoop a moat which brought the gentle waves to circle the castle. Intent on what he was doing and encouraged by the incomprehensible but eager words of the boy, he suddenly noticed at his side those unmistakable beautiful legs.

She'd stood for a full minute, observing the gentle way he'd been helping, making sure the boy was doing the building. It stirred her as nothing else about Richard had. When he stood, she wanted only to feel his arms around her. She backed into the water a little as he approached, his hands still filled with sand.

"How long were you standing there?"

"Oh, no more than five or ten minutes." She laughed. "I didn't want to interfere with your play. You looked very happy."

"If I did, it was because I knew you were coming." He washed off in the water and they stood closer, waist-deep in the surging waves. He moved forward and she turned and pushed into the water. Eagerly he dove after her and they swam abreast. "How's the party? Sounds like they've got some cool music."

"Fine, I guess. Mostly a crowd I've never met. Not very serious. Possibly even a little wild. Didn't ever know Amal very well, you know. Anyway, they're a nice change, fun. I think you could come and meet them. Do you want to? Then why not? But one thing. I'm Lebanese. I'm not telling them I'm Palestinian and Amal won't either. Oh, they wouldn't care. I don't mean that. But it would help, uh, identify me. Okay? I'll go back and then you can come after. We'll say we've met before. But we don't know each other well. All right?" Her short gasped sentences, uttered while she was keeping up with Richard's powerful crawl, had left her breathless as they stopped far out from the shore.

"All right. We don't know each other very well." He emphasized the "don't," then reached and drew her body to him, kissing her while their legs moved to keep them afloat, the rippling water adding its caresses.

"Let's go back now. I said I'd only be gone for a few minutes. Someone will think I've drowned." She swam in, Rich following in silence. She walked on up through the sand, tossing back the instruction to come "in five or ten minutes."

Deciding to walk back to the cabin to comb his hair and get a shirt, he toyed with the idea of not going. He really had no interest in the party itself, but he hadn't made any arrangements for meeting Muna again. When he appeared at the shaded sun-porch fifteen minutes later, Amal immediately came quickly to welcome him, dressed in the same explosion of color she'd worn last week. Introducing him around, Amal made no mention of his connection with Muna.

But Muna, when he shook hands, indicated they had met before. One loud and heavily-accented voice responded, "We know. We know. Just ten minutes ago, swimming together like Tarzan and Jane." There was laughter as he brandished a pair of binoculars. Rich looked at Muna, noticing her look of worry. She walked over, took the binoculars and focused them on the swimmers to see what could have been seen. Unclear whether they'd observed everything, she laughed and chided the row of bronzed hunks on the veranda railing, "I was simply showing our American how to avoid the coral reefs." This brought a whoop of laughter. "I've known Richard for some time. He's quite a nice person, considering he's from the colonies." She ended in an exaggerated British accent, appreciated they were mostly a gathering home from English schools for the summer.

Rich didn't like the way things had started. He felt vaguely that he was being made the fool, but there was no choice but to assert himself. "Any time Britain would like to join the union, we'd be glad to have them, provided they learn to speak the language properly." He moved easily into the crowd, shaking hands, nodding, saluting, waving across the room or whatever fitted until he'd made contact with all twenty or so of the noisy crowd. Beer was pressed on him. He declined and took a Seven-up which someone promptly tried to spike with Chivas Regal. Nothing but the best for this crowd so obviously rich and not so obviously anything else.

He parried with them about school, about music, about Berkeley. Was there anyone in the whole world who didn't have a relative at Berkeley? Their lightness and sophistication was like a cool relaxing breeze. He knew enough about Lebanese names to know this was a mixed bag, chiefly Maronite Christian and Sunni Moslem families which shared power in Lebanon, but also Orthodox, Druze and possibly even Shi'a. There seemed to be no problems between them and certainly no concern, not even lip service, for the tensed-up political situation. He sensed Muna's disdain for their frivolity, but she seemed to enjoy the party.

Someone cancelled out the rock tape and inserted a slow rhythmic Lebanese number that brought the slow clapping and finger-snapping response that such music always generates among Arabs. Amal had tied a scarf around her hips and stood in the center of the porch gyrating in the slow movements of the "belly dance." She swayed and dipped, her arms giving suggestive support to the hip movements. Amal was slightly heavy but her well-proportioned body was graceful and demure, providing the essential dignity that keeps oriental dancing from being lewd. Rich abruptly realized Muna was watching his reactions. He broke into a grin.

The music came to an end amidst bravos and more clapping. Then Amal took the scarf and turned to Muna. "Play the same tape again. That was just the hors d'oeuvre. Laughing, she tied the scarf around Muna's hips against the protests that are always expected in such matters. "Now, the main course, the filet mignon!" Muna, having decided to go along, undid the scarf and arranged her orange wrap-around skirt low around the hips and tied the scarf to hold it in place so that it simulated a long harem skirt hanging from her hips but open at the front. Her orange and white one-piece bathing suit completed the costume.

Taking time to feel the music, she made only tentative movements at first. Head lifted high, her arms described graceful arcs that marked the underlying rhythm. She measured the beat with the soft finger-clicks that only Arabs can do well. Rich's eyes, and probably his heart, were glued to her every movement.

The music seemed slower as she led it through each sensuous nuance. The rapt audience stopped their accompanying tympany, a hush fell over the group as they realized how good she was. Her snapping of fingers provided occasional punctuation to the sentences of love and sadness she was reading into this love poem. When Amal had danced to the same music it had been a rhythmic tune. Now it was a symphony of love, both sensuous and poignant. Her body moved as if it were an instrument being played as first she whirled like a long-skirted dervish then undulated in motions that called forth all the physical longing Rich had felt for her.

Her eyes at first avoided his, focusing above his head and letting her motions answer his gaze. But just as she would turn away, her dark shining glance would catch and hold his for a moment. This happened a dozen times in the dance until he knew when to expect it and return the emotion that her glance communicated. The delicate movements of her upper body gave only the briefest suggestion of passion but the encircling hip movements accented by the tightly drawn scarf sent sensuous signals to Rich, standing in the corner with arms folded, his mind deep within the dance. Others were commenting but he wasn't interested in discussing the performance.

In the final movement, she turned to face him, looking sadly into his eyes as she wound down the tempo in a tender finale that ended with her arms straight over her head, hands clasped. The music ended, she did a deep bow, slowly bringing her arms down as a ballerina might. They broke into applause and excited expressions of surprise and delight at the performance. Muna removed the skirt and placed it around her shoulders, coming to lean on the veranda railing by Rich, sipping from his drink.

"I'll have to go soon," she whispered.

"I'd go with you but I've already left. You sent me into orbit with that dance. I'll never touch earth again." He couldn't keep his arm from circling around her waist. She didn't move away. It wasn't possible that they didn't know how he felt about her. She must realize that. As she began to say her goodbyes and collect her things, against the protests that they were just getting ready to eat, he joined in her leave-taking, causing a new wave of protests. They left together, joining hands as soon as they were away from the cabin. The setting sun was softened by a mist on the horizon that cast a red hue on the mirrored sea and gave a rosy hue to Muna's hair that Rich would always remember.

"Can't we walk awhile? Our cabin is down there. There's no one there by now. We could sit awhile and talk." He had to try.

"Why do I always have to say 'no' to everything you want? All you'll remember about me is my no's" She tried to make a joke of it, pointing to her nose as she looked up at him, anxious.

Remember? What kind of signals was she sending now?

"Look, I've made some plans for dinner next week, okay? We'll go to the Phoenicia, the roof restaurant. A very unlikely place to meet anyone you know. Filled with American tourists and rich Lebanese businessmen. But kind of dark and nice if you haven't been there. You name the night, okay?"

"I don't know, Rich. I'm taking too many chances. I wish you could understand, but how can I expect...", not finishing the question, she went on, "I'll have to call you somewhere. When?"

"Let me call you. You name the time."

"No, you must not call. Really, it's important. I'll try to meet you Monday at AUB. No, Tuesday is better, Tuesday at three. Same place. Is that all right? I'm such a nuisance. Why do you put up with all this?"

"Because I'm trying to convert you, remember?" He smiled down, squeezing her shoulder close to him as they walked.

"To save me? I wish you could. I wish you could."

"Your talent is fantastic. Let me take you to the States and make you famous. No, just let me take you to the States and make you mine. That dance, I don't want to share that with anybody."

She started to hum a melody as they walked on down the deserted beach, then voice the lyrics in a small high voice, each measure ending with a sort of trilling refrain that he thought he understood. "Your name is in my heart." He was silent as the song's message filled his heart. He stopped and held her close. Were these words another of her attempts to say goodbye?

#########

Tuesday Rich waited for an hour and a half, pacing the small walled-in garden with its memories. Finally going home, he started twice to call her and then decided he couldn't risk causing problems for her. The next day at work, he had a call from Amal. Hurriedly saying thanks for the party, he asked her about Muna.

"That's why I'm calling. She's here and wants to talk."

"Richard?"

"Yes, are you alright? I waited for you." Why was he so tense?

"Are you alone? Can I talk to you now?"

"Oh, yes, Madame. I have a very private office, a little smaller than the Ambassador's. It measures about 6 by 8 feet. But it's private. I love you. See, now you know I'm alone."

"Richard, I can't see you any more. I want to explain." Silence. He could feel her there on the other end of the line, but what could he say? "How can I make you understand?"

"I don't think you ever can." His voice was hard, cool. "How can I make YOU understand? I love you. I want to marry you. That's important, Muna. Maybe this is more important than your other business."

He was dismissing her years of dedication and work with such a phrase! She bristled. "More important to me, yes. Americans are safe and pampered. They can't realize what Palestinians are going through." There it was again. He was bad because he was American. The same words Munir had used at the session last week. "I wanted you to know that I...I've enjoyed our...getting to know you." The phrases came out so empty. There was no way she could make it easier. For him or for her. Didn't he understand she was captive? That she knew too much? That he would be in danger if she kept this up? Did he think all this was a game? Some kind of social work?

"Muna, I have to see you again."

"It's impossible, Rich. I really can't. I shouldn't have let our...this go on as long as it has. It's my fault. I hope you won't think too badly of me. I liked you very much, Richard." Then, to keep talking so that he wouldn't counter with his insistence, his logic, "I hope the Washington Seminar goes well for you."

"Muna, I don't leave for the Seminar for a whole month." She had said "like," not "love." She had never said she loved him. He had to know. "I have to see you. I insist. You owe me that."

"Rich, it would only make it more difficult. There's nothing to discuss. Nothing more I can say. It's a decision that I won't change. I can't." Silence again. She should hang up.

"I have to see you again. Just one more time. I want you to tell me, to look at me and tell me its over. Then I'll understand, I'll give you up." His voice almost broke in forming those impossible words. He knew she couldn't look him in the eyes and tell him she didn't love him.

"I can't, Rich."

"If you don't, I'll come to the house. I'll come to the camp. I'll see you. I'm prepared to tell the Embassy about the gift, anything, Muna. I'm going to see you once more." Then, softly, "You could come tonight and have dinner like we'd planned."

"I can't. Don't you know what I'm saying? Oh, allright, I'll meet you. I'll tell you in person. A few minutes. I have work."

Was it anger, irritation, or was she as broken up underneath as he was? "At the Phoenicia, then, at seven-thirty?"

"No, not the Phoenicia. Oh, it doesn't matter. But earlier. Seven."

"Okay, seven. I'll meet you at the escalator. I love you." A pause before the receiver clicked. Rich slowly put the phone down. What could he do between now and seven that would change the situation? An ominous coldness filled him. He tried to get back to work. Finally, his watch told him it would be okay to leave. He crossed over to the Corniche, walked slowly and remembering their walks together, then found himself entering the campus and headed for the corner where they'd talked for so long. He was numb to any new thinking, devoid of any plans, except to see her, to look into those eyes. The answer would be there, he knew.

# # # # # # # #

Dressed in the same outfit she'd worn when they lunched at Pigeon Rock but without the sunglasses, she gave a forced smile and preceded him up the escalator, walking briskly at his side as he guided her out into the pool area to a table overlooking the St. George's Yacht Club with its colorful array of boats, pennants flying. Rich ordered orange juice. He was glad the swimmers had all gone, leaving the terrace empty except for a family party on the far side of the pool. Beirutis were staying home because of the troubles.

They looked not at each other but out over the sea, where graceful contrails followed a water-skier speeding along the sun-skimmed horizon. A small white ship was entering the harbor. The traffic below was quieter than usual. But the pleasant scene failed to relax the two who sat awaiting their impossible tasks. Muna, knowing what she must say and Rich, who now knew she would say it.

The orange juice appeared quickly and the waiter, leaving the bill in a small tumbler, glided away to the continuing demands of the party where happy voices mixed with the piped music in the background. Ignoring the glass placed before her, Muna finally turned, looking directly and coolly at Rich, trying to see him as a problem she had to solve, remembering that the decision was already final. "What is it that you want me to say to you in person, Rich?"

He was afraid to look into her eyes. Was he wrong? Didn't she love him? He had so many questions. "What happened since Friday, Muna? I thought…I thought everything was alright and then, pow, you hit me with that telephone call today. Did someone report seeing us? Are you in trouble?"

"Yes. Surveillance. At the party. Those weren't the only binoculars spying on us in the water. Even earlier at AUB. Yes, they know and I have to end things. It's better all around." She couldn't tell him of the trap she'd set for herself. Telling them she was getting to know him to assess him for possible recruitment, then having to tell them that she would not ask him to take an assignment and would not let them do so. They had discussed him as if he were simply a weapon to be used. When she had insisted she knew him best and that he couldn't be trusted, they had of course insisted she break off immediately.

Munir had told her privately how important it was that she follow instructions, for Munir as well as for herself. And for Rich and his family as well. Munir knew she loved Rich. A twin knows these things. But Munir didn't know what love was. He had thought they could use Rich, that Muna's hold on him would provide control. There was only one course. Now her concern was Rich.

"It's better? How is it better? You love me, Muna, I know you do. You feel the same things I feel. I know it's difficult to choose."

"No, it's not difficult to choose, Rich. I have already chosen. Don't you understand? I have loved our good times, but I….it's finished now." She looked straight into his eyes.

Rich was seeing Munir's eyes, not Muna's. That answering emotional quality he'd seen before was gone. Taking her hand, his gaze held hers, probing for the "maybe" that he knew was no longer there. He reached over the table and kissed her cheek, lingering to feel the closeness of her. Then he stood, took a five-lira note from his pocket for the waiter, and looked down at her.

"Fi Amaan Illah, Muna." The parting words he'd learned to use in Iraq were more like a benediction than a goodbye. "Go in the safety of God."

She didn't look up. "Ma'a Salameh, Rich." and then the spoken refrain of the song: "Your name is in my heart…" The words pierced his composure and he didn't turn. Muna watched his tall figure as he crossed the marbled area, turned into the lobby and disappeared. She was still there a half-hour later when the waiter came up and asked if there had been something wrong with the untouched glasses of juice. Her eyes were dry. The tears were flooding her heart. Not until she left the hotel did she notice that the sky was dark and threatening. The rain began as she entered the taxi which would take her back to the life she no longer believed in.

########

Tired and emotionally drained, Rich walked along the sea, not wanting to go home yet. Passing through the tourist area with its souvenir shops, hotels and then through the narrow street of Ain Mreisse, with its picturesque Mosque and old houses on the sea, he arrived again at the broad Corniche that started at the Embassy. The sky had darkened. Lightning flashed on the horizon. A wind was building. The pleasant shore walk was dark and foreboding.

He tried to think of his plans for travel back to the States, the stopover he'd planned in London, the Seminar with his old Washington buddies, his life at law school. In the past month, all of this planning had included Muna. Now he must get back on track. But his mind kept coming back to possibilities that would bring her back to him. He needed time. He could face what life held for him. But what of Muna? How could she give herself to this hopeless commitment? She was in danger. He knew it. What could he do? He turned up the hill toward the apartment just as the first drops of gust-driven rain hit his face, merging with the tears of his despair.

######

At home, Rich found his father and Fuad Hakim in deep discussion. Lebanon's possibilities were all negative. Another border clash between Israelis and Palestinians. Bombings in downtown Beirut and clashes in the Port area.

"Of course, David, the military government had to resign. They have no political force at all. They can't even stop the arms shipments coming in for all the factions. You've seen these militias training. The Murabitoun are right down here below us in the soccer field. What does your Embassy say?"

"They're all pessimistic, Fuad. But they don't have a full appreciation of Lebanese instincts for patching up their troubles and muddling through."

"Well, this impasse is dangerous. The Moslems have agreed that the Prime Minister should be Rashid Karami but he can't form a government. These bombings every night are only symptoms of something very dangerous. The factions are gaining military strength. And of course Israel's there to take advantage. Last night they tried to land boats at Tyre. They cross the border whenever they want, attacking the camps. But they also hit Lebanese villages. Doesn't the Embassy report these things?"

"I know, Fuad. Maybe Richard knows what the Embassy reports."

"No, I'm not on the inside of things. I did hear the Syrian Foreign Minister is coming tomorrow. But no one thinks it'll help."

"Well, it might help Syria, but not Lebanon. Richard, you don't seem very optimistic. Are you leaving soon?"

"In a few weeks. Maybe sooner. School is closing for the kids. The troubles are closing down the city. I think Dad should look into a transfer, don't you, Fuad?"

Fuad turned to David, "We'd hate to see you go, but I think Richard is speaking wisdom. Everyone's discouraged. I don't believe we can expect things to get better. Well, I've got to be going home to my own problems. Ma'a Salameh."

Seeing Fuad to the door, David turned to Richard, noting how despondent he was. The family had tried to be happy but the troubles were having their toll. Richard's summer had not been what they'd hoped and now he'd be leaving back to the U.S. soon. They'd never talked about the Palestinian girl but he was relieved at all the evidence that it was all finished. "Rich, do you need something to eat? Lora and the kids are at the school play. We haven't talked much, Rich. Why don't we talk about the future and try to forget all these Beirut problems?"

Rich hesitated. Should he unburden himself to his Dad? No, there'd be too much to explain. "I don't know, Dad. I've got two cases I have to read for the seminar. I think I'll just go back and get something done." He headed down the hallway.

David knew there was something traumatic going on with Rich. His instincts told him it had to be connected to that girl or the Front. He suddenly felt depressed and strangely alone as he looked out at the lightning flashes over the Mediterranean. He'd always felt he and Lora had built a strong fortress against the problems of the world. But now the troubles of Beirut were reaching deep inside his family. He decided to go down to the school and walk the family home.

Chapter 8

> "The righteous is not innocent of the deeds of the wicked…you can not separate the just from the unjust and the good from the wicked; For they stand together before the face of the sun even as the black thread and the white are woven together. And when the black thread breaks, the weaver shall look into the whole cloth, and he shall examine the loom also."
>
> Khalil Gibran, "The Prophet"

Dave and Lora wanted to make Rich's last weeks a fun time for the family, but it was risky to go anywhere in the city. They could go to the beach some days and the nearby tennis club was a boon. Smith's Market was blown up again. It burned all night, but was reopened after two days. An AUB friend was stricken with an inoperable brain tumor. Lora assisted the family with packing so they could take him home to the U.S. Rich spent several evenings sitting with him in his hospital room, hearing the boom of explosions downtown. It was eerie walking back to the apartment in the empty streets after curfew. On July third a truce was announced and, equally welcome, there were cooling sea breezes to break the summer heat wave.

Lora planned a Fourth of July beach party with friends as a farewell for Rich. Everyone had an exhausting good time in the high surf. There was a surge of optimism for a change. After lunch Rich wandered down the beach alone. Seeing Amal sunning in front of her cabin, he walked up and sat with her awhile. No, she hadn't seen Muna since the day of the telephone call. Wasn't Rich still seeing her? Yes, Muna had told Amal she was breaking off with Rich but hadn't said why. Wasn't Rich going back to the States anyway? "You know about her Front connections, don't you? She's been involved in some serious incidents. And you know her brother is one of the Front's leaders? He's considered a criminal in Rome. Some believe he was in the Athens Airport bombing. It's all very dangerous. I worry so much about Muna. But she would never listen to her friends. Oh, if you'd like to come, we're giving another party on Friday."

Not answering, Rich left Amal and trudged through the sand back to the family party. He played paddle ball with the young Caldwell boy and Rob, trying to keep two balls in the air. It had been fun for the family and he tried to hide how empty it had been for him. He coaxed his Mother in for a swim and, shaking off the water, gave her a big hug and kiss, realizing how much he'd miss all of them.

That night they switched on the TV news, having heard on BBC that there had been a fedayeen attack on a Jerusalem supermarket killing thirteen Israelis. The Arabic telecast included coverage from the People's Front in Beirut, taking credit for the atrocity. He sat transfixed. It was Munir who made the statement before the cameras. He was introduced as "Abu Fadhil" and his eyes flashed as he spoke the harsh Arab words. Looking in the background, Rich saw that among the group circling him was Muna, her hair drawn back straight, her face downcast.

The next day, the whole family saw him off at the airport. Before ducking to enter the plane, Rich waved goodbye. To the family, and also to the love he was leaving in this troubled place. Lora felt like her confidence in Lebanon was going with this unhappy son. "We should be sending Dannie and Rob with him. They could stay with Mother." In all their overseas living, they had never sent their children away to school, believing that close family was more important than academics. Observing British friends who always sent their children to England at an early age, the Drapers determined not to be parted from theirs until college, Then, they needed the independence. They should go.

"No, not yet, Lora. We'll be all right if we're careful." But David knew now that Lebanon was headed for outright civil war. Battles in the north between Moslem Tripoli and the Christian village of the President had taken attention away from Beirut. But the recurring bombings in the city were spreading to suburbs again. "If only Israel would stop the border attacks and the air strikes against the camps. Palestinians don't trust the Lebanese to defend the border. And now, they're trying to take control in the city as well." Fuad had told him that the acceptance and prestige the PLO had received in the UN and in European capitals had made them overconfident. The gulf between their demands and those of the Lebanese Christians wasn't wide enough to justify war. The family rode back in silence. Even Salman was somber.

# # # # # # # #

The remaining days of summer were relatively calm in Beirut. Lebanese leadership, usually adept at manipulating their political machinery over the years, seemed powerless in the present breakdown. Only Raymond Edde and Kamal Jumblatt talked of the substantive reforms that were needed. Christian rightists issued daily more and more bellicose threats from party headquarters which were being rapidly militarized. Moslem groups issued only platitudes and pledges of support for a vague Arabism and for Palestinian presence in the country.

When Israel attacked the major southern city of Tyre from the sea in mid-August it was the PFLP that mounted a swift if ineffective attack across the border into Israeli territory. It's spokesman, exaggerating the success of the attack, was again Muna's brother, now known as "Abu Fadhil".

The same day school began for Rob and Dannie, full-scale fighting erupted downtown. Classes now were accompanied by the rattle of machine gun fire and the crash of mortars only a mile away. The family settled into a discipline that was to last through the next six months. All four would keep informed where each one was at a given time. Food and water was carefully monitored. Every morning the situation was reviewed. David walked Rob and Dannie to school mornings and either he or Lora picked them up after school. They stayed indoors or in the neighborhood after five. The sharp bursts of automatic weapons, sniper shots, distant explosions and heavy smoke over the downtown skyline became a way of life.

In October, kidnappings began, each militia taking their daily quota, partly to comprise a stable of reserve prisoners that could be exchanged in the bargaining that went on at some mysterious higher level. Those were the lucky ones. Others were dragged out of cars at roadblocks and shot or tortured for information they probably didn't have. Foreigners were left scrupulously alone. Americans seemed to enjoy a protected status respected by all the groups. But the Drapers couldn't feel secure with war and violence so near.

In the last week of October foreign residents began to leave. The school enrollment, which had been near a thousand before the troubles began, declined in weeks to less than a hundred. Families of diplomats were sent home. In a matter of days the Drapers had said goodbye to most of their American and European friends. Reporting to the Institute Board, David wrote: "Even at close hand, it's unbelievable to see people making war in the midst of their city, shooting neighbors, firing into areas where friends and relatives live. All in the name of parochial politics that pretend patriotism while they deny democracy. All Lebanese knew that the Moslems are now at least sixty percent of the population, yet national leaders openly deny this fact and the necessary reform that would recognize it. Only a little compromise is needed to avoid disaster, but now that disintegration begun, there's no element strong enough to reverse it. The machinery of government has ground to a halt. Police posts are unmanned and services are unavailable, as much from lack of leadership as from necessary absenteeism. The indiscriminate sniping, bombings and kidnappings have made commuting a daily danger."

With his report, David sent news clippings that classified and enumerate the disasters of the day before: 17 bombings, 34 kidnappings, 21 killed, 63 injured. With the statistics was a listing of the trouble spots of the city, reminiscent of the traffic reports in U.S. newscasts. He ended his report with a personal reflection: "These names you hear on your TV news have become for us the symbols of senseless killing and destruction. I doubt they will ever leave the memories of those who are here: Tal Zaatar, the Rejection Front Palestinian stronghold that terrorizes the Christian Kata'ib from its key position on the perimeter of their territory; Ain Romaneh which exchanges fire across the Damascus highway with the Moslem area bordering the Sabra and Shatila camps of Palestinian refugees."

After he'd sent the report, the first big battles downtown began, fierce exchanges that pounded through the nights, destroying Beirut's three largest and most impressive high-rise hotels, the fabled Phoenicia, the new Holiday Inn and the prestigious St. George. Beirut's central business district and its famous bazaars became a blasted, burned-out and looted No-Mans-Land. The fighting now moved into adjacent residential districts. The sound of gunfire was never far away from the Drapers' ears.

Residents of the Manara district, considered one of the safe areas of the city, drew closer together in their daily exchange of information, rumor and concern. Neighbors daily offered help and advice to the Drapers and other foreigners in the community, making sure they had the necessities and were updated on the situation in the streets. Social life had ground to a halt in September but it was possible to have nearby friends for lunch. Lora preferred entertaining at lunch, anyway. Dave agreed. Conversation was more pleasant and meaningful without an evening of drinks.

The tension around them seldom intruded inside the family circle. The American Community School kept doggedly open, coping on a day to day basis with the uncertainties and problems. If students and teachers could safely find their way to the campus, classes were held, making up time on weekends and in home studies. Only a few days were missed. Most Lebanese schools, located in risky areas of the city, had ceased operating.

The American University of Beirut postponed its opening until January for all faculties except Medicine and Senior year Engineering. The other American institutions, Beirut University College and Haigazian College, began a sparsely-attended semester but the latter closed in November when the Kantari fighting engulfed its campus. Lebanese universities, in more perilous locations, simply didn't open. University students swamped the Institute office, seeking transfer to American institutions.

With half of the staff unable to commute through danger areas, Lora worked regularly now at the busy office, grateful for something to take her mind off the madness that multiplied with each new day. Safe at home by mid-afternoon as the deserted city streets offered themselves for the night work of war, the family drew closer together, finding time for each other, for books and music and games they hadn't played for years.

As the fall winds began to churn the Mediterranean and bring the splendid raging sea storms that David loved to watch, it became clear that there would be no fuel oil to provide heat for the building. The strong winds sometimes penetrated their living and dining area so the family often huddled in the small but comfortable study with a tiny electric heater which provided a low level of warmth, until the power outages began.

Angela's small apartment in Ain Romaneh had suffered a direct hit so she was invited to move in with the Drapers. Also, a young Armenian church friend, cut off from his family who were surrounded by the fighting, moved in while awaiting his U.S. student visa. The fact that he was also Palestinian held up the consulate's approval. So the family grew. Evenings in the small study were cozy, with the Arabic news on Television always a focal point of interest and, invariably, of discouragement. Trying to do their homework in the enlarged family group was a problem for Rob and Dannie. David and Lora would always remember peeking in on them in their unheated bedrooms sitting at their desks, blowing on their fingers so they could write. Who said the kids of today are pampered and unable to cope with hardship?

If there was a morale problem it was in the constant process of saying good-bye to long-time friends as the exodus continued. For Rob and Dannie it was particularly poignant to see their classes whittled down. The few remaining became close and loyal friends so that each new departure became a traumatic experience.

Businesses and careers were being damaged on all sides. Some friends were experiencing a complete loss of their life's investment. One friend had invested his entire fortune in a construction project that was wiped out in the earliest round of fighting. Most foreigners were employed by businesses or governments that bore the expense of evacuating them, but for some it was a serious economic burden. Many long-time residents postponed their departure because they didn't want to leave their possessions behind unguarded. David observed this with some surprise, how much the economic factor intervenes even when personal safety is involved. In the Drapers' case, the Institute had in early November agreed with his view that he was the best to judge what he should do and when. Budget money would be found if evacuation was necessary. Reviewing their situation daily and praying nightly, Dave and Lora decided to stay on unless and until the fighting came into the Manara area. They knew it might then be too late to leave, but somehow they felt good about the decision and had faith the family would be all right.

But there was another decision pressing on them now. Rich was insisting on coming to spend Christmas. It had been five years since the whole family had been together for the holidays and Lora began to make elaborate plans. As the fighting grew worse she became more determined that it would be over by Christmas. Her letters had renewed the holiday plans. In each of the few letters that Rich wrote he talked of the coming trip. David had reservations. "Maybe we could all spend the holiday in Cairo or in Jordan." But he quickly realized such plans were simply too expensive. Things didn't look good, but it was still safe in the airport area and in most of West Beirut. People were still traveling in and out. Lora was sure it would be alright.

An Israeli raid on two refugee camps on December 2nd had resulted in over two hundred casualties. But Dave made arrangements to send Rich the ticket. The next day, four Phalangist militiamen were found murdered on a road above the city. Enraged, Kata'ib fighters terrorized the Moslems remaining in the downtown area, killing over one hundred on this "Black Saturday". Martyr's Square had re-earned its name. Heavy firing reverberated throughout Beirut that night. TV coverage in the U.S. of the carnage brought a call from Rich. David tried to cancel the Christmas visit, but Lora was sure there would be a truce.

Amazingly, Lora's truce materialized. An agreement was signed in Cairo. The many previous cease-fires hadn't held, but this one looked better. By mid-December the fighting had pretty much stopped with the airport still firmly in Moslem hands and a safe area all the way to Ras Beirut. But the 5 p.m. curfew would be maintained. David sent a cable telling Rich to come but specifying that he should connect with the Middle East Airlines flight from Paris. It was scheduled to arrive before curfew and before the sun would set, taking safety with it.

Chapter 9

> "…joy and sorrow are inseparable. Together they come, and when one sits alone with you at your board, remember that the other is asleep upon your bed."
>
> Khalil Gibran, "The Prophet"

The airport was almost deserted. Dave and Salman had been stopped by eight roadblocks, first by Lebanese security forces, then Druze militia and finally the PLO's coolly efficient militia, Al Fatah, which guarded the Palestinian camps along the airport road. David was relieved to see MEA's cedar-marked jet gliding low through the setting sun to a graceful landing. A trickle of passengers came through the Arrivals gate. With few airport staff willing to report for work, procedures were perfunctory. The group cleared, but there was no sight of Rich. He'd missed the flight.

"What about Air France's flight at 8:30?" David asked the Passport official. "The curfew, sir, no Beirut passengers." Rich had plenty of connecting time in Paris. Somehow he'd decided he could wait for the later flight. Angry, David reviewed what his cable had instructed. Well, he couldn't risk Rich's making some wrong decision about how to get into the city. He would meet the Air France flight. Salman offered to stay, but David insisted he return before curfew. He didn't see any other taxis. They could stay the night in the terminal. He couldn't telephone Lora.

He wished Salman hadn't told her how risky it was on the airport road. They'd stopped shooting, but not robbing and kidnapping.

Finding a place to sit out of the cold, he looked for something to read. Upstairs, the departure area was closed and the news kiosk hadn't operated for months. Trying to rid his mind of the worrisome possibilities, he let memory take over.

Other Christmases. The best were snowy ones, the kind he'd grown up with in Idaho. That year in Washington when Christmas fell on Sunday. A raging blizzard had closed the roads and the family had walked two miles through the drifts to spend Christmas morning where it ought to be celebrated, in Church. They'd had three great days of snowbound fun and games. He thought of their first year back from Baghdad when young Rob had seen his first snow: "Look, Daddy, its on the houses, too!" He recalled exasperating Christmas Eves assembling toys from kits that were always missing nuts or bolts or directions.

Those simpler days were finished. Now you worried about all the pitfalls the world placed in the path of the young. There wasn't much you could do for them after high school. What of Rich's relationship with the Palestinian girl? What had really happened? Was she the reason he'd insisted on coming?

The plane roared out of the dark sky onto the runway at exactly 8:30. Anxious as much for the risks in going back home as for the arrival of his son, David spied Rich's familiar form, laden with carry-ons and Christmas-wrapped packages. A smiling Santa Claus. Watching him approach the visa counter, he was glad he'd sent the Lebanese lira to pay the fee, since the Exchange office had long since closed down. The security officer, taken aback at this Christmas vacationer who apparently didn't realize there was a war on, questioned him and then stared at David through the glass partition as Rich pointed out who was meeting him. He quickly issued a 15-day visa and passed him through with two other Beirut passengers. Rich hurried through the unattended customs channel and hugged his tired and strained-looking Father.

"Did you get my cable, Dad? Decided to switch to Air France so I wouldn't have to change airports in Paris."

"Cables aren't arriving these days, Rich. There were important reasons why I..." He stopped. Why push the matter?

They left the building, which provided the only light. One old Mercedes taxi was there, the driver dozing inside.

"Taxi? We want to go to Manara."

"Fifty pounds." The pre-war price was seven. Dave got in front by the surly driver, who backed the car and shot up the wrong side of the street, his lights off in the moonless night. Another car suddenly cut in front and then sped ahead. Rich noted his father's worry. With curfew and no street lights, this was an eerie experience. The situation was much different from when he'd left in July.

The driver floored the gas and hunched low over the steering wheel to see the chuckholes and shellholes that pocked the wide throughway leading from the airport. Suddenly he slowed and pulled off to the side of the road. Up ahead, the tail-lights of another vehicle were visible. "What's wrong," asked Dave. A stream of guttural Arabic. The driver believed that the car ahead was going to try to cut them off and rob them. He didn't want to go further, saying they'd have to turn back.

At that moment, a motorcycle passed. "No, it's alright, I'm sure. Look. Follow the cycle." The driver started up, slowly, then regained speed. He rounded the traffic circle almost on two wheels. Another car waited. They passed. It started up and followed. The nervous driver grumbled. How stupid he was, letting this foreigner talk him into this trip. The car ahead slowed. Rich sensed the danger, and the adventure.

They sped up the hill and the car ahead circled around as they went on through. David breathed a sigh of relief. Rich looked back. "The car's behind us again, Dad."

David was convinced the car was pursuing them. With a curse, the angry driver floored the gas pedal and the old taxi careened down the hill toward the sea. No conversation. Rich's comments and questions were ignored as David concentrated on what might lie ahead. They turned onto the Corniche and braked to a sudden stop. Being out at night was nerve-wracking. You didn't know where a roadblock would be until it was in your face. Even then there was no way of telling which of the myriad groups was stopping you. Only one element was needed: armed men.

When they pointed their guns you stopped. You turned on your lights in the car so they could look at you. You couldn't see them, just the muzzles of their varied weapons poking their authority at you. You answered their questions, let them search the car, your luggage and yourself. then waited for permission to leave. If they were friendly, you got advice on what lay ahead.

The first roadblock was just a peremptory stop asking who they were and where they wanted to go. The driver was told he shouldn't go into the city, it was dangerous. At the second road-block he was told he could go only to the Continental Hotel nearby, still a long way from the Drapers' apartment. He pulled up at the hotel. Dave pleaded with him to go on in, finally persuading him with another twenty-five lira. They got to Raouche where another roadblock warned of trouble up ahead.

Now they were only a half-mile from home. Cursing all foreigners and the war he believed they were visiting on his country, the nervous driver edged down the final curve of the Corniche road to the darkened Mediterranean Hotel. "I stop here. You stay hotel." He couldn't be persuaded, so David paid him. They could walk. A militia post beyond the hotel stopped them, loaded down with baggage. One gunman recognized David and they were cleared to trudge the back road up the hill to the lighthouse.

"They're here, Mom," Rob whooped, leaning out the window. As the family descended, neighbors who were still in the city opened windows to join in the greeting. From their high balcony the Hakims called down "Ilhamd'Allah! Thank God! We were worried." Having agreed with neighbors that David and Lora must be daft to bring their son home when everyone else had been sending their families out, Fuad was happy it had worked out. How tall this Richard was! Was he serious about Abu Fadhil's twin sister? Distant shots punctuated his thoughts. The glow of the port fire, raging for the second day, was a halo over the burnt-out buildings. He leaned on the rail, pensive as he watched the Drapers enter their building. When will Beirut see peace again?

David, exhausted from the evening's worries, allowed the others to handle both the luggage and the welcome home. Lora's questions brought half-answers quickly submerged by new questions. Angela hugged Richard and caressed him with the Arabic litany of welcome, big tears coursing her cheeks as she thought of her own two sons, two miles away in the divided city. Rob inspected parcels for hints of what Rich had brought for Christmas. Dannie was intent on telling him the school's war routine. David dropped into a chair. It came to him that he wouldn't really relax until he had the whole family out of Beirut.

##########

The holidays were both pleasurable and tense, not alternately but in an odd continuous mixture of both. Since the Moslem Id al Fitr holiday had been marked by Christian militia attacks, most Christians were expecting their holiday would be the occasion for Moslem attacks. Though there was fighting in the downtown area, the attacks never came. The days were peaceful enough for the Drapers to make forays into the city for Christmas shopping. Work at the office consumed their mornings. Rich gave a hand, helping students in filling out forms and providing informal orientation and advice on U. S. university life. Dannie and Rob helped, too.

Evenings featured "curfew parties". Wives would coordinate what each could bring to these potluck dinners and an evening's battle against the boredom of a besieged Beirut would be waged and sometimes won. Other evenings the family gathered in the kitchen helping Lora and Angela make maximum use of the dwindling supply of cooking gas. Lora would never put a single item in the oven any more and during the holidays managed to keep it efficiently filled with holiday baking each time it was lit. They'd managed to get a canister of gas for hot-water showers, their first in over a month. Rich loved prolonged showers and had to be carefully monitored so the supply would last. Lora hated the morning ordeals under the cold cascade of the mountain-fed water supply.

The sun favored Beirut over the holidays and the living room was comfortable with bright warming rays streaming in. The small veranda on the west took the full force of sun in winter and its yellow-cushioned couch and chairs provided a great place for relaxed reading, dozing and lazy conversation.

Krikor, who'd been such a cheerful member of the family for the past two months, learned that his family had fled Ashrafiyah where their home was part of the battle-front and had gone to relatives in the mountains. He left to spend Christmas there.

A holiday party brought together the Drapers, the Hakims and the Moores whose daughters were now safely down from their school in the mountain village of Broumana. Several single friends, an American AUB student who had stayed on after his parents left and a couple of correspondent associates of the Moores, made up the large friendly group, determined to forget the war and have a good time. The Moores came up early, bearing wine, a large casserole and assorted other goodies carried by their two self-assured blond daughters aged eleven and thirteen.

The Hakims arrived bringing tabouleh, the Lebanese parsley salad, stuffed grape leaves that Nadia did so well and some date-filled cookies. Fuad, in an expansive mood, recited the Arab proverb: "These three things bring long life: A spacious house, an obedient wife and a swift mare."

"An obedient wife, eh? Well, I have a swift wife. Now what I need is an obedient mare." Allen smiled wryly at Inga, whose green eyes flashed a welcoming smile to the Hakims.

"I'm your obedient mare and you know it. These days, with no servis-taxis running, I'm a pack-horse, bringing the food to keep the Moores from being less." Grabbing Allen around the middle, she added, "And you should be a little less, right around here."

The main business of the evening was in the kitchen where all the evening's culinary contributions were organized into a meal of gigantic and delicious proportions. Rich was anxious to talk with Fuad and get news of the Front. He found him less informative than the correspondents and gravely pessimistic.

"If the PLO supports the Moslem militias it will escalate the situation. PLO Al Fatah troops are the best-trained and best-equipped forces here. I think, Rich, we must be worried now."

"Why doesn't the Front cooperate with the PLO?"

"The Front thinks the PLO has sold out. They all have their own wars to fight, Richard. The Front groups are dangerous."

David had promised Lora to keep the conversation off politics and war and now made a conscious effort to do so. He organized games for the younger ones in the study where it was warm. Trying to cheer up the living-room conversation was difficult. The evening's humor was mostly war-connected. There were things to laugh about in Beirut. The night before, a man had telephoned the concierge of a luxurious apartment high-rise, telling him a bomb had been planted and that he must get all tenants out in ten minutes. The frightened concierge raced through the building warning the wealthy tenants, telling them to evacuate immediately.

When they appeared in the lobby, laden with all the money and valuables they could carry, an armed group met them and relieved them of their possessions. The leader then thanked them for selecting their most valuable possessions, saving his group from having to search and make a mess of their beautiful apartments.

This story brought a review of other robberies. A good friend of Inga, living in a penthouse in Kantari, had watched through the day as a neighboring building was looted, the thieves lowering rugs, antique furniture and costly appliances with a block-and-tackle rigged across to the roof opposite.

Some of these incidents were "fund-raising" operations and some were simple thievery. There was little control by the command level over their militias. In a Beirut with no police protection, knocks and doorbells were now challenged before doors were opened. But intruders could force a concierge to front for them.

Seeing the evening deteriorate into a repetition of the many nights spent exchanging horror stories with neighbors, Lora hurried the food onto the table, called in the guests and David offered a prayer of thanks, invoking God's blessings on the food and guests, echoed by Fuad's "B'isim Illah, al Rahman al Rahim", the Moslem dedication to God that accompanied all daily activity. The food was plentiful, delicious and the subject was changed to lighter matters. Allen sensed Lora's almost desperate wish to make the evening a happy one and spread his repertoire of funny stories and experiences before the responsive group, finally convulsing them with laughter when he gave a straight-faced replay of what he claimed he had filed earlier that evening to the network. "This is Allen Moore from embattled Beirut, where the small Christian community is being joined by millions of Moslems and Druze in celebrating the Christmas season with the traditional firing of guns and the more recent practice of ritual sacrifice. It's the day before the feast and fighting units on both sides spent long hours of overtime killing, racking up a reserve of casualties so that they can take the holiday off. This is Moore from Beirut…actually less from Beirut because I'm not about to get my tail shot off in this crazy town."

Rich found himself more interested than entertained. He'd watched nightly at Berkeley the responsible reporting of Moore, with the dramatic background view of the savaged, burning city.

"Allen, I think you and your colleagues are really selling our war here in Beirut." Fuad, always digging for substance in a social evening, cautiously introduced a point of controversy.

"Sure, we sell the war, we sell the news. We're like the merchants in the souq here. We sell anything the people want, for a profit." He didn't bristle. It was simply his guileless estimate of his job.

"But a good merchant worries about the quality of the merchandise. Isn't the quality of news reporting its accuracy?"

Lora interrupted. She wasn't about to let the evening get serious again. Shooing them into the living room, she served a buffet of desserts with coffee and spiced hot apple juice. The room grew cold, the conversation lagged and the party broke up. The Moores would leave the next day to spend the holidays with her parents in Munich. The Hakims issued an invitation for lunch the next week and left, Fuad reminding Dave to call him if there were ever any problems. It was decided that the student friend should spend the night rather than risk the short walk back to campus. The next morning they woke to sounds of random firing.

#########

The day before Christmas was sunny and there was shopping to do. Shops now closed at three so everyone could get home before dusk brought out the armed gangs that ruled Beirut's night. As they set out, they heard shots on Bliss Street. Dave considered cancelling. But Rich had shopping lists of things he'd promised to bring to Arab friends at college. Dave and Lora were still trying to balance the small gifts they'd gotten for the family.

Rich was the hard one to buy for. Coolly particular though simple in his tastes about the things he would wear, it was just about impossible to buy him clothes. Lora had learned that, for some strange reason, he wanted a pearl stick-pin for ties. Knowing a place where Gulf pearls were inexpensive, she and Dave had planned to leave the others to do their shopping and visit a shop in Hamra. They went first to two shops on Bliss Street near the University and learned that shots they'd heard earlier had badly wounded an AUB security official. A carload of gunmen had been waiting on the street when he left his apartment.

Unnerved, they decided to quickly wind up their errands and meet in an hour at a Florist's on Jean D'Arc Street.

The main shopping street of Hamra was busy, crowded with people determined to make an enjoyable holiday. Sidewalk salesmen were supplementing the offerings of the shops and boutiques. Entering the jewelry shop and exchanging greetings, pleasantries and news with the owners, they waited while the jeweler sent for additional goods. Merchants now kept minimal stocks in their shops. An employee could be dispatched to bring what was desired.

The tray of pearl-encrusted pins and earrings had only two of the old-fashioned stickpins that Rich so incongruously wanted. Agreeing on one, Lora looked for flaws while Dave arranged to pay. Suddenly a burst of automatic gunfire rang close and sharp in their ears. Immediately the street outside was a storm of motion, with people running, shouting, colliding, scrambling to move through the crowded street. Cars screeched and honked in a confusion so immediate and frantic that it immobilized everyone in the shop. Then, in an instant, the owners were outside, lowering the metal shutter that protected the shop. David tried to pay for the gift which Lora held, but were ushered out with a curt "Pay later." They were pushed into the mob now milling in the street.

The firing stopped and David restrained Lora from running, pulling her close along the buildings and turning off at the first alleyway to escape the crush. Coming out on Jeanne d'Arc Street, they glimpsed their three, Rich watching anxiously above the heads of the crowd for his parents and Dannie still picking out Christmas flowers as she'd been requested. The tiny grocery near the apartment would have to provide what was still needed for Christmas dinner.

########

Christmas came and went with a relaxed family routine unbroken by the intrusion of the war. They were thankful for the gale that blew off the Mediterranean. It carried the sounds of shooting and the periodic bomb and rocket blasts away from Manara. They didn't hear the fighting raging downtown through the nights, laying waste to the old buildings of central Beirut.

When Rich insisted on visiting the beach cabin the day after Christmas and enlisted the support of the taxi-driver Salman in taking him, David uneasily agreed. He wanted to go along but work intervened. Rich took Dannie and Rob to spend the sunny but still windy day. Deserted and unserviced in the winter months, the cabin with its sandy beach was still pleasant in December. Lora was hesitant but decided she had to trust Rich. She asked them to check and straighten the cabin, air the mattresses and store away things for the heavier weather to come. They finished all this in a few minutes and Rob waded into the surf for a swim, trying to lure them into the cold water. Occasional explosions and bursts of rifle fire reminded them of Beirut's war with itself.

His jeans rolled to his knees, Rich ambled slowly down the beach, his feet sinking into the surf-softened sand and his mind drinking in the overpowering peace of the lonely shore. Only at the far end, near Acapulco, did he see any other activity or people. Time, like a twisted swing that unwinds itself, quickly returned to that happy few weeks of early summer with Muna. His pace quickened. That place where they'd been might somehow bring her back, but instead it just confirmed his loss. He thought he could learn to live with what had happened, but it had left him in limbo, able to study and work but lethargic and listless about his personal life. His roommate dubbed him the "old man".

The sun sparkled on the water. Its shower of sequins moved along the surface as Rich walked, painfully piecing together his memories of Muna. As he passed the shuttered cabin where she'd danced at the party, Rich recalled the subtle personal overtures of the dance. His eyes moistened as he tried again to cope with her decision to cut him out of her life.

Looking up to clear his mind, he noted the figure walking ahead of him, a jacket around her shoulders and loose-fitting worn pants rolled like his to the knees, her hips swaying slightly as she picked her way in the yielding sand. A way of walking particular to girls on the beach, he thought. Then something about the walk grabbed at his memory and before he realized it, he had called her name.

"Muna. Muna!" A momentary hesitation, a stiffening and turning of the neck, then a quickened pace as she hurried on. He was convinced it was her. Starting to run, he shouted "Muna, I just want to talk with you. Muna, it's Rich." She must know it was him. That was why she was hurrying. He was gaining on her and when her profile turned to discover this, she suddenly broke into a run, cutting through the open area between the two beach clubs. Shouting once more, "Muna", Rich stood with hands on hips watching the fleeting form, hair streaming behind as she reached the highway, entered a small white car and drove off. Rich knew it was her. She had visited the beach for the same reason that he had. How could he talk to her? Telephone? Go to the Masmoudi house again? He had to work something out. He must see her.

Back at the cabin he persuaded the others to leave, though it was still early and the sun pleasant. Salman was waiting for them and Rich said he knew their mother was worrying. Dannie dressed while Rob and Rich stowed away the sun-baked mattresses and the beach chairs and checked the shutters. They ate the snacks they'd brought in the taxi, sending some for Salman's children.

After the others had left the taxi, Rich asked Salman if he would take him to Patriarchiyah tomorrow. Salman's reply was that he could never predict the situation but maybe. As Rich described the place, Salman ticked off the dangers, including the nearness to an entrenched Moslem quarter and the presence of Kata'ib roadblocks on the main throughway. If Rich came to the taxi office the next day at eleven they'd decide, Salman agreeing that the trip was to be kept between the two of them.

Twice that evening, Rich tried to telephone the old house where Muna lived. Both times he heard noise on the line but had not been connected. He asked his father to listen. "What does this noise mean, Dad? I need a translation of Beirut's telephone system."

David listened, perplexed. "I don't know. Sounds like someone's there. Did the number ring? Did someone pick up?" Rich didn't know. "Maybe we're being bugged, eh? But we haven't heard that on other calls. Who are you calling?"

"Uh, it's Jim Powell's number. He had to move closer in."

"I'd have thought he'd just move into the Embassy. Most of the singles have. Well, you can get him at the Embassy tomorrow."

########

After a big breakfast and some work on a law paper he'd brought with him, Rich walked to the taxi office. Salman wasn't there. Waiting for a quarter hour, he talked with another driver. Hearing where Rich wanted to go, he agreed, "as far as I can go without meeting any Kata'ib roadblocks." They drove quickly, the streets of Ras Beirut easier to traverse with the reduced traffic. Only the gun-mounted vehicles and cars of the fighting factions travelled the city, bullying traffic, ignoring one-way signs and generally taking over the streets. With cars and vans "commandeered" from their owners, the groups pressed all ranks into service as drivers. The taxi man complained, "They don't know how to drive. No license. Just boys."

As they reached the broad throughway cut through the crowded old-town area, a road-block materialized with sandbag barricade and five or six gun-laden fighters at the side of the road. No visible indication of what group. The driver slowed, pronouncing the one word that Rich knew was bringing his ride to an end. "Kata'ib". This was the well-trained fanatic militia of tough young Maronite Christians who followed the rightist political "Lebanese, not Arab" views of Pierre Gemayel and his sons Bashir and Amin, both actively involved in the militia. Could he go ahead on foot? There was probably a side street he could use. The taxi-driver was of no help, although his English was quite good.

The taxi turned into a side street and Rich got out, paid and walked up a short hill on the street paralleling the throughway. The shoppers, sidewalk vendors and even the gossiping neighbors in this mixed business-residential area were tense, watchful and worried looking. After eight or nine blocks, he turned over to the throughway again and walked along its deserted sidewalk. A car pulled up alongside and two armed men stepped out.

One spoke to him in French. What was his nationality? What was he doing in Lebanon? Where was he going? His school French helped him answer but the fact that he had no passport with him resulted in an insistent invitation to come with them. They had the authority of weapons they seemed perfectly willing to use, so he decided to accept their invitation, repeating that he was American. This information was of only marginal interest to the two warriors, who were probably younger than he. They asked him again to point to the house he was visiting and then pushed him into the back seat of the car. The driver, older and not in uniform, said in broken English they would take him to the office.

After ten minutes of driving around the edge of Moslem Basta, Rich recognized they were in Ashrafiyah, the Christian sector. If he'd been observant, he would also have recognized Ibrahim, sitting at a sidewalk table, then standing excitedly to get a better look at this familiar American face in the company of the enemy.

########

Returning to Tal Zaatar, Ibrahim was agitated. This young American, so obviously CIA, was now openly in the company of the Kata'ib. And only a day after he'd tried to contact Muna at the beach. Ibrahim had warned Abu Fadhil that Richard Draper was not to be trusted, insisting that Muna's contact with him was suspicious. He suspected the American had recruited Muna. After the night at that silly AUB professor's apartment it was clear that young Draper was working for the American service. His father was undeniably an agent, also. The Front's contact in the Embassy had confirmed that Rich was doing secret work on the Palestinians in Lebanon. Now he was back, openly consorting with the Phalangists. Hurrying, he found Munir answering the telephone.

"An American at Kata'ib headquarters? How do you know he's American?" Munir listened to the description and the report, which claimed the American was from the Embassy. The Kata'ib driver had also said he was American. Munir's agents had been watching the Kata'ib buildings closely for some indication of who they were working with, who was supporting them. They knew there were a number of young Frenchmen who were apparently volunteers and they had seen a mysterious delegation of two who were later identified as officers in the Israeli Defense Force. Others that appeared to be foreigners were young Maronites from the U.S. and South America who had returned to join the fight. This was the first information Munir had of U.S. official contact with Kata'ib.

Hearing Munir's queries, Ibrahim signalled him and picked up the other phone. He knew the informant, a Christian Palestinian who lived in the Armenian quarter, a Communist before he agreed to work with the Front. He'd moved his small fruit-juice and coffee cart into the street where Kata'ib headquarters was located, making friends with the guards, drivers and hangers-on that clustered around the offices. He'd left his cart with his boy while he phoned.

Ibrahim had seen that it was Richard and the man said he was taken directly to the captain in charge. "Watch closely and report when the American leaves." They hung up.

Ibrahim excitedly reviewed with Munir all the reasons why he suspected that this friend of Muna's was more than just the naive young student that Munir believed. Why had he claimed he hadn't reported the bomb attempt to the Embassy? Of course he had, but the CIA had decided to play along. Hadn't he offered to join the Front? What about his pursuit of Muna? An American wouldn't be that devoted to a Palestinian. There were plenty of girls in America willing to do anything. He remembered well from his year in New York. And what about Richard's father, his long residence in Arab countries? Obviously a deep-cover CIA man. He pressed his view that Muna may have been recruited. She'd met him secretly for over a month. Hadn't she telephoned him after promising she wouldn't? Why did she go to the beach yesterday? How much did Munir know about his sister? Her loyalty was only to him, not the Front. And what about Um Ali? She might be their contact.

Munir angrily rejected Ibrahim's suspicions. They would watch Rich, but it was laughable that he was an agent. He might be as intellectual as Muna had claimed but he was too idealistic to be with CIA. Munir trusted Um Ali. She'd always reported Muna's activity, believing his concern was for his sister's safety.

Ibrahim was building a fantasy. His jealousy and pride were turning to vengeance. Munir now suspected that his sister's regard for the American was genuine. It worried him. They'd watch Richard but he was more concerned now with what Ibrahim might do.

#########

Trying to find out why he was being taken to the "office", Rich realized that neither his elementary French nor his sparse Arabic were of much use. Arriving, he strode ahead into the Kata'ib command post. Dad's advice was sensible: if they have weapons, don't argue. The guntoter is always right. Smile. Be patient with the bastards. As they entered the building he looked more like an important guest than a prisoner. When they indicated the stairs he took them two at a time. Soon, he was ushered into an office filled with uniformed spit-and-polish militia types.

Their chief, a young man about Rich's age, was seated behind a large desk in front of a huge symbol of the party. Why did the quick vision of a swastika pass through his mind?

Although educated in the French St. Joseph University, the young commander dismissed the group in French, then spoke fluent English to Rich. The conversation was friendly but constantly interrupted by underlings, their short visits marked by a display of salutes and military formality, with stiffened bodies at rigid attention and eyes ahead. Did he hear heels clicking? The commander's smile told Rich that he thought it overdone, too. "Sorry, Mister….? My name is Khouri. Roger Khouri."

"Draper, Richard Draper." He paused. "American."

"I hope my men have not troubled you. We must check everyone in these difficult times."

"Is this the Lebanese Army?" Rich knew it wasn't.

"No, but in our area we must be careful. My men don't have the knowledge to make judgments. I hope they were polite. I'm surprised to find Americans strolling in our area."

"I'm visiting my family for the holidays."

"Well, that should be encouraging to us Lebanese who stay on in Beirut. What do you do, Mr. Draper?"

"I'm studying law at University of California."

"I'm a law graduate myself. Not yet practicing."

You can say that again, Rich thought. The interrogation continued. Why did he want to visit that particular house?

Rich explained that he'd known the Atallah and Masmoudi families, claiming he'd known them in London and wanted to look them up. More about Rich's family and where they lived. "How are things in Ras Beirut now? I haven't been to Hamra for some time." The young officer returned to the subject of the Atallahs. "Do you know that they are radical Palestinian terrorists? Who are really the basic cause of the war in Lebanon?"

What should he answer? "Yes, I've heard they were involved in the Rejection Front. They were known in London as activists, idealistic, reactionary, involved in Palestinian politics, as you are involved in Lebanese politics." He shouldn't have added the last, from the frowning response it brought.

"You may compare us. I wouldn't. After all, this is my country. It is not theirs. When Palestinians realize they are guests here and act like guests, there will be no problem."

"You mean no problem in Lebanon. For the Palestinians there will always be problems until they get their own country."

"Of course, and we all want that, except maybe your country."

"Oh, I think the U.S. wants it. But Israel doesn't and what Israel wants is very important in the U.S."

"Well, the true Lebanese understand the Israeli position. They are surrounded by enemies, as we now realize we are, too." Rich was surprised at the strong view. He'd heard his parents talk of things they'd heard Maronites say about preferring Israel over the Arabs, about pushing the Palestinians back into Syria and Jordan so that Lebanon and Israel could have a peaceful border and good commercial relations. The tone of his interrogator was friendly. He decided to probe his views further.

"But I thought the real problem here is representation. Isn't it true that the Moslems are now a majority in the country? I thought they only wanted a census and then to have proportional representation, democracy." He shouldn't have added the last word. The young lawyer across the desk bristled.

"Who is a Lebanese? Are the people who have come here to work from Syria and Iraq Lebanese? Are the Palestinians? The Kurds who work in the port? The Armenians who flooded in from Aleppo? We have hundreds of thousands of pure Lebanese all over the world, in your country, in South America, and in Africa. They will all want to come back some day. You count all of those abroad who are still loyal to Lebanon and there will be no Moslem majority. We are fighting to save Lebanon as a Christian country. Can't there be a Christian country in the Middle East? I think America would want to have a Christian country here."

"In American law you don't even mention religion. So, I don't know about that. I just hope this can be worked out without destroying Lebanon. We just tried to help save a country and almost destroyed it. We failed and the Vietnamese failed. There doesn't seem to be any progress here, just a lot of killing." Rich stopped, deciding he'd better try to get back home.

"There's progress. We know what we are doing. Our civil war is like your's was. We're trying to preserve the nation. We are strong enough. Our side is winning. You'll see. Lebanese all over the world are helping us. Governments, too." A true believer.

"Could I telephone my family? My Mother may be worried."

"Of course, here, use this telephone." Rich dialed the number several times, each time the call aborted half way through the dialing to produce a constant beeping. He'd never understand the telephone system here. He waited, tried again. The chief took the phone and tried the number. Unsuccessful. Then he dialed some assistant in the building and asked him to get the number and to send in some coffee. "They'll get the number for us. Is there another number? Maybe yours is out of order."

Consulting his watch, he remembered that the family was invited for lunch at the Hakims. "No, I don't know any other number to reach them now. Are we finished, captain? I could call the Embassy and ask someone to contact my family."

His host looked at him sharply. Rich intended the suggestion as a threat. "We would prefer not to call your Embassy from this office. In fact, I would prefer if you didn't inform your Embassy about this. You understand. My men should never have arrested you. Mistakes are better forgotten, isn't that right?"

"Of course. I can leave then? Because my family is invited for lunch at friends'. I could find a taxi down here someplace."

"No, I'll make arrangements. Ah, here's the coffee." Rich asked for a glass of water and it was another half-hour of interruptions before the chief asked someone to get a car for Rich. The operator had reported he couldn't get the Drapers' number. Finally, the commander—Rich still didn't know what title or rank he used—rose and took an automatic rifle from behind the desk in preparation to go. "I'll accompany you. I have to go into the city anyway. Have you ever fired these kinds of weapons?" He held it for Rich to examine. Russian markings.

"Russian?"

"Yes, Kalashnikov."

"I thought the other side was getting Russian arms."

"Oh, it means nothing. You buy arms from everywhere, through channels. We know an American who sells Russian arms. We're trying to get Uzzi sub-machine guns, you know, from Israel? But they're hard to get. Maybe the Israelis will decide we should have them. What do you think?"

"I think they already have." No response. Rich preceded the commander and his retinue down the stairs to the street, all the guards and party functionaries paying deference to the Kata'ib chief. In the street, soldiers scurried to open car doors, to check the street traffic and wave them away in the sudden burst of speed that characterized all militia traffic on both sides of the city. As they left, he noticed the neat pile of oranges on the juice-cart near the entrance and thought how delicious a glass of juice would be.

#########

The poorly-dressed man behind the cart called to his son who was being shown the workings of a machine-gun by a Kata'ib soldier. He left the boy in charge while he went up the street and into an alleyway, where an Armenian tailor allowed him to phone in his report. Soon after, telephone calls from agents surveilling two other Kata'ib installations had indicated that a tall young American was being shown Phalangist military bases. Another call reported to Ibrahim that Rich was being taken to what the Front knew was the major arms warehouse of the party, a place kept secret even from the Party's own members. Ibrahim was convinced this proved that Rich was working openly with the Kata'ib, that he was a CIA liaison man helping to arrange arms shipments. Munir was still not sure, but the events of the day were strange.

# # # # # # # # # #

Rich also thought it strange that he was taken to a military position. He objected when the young Maronite leader had insisted he leave the car and come along on a trip through a small alley to an old building obscured by new construction around it. Waiting in the doorway while the others entered, he could see that it was some kind of warehouse. The crates he saw contained ammunition. A shouting match ensued, the man in charge claiming something was not in stock, a fact the commander had come to confirm.

"I am sorry to delay your return but it's very important. I have to be at a meeting near where we are taking you."

Rich nodded. It was clear that the commander wanted his men to see this man so obviously American touring their area. Helped the cause to show Americans were with them, even if they weren't. He was glad he'd spoken up for the Palestinians. "Look, I've got to get home. If there are more stops I'll get a taxi."

The commander decided he'd better get to the cross-over point and make sure his guest got safely across. There'd be trouble if anything happened to an American held by Kata'ib. As if to punctuate his thinking, a shell landed in the street ahead and the windshield was shattered by shrapnel or debris. Rich had been given the front seat in the small car because of his long legs. There was no way to duck and as the car braked to a sudden stop, his forehead hit the metal frame above the windshield in a painful wrenching of his neck. Something rough had cut through the skin and blood trickled down his forehead.

Assuring the others he was alright, he pressed a handkerchief to the wound and they drove on. In the next block, they heard close shooting and the driver again braked. This time he was braced for it. A quick exchange between the other four in the car produced the order in English to "get out...we'll go into this building." They quickly did and Rich saw that the firing was from the roof of a building ahead. Sniping. "We'll have to wait here awhile until we find out what's the situation."

They waited two hours. The firing stopped a few minutes after they'd stopped, but the commander wouldn't agree to leave until his aide had returned to tell him it was clear ahead. As they waited, the military situation was explained in detail by the "Ra'iss." Rich knew that was an army rank, but couldn't remember if it was Captain or Major. It also meant president, chief or head. So maybe it was just the equivalent of "Sir."

It was unnervingly quiet in this once bustling downtown area. The only sound was water gurgling from a broken pipe. Damage to buildings was superficial but there was no sign of life. Asking where they were, Rich learned they were near the seafront section held by Murabitoun, the Nasirist Moslem militia. Inactive for the past week, the battle was now heating up again. The Captain hoped to get Rich past the hotel area where he could taxi home.

###########

David and Lora hadn't worried when Dannie told them Rich had gone to AUB to find his friend. When he didn't return at 1:30, they went to the Hakims'. At 2:30 David went back to the apartment but found he hadn't returned. Dave felt uneasy as he hurried back to Fuad's. They persuaded Nadia to serve lunch without Rich. Afterward, David walked down to the campus. Lora helped Nadia in the kitchen. Rob and Dannie were engrossed in the new Beirut Monopoly game, the Hakim's son explaining the Arabic names and directions.

After a quick check of the campus, partially closed for the holidays, David realized there were dozens of places Rich could be. The

Registrar's office was closed so they couldn't locate his friend. They walked quickly back and took the elevator to the Hakim's. It was almost five, curfew time. Dave was worried but didn't want Lora to realize how much. Fuad called the PLO which was increasingly responsible in West Beirut for police matters, helping with missing persons, kidnappings and even war damage. His friends at the main office agreed to send out feelers. At six-thirty, they reported there were no clues.

###########

It was Fuad's query that provided the final report of the day to Ibrahim on Rich's mysterious goings and comings. Hearing of the PLO search, he was convinced that PLO had discovered that Richard Draper was some kind of agent. He was still with the Kata'ib, ignoring the curfew. Adding that fact to the others, Munir began to believe Rich was in some way involved with U.S. intelligence. Should he confront Muna with this?

###########

Deciding finally that they could venture into the street, the Kata'ib leader helped the driver break out the glass from the windshield so they could see. They backed the car, maneuvering up a side street away from the port area and circled the upper end of the devastated Martyr's Square. Driving slowly in darkened streets, they arrived at militia headquarters near the towering Holiday Inn. Not far away was the unfinished Murr Tower, a building intended to house the communications ministry and provide the city's tallest TV antennae. For the past month it had been used as a commanding gun emplacement where leftist forces had clear access for their nightly barrage against the gutted Holiday Inn, Phoenicia, and St.Georges Hotels. This was now the major front. These imposing buildings commanded the whole downtown.

A civilian with an aging Peugeot was found and persuaded to drive Rich to Hamra. Rich shook hands, again refused first aid for the cut on his head. He wanted to be out of this complicated adventure. And out of this demoralizing city. The driver was a Christian unwilling to penetrate the Hamra area so Rich found himself walking after only a few blocks in the car, short twenty-five lira the man had demanded. Staying close to the buildings, he walked the remaining mile along the dark empty street past shuttered shops his family had patronized for years. Twice he was eyed by gunmen waiting in clusters along the way. Once a land-rover bristling with armed men slowed to look him over. He was tired and didn't really give a damn what these crazy people did with their lives but he wanted to get home and the home he was thinking about was the U.S.A. He reviewed how he might continue the search for Muna and decided he'd try the telephone again. The telephone. Look what the day had done to his determination.

When he finally unlocked the apartment door, standing in the half-lit foyer, Dave rushed out and grabbed him by the shoulders, shouting "He's here. It's Rich." The others gathered around. It was Angela who noticed the bloodied scar on his forehead, uttering a high screech. Amid excited questions, they followed him to the bathroom where Lora bathed the slight wound with alcohol and applied a bandage.

He recounted the Kata'ib adventure after a clumsy start explaining that he was walking too far downtown. David knew there was more to the story. He needed to talk with Rich. But not now. Not able to get the Hakims on the phone, he walked over to their apartment so they'd know and not worry, an errand that he'd have used Robbie for in normal times. When he returned he found them laughing and talking over Lora's hastily-assembled supper. The tensions that had clawed into their minds now skittered back into those dark corners that house our worry, imagination and fear. The Drapers were a family, cemented even more firmly together by crisis. Watching Rich, he thought of the Lebanese proverb that answers "Who is your favorite child? The youngest until he is grown. The sick one, until he recovers. The absent one until he returns." He joined them, contributing the news that the Hakims would drive to Jordan and the West Bank for the New Year Holiday.

Lora was disappointed. "The Moores, now the Hakims, and the Issawis joining his brother's family in the mountains. Everybody's leaving. I wanted a New Years party, but who could come?"

# # # # # # # # #

Lora's party included friends of Dannie who could sleep over in the Moores' apartment. The main attraction was an incredible light show acrossd the city. The Lebanese celebrated holidays and events with the firing of guns. This year there were so many weapons in the city that it was as if the war had suddenly come to life in every sector of Beirut. Grabbing the roof key and telling the young people to follow, David herded them up the stairs and led them onto the flat roof with its unimpeded view of the whole city. The display was incredible, a light-and-sound fireworks display beautiful to behold but awful to contemplate. Better to have the ammunition used in this way, he mused, expressing their hopes in the New Year. The barrage continued for a full five minutes, the varicolored tracer-trails filling the sky.

"Happy New Year!" The anxious loving kiss of Lora and Dave were followed by hugs and kisses all around. Did anyone hear the "Auld Lang Syne" from this small group on a Beirut rooftop? Others might see the wild firing as Beirut gone berserk. David hoped it was a benediction for the year of madness, a prelude for new year of peace. But he saw the broader streaks of light, rockets aimed at targets across the city . Not all the shooting was celebration. The cease-fire was breaking up.

# # # # # # # # #

The day following the uneventful departure of Rich on an early-morning MEA flight to Paris, the Kata'ib imposed a blockade of the Tal Zaatar camp and its environs. David had already postponed some necessary area travel for a month now and it was important that he leave soon. Booking his ticket for Egypt and the gulf states, he felt uneasy about leaving but knew the neighbors and the office staff would take care of the family in an emergency. Always before, his short trips out had been without problems. He'd developed a respect for the judgment of the Radio Taxi people and especially Salman. If they felt it was safe to go to the airport he went. Once in the fall they had advised him to postpone a departure. He'd been reluctant to accept their advice. On that day two taxis had been fired on near the airport.

What Dave really dreaded was the ever-present possibility that the airport would close while he was away. The trips were important for the Institute's programs in other countries. You had to have faith. "Ilhamd'Allah" as the Arabs say. So he went, leaving detailed cautionary instructions which brought brave reassurances from Lora. She worried more for his safe arrival at the airport than for her and the childrens' safety.

After three days in Cairo, David was waiting in the airport for his delayed flight to Muscat. Conversing with an Egyptian professor, he learned the details of the Kata'ib capture of Beirut's Dbaiyeh refugee camp. Finally, the flight was announced and he joined the pushing crowd at the gate. If there were any possibility that the flight was fully booked, one had to be sure not to be the last aboard. Experienced as he was in trying to hold his ground in the melee that passes for a queue in the Arab world, David slowly lost ground to the more aggressive. The most formidable opponents in such a situation were women, the best-dressed and most finely-mannered being the most ruthless.

Battered, shoved, nearly asphyxiated by the constant smoking in Arab airports, then inspected and again frisked, he boarded the bus only to wait another ten minutes for late arrivals. When the bus disgorged its passengers at the plane there was another comic opera scramble. You had to identify your luggage on the tarmac, see it put on the plane and then join another line to slowly ascend the ramp. Frayed and exhausted, he sank into his seat for the takeoff, four hours after he'd left the Cairo office for the airport. Travel was his most exhausting work.

########

At about this time in Beirut, Munir and Ibrahim were poring over a report from an agent on the Berkeley campus about the activities and associations of one Richard Draper, concluding that he was seeing too many Arabs on campus not to be involved in something suspicious. Their agent inside the PLO office had told Ibrahim that the senior Draper was being monitored in his travels to other Arab capitals. He was seeing cabinet ministers and then always meeting with American embassies.

Munir decided the Front should make a full investigation of Richard's father and that the Front representative at Berkley should keep Rich under "random surveillance."

Chapter 10

> "For even as love crowns you so shall he crucify you. Even as he is for your growth so is he for your pruning. Even as he ascends to your height and caresses your tenderest branches that quiver in the sun, so shall he descend to your roots and shake them in their clinging to the earth."
>
> Khalil Gibran, "The Prophet"

Ten days later David was in Bahrein, helping the Ministry organize a U.S. graduate study program. News of Beirut was daily more alarming. Karantina, deriving its name from its early use as a quarantine area for the Beirut port, was a slum area filled with the squatters' huts of thousands of Kurdish port workers and Shi'a Moslems, a few of which were Palestinian. Occupying a strategic coast area adjacent to the large port facilities, it had been yet another thorn in the side of the Christian Kata'ib command, which was seeking hegemony over all of East Beirut. Their solution was an "ethnic cleansing" which, filmed at shocking close range with Kata'ib approval, stunned TV audiences in Europe and the area. Men were indiscriminately lined up against walls and shot, women and children killed, the shacks filled with hundreds of dead.

In answer, Palestinian and Moslem forces besieged the picturesque Christian beach town of Damour south of Beirut and visited similar death and destruction, the atrocities equal in number, but wisely away from the TV cameras. The slicing of tendons and nerves in young boys' right hands so they "would never fire a gun against the Palestinians again" was a brutal feature of this three-day nightmare. The nearby beach estate of the Christian ex-President, Camille Chamoun, was looted and destroyed. But his life was spared in the high-level tradeoff of security the war afforded those leaders most responsible for it.

The forces of Sa'iqa, the Syrian-controlled Palestinian force welcomed into Lebanon, surprisingly did not join the PLO forces. In fact, its first use was as a Syrian peace force, restraining Palestinian support for the Lebanese Moslems. The situation was always muddled, David thought, whether you were inside or out of the country. The Arab states were of no help. Each had its own partisan view of the conflict, its own interests to be served. Many actively supported one or another of the factions.

Finished with consultations in Oman and Dubai, Dave hoped his stay in Bahrein would be brief. He was booked to return to Beirut the next day. It was at the Bahreini Education Minister's lunch that he learned the Beirut airport had been closed by heavy fighting in the area. His heart seemed to fall into his stomach as he realized his luck had finally run out. The family was stranded in Beirut without him. Asking his host to excuse him, he taxied to the airline office. A flight was available in two hours to Amman. Dave hurried to his hotel to pack and check out.

On the plane, he sank into a funk of despair, wondering how he was going to get back to the family in this self-destroying city. From the beginning, this worry had dogged him every time he had to travel. Now it had happened.

In Amman, the resourceful Director of the Institute office reported that neither ALIA, the Jordanian airline, nor MEA had any reading of when, or even whether, the airport would reopen. Asking about taxis he found that no one was making the Damascus-Beirut run. Fighting had cut off the mountain approaches. The beach road from the south was cut by the Damour fighting.

Three days and no contact with Lora. Dave stayed in the office guestroom, set aside when hotels filled up with Beirut refugees. Each afternoon he took a long walk, traversing two of the city's seven hills or "jebels" as he worried the problem. At the Intercontinental Hotel on Jebel Amman he read the pressroom teletype for detailed reports on where the day's fighting was located. The battle was raging on all sides but Manara was still safe. The army, still weakly trying to exert some authority, was plagued by large-scale defections. A Lieutenant named Ahmad al Khatib had taken his whole camp with him to join the Moslem insurgents.

The office located a company telex line which miraculously was still working. A secretary on the Beirut end agreed to telephone Lora. A few hours later, her reassuring telex back reported all was well and not to worry. At six the next morning David left in a share-taxi winding through Amman's awakening business area, nestled between the steep hills. The air was crisp and the sun was bright but he wondered what prospects there would be for getting back to Beirut once he reached Damascus. There was a long wait at the Syrian border town of Deraa. Deraa, the village where Lawrence of Arabia had been captured attempting to spy on the Turkish garrison in the first World War. On his first visit there twenty years ago he'd waited in the passport control line behind two English businessmen. The whole "Seven Pillars of Wisdom" had been toppled for Dave as he overheard the blustery Britisher say "This is the place where Lawrence got buggered by the Turks, you know".

After two hours of the pot-holed road from the Jordanian border into Damascus, Dave was happy to be in the noisy hot traffic of the city's grimy downtown streets. The upper part of Damascus was beautiful, boasting residential areas as pleasant as any in Europe but the business district and the square where the taxis for Amman and Beirut gathered, was always an ordeal, with its noise, dust and confusion.

Unloading his bag, he fought off the swarm of boys that insisted on providing help he didn't need, and went inside to inquire about transport to Beirut. As he'd expected there were no taxis running….officially. The next step was to word it about that he would pay the asking price for Beirut. Soon, he was taken by the elbow and urged outside the congested compound to where a big battered Chevrolet was sitting. For one hundred Syrian pounds or twenty-five dollars he could have one seat. After the usual bargaining, Dave talked him into the front two seats for the same price, since both he and the driver wanted to get on the way before darkness hit the mountain roads.

Exchanging salaams with the family that occupied the back, Dave explained his family was in Beirut and he wanted to rejoin them as soon as possible, having been caught out when the airport closed. The man, a Beirut merchant, said the airport was now open. All this trouble and I could have arrived on the morning flight from Amman, Dave thought, but then realized he couldn't have, with a waiting list of delayed passengers. At the breakneck speed and aggressive recklessness with which all taxi drivers in the area functioned, they arrived quickly at the Lebanese border.

With almost no traffic, formalities were rapid, including the bribes taxis paid to be allowed through. Driving down the valley into Zahle and then Shtoura, it was clear that the Sa'iqa troops moving into Lebanon were Syrian, not Palestinian. As predicted, Lebanon had fallen under a Syrian mandate.

All taxis stopped in Shtoura for their famous sandwiches, made by spreading a thick layer of "lebneh", the thick ripened yoghurt, on a fresh round of paper-thin mountain bread, adding a sprinkling of oil and herbs, then rolling the whole. Having no food since the night before, Dave wished he'd taken two as they sped up the mountain and down the precarious Beirut highway.

There was little evidence of fighting in these villages that had become resorts. Syrian roadblocks gave the taxi a relaxed wave-through. None were manned by Lebanese army now. The family in the back seat were delivered and Dave made a deal with the driver to take him directly to the apartment.

At a roadblock near the Sabra Palestinian camp, they were stopped. Asked to produce his passport by the young, curt commando, he did so and was surprised when the commando took it into the camp. While they waited, the driver more nervous than Dave, another swaggering youngster asked to see the luggage. He went thoroughly through Dave's things, taking particular interest in the electric shaver. Dave demonstrated it. The boy obviously knew little of how to go about a search. When he had finished, Dave repacked in order to close the suitcase. The driver said nothing but he looked furiously at this upstart who was delaying him. Lebanese, whether Christian or Moslem, deeply resented the way the Palestinians were assuming authority in their country.

After fifteen minutes, an older commando, machine-gun slung casually over his shoulder, came with the passport. Asking full details of where Dave lived, what he did, where he'd been, why was he returning? Mulling over the answers, he delivered the passport and started grueling the driver, who again had to open his trunk. Another search of his suitcase? No, they were waved on.

At the apartment, no one was home and the phone didn't work. Leaving his bags, he walked to the office. Lora was surrounded by students seeking transfers to the U.S. Leaving them, she came in his office for a quick embrace and exchange of news and then returned to her work outside. School was in session. Beirut was functioning. Drapers were coping. The war had become commonplace.

# # # # # # # # # #

That evening, the events of the past weeks were reviewed: bombings, new damage, facts and rumors fed by the conflict. The French were sending troops. The Americans were arming the Kata'ib. A hundred Libyan soldiers had arrived yesterday on a military plane. King Hussein was training Christian forces in Jordan. Israel was selling arms to the Kata'ib. Iraqi soldiers in PFLP uniforms were seen in Tal Zaatar. The President had moved out of the palace to the Maronite-controlled sector. Israel was moving troops to take South Lebanon up to the Litani River.

This last rumor was becoming a possibility that all but the Kata'ib feared. Almost daily, the air-raid siren located atop a nearby building announced the overflight of Israeli phantoms whose contrails and sonic booms were reminders of the distant but no less threatening enemy.

Hearing the recap of damage that continued through the city, it was clear at least two businesses were flourishing: glaziers and providers of the roll-down metal shutters now essential for all businesses. Glass was replaced in most buildings within a few days of its being broken. Damaged shops replaced the mesh roll-down shutters with the solid metal type that hid completely from view the contents and identity of the city's shops.

The exodus of Lebanon's wealthy class began before Christmas. Now jet-set refugee colonies of high-living Lebanese in Paris and London provided daily comment and criticism. Thousands of less fortunate Beirutis forced out by the fighting were barely existing in major cities of the Arab world and Europe. Damascus had the greatest number, but Amman and Cairo now housed tens of thousands. A steady flow of visitors, students and emigrants received U.S. visas. The worldwide Lebanese diaspora worked unceasingly to bring their relatives out of the war-torn country.

Extensive damage in the business areas of the city and destruction of inventory stocks in the port was wiping out the fortunes of many families considered affluent. When the gold and jewelry souks were threatened by the fighting, merchants deposited money and merchandise in safety-deposit boxes of downtown banks. When the British Bank of the Middle East, boasting the city's largest safety-deposit facility, was blasted open and robbed, many more were wiped out. This robbery, carried out by professionals brought in by one of the factions seeking funds to buy arms, was probably the largest bank robbery in history. One vault was opened professionally, the wall of the other simply blasted open with explosives. David's neighbor, the bank manager opined that no bank is safe when it can be worked on for twenty-four hours without interference.

The downtown area was totally uncontrolled, a moveable frontline where military force temporarily applied could cover the looting and stripping of any building or area. Thus, while most of the looting was done by combatant groups as a "fund-raising activity", there was also a wave of simple robberies. Hundreds of cars were stolen or expropriated each day around the city. Almost everyone the Drapers knew had lost their car at least once. The lucky ones got them back, sometimes stripped, always inoperable.

As if to meet the psychological need for leadership that was certainly not indicated in the nightly pious and repetitious cliches of the Prime Minister, an obscure radio commentator named Shafif al Akawi became the folk-hero of the city for a time. His vituperative criticism of the authorities and his benevolent advice displayed a concern for listeners. They would easily have propelled him into Parliament had elections been possible. The government simply disintegrated. Ministers and Parliament members made ineffectual statements but the leadership vacuum continued.

February brought another truce. Banks opened for a few weeks and produced account statements for the first time since September. There was a breathing spell and Beirutis wandered in to view with disbelief the destruction of their downtown area, the blasting of the beautiful hotels, high-rise business buildings and tourist facilities. People were dazed, not daring to be hopeful. Benumbed by their close-up experience with war, they accomplished little during the lull. The city remained without services and shops continued to close in mid-afternoon. A few cinemas screened films from three to five in the afternoon.

Friends called and invited the Drapers to dinner. An idea that not many tried, the dinner would be at five so everyone would be home early. Their apartment was in Ramlat al Beida, where the new Embassy was being built. Taxis were again available at night, so they accepted. Dannie and Rob could come too. Their son was one of Rob's four remaining classmates at school.

Art Torelli was Air Force when he'd been assigned as an Attache at the embassy in the sixties. Retiring early, he was now area representative for a well-drilling company and they had settled into the Beirut social life just before the war began. Mary Torelli and Lora worked together on a hospital project but they moved mostly in different worlds. Their taxi arrived late at the posh apartment with its unobstructed view of city and sea. Drinks in hand, guests on the room-sized balcony were discussing, what else?, The War. The Syrians had negotiated the cease-fire and now were receiving Lebanese leaders in Damascus. Yassir Arafat had arrived, charging that the CIA and Israel were behind the Lebanese crisis. The President agreed to the "Baabda Document", a listing of half-reforms intended to meet demands for Moslem power-sharing and assistance to Lebanon's disadvantaged. Introduced around, Dave realized that all present were Americans, mostly Embassy staff whose wives and children had left in November. Some were service attaches David had not met and some were newly arrived, including the new security officer who expressed surprise that Dave had not sent his family out.

"Where did you get such handsome men?" Lora teased.

"Oh, Lora, they're the leanest and hungriest I could find. We have to see that these poor guys get a decent meal now that the shooting has stopped long enough for us to find groceries." She and Lora went off to the kitchen, the only two women at the party. Dave joined his friend the Consul, Mack Pauley.

"Dave here is bound to have a different view of things. I've never known him to agree with me on anything in the Middle East. What do you think, will the Baabda Document defuse things, Dave?"

"No. It's just badly-conceived tokenism. Too little and too late. It would have worked if they had offered it a year ago. Is that pessimistic enough, Mack?"

"Yep, that'll do for now. I like the Colonel's version a lot better. He says it was dictated by the Syrians and they already know it will satisfy the leftists."

"Perhaps. It's what the establishment wants. Franjieh has been lucky thus far just to stay in power. Like the Lebanese say, if he'd fall into the sea, he'd get out with a fish in his mouth."

"He still has the army and they're finally being used." This from Jim Powell, Rich's young colleague of last summer, who'd asked about Rich when they'd greeted him earlier.

"The Army? What army? Is there an effective army in Lebanon any more? For that matter, was there ever an effective army?"

"No, it's falling apart," the Colonel said. "Should have reorganized when the trouble started. Probably too late now."

Powell countered. "Franjieh knows what he's doing, should be given a chance. He'd been very good at survival thus far."

"Yes," Dave interjected, "survival for himself, not for Lebanon. I have no respect for him whatsoever. He should resign and let someone else try. No one respects him. My neighbor quotes an Arab proverb: 'He has no secret friend nor open enemy.'"

"What's needed, of course, is a military coup. If Lebanese officers had been trained at Fort Benning instead of by the French they'd have taken over by now." The colonel, tough-looking but intelligent and sensitive, summed up everyone's impatience. David's experiences in Iraq, Turkey and Egypt where he'd seen coups or "Middle East elections" had led him to predict a coup in Lebanon months before. But Lebanon was proving very different.

Lora interrupted, carrying a tray of hot snacks which were instantly consumed by the hungry males. "Hey, this is a party, not a seminar. Let's talk about somewhere else. What's the news from the States? They say Reagan will get the Republican nomination."

The colonel, anxious to rid his mind of Lebanon too, joined in. "It doesn't matter. Republicans can't win after Watergate."

Dave agreed. "What would this man Carter do about the Middle East? He'd have to learn from the ground up, but he seems teachable, more honest than the others. And he's religious."

Escaping the pros and cons, Dave drew Lora onto the balcony, looking over the darkened city. The sea was luminescent, as if lighted below its surface. David's arm drew her to him and they kissed. He sensed their time together was drawing to a close.

"I understand that you do a lot of traveling in and out, Mr. Draper." It was the Embassy security man who'd made such a thing of bringing his walkie-talkie with him as he moved around the the spacious rooms. Its staccato chatter intruded as the crew-cut ex-Marine leaned on the veranda beside Dave, smoking a thin cigar.

"Yes, about every two or three weeks. We have projects in Sudan and the Gulf and I supervise offices in Jordan, Syria, Egypt and the West Bank. Miscalculated last time. Caught in Bahrein when the airport closed. Not sure I'll go again very soon."

"No, you shouldn't. We don't advise it."

Something about the way he spoke indicated to Dave that he was receiving an order and it irritated him. "I'm pretty careful. I only go when things look okay."

"But how can you possibly know? If people like you had any idea of the situation, of the risks, there wouldn't be any Americans left in Beirut."

"I've lived in the Middle East a long time. I have a pretty good idea of the risks. You know, you can walk into the lobby of the Hilton Hotel in London and get blown up. I'm not the only American using Beirut airport. I see Embassy people quite regularly on flights in and out."

"Yes, but they're on official business. Quite different."

Dave, who'd flown out on his last trip with the embassy personnel officer going to Cairo to "get away from the war", wasn't about to be put down by this man.

"Well, Embassy business may be more important to you but I'm not sure it is to me, or to others who still have work here. AUB, for instance, or business types like our host."

"You'd do well to take my advice, Mr. Draper. In 'Nam we had to simply put a stop to non-approved travel."

"In Vietnam you were an occupying power, apparently. That's not the case here. I appreciate your concern. I really do."

"If you must make trips, check with me. There's an Embassy convoy to the airport every day and another after flights arrive in the afternoon. I can fit others in if their travel is urgent."

The man was just doing his job. Why did Dave feel so belligerent? "Look, I don't know how to say this without having you misunderstand. But my experience over the years is that American embassies haven't been any closer to the situation in the Middle East than I myself have been. I'm not sure that the Embassy, as cut off and protected as it becomes in these situations, has as full and realistic view of things as I do with my contacts. And now I'm going to appear really ungrateful. I appreciate your offer of escorted transportation in Embassy vehicles, but I think such vehicles are much more of a target than I would be if I simply make my own arrangements. Radio Taxi's view of whether its safe to go has been pretty dependable."

"How can you be so sure? You have some special sixth sense?"

Oh, well, why not? The guy thinks of me as a kind of kook already, David thought. "Well, if you want to know, a part of my confidence comes from the fact that I pray about it. After that, if it seems alright, I go ahead. A couple of times I've delayed my trips." He looked straight at the incredulous security man, barely able to stifle a smile at the reaction. It would be interesting if Jimmy Carter became President. The country would have to deal with a man who believed in the power of prayer.

Mary's call to dinner was not needed to end the conversation. The open-mouthed speechlessness of the security man had already terminated the exchange. Dave joined Lora at the table, wishing that she'd been there to hear the last part of the discussion.

When nine o'clock arrived, everyone left. There were still roadblocks where one was stopped by who-knew-whom. Being robbed, kidnapped or relieved of your car was an increasing possibility. No one had confidence the truce would last. It didn't.

###########

The following Tuesday as David and Lora were working at the office, a student rushed in with tragic news. The American-born Lebanese Dean of Students at AUB, a good friend, had been killed. A radical student, dismissed after the campus takeover, shot the Dean and then raced to Engineering building where he killed its Dean as well. AUB's President was spirited out a back entrance as the deranged student burst into the Executive office, where he was finally captured.

The joint funeral of these two academics was an emotional release for the all-pervading despair of Beirut life. Held in the Assembly Hall, as the campus chapel is now called, the service provided an incongruous opportunity to see friends and associates isolated by the war. An air of gloom pervaded the large gathering.

School life for Rob and Dannie was a deteriorating situation, too. Some of the newer, younger teachers were dwelling on the war in their classes, skimming over lessons in favor of never-ending reviews of the day's fighting. The headmaster, staff and a few parents tried valiantly to keep students' spirits up with activities but it wasn't an effective educational year.

Scheduled to chair an Institute conference in Cairo in late February, David decided he couldn't leave the family and so they all went for this five-day visit. The children stayed with a professor-friend at American University in Cairo and Dave and Lora stayed at the conference hotel. In spite of the hectic schedule they enjoyed the much-needed change from the gloom of Beirut. Celebrating their twenty-fifth anniversary at the new Meridian Hotel's supper club, they mostly ignored their Institute friends as they danced away the evening.

Rob and Dannie were able to join in a day at the Pyramids and got a lot of attention from the adults. At a family dinner given by Egyptian friends from Washington days, the two families enjoyed their reunion over a sumptuous feast. But again the talk was the Beirut war. Early the next morning they boarded the plane bound for home. EgyptAir had leased a World-Air plane with a Texas crew. The co-pilot invited Rob up to the cockpit for almost the whole flight. Allowed to remain in the cockpit during the landing in Beirut, Rob was in a state of rapture for days after.

##########

On returning, Lora involved herself in relief work and spent a number of afternoons with a group of Americans and European women helping overworked Lebanese institutions provide aid to the homeless victims of the fighting. The refugees from Karantina and some of the other areas overrun by Kata'ib forces had been moved into the beach clubs. The small cabanas, built to serve mainly as changing rooms with tiny kitchens and bathrooms, were now housing large families who were destitute of belongings and livelihood. Collecting money and donations from the dwindling foreign community, the small group elected a delegation of three including Lora to take their contribution to the loosely-organized camp that now occupied San Michel, San Simon and Acapulco beach clubs. Their visit was coordinated with the PLO, now in charge of just about everything in West Beirut. Dave agreed she should go but worried about it. When she hadn't returned in four hours, he decided he'd better do something. As he was dialing the number of the committee head at AUB, Lora walked in, looking exhausted.

"Oh, what an experience!" She sank into a chair by the window. "The way they are living out there. They don't have enough clothes to keep warm. There isn't water most of the time now. You should see what they're feeding them. But at least there seems to be enough food." The narrative flowed out like water over the top of a dam, phrases and reactions spilling out so there'd be room again for the order and security of her own life.

"We hadn't nearly enough diaper material, but it was a good start. The other clothing was grabbed up within minutes and immediately put on. They're cold. I hadn't remembered the almost-constant wind you get at San Michel. We worked with the children mostly. Some of the Palestinian women I knew from the embroidery project were there. They looked exhausted. The families in San Michel were mostly Kurds from Karantina. No, I didn't get to see our cabin. After I was there, I didn't really want to. Oh, Dave, if you could have heard this one old Kurdish man, his back all bent like the porters in Baghdad, remember? He told us in broken English, guess he'd learned it from the ship crews, how he'd seen his wife and two sons shot. He just babbled.

I don't think he'll ever forget. I'm not sure I will."

Dave took her hand. "You should go lie down for awhile."

"No, I'm alright. I think we accomplished something but not nearly enough. I'm glad I went. They appreciated it. When they learned I was American they all crowded around. I was glad we'd taken the baby supplies. There were so many who needed just simple first-aid, baby oil, salve, eye-medicine." She paused, emptied of her emotion. "I've got to get something for dinner. Where are the kids?"

"Studying. They're quiet these days, have you noticed?"

"Yes. So serious. Oh, I almost forgot. You know Fawzia's niece, Muna? She was there. Muna and two young girls were having some kind of argument with the camp director. They brought a pick-up filled with bags of bread and some other things. Later, she came over and joined me. Worked with me, helping dress the children. Then we cleaned the room they have for a clinic."

"What did she say? Did she mention Rich at all?"

"No. Said Fawzia is in Cairo. I could have called her there."

"And no mention of Rich?"

"Not by her. I told her Rich had been here for Christmas, that he'd tried to call her."

"I didn't know you knew that. Rich didn't say anything."

"A mother knows a lot of things about her sons that they don't tell her. I was hoping there would be some indication from her. It's a worry for me. I know Rich still cares for her."

"How long were you with her?"

"Oh, over an hour. She left early. I have the impression that the PLO people didn't want her group there. They don't like the Rejection Front. Dave, when she left she gave me a hug and kissed me, and then quickly ran off. I couldn't even return the gesture, it was so quick. She seems so sad, so delicate. Such a tender person for what they say about her."

"Yes." They were joined by Dannie. Rob came in and their mother took them to the kitchen, telling them about the camp while she prepared dinner. Looking out at the blue Mediterranean, Dave pondered the end of the surf-sand-and-sun good times San Michel had provided before the refugees moved in.

# # # # # # # # # #

The next few days saw the final collapse of the Lebanese Army. A steady stream of small units, with stores of weapons, joined Christian forces. The mutiny of Ahmad Khatib had drawn Moslem troops into what was now called the Lebanese Arab Army. Occupying Bain Militaire, the Officer's Club beach installation below, they commanded the Draper's area. After a telephoned threat that a bomb would explode in the lighthouse, they placed a twenty-four-hour guard at the lighthouse, providing an uneasy daily reminder that the area was now militarized. The fighting started again, slowly increasing its area and intensity. Nights were filled with the noise of shelling and the days with intermittent gunfire in the distance. Varicolored columns of smoke marked the burning in the central city and port. One day it would be a warehouse filled with butter, another time fuel-oil, another of blacker density was new rubber tires.

Sleep still came easily for Dave and Lora. Most evenings they retired early because of power failures. Occasionally, heavier gunfire awoke them. If it sounded close, Dave plodded around the apartment, opening windows to prevent the blast damage that could occur with a close explosion. A direct hit, of course, you didn't think about. The apartment was protected from the line of fire to the East by an adjoining building. They slept in their usual bedrooms, with the slatted roll-shutters down and drapes pulled across against the danger of window glass. Many friends were not so fortunate, moving beds to hallways, inside foyers, or even outside in the stairwell of their apartment structures.

On 11 March, the Drapers tuned to the TV news, expecting to hear another intense and sincere harangue by the Prime Minister, whose nightly sing-song exhortations for compromise and settlement were ridiculed and mimicked. The news was suddenly interrupted. Commotion seized the TV studio and then a camera focused on a relatively-unknown Lebanese Brigadier named Aziz al Ahdab as he announced a coup d'etat. "Well, finally," Dave sighed, "maybe this guy will take charge and govern the country."

The "Television Coup" as it came to be known, was an empty gesture. Apparently thinking that he could simply announce a takeover and it would materialize, the unfortunate officer hadn't enough military support to capture even the TV station. He was announcing a coup and then expecting to negotiate it. After experiencing two coups in Iraq, Dave knew the essential elements: the takeover of radio and TV stations and of at least one military installation in the city. Then the announcements of military camps and commands that, previously committed, pledge their support. None of this was forthcoming. Rob's classification was probably right. This had been a "chicken coup."

Security was nowhere in Beirut. Random shelling of the nearby Hamra area made every day a Russian Roulette. Manara remained an enclave of relative safety, though an apartment building just two doors away from Dave's office had taken a shell which opened a ten-foot-wide hole in the apartment of an absent American tenant. Shrapnel from another shell riddled offices, shops and the Turkish Embassy. A fragment ricocheted into the Institute office where Lora was helping a student with forms.

Late the next afternoon, a frantic call from the assistant director of the office brought the war closer still. A rocket explosion had wrecked her apartment. She'd been sitting on the sofa in front of the window-wall and got up to turn on the radio news in the bedroom. The blast hurled heavy plate glass across the room, shredding the drapes, sofa and chairs. Then the implosion sucked in the hallway door, splintering the doorframe. Dave and Lora walked over, helped her collect some clothes and brought her home to stay with them. After two nights sleeping at the Drapers', they decided she should leave. She was still shaky and dazed when David found her a taxi for Damascus.

On Sunday the family visited Robbie's first Beirut teacher who was dying of cancer at AUB Hospital. A legendary figure who had been with the school for eighteen years, Mrs. Churchill was beloved by all who knew her. A small thin woman, her mind raced at such speed it quickened the thinking of all with whom it made contact, planting seeds of curiosity in her fourth graders and tilling their minds to provide independent growth. Whatever it is that makes great teachers was hers in abundance and the Board had already decided the grade school should be renamed in her honor.

She lay now, nearer death than life, but managed the encouraging smile that Rob remembered. He didn't want to stay, seeing her emaciated face and wispy hair. Lora, seeing tears in his eyes, told him to leave the flowers and wait for them in the lobby. Distant gunfire punctuated their sentences and the frail patient whispered in a breathy voice, "Oh, Lora, I believe my cancer has spread to all of Beirut. This city has seen the largest part of my life. To see it now, destroying itself. I wish I hadn't lived to see this." She was tiring and they left.

The hospital was operating with as much efficiency as it could muster, considering that many of the physicians and most nurses had left the country and that staff living in the Eastern part of the city had not been able to report for work for months. Those who lived nearby worked long hours coping with the growing list of casualties. Luxury suites, built to house the oil sheikhs and VIPs from abroad, were now living quarters for physicians and teaching staff. The once-prestigious hospital was not very clean. The PLO was in charge of hospital security. This solved supply problems and provided protection, but it also meant that many decisions on medical priorities were imposed by the commandos. Nevertheless, the university and staff could be proud of their crucial contribution. "What a waste of surgical talent," Dave commented, arm around Robbie as they left to walk the mile home. "Most of the patients are innocent victims, non-combatants."

Monday morning the firing downtown started early, its slow rumble and staccato accompaniment slowly waking Dave from a sound sleep. He roused the kids for breakfast and school. The firing continued unabated. As Lora picked up the phone to inquire if school was cancelled, it rang. School wouldn't be held. The situation looked very serious. Would she please call those on her list to inform them. As a Board member, she shared in the job of communicating changes in the school schedule.

At eight-thirty when she'd made the last of her calls, a loud blast shook the building and rattled the windows. Smoke curled up from the Military Beach below and then another shell swooshed over, landing in the sea and roiling the waters in a great white circle. Dave drew back from the window. They usually fired three volleys before changing their aim. The third shot blasted the Corniche, tearing the rail and riddling an armored vehicle.

Expecting a letup, Dave started to leave for the office but another deafening blast shook the area. Then more. Neighbors came on balconies calling to each other and then ducked inside as the barrage continued. The Drapers' bell rang and the Moores came in, Allen asking Dave to get his roof key to see what was happening. They climbed the stairs, deciding the elevator was a risk. The blasts continued. Was the office getting it?

Deciding against the exposed roof, Dave used the key left by the tenants of the penthouse apartment. They entered, taken aback by the noise and vibration in this upper exposure. The circular view of the area revealed a row of smoking targets along the Corniche road. Going to the kitchen balcony, Dave saw that Robbie had joined them. Lora was calling to be careful from the stairwell where Dannie also waited. "Looks like it hit the school. Good thing you cancelled classes today. That one's got to be the Riviera Hotel." Shells were coming about one a minute.

Allen had brought binoculars and confirmed that the Hotel and another building had received direct hits, and the school a block away. Rob peered wide-eyed over the balcony next to his dad, who hugged him close and drew him back. Allen was ticking off the buildings and locations hit. "About half are on the Corniche or in the water. AUB is certainly getting it. And the school. They've gone crazy over there. What are the Kata'ib trying to prove? Half the people living in this area are foreigners." Lora called again, pleading with them to come back inside.

A sudden whoosh filled their ears as the targeting changed back to the military headquarters below their building. It froze all of them for a moment. They moved to the doorway, Allen reminding them "You don't worry about the ones you hear", then reflexively ducking as a second louder whoosh was followed by the crack of an explosion and the sound of flying shrapnel hitting close. "I thought you heard the whoosh only if it passed over." Another rush of air and sound as a shell fell just short of their building, the debris and shrapnel blasting the ground floor.

Inga looked grim. Allen would insist she leave. Their two girls hadn't been able to return to school in Broumana. She wanted them to stay in the apartment but hearing Rob and Dannie, they'd crept up the stairs and were standing now with Lora. Another bone-chilling whoosh, so loud it filled their whole consciousness, was followed instantly by a second. The explosions reverberated through the rocky foundation of the building. Lora, arm around Dannie, looked at Rob at the same instant that Dave did. Unconcealed fright shaped his expression, a rigidity and whiteness, a staring of eyes that brought Dave to his side. David looked into Lora's sad eyes. The time had come.

They drew back into the empty apartment, "We'd better get down below where it's safer. They've got us bracketed. If this goes on much longer, the law of averages alone will mean a hit on the building." Allen grabbed his two small girls' heads and drew them close. David opened windows to prevent blast breakage, then gripped Rob's shoulder as they followed the others downstairs.

"Well, son, we've got plans to make. We promised we'd leave when it came to our area and it has."

Rob hadn't told the family about what he'd seen in the hospital corridor, when they'd visited Mrs. Churchill. A patient in a wheel chair had uncovered his wounds, showing his whole side riddled with deep cuts stitched together but not yet healed. He saw again the sliced and scarred body as explosions had engulfed them on the roof. But now, the fortifying flow of adrenaline that accompanies excitement and danger was injecting confidence into his thin straight form. "We don't have to leave, Dad. Unless you think they'll close the school. Allen says it got a hit, but maybe not. Do we really have to go?"

"Yes, you have to go." As certain as he was, it was hard for David to say it. He hated to see the family broken apart, even in this kind of circumstance. Neishbor families, close friends, even the Institute officers in Washington couldn't understand why he would continue exposing the family to danger. Now the war had reached unacceptable risk-taking proportions. Before, sensible precautions and discipline had, he felt, provided protection and security. He'd felt confident. Both he and Lora, in their daily reviews and in what they felt was inspired prayer-sought guidance, had felt a quiet calm about their experience. They'd also noted the uses this adversity had in strengthening the children, in teaching them some of the necessary lessons in life. Had he lived in the area so long he'd become fatalistic? Maybe.

The shelling continued through the day but they ignored it as they packed and made plans. Lora's worst fear was confirmed. Dave was not coming with them. When they could leave depended on contact with the few airlines still operating. The question of where was harder, depending on what the future might hold. Who could predict the length of this inexplicable conflict? Finally, it was decided they'd go to Utah, where they owned a house they could use when students moved out at the end of the winter trimester. They'd be close to relatives, not too far from Rich.

The schools were good.

Lora agonized over her "desertion" of ACS. As a Board member she had urged continued operation of the school in the war. Now she was abandoning them. Dave felt the school should close. The Board voted to recess early for the annual Easter vacation and to prepare for permanent shutdown.

The earliest flight was on Friday. The week of preparations was complicated by shelling that now made even the smallest errand out of the apartment an adventure. On Wednesday, walking the short distance from the office where Dannie and Rob had been helping with filing and other chores, the four of them were showered with debris from a mortar shell exploding a hundred feet ahead, leaving the star-shaped crater that pocked the streets. Thursday morning Dave walked a mile to the Carleton Hotel, where Middle East Airlines was temporarily holding forth in a wing of the lobby, their beautifully appointed offices now abandoned in the battle area. Everyone was seeking flights out of the city and it took two hours to buy the tickets, which were only to Amman. From there, Lora would buy U.S. tickets. They would sleep in the office guestroom, hotels filled with the exodus from Beirut.

Friday morning, Salman's taxi appeared on schedule at seven-thirty in spite of the random shelling still continuing. The neighbors waved from balconies or gathered in the street to say good-byes. Mrs. Issawi had called across from her balcony yesterday, urging Lora to reconsider, promising the Syrians were coming to bring peace. Coming down, she hugged Lora and the children, tears in her eyes. "As long as you stayed, we hoped. Now, I think there is no end, just war, war. Don't forget us. God bless you." The Moores came down. They would fly to Greece the next day. Luggage in the trunk and with Rob and Dannie in the back, Dave and Lora sat with an anxious Salman.

The trip to the airport was marked by seven roadblocks, each including a careful inspection of the car. The final one required a full baggage inspection by the Sa'iqa troops from Syria. Just before rounding the last circle, they heard a large blast which felled a tree at the side of the road fifty yards behind.

"Well, I was just about to have second thoughts. Maybe that was to assure me this is the right decision," Lora's arm held Dave closer. After the delay of the baggage search, they pulled up to a frenzied crowd at the airport. David, using the ticket he always carried so he could be admitted to the check-in area, rushed the porter and the kids in with the luggage. Salman would wait. A shooting fracas had left broken glass and damage everywhere.

Meeting others they knew leaving on the same flight, they jockeyed for position in the undisciplined melee, suspecting the flight was oversold. Coming two hours early had been wise, but everyone else had the same plan. David stood in one line, Lora in another. Finally, with Rob's help in moving luggage, they were entered on the passenger list. Quick good-byes parted them at passport control. Lora's tears would come later. A new fear now gripped her as she shepherded her children through the airport chaos. A fear for David, this man she had loved so long but still didn't really understand. Why was he so insistent on staying?

Chapter 11

"What have you in these houses? What is it you guard with fastened doors? Have you remembrances, the glimmering arches that span the summits of the mind? Or have you only comfort, and the lust for comfort, that stealthy thing that enters the house a guest, and then becomes a host, and then a master?"

Khalil Gibran, "The Prophet"

Trusting the amazingly efficient performance of MEA once again, David exited the Airport building and waved to Salman. He should have stayed to see them on the plane but Salman said they must be back before the road was cut. The shelling of the Palestinian camp area was increasing. The blast in the road had just missed them, a close call. Now he was relieved. The responsibility of the family's safety would no longer be a daily pressure.

Salman confirmed that the Damascus-based refugee army Sa'iqa was more Syrian than Palestinian. "They're actually helping Kata'ib against the Palestinians." The hotel battle was on again. "The PLO now has the Murr Tower again. They blasted the Holiday Inn all last night." Later, Allen would tell him the PLO's Fatah forces had captured the luxurious hotel and savagely hurled trapped Kata'ib fighters from its 19-story roof.

Salman was almost tongue-tied with anger and frustration. No longer could he mouth the clever comments and anecdotes that had made fun of his country's politics in the past. What could one say to explain this madness? "I'm going to work for the newsmen, Mr. Draper. I'll be at the Commodore." The war had months ago enveloped the St. George Hotel which had been foreign press and media headquarters for a quarter-century. Ras Beirut's Hotel Commodore, a comfortable if less prestigious establishment, now offered the specialized telex access and personalized services the news nomads required. The war brought in a horde of journalists including most of those who specialize in the world's ever-replenishing supply of big and little wars. Lebanon's little war was becoming big enough for the world's attention finally.

Not until he entered the empty quiet apartment did David feel the impact of the parting. The family was gone and now it hit him that most of his friends and associates had also quietly departed. AUB was badly hit and one shell had killed a student who'd been in the office a week before. It had also injured eight others, including the young man who had come for New Year's Eve. Both professors and students were leaving and work accelerated at the office, arranging transfers. Mack Pauley, Dave's friend who was Consul, began issuing "Prospective-student" visas to those the Institute would certify met U.S. admission requirements.

Without either the Assistant Director or Lora to help out, and regular staff not reporting for work in months, David worked long hours with the help of a Palestinian AUB student living in the neighborhood. His aunt, a resourceful woman who was willing to brave the streets, helped with translating credentials. At the apartment, dinginess took over. The bright cheeriness faded, though the spring sun shone brightly through the taped windows.

The fighting let up and a special U.S. emissary arrived, assuring the failure of his mission by announcing on arrival that, of course, he couldn't talk with the PLO. The entire hotel area and south waterfront had fallen into the hands of the Moslem-Palestinian militia coalition, which also captured the strategic mountain villages of Mtein and Ain Tura. The President had fled his palace and established himself in the Christian stronghold, vowing again that he wouldn't resign. It was a good time to get away. Since there was no mail service, everyone depended on special channels. With the family gone, Dave was free to catch up on the area work that was part of his job and to take out mail for the office and friends. He went to Cairo, Khartoum and Amman.

Returning in eight days, he was glad to find Allen back.

"Dave, you came in on the same plane with the French mediator. Our American couldn't do anything, not being able to contact PLO. Maybe the Frenchman can, but I doubt it. France only has influence with the Christian side." Allen had just come from the Parliament meeting. "They decided they'd elect a new President but now they have to wait so there can be a campaign."

"Incredible, Allen. The whole year's been a campaign."

Fighting continued in the Port area, where Kata'ib occupiers looted the port warehouses. "They're driving through East Beirut in hundreds of new Fords and Chevies intended for transhipment to Iraq and the Gulf. So, the insanity still reigns. An equal mix of Oz, Wonderland and the third level of Dante's Inferno."

# # # # # # # # #

Dave had brought a new novel to read, but with power failures almost nightly, the madness of Beirut pressed in upon all his waking moments. One night, Allen appeared with a mock-formal request for the pleasure of Mr. Draper's company at a spaghetti dinner with the correspondent crowd, to which Dave would bring the salad and anything else he could find. The spaghetti was to be cooked by a German TV newsman, self-acknowledged expert. Allen had the sauce on the stove already. Dave gathered up what he could find for a salad and took the dressing Lora had mixed. Searching the cupboard, he grabbed cans of apricots and pears.

Though some of the characters were new, it was the same relaxed and casually-dressed crew he'd met on other evenings at Allen's. Dave welcomed their insistent hilarious banter. It helped to put Beirut into perspective, no, out of perspective. He was weary of perspective and certainly weary of Beirut.

"We're celebrating, Dave. Franjieh has agreed that Lebanon can have a President of its own choice. We're here to rejoice."

"Did you say re-juice? That's what I'm here for. I hope, Allen, you haven't hidden away all that NBC liquor. I came to drink." The new Times man headed for the victorian chiffonier that Inga had converted into a bar.

David had met Gunther, the German TV commentator, who was defending his skill in cooking pasta. "I cook spaghetti like you have never tasted before."

"Exactly what I'm afraid of." Allen was not convinced.

"It's practically the only thing I learned from the Italians in four years in Rome. Certainly the only worthwhile thing. You are not to worry about my spaghetti. You go back to your sauce."

"Exactly what I had in mind," Allen retorted, picking up his glass. "I plan to stick very close to my sauce all evening as a matter of fact." A heavier-than-usual distant explosion interrupted for a moment. "Where do you suppose that was?"

"It doesn't matter. There's nothing left down there to destroy. I was downtown today. Looks like Munich in forty-five."

"You can't use that. I already have." Nigel, the Guardian correspondent, was still trying to get a fix on the day's story and was interested in something Dave had said about Syrian intentions not seeming so ulterior if one considered what they had not done, rather than what they had. After their discussion, Dave felt he'd helped, if only by listening. Nigel then went to Allen's study and put it down in ten minutes of furious typing. David went to the kitchen, where war had broken out.

"I tell you, Allen, it is cooked and overcooked". Gunther wrenched the heavy pan away, almost spilling the boiling pasta as he drained the boiling water, quickly rinsed the pasta and returned it to the hot pan, putting a slab of butter on top.

Allen's loud "Comen ze now. Ze German-Italian spaghetti, she is on ze table," brought everyone to the long table set with various pans, plates, bottles and a general clutter that would have horrified Lora or Inga. Gunther was right. The spaghetti was overdone, and his Teutonic fury lasted through the meal.

"Don't you Americans understand scientific principles? The spaghetti continues to cook after you remove it from the flame. You must stop the cooking before it is fully tender. Your American stubbornness has ruined my reputation."

Sticky spaghetti aside, stomachs were soon filled and conversation grew more mellow. The talk wound down, most of the men around the table staring into their refilled wine glasses. Allen had already sent his filmed report on the Tal Zaatar camp. The evening was languid and unpressured as they grazed over the food and the situation, nibbling at some of the new rumors and unconfirmed reports. Dave didn't usually stay on as the heavy drinking drained the substance from the conversation, but tonight he dreaded the return to the apartment above.

Nigel, leaving to telex his story to the Guardian, asked if anyone was up to some eight o'clock tennis. "Probably without a net…but also without paying. They've simply stopped coming, but left the courts open."

Allen wanted to make it nine-thirty or ten, "after the shelling. I sleep best knowing that the war for liberation, truth and democracy is proceeding without interruption."

"Not me. I'm bonkers as soon as it starts. I'm always an early bird and now I'm a very early bird."

"Exactly." Allen opened the door for Nigel. "You, Nigel, are the early bird and I'm the worm, in bed where I won't get caught." The others gone, David and Allen looked at the party's devastation and hoped that Allen's maid would come the next day. At the door, Allen asked a surprising question. "How did you get to know the Tal Zaatar crowd, Dave?"

Stumped for a minute, Dave's response was puzzled. "I don't think I do. What do you mean, the Tal Zaatar crowd?"

"Well, the guy I talked to is Abu Fadhil. He's become the spokesman. Articulate, cool, British educated, actually moderate for PFLP. No, not moderate, sensible. When his sidekick asked about you, he seemed to know you, too. Asked me what you do, why you travel so much? Not friendy questioning. I asked them why they wanted to know. Abu Fadhil said they'd heard you were helping Palestinian students leave Lebanon and wanted to know more about you. But there's something else. This other character asked about your son that works for the American government. You don't have any sons except Rich and Robbie, do you?"

"No, Rich worked at the Embassy. But he's in law school."

"I told them that. They pressed the point, saying no he was still working. Was it for the State Department or the CIA, they asked me." Allen's eyes searched Dave's face. Was his neighbor hiding something? "I thought you'd want to know. They aren't the PLO, you know. These guys are a whole different kind of animal. The conversation worries me, pal."

"Allen, I think Abu Farid."

"Abu Fadhil," he corrected.

"Abu Fadhil. He's the brother of a girl that Rich was very taken with last summer. He also met Rich at a meeting with an Embassy friend and that Americans for Justice group. The brother was invited to speak. That's all I can figure out. I haven't met any of them." He couldn't tell Allen about the bomb incident. He'd want to do a story on it. "American Student Delivers PFLP Gift Bomb to U.S. Embassy."

"Well then, not to worry. Thought you'd want to know."

"Yeah. Thanks for a good time. Enjoyed your "Choiman" friends, though they do come on strong."

"A pain in the ass when you're discussing politics, otherwise nice guys. When do you travel? I've got a letter for Inga."

"Day after tomorrow. My first visit to Baghdad since sixty-six. I spent so damned many hours getting the visa I'm determined to use it. Going to Amman first. I'll pick up your mail tomorrow night." Back in his apartment, Dave worried about Allen's strange report. He wished he knew more about this Abu Fadhil.

# # # # # # # # # #

Frequent trips out to the real world of business as usual in the prosperous and peaceful countries of the area helped to save Dave's sanity. But each return was more difficult, the despond and despair a little deeper. Flying in from Baghdad, passengers pointed out the smoke-swirling fires as war damage. But most were the burning garbage heaps on every street corner.

Dave knocked at the Moore's door and was surprised by Inga who'd returned to bring things needed in Athens. Allen would be home soon. The power was off. Clothes spread over the furniture. "Hey, I've got some steaks from Smith's. Their freezer's given up. I'll broil them and bring them down." David still had cooking gas and knew Allen had run out.

Steaks under the oven broiler, a vegetable casserole Inga had prepared and frozen before leaving for Athens in the oven above, David was stirring rice in boiling water when suddenly a shell swooshed down in the small courtyard below the kitchen balcony. The blast jolted the building. The heavy plate glass in the kitchen door blasted in, luckily not reaching where he was standing. The open windows banged back into the room and a spray of glass and rubble fell like heavy hail. Then, instantly, a second explosion threw Dave back across the room, the stove jumped toward him and the oven door crashed against the refrigerator. The burner-grills were tossed into the air.

Stunned but realizing the butagas had exploded, he managed to shut the valve. Rice was everywhere, grains flung to every corner. The broken casserole sat empty at Dave's feet, slices of eggplant, tomato, zuchini and onion mixed with rice on the floor. The steaks remained in the broiler drawer of the stove which now sat diagonally in the center of the large kitchen. Still holding the spoon aloft, he'd used his left hand to close the gas valve as if the spoon were somehow too important to put down. Counting off the potential dangers he'd escaped, he rubbed his bruised leg where the oven door hit him. "Dammit, what are we going to eat now?" he said aloud.

Heavy knocking at the door. In the failing light he opened the door, spoon still in hand. "Thank God you're alright. I knew you were in the kitchen." Inga, a gas light in hand, hugged him, Allen behind her. Seeing Dave was in good shape, he rushed in. "I don't care about Draper. I want to know about the steaks! What happened? Have you got a mortar out there in the kitchen? Sounded like you returned their fire. Luckily we were in the living room making love."

"Oh, Allen! Are you hurt, Dave? We heard a second bomb up here." She held up the lantern and went down the hallway. Dave, shell-shocked, followed, spoon in hand. They surveyed the wreckage: the stove at its crazy angle, top askew, pans, dishes and a bouillabaisse of vegetables on the floor. Dave began to chuckle, still holding the spoon.

"I don't think you need that spoon, Dave, at this point in time, that is." Allen took the lantern to inspect the uncooked steaks. "The bastards could at least have waited until the steaks were cooked. Do you think we can get your stove working again?"

"I don't think I'd like to try, not in the dark anyway. That second blast was the stove blowing up on me. Did you get much damage?"

"Yeah, same as up here. The kitchen and two rooms along the hall. Windows. Shrapnel. I was afraid you'd gotten it, Dave. Damned strange, that second explosion. Maybe the first one blew out the flame and gas built up. Anyway, supper is gone to hell and back. Inga, can't we finish the steaks in our toaster-oven?"

"Of course we can…when the electricity is restored. Now, when do you suppose that might be? There might be glass in them now, anyway. Well, let's clean up this mess."

Just then there was a pounding on the door and a voice calling "Mr. Draper! Mr. Draper!" The building's laconic concierge appeared. They weren't prepared for this new Abu Ahmed in his sad-sack uniform. Somewhere he'd gotten an American army helmet, without the liner. Eyes hidden by the too-large helmet, he had an old rifle slung unconvincingly over his shoulder.

"Abu Ahmed, the good soldier. Welcome my man. What news do you bring from the front?" Allen couldn't keep a straight face. The concierge's flashlight beam led him into the room as he instructed them to stay away from windows and told of the damage to his flat. "Ilhamd'Allah" his wife and children were safe. Dave decided against showing him the kitchen. Abu Ahmed left, unable to understand why these Americans were laughing.

"We've got some very good Gruyere, some crackers and some apples. Come on down, Dave, and we'll talk about the war." Dave grabbed his key and followed them downstairs. They made a quick inspection of the glass-spattered rooms and traced the pattern of shrapnel in the kitchen ceiling from the blast below. Liberating a tray of things to eat, they stepped carefully over the mess and settled around a coffee table holding the lamp and their dinner. Inga had hoped to stay longer but now agreed to leave on schedule.

"Well, David, we have a President again. The Parliament just finished electing Elias Sarkis."

"Somehow, that doesn't make me any happier. I'm ready for my vacation. But I still have make a trip to Kuwait."

###########

It was a wild ride to the airport. Salman had agreed to take him. The fighting groups patrolled every street. There was a sudden fad of Western-style gun holsters slung low on the hip. Shooting incidents unconnected to the war as more weapons became available to the gangs which controlled the streets. The motley collection of undisciplined gunmen in West Beirut were united only in their opposition to the Christian rightists. Would they take over the country? The revolutionaries always win. They capture the young and frighten the old. The in-between ages remain apart from the struggle, allowing the anarchists free access to do their dirty work.

"Look at this, Mr. Draper. They call this the 'Bridge of Death' The fedayeen drop bodies over the side and set fire to them. The little kids come and watch."

"It's awful. I was at AUB hospital yesterday. Went to the children's ward with a friend. A roomful of kids torn up and maimed by the bullets and schrapnel. You know what? Parents were bringing toy machine-guns and pistols as gifts." With schools closed, children were ever-present at militia posts. Their fascination was fed by the adolescent fighters, always eager for an audience, even if it was only children.

At the airport, the ticket agent said Syria was mobilizing, to assist in a Moslem-Palestinian takeover of the country. He was wrong. Dave flew back from Amman the same day six thousand Syrian troops poured across the border, taking up positions in opposition to the Druze and Palestinian troops. Moslems such as the neighboring Issawis were alarmed at this serious reversal of the conflict. Dave resolved to get the office mothballed and get the hell out. Few students could now come to the office. Fall admissions were finalized. Beirut was ready for more fighting.

At a nearby small hotel where Pan American was handling its business out of a second-floor bedroom, Dave charged a round-trip ticket to the States. There was one flight to Damascus still open, June ninth, connecting with PanAm to London and then home. The act of finalizing these arrangements cheered him and he stayed on at the office that afternoon, hoping to do the final drafting of an article he'd promised for the Chronicle, reporting on the disastrous education year in Lebanon. It was slow work, checking his notes from talks and visits, complicated by the intricate mosaic of Lebanon's public-private educational system. It was past curfew, but the old Royal typewriter he used at the office stimulated his thinking. He was almost finished.

As he began the summary paragraph there was a sudden noise in the street, a screech of brakes, shouting and men running into his building. Jumping up and looking out the window, he saw a gun-mounted Land Rover pulled around with its gun pointed up at his office. Dave waited, certain they'd decided this American office deserved their attention. Shouted commands and commotion filled the empty street below. A heavy-booted scuffle up the stairs paused, then went on up the stairs. Maybe they just want the roof for a gun position. A banging on the floor above and, finally, machine-gun bursts. Who were they shooting at? The floors above were all empty. He waited. More commotion, excited voices. More men coming up. He peered out the window. Two jeeps disgorging men with boxes. They didn't seem interested in the Institute office. He nervously typed the final paragraph, concluding that the quantitative loss to education was considerable, but qualitative and psychological damage was greater. It would be felt in Lebanon for years. Dusk having dimmed the street, he worried what the group downstairs would do about this foreigner out after curfew. Taking everything he'd need if he couldn't return, he locked the door, listened to the continuing commotion upstairs and descended, passing gunmen carrying boxes. He greeted them, "Marhaba". On the street he turned homeward, expecting to be called back. He wasn't.

The next day he learned that the Nasirist group "Murabitoun", had needed more headquarters space. They'd blasted the locks of the fourth and fifth floors and expropriated these two private apartments, plastering the hallway and building entrance with slogans and pictures of Nasir. Strange, since rumors indicated that Egypt was now supporting the Christian right.

# # # # # # # # # #

Saturday, his birthday. He switched on BBC with a certain dread. So many tragic incidents had occurred on June 5 that he had learned to expect bad news somewhere on his birthday. In '67 the Arab-Israeli War had started. In '68 Robert Kennedy had been assassinated. Several years ago, a devastating Israeli attack had wiped out two Lebanese villages. Last year they had attempted a landing at the southern city of Tyre. But today, nothing thus far. Looking for breakfast, he met Nadia Hakim picking vegetables from the meager supply on a vendor's cart.

"Did you hear? They've closed the airport."

"Really closed it? Or just suspended flights for today?"

"No, our neighbor says closed. You were leaving today?"

"Wednesday. It'll be open again by then."

"David, don't count on it. Come over for lunch. Let's ask Fuad. You should leave. It's going to be much worse, I fear."

"Thanks. You have me so often. What can I bring? I'm going up to Hamra." He was preoccupied with this birthday bad news. The PanAm office confirmed that the airport was closed and suggested he cross over the line and leave by boat to Cyprus where he could get a flight. They had a taxi-man who would take people to the Museum cross-over point.

The lunch was pleasant, filled with small talk. They sat on the plant-framed balcony high above the smaller houses and buildings that crowd the Manara cul-de-sac. Only the black and white lighthouse reached above them, the Hakims' apartment just below the glare of its rotating light. Now it was extinguished, too easy a target for Kata'ib rockets.

A neighbor that David had not previously met, Mrs. Tawfik, joined them after-lunch. Introduced to David, she mentioned that she knew Lora. In Arabic, she said something that brought a laughing response, Fuad commenting that we must always give Allah the benefit of the doubt. Nadia explained: Madame Tawfik had suddenly felt she should visit the Hakims but she didn't know why. Learning that her husband was the airport civil manager, Dave asked "When will the airport open? Maybe that's why you're here, to tell me when I can leave." But she explained that her husband had closed it down for good. It was not possible any longer to be responsible for it. There were no supplies, not even food for the staff. Equipment was beginning to malfunction and security was a constant worry. MEA was less and less willing to subject their crews and particularly their passengers to the random shelling. Two planes had been hit and the building had taken three shells, one in the main waiting room. Two hangars were damaged.

Fuad, seeing David's growing worry, said he'd help. "I'm not sure you should cross over at the Museum. Its a risk."

Dave left. There had to be some way to leave this unhappy city. The next morning BBC reported more bad birthday news. The Teton Dam in Idaho had burst, spilling destruction over a wide area of the valley and flooding the town where he'd grown up. He wondered if any of his cousins were affected. Sunday, two ladies from the Church visited to see if David needed anything, bringing him some roasted chicken. Each spoke movingly of their experience and their faith in coping with the war situation. Their long-time friend, the head surgical nurse of the AUB hospital said she was now doing "triage", helping decide which of the shrapnel-torn bodies brought into the hospital could be allotted the surgical care that was now insufficient to serve all. Emotion shook her slight frame as well as her voice. "I've always found time to speak, to give sympathy to the hopeless cases, the ones we have to delay. Most of them just die on their stretchers. But now, these deaths are so commonplace, I just leave them. There isn't time. What is this war doing to me?"

As they left, Dave walked partway with them and went on to check on possibilities for leaving. But Radio taxi was unwilling to take him either to the Museum crossing or over the mountains. They noted his request if the situation should change. Walking back, he saw a fresh flowering of martyrs' posters on the streets. Beirut's printers had turned their talents to the daily production of these photo-sheets, hailing the heroic death of some stalwart fighter. Always young, the faces on the posters with their prose lauding their brave sacrifice and noble cause stared sadly, accusingly, from every wall.

He puttered with packing and then watched the fifteen-minute shelling by the field gun in the soccer field below. First the muzzle flashes and the boom-swoosh of the shell over the building and then the laconic response from the Kata'ib guns across the city, lobbing shells which landed mostly in the sea. The electricity came on so he tried to read, but his mind wondered what the family might be doing. Time ticked slowly by. He only half heard the heavy vehicle draw up in the street below. When the pounding knock rattled the door he knew he'd been expecting it.

Chapter 12

> "Shall the day of parting be the day of gathering? And shall it be said that my eve was in truth my dawn?
>
> Khalil Gibran, "The Prophet"

Opening the door, David was pushed back into the room by the barrel of a machine gun. Two commandos rushed in, a third in the foyer with gun pointed as if to cover them. The one with an insignia on his sleeve quickly circled through the front rooms, kitchen and back into the hallway, opening bedrooms and bath. The other kept his gun in David's chest, pushing him further into the apartment. The third man entered, closing the door.

"Your name?" His guttural Arabic sounded tribal. "Give me your passport." David went to his packed briefcase on the sofa and extracted the thick, much-used booklet. The commando grabbed it from him, opening it so that the extension pages unfolded in long trailing strips. Dave tried to show him how to fold them back in but was shoved aside. He'd found the first page. "Draper David?" The man scowled, wanting to be tough.

"Yes, Draper. David Draper. What do you want of me?"

"You come. We go to markaz." They wanted him at their headquarters. David repeated his question in Arabic, this time asking why he was being taken.

The "Ra'iss", as they called him later, ignored him. The one who still had his gun prodding David's chest, said "You come now." Then, in English, "Not worry." They pushed him out the door.

Well, he wasn't worried. Somehow he felt exhilarated, calm and in control. Not really afraid and glad to know it.

The very cursory search of the apartment gave no clue of what this gun-threatening threesome wanted. They herded him downstairs and into the street with its crowd of concerned, or curious, neighbors. David saw the crudely-painted "Fatah" on the side of a weapons carrier with six other kaffiyah-wrapped commandos. They were PLO and that was a relief. Al Fatah was well-disciplined, responsible. They wouldn't harm him unless it was policy and he was sure it wasn't. There was some mistake.

Maybe it was just his turn. Over the past six months almost everyone he knew had experienced some kind of run-in with one or another of the fighting groups. He couldn't think of anyone whose car hadn't been expropriated, apartment robbed or "visited for contributions". He'd laughingly told Lora that the law of averages would probably catch up with him. Others hadn't been taken to "headquarters" but at least there he'd get answers.

The three commandos followed him to the weapons carrier with its mounted gun. But they pushed him on to a dirty-white Taunus and his "personal guard" squeezed into the back seat with him. The captain barked orders and they roared down to the beach road. Raouche. Beirut's St. Tropez. In other summers it was a swinging happy place, vacationers filling its sidewalk cafes and sea-side restaurants, spilling over onto the highway or Corniche which crowned the pink sea-cliffs and Pigeon Rock islands rising sheer out of the coastal waters. They stopped in front of a vacant apartment building and dismissed the vehicle with the commandos. Roughly, his guard pulled him out of the small car and hustled him forward through a now-derelict cafe. He stumbled over broken curbstone. The sea-wind fluttered the fringes of the ever-present garbage heap with its familiar stench of the neglected city. He slipped, stumbling in its slime.

The captain pulled him by the arm into the unlighted building, gave instructions to take him upstairs and turned to go. "My passport. You have my passport." Somehow it was wrong to be left here without his passport. When they had knocked and rushed in upon him at the apartment, he'd handed it over. Now, using his somewhat bookish Arabic, a mixture of the classical and Iraqi dialect which usually convinced Lebanese that he was an oil executive from Saudi Arabia, he raised his voice. He insisted on having the passport and used very direct Arabic phrasing. "If you want to find out about me, I'll give you the names of people I know. But you must leave the passport with me." Conversations between them, the young boy with the rifle taking his side, the other smiling his constant "Not worry. Not worry." as he waited the Captain's decision.

"I demand that you take me to your main office, where I can talk to someone who knows English." Either the use of the Arabic word for demand or the slur on the Captain's language ability angered him and he shoved his captor toward the elevator and left. Breaking his fall and regaining his balance, David was more angry than afraid. He ignored the machine gun nudging his back. The elevator showed no sign of life. Its door wouldn't open. Suddenly there appeared out of the darkness a small boy of six or seven who crawled through the broken glass of the elevator door and opened it from inside with what looked like a tire-iron. The four pressed inside the small cubicle. After some connecting of wires, a feeble light appeared above and the elevator spurted upward, stopping several times when the connection broke. Faces close to his, the two guards introduced themselves. Khalil, about 25, unshaven with a large moustache and a grin equally as wide. Andre, a boy of no more than 17 with an oversized rifle. Both smiled, trying to make David feel at ease. The boy suddenly disconnected wires and the elevator stopped near enough to the fifth floor that they could step up and out of it. The tire-iron was applied to the door again by the youngster, whose wide eyes classified Dave as the enemy.

A long hallway ended with a dim light. The entire floor seemed deserted, but a door opened at the end to reveal another gun-bearing type dressed in jeans and an undershirt, a kaffiyah wrapped around his head. Saying nothing he backed into the well-furnished living room and Khalil told his prisoner, "Sit now."

David sat with his back to the open terrace doors. The Mediterranean breeze felt refreshingly cool but he wished he'd brought a jacket. Looking around at the poorly-lit room, he regretted he hadn't insisted on getting his glasses. Without them, the other side of the room was a haze and he felt his whole situation was out of focus.

Khalil sat on a sofa at right angles, a wide smile and "Not worry. Not worry" on his lips. "We bring tea. Everything okay." David tried in simple Arabic to question him: "What is it you want of me? How long do I have to stay here? Can't you bring someone so I can find out what it is you want?"

"Not worry. Okay? Relax, yes. We not bad. We friend. You like Palestine? What you do in Beirut?" He wouldn't use Arabic and didn't understand enough of English, so the conversation continued with Khalil speaking English and David using Arabic. Explaining his work with Arab students and education, he again asked the questions that were foremost in his mind, "Will I be here long? What is it you want to know? Can I see someone from your headquarters?" Tea was brought. The warm liquid felt good in the cool night-breezes.

"You have children?" For the first time Andre joined the conversation. In Arabic, the question asks if you have any boys but it has come to refer to children of both sexes.

"Yes, three. Two boys and a girl. They're all in America."

"It's better for them", Andre wistfully responded. "Beirut is bad for families."

"Where is your family?"

"In Ain Romaneh...but I haven't seen them for four months. They live with my uncle. We're Christians and he's Lebanese. His son is in the Kata'ib so our family is like Lebanon now, split from the middle." His hands gestured the split and the expression on his young face continued the thoughts he didn't express.

Khalil broke in: "How old your daughter? You have daughter me marry?" Grinning, he watched for David's reaction. "I marry your daughter, okay?"

"American fathers don't choose who their daughters marry. My daughter will marry who she wants to marry, not who I want."

"Your daughter no like Falastin?"

Using the Arabic phrase for "on the contrary", David assured him that his family had lived among the Arabs most of their lives and supported "Falastin" or Palestine. It was a wasted exercise. Khalil wanted to talk but not to listen. Andre told him what David had said and Khalil smiled broadly. "Okay, I marry your daughter, okay?"

"Inshallah", the all-purpose Arabic response "God willing". Then they had both left, with Khalil's Kalashnikov pointedly aimed at their prisoner, maybe for some psychological effect. An hour passed. David pondered the situation, wondering how long he'd be held. When he'd left the apartment ahead of the three fedayeen, the neighbors looked on, silent, frightened or, with some, only interested. The two Issawi sons had tried to tell the Fatah men of David's good record but were rudely ignored. The Christian Malek family peered out, the mother looking so worried. Abu Ahmed, the concierge, told him not to worry but his wife cried and wrung her hands. Others looked on mutely, some accusingly. He had looked up, but there was no sign of the Hakims. Fuad's influence and contacts would be helpful.

But his confidence surged as he balanced all the factors. This was just another unpleasant part of what Beirut had become. The commandos that confronted him when he answered the door at least promised a different evening than he'd grown so tired of.

The black gunmetal glowed against the dirty sofa cushion, as if it had power to guard him in the absence of its owner. Why did they leave him alone after the dramatic "arrest"? He looked at the weapon. Was it a

Kalashnikov? He'd seen hundreds of weapons in Beirut. In the streets, in restaurants, in cars and even in friends' homes, but he still didn't know a Kalashnikov from its American or French or Czech counterpart. For a foolish moment he considered grabbing the weapon and shooting his way out.

The weapon continued its guard duty and he sank back in the uncomfortably low chair he'd been assigned. David Draper, friend of the Arabs, outspoken partisan of the Palestinian cause. For twenty years, he had lived and agonized the Palestine problem. Now it was producing another crisis, not in Palestine. In Lebanon, this land he had grown to love that was now becoming a vast burial ground. Would it be his? The gun glinted in the half-light. Another hour passed. Abruptly he realized he wasn't alone. In the corner, seated on the floor, was a young African, whose fine featured face shone in the lamplight. Had he been there all along? His weapon, an automatic rifle, lay across his knees and he held David's glance. Without glasses, David guessed the gunman was curious. "Do you speak English?"

"Non. Je parle Francais." His accent was impressive but David didn't want to get into another language he couldn't fully handle, so he switched to Arabic.

"Are you Palestinian?"

"I'm from Chad. Now I'm Palestinian until the war is won. Then I'll go back to Chad." In strongly-accented Egyptian Arabic, he continued, coming over to sit next to the pointing Kalashnikov. "You are American. Why doesn't America help the Palestinians?"

"Because the people who decide these things have wrong information. They don't know the problem like you and I do." He had long since given up defending America's Middle East policy. What he wanted was information from this friendly fellow. "Where have the others gone?"

"A little rest and some food."

"But the captain. Where did he go? He has my passport."

"Headquarters." He began to tighten up a bit. "He will come. They go to find radio."

"Radio? What radio?"

"Radio your house. You have radio? Where is radio?"

So that was it. They thought he was some kind of spy with a wireless set and the whole works. How the hell did all this develop? Oh, well, they can scour the place and satisfy themselves on that score. Why hadn't they searched when he was there? Another hour went by. He asked to use the bathroom. As he re-entered the room, Khalil and Andre came in, probably hearing the toilet flush. Andre offered a thick sandwich from a plate but David thanked him with the polite repetitions Arabs use in turning down offers of food and drink.

They walked out on the balcony, looking down on the darkened deserted boulevard below. Khalil picked up the Kalashnikov, swept the area with the gun, smiling. "When the Israelis come, we will shoot them like dogs." His fevered eyes and sudden disconnected smiles suggested either drugs or mental problems. Khalil was unpredictable, the dangerous one, the one to watch. His eyes seemed to burn, yet they looked strained, tired. "No sleep fifty days. Work very hard." If what he said meant he'd been on duty nights for that long with only brief daytime naps then he was probably on drugs, or enough of the strong Arabic coffee to have the same effect.

Walking back in, Khalil sat, again placing his gun as if it could guard the American. He stretched along the other end of the sofa. The adopted black feda'i from Chad took up his position on the floor and Andre sat in the remaining armchair, fondling his rifle as if it were that other phallus that so preoccupies teenage boys. David's mind considered the sexual signs and symbols in the war. These adolescent would-be soldiers strutting in the streets had replaced the parading, ogling, pinching and suggestive taunts of teenagers in past years. Hamra street had changed from a sexual to a military parade ground. Maybe wars were accountable to the sex drive.

The Kalashnikov reigned over the room, its assembly of intricately machined metal designed to maim or destroy. Only the most destructive blunted bullets were used, leaving bodies torn, exploded, shredded. Why does man, why does God allow man, to develop such easy ways to destroy that which we can't create? Why hasn't man learned the futility of killing?

A knock on the door. Both Andre and Khalil went, admitting several, the open door blocking David's view as they went into the hallway. Voices, quiet at first, then raised. One higher voice. A woman? Somehow familiar. The high voice insistent, demanding. "But you must...a mistake. I know....couldn't possibly...." and something about the central office. Khalil shouting something, a glimpse of two of them as they leave, both with kaffiyahs wrapped around their heads and the loose-fitting fatigues that disguised the wearer, leaving only the eyes for identification. Andre whispering, then pulling back as Khalil vented his anger, ending with a phrase David heard well: "We take our orders from the Captain. She knows that."

His stomach muscles tightened. Was he now really going to be a hostage? Local hostages had been taken by all the groups and random kidnappings were used daily as part of the battle plan on both sides. But foreigners had been left out of these actions, even protected. Fatah was particularly noted for assuring that Europeans and Americans were not targeted. Fatah had discipline. They were responsible. Nothing would be done at a lower level that wasn't ordered by the top command. Buoyed by this thought, he relaxed and tried to close out the present by thinking about the family, but the question persisted: was there now a change in that policy?

He hadn't any answers so he thought of Lora. He pictured his wife on her last day getting ready to leave, with so many people coming to say goodbye that he had to do all her packing. Old friends and new. He marveled still at her constant reaching out to people. She'd still be making new friends and commitments on her deathbed. By now, she was undoubtedly involved with a busy schedule of new people, projects and promises in Utah. Not a people person, David tended to protect his time and options. His thoughts drifted into drowsiness and he caught himself falling into sleep. He looked at his watch. It had been over four hours since he opened the apartment door to this adventure. Was anyone trying to check where he was? If not, how long would it take? There were few people left to be concerned about his absence. Neighbors might feel it was risky to talk. As for Fatah, had the captain simply forgotten him and gotten involved with something else? Would they really hold him hostage? Had the PLO decided on a new get-tough policy with Americans?

The door opened suddenly and the captain walked in, followed by five or six others. Across the room it was difficult to make out who they were but one large figure headed straight for him.

"David! I'm sorry. I came as quickly as I could. There's nothing to worry about. They are just checking on something. I'm very sorry. You've been here how long?" The familiar voice was like sunshine in the room. The concern in Fuad's searching eyes and his hand grasping David's shoulder brought an answering grin.

"Fuad. It's good to see you at this particular moment, I must say. I'm fine, just mystified. Can't seem to find out what it's all about. Thanks for coming."

"You're alright? Were they treating you alright?"

"Yes, of course. I just want to find out what its all about."

"Well, that's what I've been trying to do, but they insisted wait at the Hamra office all this time. I think they've been searching your apartment."

"Fine. I hope they have. There isn't anything there."

"But for this to happen to you, David. I'm truly sorry. I've told them. But you know how it is."

"Of course, Fuad. It's a war. I have no objection to their searching. They should have checked us out before, it seems to me. After all, our building looks out on the whole coast area."

"They said you are directly above the Khatib faction's headquarters at Bain Militaire. They had a report there might be a radio in your building, directing the fire to the target? I told them they don't need a radio. All the Phalange needs to do is aim at the lighthouse. One of these days we're all going to get it because of that lighthouse." His familiar eye-creasing smile lighted the whole room.

They sat down together after Fuad had introduced Mahmoud, the driver for Gordon Brown, the Times correspondent who lived in Fuad's building.

"Mahmoud was a big help with his Press credentials to get us through. David, you remember Madame Tawfik from yesterday at lunch? Remember what she said when she left? You know she's famous. She reads tea leaves. Yesterday she wasn't going to stay for lunch but when she read her cup she said she would stay after all. Then, when she left, remember she said 'Mr. Draper, I believe I stayed for lunch so that I could meet you.' I remember you were embarrassed, right? Well, it was Madame Tawfik who saw them take you away. She was the one who came to me and told me.

If she hadn't known we were friends, I probably wouldn't have known. You see, like I've told you, it is fate. You don't give fate enough attention in your life, David." David laughed, but caught a glint of more serious meaning, too. Was Fuad telling him his situation was more serious than it appeared?

"I'm fully prepared to give fate its due. I must thank her for her concern. You know, she told me I must leave soon. She pressed me about it. Strange. But, Fuad, what do they want?"

"They insist that you stay until they come back. They've sent someone to search your building. They want to talk to you. This is my friend Hashim who works with WAFA, the news agency. Fluent English, he'll help when they question you. You can tell them all they want to know, eh? Do you have any secrets, David?," he teased. Then, noting the reaction, he sobered. "Don't be concerned. I'm sure it's nothing…you will go home with me." He got up, talked with the circle of men, including Khalil, the only one remaining who was armed. Tea was brought again. The discussion lengthened but David gave up trying to understand their truncated Arabic. Abruptly, Fuad returned, his expression grim.

"Did you talk with Muna Atallah when she was here?"

"Who? No one was here."

"They say she was was here. It's important, David. She's not with Fatah." David frowned. "You know, the girl who knows your son. I met her at your party. The niece of Fawzia. She wanted them to release you. They think it was very suspicious."

"I didn't know she was here. Someone came...I thought I heard a female voice, but...What do you mean, suspicious? I didn't see or talk to her. I hardly know her."

Fuad relayed David's answer. "Don't worry. They're just curious how she found out you were here. Did you contact her when the man came to the apartment?"

"Tell them to ask the men. There were three of them. They know I couldn't have. Besides, the telephone isn't working again. I hardly know her." This was curious. Since Lora had seen her working with the refugees he hadn't heard anything of her, though her brother was frequently in the news. Every letter from Rich asked for news of her. Her delicate and graceful beauty had completely captivated Rich. But his attempts to break through her flint-hard dedication to the fedayeen had ended with political rejection of him as an American, a trauma for Rich that was probably deeper than the family realized. He couldn't tell Fuad about their attempt to use Rich in the foolishly-contrived bomb scheme. What was her possible interest now in his arrest? Was she really trying to secure his release? He remembered now the urgency of that voice in the next room. Somehow it chilled him.

"David, don't be concerned. They think she heard about you from her brother. The Front has informers in the PLO office. They wonder why the Front should want your release. They'll work it out. I think she must still have feelings for Richard, eh?" He smiled and David relaxed.

"I didn't know she had any real feelings for him. It seemed to Lora and me that it was a one-sided infatuation." His answer was not quite candid.

"David, they want me to leave now. I'm sure there is no problem. They say that as soon as the men searching the apartment have returned, you will be released. I think they simply don't want it to appear that I can come in and take you away. It makes them look weak, like they aren't responsible. You understand? I'll be home and watching for your return. Keep your spirits. You'll be home soon. Okay?"

"Sure. Thanks so much, Fuad. Give Nadia my best." Somehow, he mustered some outward cheer to mask the bleakness within. "Shukran, Mahmoud. Thanks for your help. I hope it hasn't taken your whole evening" The driver, used as he was to running interference for the daily risk-taking of correspondents, brushed aside the thanks. "Wa laa shi", It is nothing. They left, Fuad looking back with a smile that reassured and eyes that didn't.

The WAFA man Hashim came over and sat down. Well educated and articulate, the Palestinian assured David that they were doing their necessary work. David agreed that if there were such reports they should be thoroughly checked out. Hashim knew of David's work, his long support of the Palestinian cause and his help for students from the area. They talked about the situation, the dearth of new Lebanese leadership, the strange uncaring policy of the big powers, the enigmatic Syrian moves which appeared to support the Christian rightist minority's demands. The WAFA man's bitterness revealed itself in every comment.

"Palestinians have no real friends. We've learned not to trust anyone. It's hard even to trust each other any more. Even this report about you that we're checking out may be something intended to do the movement harm. Your government refuses even to acknowledge that we exist. Others probably recognize us because they know that, with American policy the way it is, there's no commitment required by paying lip service. Arab leaders never really respected us. Now I believe they hate us. Certainly the Lebanese do. Even our Lebanese Moslem brothers that depend on us to do their fighting and make their decisions. Resentment. I've lived with it everyplace I've been since I got my degree at UCLA. People simply wish we'd go away. Where do we go?" He looked out the window to the Mediterranean shore, extending his arm. "West, I guess. Go West, young Palestinian. Swim."

What had happened, David wondered, to cause such pessimism in PLO leadership? Six months ago, they'd been on top of the world, accepted by the UN, recognized in many countries, even acclaimed in Europe and the third world.

"It's not the Jews they want to drive into the sea…it's the Palestinians. No, they can't drive us anywhere. There's no place left to go. They just want to bury us here in Beirut."

It was partly true. Over the years it had become clear that none of the Arab countries really wanted Palestinians in their midst. Even Iraq, Libya and Algeria, the most vocal supporters of the cause, made sure Palestinians didn't get a toe-hold in their cities. The Arab establishment had decided long ago that Palestinians were too radical, too clever, too threatening to be allowed anywhere but Jordan and Lebanon. In 1969 Hussein had decided he couldn't take any more risks with Palestinian activity in Jordan. So Lebanon, never able to muster either policy or leadership with its Arab neighbors, suddenly found its comfortable nation turned into a headquarters for aggression and subversion by Palestinian cousins, supported with the tribute of money and political support that the oil kingdoms could so easily supply.

David had often said the problems that caused the civil war were Lebanese but the fuse that set it off and the live coals that continued to rekindle the flame was the Palestinian presence. There was little likelihood of a Lebanese settlement without some solution to the Palestine problem. As he had for twenty years, David fumed at a U.S. policy that prevented a settlement.

The WAFA man left to talk in the kitchen with the others. When were they going to question him? After a few minutes two armed men entered and were ushered in with the group in the kitchen. Maybe this was the search party. After some discussion, Hashim and his companion came in.

"I think everything is all right now, Mr. Draper." Then the captain pulled him back into the kitchen. There was an argument: "We must not do this. It has always been our policy with Americans…" They were arguing about whether he would be released. For the first time, Dave began to worry. He listened.

"But you looked. There was nothing." The WAFA man's voice, his Arabic easier to understand, "This is only the plan of a faction. Not approved. Headquarters has given its promise to Dr. Hakim." The other man grunted. "All right, but…"

They entered, the WAFA man now relaxed. "We are very sorry for detaining you. I apologize on behalf of the organization. It's necessary we check every possibility. We know you are a friend, but we have to satisfy all of our people. The Major will take you back to your apartment." He indicated the captain, probably thinking to flatter him with the title of Major.

David rose. "I understand. I'll be glad to answer any questions." There had been no interrogation, but he damned well wasn't asking for one. The captain beckoned him, waiting while David shook Hashim's hand, then Khalil's, then Andre's, and finally the adopted Palestinian from Chad. Khalil's wild grin accompanied his reminder "Remember, I marry your daughter, okay?" The boy with his tire-iron appeared to operate the elevator.

In the street below, there was enough moon to illuminate some twenty or so armed men in the area around the building. The captain motioned him into the battered Taunus, laid the Kalashnikov between them, and drove without lights down the Corniche road, through the two roadblocks and up the hill to Manara, the lighthouse, home. They were in front of Fuad's building and David wanted to make sure Fuad knew he was home. He glanced up, not wanting the Captain to see, but the commando's eye followed his, seeing Fuad's face above the ferns on his balcony. Fuad waved, saying nothing. The Captain waved back, then shook hands solemnly with David and went back to his car. David fumbled for the key that was now necessary to open the door to the lobby and took the steps two at a time to his apartment.

Once inside, he paused, thinking of Lora and the family. "Thank God, they're not here." Electicity off, he brushed his teeth by moonlight. Relieved but very tired, he undressed and fell into Robbie's single bed that he'd exchanged for the large one after Lora had left. Asleep, his mind continued to process the worries of the day and of tomorrow.

Chapter 13

"The veil that clouds the eyes shall be lifted by the hands that wove it."

Khalil Gibran, "The Prophet"

At four David awoke to the whoosh and boom of firing below the apartment as they answered the Kata'ib's nightly barrage. Half the windows of the veranda were broken. The field gun pointed directly at the apartment but its shells passed over the building to land somewhere across the city. Like Allen said, "I know they're not aiming at us, but they're such lousy shots we're going to get it one of these days." David found sleep again.

At seven, the telephone jolted him awake, clearing the sleepwebs from his tired brain. "Hello. Hello. Hello. Monsieur Draper?"

"Yes. Yes, this is Draper."

"Please hang up. I have a long distance call." He'd never understand this nonsensical request when there was an overseas call, but he obeyed. Strange, the telephone hadn't worked for days. Who could this be? "Hello. Yes, hello, hello, yes this is Mr. Draper. Hello….Lora? Lora! Is it really you? No one's been able to call."

"I was thinking of you. Worried. Just decided to try—-I told the operator it was an emergency. It came through in ten minutes. How are you? I love you. When are you leaving?"

"I'm fine. How are all of you. Are the kids all right? How's the school? Are they finishing the year okay? And you? Did you get my letters from Amman? I write you every week."

"When are you leaving? You said you'd be leaving now. Come home. We want you out of there, dear. Now!"

"This is a miracle, hearing your voice. No one's getting through. Lora, they've closed the airport. My reservation was Wednesday. I'm all packed, but…"

"When will it open? There's been nothing in the news here. Was it bombed? When will it open?"

"Well, no way to tell." He couldn't tell her how permanently closed the airport now was. "Maybe I can get out by taxi."

"Oh. Be careful. Don't take chances, Dave. We want you but don't take chances. How's everyone? Who's left now?"

He ticked off the growing list of departees. "I've written all this. How is Rich doing? How's the job?" He was interning with the Justice Deptartment in Washington.

"Fine, not making much money. You'll see him first." Lora knew Dave would stop at the Institute before coming West. "Rich called last night. He wants you to find out about Muna." The name came as a shock. "You know, Muna, his summer love affair. The lovely mixed-up girl we all loved until she treated him like she did. He can't get her off his mind and wants you to find out how she is if you can. I've written you about it. I think he has, too. But you won't get those letters." Static on the line.

"I miss all of you so much." His voice almost broke.

"You're sure you're alright?"

How could he describe last night in this crackling static? The line was failing. "Lora my love, I'll come soon. I won't take chances. Tell Rich I'll try to see the girl. I love you, Lora."

"We pray for you, Dave. I need you. Come soon, okay? But be care—" The line went dead. He hung up. Amazing. Maybe the call came through because he so badly needed it. Shaking loose from the euphoria of his contact with family, he tried to call Radio Taxi. The phone was dead again. Dressing quickly, he went to the kitchen. With no power for over a month, he'd cleaned out the frig but the door was shut again. He took a warm 7-up and a wrapped wedge of cheese. Rummaging, he found a partial round of the paper-thin mountain bread that Um Ahmed, the concierge's wife, had cooked with the flour he'd given her. A package of fig newtons completed the unappetizing repast. The dining table, covered with the same flowered tablecloth that Lora had left three months ago, now looked faded and worn.

As did David, now a half century old, in his badly laundered blue shirt, pants and sandals. Shaving only every third or fourth day, he hated shaving with a blade and cold water. The battery in his Norelco wouldn't charge anymore. The 7-up tasted awful. He opened the last bottle of Sohat, the bottled water they'd stored for the days when water was cut off.

Munching a fig bar, he started down to see Allen. Someone should probably know that he was back and alright. With all the neighbors lined up to watch his escorted departure the night before, they might think he was still being held. But, first and not knowing why, he went into the study where Lora kept her neatly arranged picture file. Opening the dust-covered box, he found the photo of Muna Atallah, taken at Mathew Knoll's reception. Darkly beautiful and serious, her countenance stared at him from the pleasant setting. Her aunt Fawzia stood beside her, then Lora, and, in the background, Richard, his eyes seeing only Muna while he talked to someone else. How would he find Muna?

After repeated knocking, Allen opened the door, a mug of coffee in one hand, unshaven and in pajamas. "Come in. The BBC's eight o'clock is on. I heard you upstairs. Want to hear all about it. Maybe we can do a story, eh?"

David smiled: "Got in about two. Fuad helped. I'm fine." Absorbing the BBC recitation of the night's horrors from Beirut, Allen indicated a chair and watched his friend for an indication of the effect of last night. He liked this straight-arrow do-gooder. Not the usual idealist, anything but naive, but did he know the risks he was taking? "Can I get you some

Nescafe? I got some decaf especially for you." Then, waving to indicate he wanted to hear BBC's next item instead of David's answer, he leaned toward the set, fiddling with the tuning knob. The newscast finished and he switched off, sinking into the sofa with the still-full mug precariously balanced. "BBC says the Syrians are coming into Beirut. They're wrong again. Strange. They have a pretty good man here, too. The Syrians will stay out of the city itself. Well, what happened, Dave? They finally realized you were supporting the Armenian uprising?"

"No, it's that secret transmitter you have in the bedroom that's got me into trouble. But I didn't talk, Allen, although you can see how they tortured me. Not even CBS can make me tell."

"Seriously, I came home about nine and Gordon was downstairs with his driver and your friend Fuad. They were trying to locate you. Gordon said you marched away with those three gunmen as if you were leading them on a mission. He's made some notes already. calling you a 'gentle American'. How about that? Shall I tell him what you're really like?" Allen was never serious for longer than a sentence. How did he write those profound and lucid commentaries he called the "night's bullshit"? "Did Fuad find you? Or did you break out on your own, guns blazing and tall in the saddle? Tell me, Dave. We worried."

A quick overview filled in the basics and convinced Allen that there were no story angles for him. They fell into bantering discussion about how one might get out of Beirut overland. "The Reuters man came in from Damascus yesterday, detoured South almost to Marjeyoun on the Israeli border. I'll try to find out more, but getting out now is going to be a hassle. When are you leaving?"

"Well, I don't have any reason for sticking around."

"Seems to me you have a few extra reasons for leaving after last night."

"What about crossing over and going out to Cyprus?"

"It's risky, Dave. That damned no-man's land at the Museum. Too many incidents there. Snipers on both sides. You're left completely on your own, got to carry your bags for about a hundred yards from the

West Beirut taxi to the East Beirut taxi. They're calling it the Mandelbaum Gate but I remember Jerusalem and the Gate was simple, just ten feet and it was policed on both sides. Another thing about crossing over, the boats are charging pure gold for tickets to Cyprus. You even have to pay to get into the port area."

"Well, I'll check it out. I've got money for some of our church members that I should deliver in East Beirut. I'll ask around. If you get any info, I'm interested, okay?"

"Why don't you ask the Embassy? Hey, reminds me. Have you checked in with them? I heard they're setting up a search."

"No, really? I didn't think they knew anything about it. Who told them? Well, I ought to tell the Consulate I'm leaving. Your phone working?"

"Dead when I got up. Let me check. Maybe it's back on." He went into his office. "Still dead. Look, I'll drive you. Let me get some clothes on and a piece of toast."

"You don't need to drive me. I'll walk down later."

"No, I'll drive you. I want to see the press office anyway." Allen wanted David's situation taken care of. Much more cautious and orthodox than his manner indicated, his long success as a media reporter had resulted from a carefully-developed method of research, covering all the angles. Dotting the T's and crossing the I's, as he put it.

The view of the morning-green Mediterranean through Allen's neatly-taped picture window was like looking through the Union Jack. The picture of Muna came to David's mind. How was he going to handle Rich's request? He'd have to visit her Aunt's house. He could thank her for what she had tried last night.

They crowded into Allen's scarred MG. "You know, if it hadn't been for this car, I'd have been taken along with you last night. Mahmoud told me. Remember, when it was stolen I went to the PLO and they got it back for me. Their man came to check on the car. Remember, I introduced you? He probably searched my place." Driving away, they waved to Abu Ahmed who was pleased to see that

Mr. Draper was safe. Mrs. Issawi leaned over the balcony and called a greeting and a "thank God". Others gathered around to be reassured. Even the militiaman posted at the lighthouse seemed happy to see him. Manara was a great neighborhood.

David waved to Nadia who was walking her two girls to school.

"Tell Fuad thanks. I'll come over later." Her answering smile and wave spoke her relief at seeing him safe. "You know, Allen, I think Fuad was taking a risk coming last night. Life is very basic now."

"Yeah, the survival instinct is taking over." Allen's driving fit very well into Beirut traffic. The nervous energy he applied to wheel, accelerator and brake would have easily controlled a truckload of cement. Dave's rangy frame crowded into the low-slung MG was only inches above the rubble-strewn surface and he thought of Spiro Agnew's reference to "tightening the sphincter" as the car sped around the curve.

The city was waking up. Not in the happy, hurrying, vending way that Beirut used to greet the morning, but with militia cars and trucks driven recklessly by adolescent revolutionaries. Few residents used their cars now. Haggard-looking, they hugged the walls and buildings as they walked to markets to search for the day's food.

Waved through to the wrong side of the divided boulevard with its now-mangy palms and overgrown grass islands, they were stopped at the "Ishtiraqiyah" or Socialist party roadblock, with its hammer-and-sickle-like decals. Ironically, the nearby American Community School was under the protection of this vociferously anti-American faction. Further on, the Lebanese Army roadblock that Beirut's Corniche traffic had endured for years was deserted, its tanks probably spirited away by officers defecting to one of the factions. As Allen screeched to a stop at the Embassy, David half expected the Marine guards to fire on them. Instead, they heard the familiar shots and answering rattle of machine-guns somewhere in the Ain Mreisse area beyond the Embassy, now controlled by the Nasirist Murabitoun militia. In the short drive of less than a mile, they had crossed through four military jurisdictions and were now entering a fifth. The U.S. Marine guard greeted them at the reception desk, recognizing Moore from U.S. television news-shows.

Each time David visited the Embassy there were new, more forbidding reception arrangements. Now the lobby was stripped of anything but protective equipment. The iron-barred entrance door opened electronically from the inside. They ascended a dozen steps to a high-countered reception console, the bullet-proof front of which hid TV monitors covering all sides of the building and showing closeups of those seeking entry. Briefcases, handbags, or thick envelopes were inspected there. They were waved on to a second glassed-in reception and David asked to see the Consul. After telephoning the Consulate, badges were issued and they were sent back to the Marines for frisking.

They were finally rescued by the booming voice of Mack Pauley, the U.S. Consul. "Dave! When did you…we had a report…didn't you get picked up last night by the fedayeen? I've just sent somebody out to look for you."

"Yes, Mack. I thought you'd want to know."

"Want to know? Sure, I want to know. I was worried. But I'm supposed to know, Dave. It's my job to know. The Ambassador heard about it some way and called me at six this morning. Gave me hell cause I hadn't called him last night when I got the call from the duty officer. Come on up and tell me about it." Then, looking at Allen, "Is this gentleman with you?" Mack hadn't served Stateside long enough to recognize Allen's famous visage. "I'm Mack Pauley."

"This is Allen Moore, correspondent. Friend. Neighbor."

"Chauffeur," Allen added. They shook hands. "Look, I'll go to the Press office if this Marine will let me."

In Mack's large office with its American flag and newly shatter-proof view of the sea, David wondered how much to tell. "What do you hear from Sally? Still in London with the girls?" The Pauleys and Drapers had maintained a friendship over the years, sharing the mystical bond that unites expatriates who've endured a worse place together, in their case Baghdad.

"They're headed for Seattle. I'm going there in two weeks. It's time you travel too, Dave."

"Yeah, I was ticketed for yesterday. You don't have a helicopter I can take off the Embassy roof, do you?"

"You kidding? That roof is the most exposed place in Beirut. I was up there last week. You're looking straight into the guns at the Holiday Inn. No news about the airport today but the Embassy thinks MEA will get flights going again."

"Don't count on it, Mack The airport manager is my neighbor. He says they've cleared out. Funny, the real reason they closed Saturday, he didn't have any money to buy food for the staff and customs. So when the Syrians in Sa'iqa uniforms crowded into the chowlines, he just gave orders to close up the place."

Mack intercommed his secretary. "Mary, see if you can reach Bill Rawson on his squawk-box." Turning again to David, "He's my only man with Palestinian contacts. He's trying to locate you."

Wouldn't you know, Dave thought, it had to be someone who probably hated his guts. Just the Friday before he'd quarreled hotly with Rawson on the telephone over the denial of visas to two Palestinian students who had grants from the PLO Student Fund. The office had processed their applications. Acceptable grades. Admitted to Mississippi University. Dave was sure they were denied visas because of their PLO sponsorship. He'd questioned the decision and told Rawson that he didn't know enough about Lebanese or American education to judge academic qualifications.

Now he'd have to thank this young man for trying to help him.

Briefly, Dave related last night's adventure, leaving out the details except for credits to Fuad and Gordon's driver. He was relieved when his friend didn't ask for identities, intelligence details, or request a written report.

Mack examined the Drapers' card his secretary had brought, chided Dave for not reporting the departure of his family, marked their departure in March, then paper-clipped a note to the card with "principal departing mid-June" scribbled on it. "So, how are we going to get you out of this madhouse? If I were in your shoes I'd be trying to get a boat for Cyprus today."

"Well, I'm ready to go. No reason to stay on. Anyone going through the Museum crossing?"

"Some of our locals still make it back and forth. But you heard about the French couple that were shot at the crossing last week? There was a kidnapping yesterday, too. Canadian. Don't know if he was trying to cross or not. The Ambassador has been over the line twice, but that was elaborately planned. The PLO provided cover. Our security officer plans these things and goes along. I don't know, Dave. We're supposed to be making new evacuation plans. Don't know about the museum. Over the mountains to Syria would be better, but there's serious fighting up there now. The Brits say the roads are all mined. Look, Dave, let me know your plans. Don't leave without our knowing it. You've been taking trips out, haven't you?"

"While the airport was open, yes. Every week or so since the family left, but I came back in two weeks ago."

"And we didn't know whether you were here or not. In fact, last night if somebody had just reported you missing—if the second report hadn't said you were taken away—we might have assumed you'd simply left on another trip. Keep me posted, Dave. Have you heard from the family?"

"You won't believe it. Lora phoned this morning. I was dumbfounded…came through clear as a bell. Said to tell all the friends "hello". So 'hello' from Lora. She misses Beirut."

"She doesn't miss Beirut. She misses you."

"No, she misses Beirut too…she has more friends here than anybody I know. She really agonized over leaving. Mack, you said 'two reports'. Who called the Embassy last night?"

"Well, the first one was strange. The marine guard got a call. It was a woman. She said the fedayeen had picked you up. She said the Embassy should find out about it. The Marine tried to get more information but she hung up. He reported she sounded very emotional. British accent. The second one was from Poston of the University. He asked for the duty officer, knowing the duty officer now has to stay inside the Embassy. One of his local staff had called to say that 'Professor' Draper was taken from his apartment by an armed guard about 8 p.m. Said the soldiers had 'Fatah' written on their jeep. The man thought you were AUB."

David didn't really hear the latter information, his mind dealing instead with the first call, the continuing involvement of this girl. It had to be Muna. Why was she so willing to put herself out for him? Was she, after all, in love with Rich? He'd thought Rich's infatuation was hopelessly one-sided. She'd continually rebuffed him. Maybe there was more to know about the enigmatic Muna. He had to meet her.

"….so I don't really eat at home, except for snacks." Regaining the conversation, he realized that Mack was apologizing for not getting him over for lunch.

"I'd better get going. Allen has a trip to Sidon planned for this morning. I'll let you know when I've found a way to leave. Mack, please tell Bill Rawson I very much appreciate his going out to help me this morning. I came on pretty strong with him on a visa problem last week."

"I know. He told me. I appreciate that you didn't involve me. The head of the Palestine Fund did call. Your two students have their visas. I guess the PLO can get them out. At least it means they won't be Fatah gunmen, eh? Hey, maybe you ought to ask if you can go with them."

"Uh…no, I don't think that's a good idea. At least not yet. What do you know about the Patriarchiyah area?"

"Nothing. Why? There aren't any Americans there anymore. At least we don't know of any. Do you?"

"No, I just wondered how it is this week. I was planning to visit somebody there before I leave."

"Well, don't. That's my advice. I hope you'll take it."

"Thanks, Mack. I'll be in touch. Do you have to walk me out, or just sign my slip?"

"Both. Let's go down the hall and get your friend."

# # # # # # # # # #

At the office, David reviewed the financial arrangements and hoped-for mailing opportunities that would keep things functioning one day a week until the situation improved. Ramzi, the student assistant who would be left in charge, was thoroughly capable of handling things. Mrs. Hani, whose chief work now was translating and certifying educational transcripts, was helpful with her more mature judgment. Both lived nearby. Both were Palestinians.

Everything in West Beirut seemed to be run by Palestinians now. Fatah was handling police matters, repairing electric lines and keeping what telephones they could in order. They had reopened the major water line into West Beirut after it had been bombed. Fatah used its own and other groups' members in an organized garbage pickup a month ago. Bakeries were now under guard, either by Palestinian regulars or organized by the PLO.

In Amman he'd talked with an old friend, a former Ambassador who had visited Lebanon as a special U.S. mediator. The Embassy had depended on the PLO to set up and police almost every meeting in the Moslem areas of the city. What a farce, this U.S. policy not to recognize or deal with the PLO?

At noon, he closed the office, declining Mrs. Hani's invitation to lunch. It would be a delicious repast with her extended family but her food supply would be scarce through the summer. He was getting out and he could certainly wait for some good food. He'd buy some tomatoes and apricots and do fine with what he had at home. They said goodbye. He didn't discuss last night. They'd hear later. He was tired of thinking about it. In the apartment, the slow revolution of a ceiling fan told him the electricity was on, so he quickly shaved. Then he put stale breaad and cheese in the toaster oven they'd bought when the butagas ran out. With a cucumber and tomato, he brought his meal to the marble table near the veranda, said a brief prayer of thanks and played the record of "Zorba" that he liked so well.

The music's throbbing optimism filled the room. When they'd first married, they'd gone to Athens to live, his work with the American college there providing a purposeful background to an almost hedonistic existence. Afternoon swims and evening strolls, weekend boat-trips in the islands and day-trips walking and reading among the ancient ruins that were still uncrowded then. Happiness is an Attic evening. In the morning, Greeks were curt and difficult. By noon, they warmed a little but after their large lunch and the following siesta, they became beautiful people: articulate, witty, sociable. Life in Athens had a magic that would always remain just under the surface of Dave's consciousness. Of course a large part of this was the loving that he and Lora had learned there, where Rich was conceived and their marriage had progressed from its physical and emotional components into an almost spiritual structure.

As the music soared, Dave's morale edged upward. Leaving the food, he rose and almost unconsciously traced the cadenced steps of the "hora" they had learned with Greek friends in those earlier years. Zorba's booming voice: "Am I married? Of course I'm married. Wife, children, house, the full catastrophe!" Dear God, how he missed the family that made this apartment so alive when here…and so empty when gone. The record slurred, then ground to a stop as the power failed.

Remembering as he placed the dishes in the sink, he took a cursory look around to see what the fedayeen had done in searching the apartment. There was not much evidence they'd been there, no locks forced in the closets where he'd stored valuables. They'd spurned his offer of keys and looked very amateurish with their rummaging while he was there. Probably used experts. In his briefcase, the envelope of money was untouched. The family's residence permits, his notes for the Washington office, his report to the Board, even his draft of the article on the war's impact on the educational year; all undisturbed.

Ah, but wait, where was the watch he'd bought for Robbie in Kuwait, a handsome rugged Orient wristwatch with all the sports functions? Gone. Had he put it somewhere else? No, it had been in his briefcase. Well, they're only human. He could picture the Captain opening the box and seeing the watch, exactly the kind of timepiece for a commando. Too big a temptation. He could report this. If he told Fuad it would be located and returned. No, let him have it. Robbie probably wanted skis more, anyway. It looks like he'll be staying in the states next year to use them, too.

Time to get out and make the rounds before the city locks itself up. It was almost one-thirty. He had to find a way out of this unhappy place. He also had to go to Fawzia's house in Patriarchiyah. The phone was still dead as it had been at the office. Picking up sunglasses, he stuffed a fifty and a five lira note in his pocket, checked his keys and left, walking rapidly up the small lane called Manara Street.

The line of abandoned or stripped cars along one side, didn't change the beauty of the opposite wall. Cascades of royal blue bouganvillea lined the street and less bounteous blossoms offered alternating hues of pink and white. Manara was too narrow for the dumping of garbage so its heady flower smells could still compete with car exhaust. Uphill, head-down, go-around, step-up, the kind of walking that Beirut now required, with its broken sidewalks, litter, parked autos blocking the walks and traffic coming at you from all directions. Pedestrians had no rights at all in Beirut and the whole family worried about David's assertion of such rights. He missed Lora's pulling his arm and cautioning him on their walks.

Descending stairs to the street below, he cut across to the lower end of Hamra Street and dodged the traffic at the taxi office. Maybe Salman was there. He had used the Radio Taxi company for five years and relied on the judgment and advice of their drivers. A Lebanese satirist had proposed that Radio Taxi, surely the most efficient organization in the country, be contracted to run the government.

"Marhaba, Sayyid Draper. You look tired. Have a Pepsi with me." Salman's brother handed him the bottle.

David thanked him and drank the over-sweet beverage. "It's cold. You have electricity?"

"Na'am. We have a generator." He reminded David that Salman was now full-time with the journalists at the hotel. Hearing David's request, he indicated a driver sitting outside. David described where Fawzia lived. "I can let you off there but I can't wait."

##########

The taxi wound its way to Hamra through Kantari, then along Avenue Clemenceau and down to the newly-built 12-story Holiday Inn. Destruction was everywhere and grew worse as they descended into the war-scarred city. Looting had cleaned out showrooms and shops. The streets were lined with burned-out hulks of cars and debris from the buildings. Broken water pipes poured out Beirut's dwindling water supply. He'd seen the ruined hotels in February and again in April so they were no longer a shock, their gutted shell-pocked towers marking the front lines of the downtown battle. Maybe it was justice that these symbols of the former Beirut should be so targeted. How transitory are the furnishings, the materials we live with. Never again would a favorite chair or house or car have real importance in his life.

They entered the broad boulevard that had been cut through the city ten years before and the taxi veered off on another thoroughfare to the Moslem sector called Basta. Soon they were in Patriarchiyah, which belonged to neither side. "Here will be fine."

"Are you sure, Mr. Draper? Well, when you're through I'll be at the petrol station up ahead. But before five."

David quickly climbed the unrailed steps and followed the stone-paved path to a high wall. Hardy clumps of flowers fought for a place in the rough hillside, as determined as the Beirutis themselves to survive. A strange place, land Fawzia's family had owned since Ottoman days. Had Muna's brother turned the place into a commando outpost? The ancient iron door, with a tiny grill-piece in the center, had no handle, just a keyhole. He rang the bell. There was probably no electricity. He rapped on the door, calling "Raja'an, Sit Fawzia maujoud?" Silence. He tried again, then took a stone and struck the iron grill. Distantly, a door shut. Slow footsteps. A high, shrill old woman's voice called from the other side of the door.

"Meen?"

David answered in a jumbled Arabic explanation of who he was and that he wanted news of Fawzia and her family. The door slowly opened. The tiny woman he'd remembered from their visit last year….she'd almost spilled the rose tea she'd served him….admitted him, closing the door and leading the way to the ornate veranda that had been cut in two when the house was halved by freeway construction. She indicated an ancient rattan chair with faded floral cushions and went inside.

The garden offered restful shade from the heat. Its walls gathered in the sweet jasmine smell that mixed with the sumptuous odor of closely-planted roses. He remembered the earlier visit with his family to this Victorian setting. Crumbling statuary, mossy fish ponds and a fountain that gurgled impotently in a tangle of unpruned greenery.

The house was a veritable museum of the family's heirlooms, furnishings that reportedly had served the Sultan Hamid in Istanbul. Narrow pathways led one in circles through the maze of gilded wood and marble. He had peered at Madame Masmoudi through the legs of a marble nymph as they discussed religion.

The bent old woman brought a glass of water with rose-drops visible on the surface. Having performed the routine of welcome, she sat wearily on the edge of the fountain.

"I remember you. You are his father."

"…and I remember you, Um Ali. Thank you." He recalled her name because he'd thought it strange that she was called the Mother of Ali when Ali was Fawzia's son. He drank the rose-water reluctantly. It was the one flavor in Middle East cooking that he disliked. This aging garden must have been planted a hundred years ago. But in the corner a jagged hole in the wall and broken pieces of marble gave evidence of the present reality.

She noted his glance. "Two nights ago. It woke me and I feared there would be another on the house. I must fill the hole." She rose as if to start the task, then stopped and sat again. She sighed. The silence worked its sensory magic. She dozed for a moment. Then, momentarily confused. "Is your family well?"

"All of them are in America now…since March."

"It is better. Beirut is a bad place."

"When did Madame Fawzia leave?" It would not be proper to ask for Muna immediately.

"Before the New Year. She wanted to visit you. There is a letter. I must find it."

David watched as she hobbled inside again. He felt refreshed in this peaceful setting, his problems far away. But firing in the distance reminded him of his mission. Um Ali appeared with a letter and a news clipping on a silver tray. From an old Daily Star social column, it pictured Lora and Dave at a party.

"Sit Fawzia wanted me to bring the letter but I am too old to go out. She told me I'd recognize you from this. But I didn't need it because I remember your son."

"To Mr. Richard Draper," the envelope read. No return address. "Fawzia gave this to you?…or Muna?" She smiled. "Muna. For your Rishard." Then, remembering, "Ah, but there is one from Fawzia, too." She slowly hobbled out again and brought a note addressed to Lora.

"When did Muna give you this letter?"

"A month, two months."

"Does she live here with you? I must see her."

"No. She wrote the letter when she left. They came and took her off to Tel Zaatar. I wanted her to stay with me. Her brother came." Her voice harshened at the mention of Munir. "She should not be with them. She is delicate, like her mother, God protect her." Her voice broke and tears appeared on her wrinkled cheeks. A pair of pigeons landed on a stone bench. "They sat there. Your son is taller than you." Her eyes measured how much. "She loves him very much. From her eyes I can tell." A softness lit her eyes and raised the crinkled corners of her pale dry lips.

She busied herself picking dry leaves from a dying vine.

David followed a number of conversational paths leading to some further knowledge of where he might find Muna, but Um Ali apparently didn't know, except to mutter "with the fedayeen." Well, he had the letter. At least she'd written Rich. Maybe the letter would finish the affair and the boy could get his mind on his future. He rose to go, speaking the elaborate Arabic words of thanks and parting. He offered help or money if she needed it. She proudly reassured him. She needed nothing. It was hard to understand her mutterings and chirpings. She told him the neighbors looked in on her. Knowing Beirut, this was probable.

He left, hurrying down the steps to find the taxi pulling up as he reached the bottom, the driver anxious to get home. A hazy red sun was setting over the water as he entered the apartment. Overcoming the temptation to read Muna's letter, he stashed it in his briefcase and picked up the Michener novel. But his mind kept grazing over the discouraging field of possibilities. He went to bed and worried his way into unconsciousness.

Chapter 14

"If this is my day of harvest, in what fields have I sowed the seed, and in what unremembered seasons? If this indeed be the hour in which I lift up my lantern, it is not my flame that shall burn therein."

Khalil Gibran, "The Prophet"

David slept soundly and awoke determined to find a way to leave. But the visit to Madame Masmoudi's strange old house dwelt in his mind. Why did he feel uneasy after talking with the old woman servant? And who had reported him to the PLO? Had Muna tried to help with her visit to his captors? Washing in cold water, he tried to put the questions aside, to move his mind to make decisions. Should he go through the cross-over point in the hope of getting a boat to Cyprus or should he take the longer route over the mountain detours that would lead to the Syrian forces and on to Damascus airport? Allen and Fuad favored the "Mandelbaum Gate" as Allen called the Museum crossing. Dave had crossed that pre-'67 border between Arab and Jewish Jerusalem. It was easy. The museum crossing was an active battlefront.

He tried to call the Swiss social worker who'd delivered funds to church members on the East side and helped David to keep in touch with families he was assigned to care for. The phone was dead so he walked the short distance to the mission office in Hamra. Closed. He would try the helpful PanAm man again, a short walk down the hill. He might know a driver who would go.

"Yes. Hassan called me an hour ago, on something else. I'll try to get him. Sit down here." With the airport closed, the PanAm man wasn't selling many tickets but he was certainly helpful. The maxim to "entertain like brothers but deal like strangers" had been set aside by the shared dangers of the conflict. The rule now required that people also deal like brothers. How many times had he been able to hand over a problem to the optimistic effort of total strangers in Beirut.

On the phone, Hassan said yes, he would take Dave at seven the next morning, picking him up at the lighthouse corner. He wanted full details on his passenger, his work, where he lived, including how to recognize him. This seemed a little strange but was laughed off as the PanAm rep gave an exaggeratedly handsome description of David. Changing the ticket to provide a routing through Nicosia and Athens, he assured Dave. "Hassan is a good driver, has contacts. Palestinian. He'll deliver you as close as possible. Ask him where you should walk to get the other taxi."

Thanking the amiable PanAm man, Dave hurried home to finish packing, glad the arrangement was finalized but still troubled. Most of his packing was done. He wondered if he should take one or two of the things that meant most to them. Their best paintings were not their favorites. Lora had grown to love a rather classical-style copy by a Turkish artist of "The Dervishes", the work of an Italian named Zonaro, which was hanging in the Dolma Bahce Palace in Istanbul. It could be removed from the frame and packed with his things. Dave's own favorite was a starkly impressionist painting by an Iraqi art student of two figures clasping hands on a clouded sand-colored background. Dave jokingly called it their wedding portrait, since the figures were devoid of expression and experience, empty of substance. The real substance of life was after marriage, family and parenthood. The item that Lora would most appreciate knowing was safe, though, was the small Isfahan carpet, framed in white and hanging on the pale blue wall of the dining room. He'd bought it in Tehran as a fifteenth anniversary gift. For Lora, its delicate ivory and blue prayer-rug design, with the symmetrical twists and turns of its ornate Persian pattern symbolized the intricate history of their life together. But, viewing this now forlorn room with its blue echoes of family, friends and the laughter of good times, he decided to leave all these things. He didn't want to change this room or any other in the apartment with its dingy taped windows and patina of dust. To do so would be saying that their life here was finished.

Taking a snack to the study away from the bright empty echoes of the larger rooms, he found the telephone working. He called the office assistant Ramzi to confirm his departure and give final instructions. He also managed to get Mack Pauley, working late at the Consulate, who referred to his penciled note, "departed June 9. You're right on schedule."

"Yes, that was when I'd planned to leave by air. I'm taking a taxi to the other side."

"Good, but be careful. We still get reports of sniping and kidnapping in the Museum area."

After saying goodbye to neighbors, he stopped to talk with Allen, who'd spent the day trying to get Lebanese reaction to the Arab League's proposal to send a League peacekeeping force. Under a deadline to finish his commentary, he expressed surprise that Dave had decided on the Museum crossing and wanted to hear the details. Echoing the Consul's cautioning advice, he said he'd wave from his bedroom window if the taxi woke him when it came. Then he went back to his lantern-lit notes and Dave went upstairs to do the things that kept popping into his mind for "mothballing" the place. At eight-thirty he blew out his last remaining candle, crawled into bed and was instantly asleep.

# # # # # # # # # #

In a basement room of a bullet-scarred building on the fringes of the Tal Zaatar camp across the city, Ibrahim began arranging a project he would keep secret from the leadership. He had to act independently on this. He'd known for months that this American was working against them. Now he had the information he needed to do something about him. The report about the radio had gone through the wrong channels.

The PLO "diplomats" had passed up the opportunity to interrogate Draper and learn his real identity. Released, even after the report he'd sent the Front's channel. When would the Fatah fools accept the realities of the conflict?

Carefully removing the wooden box from the closet, he placed it on the table. A sputtering Coleman lamp distorted his sight. He moved the lamp to a higher perch on an old file cabinet and opened the hinged lid to reveal the careful styrofoam packing. The German support group had done their work with accuracy and efficiency. One could almost relax when handling the devices they provided. He shuddered at the memory of the Iraqi-supplied bomb that had exploded across this very room. His fingers traversed his facial scars, scars that he knew had repulsed Muna.

The room's only window had been sandbagged and the door led to a hall corridor, where he now heard footsteps. Admitting the two young commandos, their dirt-stained kaffiyahs hiding their faces, Ibrahim ordered the one to douse his cigarette before entering. He'd been assured by the chain-smoking explosives expert of the Front that all modern devices are totally protected from anything a cigarette could do, but it was a way of wakening them to the risks of handling explosives.

When they had closed the door, he removed the semi-circular device and unwrapped the two meters of rubber tubing that led into it. Gruffly, he explained that it was a converted land-mine and was to be placed as near the roadway as possible, the circular side toward the road and the straight reinforced side against the curb where it would direct the explosive power outward into the road. The tubing should extend into the road and would operate like the bell-signal you drive over in a petrol station. He had each of them handle the deadly device to assure them and to acquaint them with its weight. Demonstrating the safety mechanism and activating it, he replaced it carefully in the box, closed the lid and fastened its hasp.

They sat while he gave the final instructions and identifying details of the targeted automobile. The younger one took some notes on the back of his cigarette box. After an eye-argument over who should carry the lethal load, the younger one picked it up and they left.

Ibrahim sat for a moment, relaxed now that all was arranged. Hassan always called him before going to the crossing since he didn't want to take chances if something was planned there. But this call had been an unexpected gift. Unbelieving at first, he had reviewed the name and full description of Hassan's scheduled passenger. It had been easy to suggest that Hassan ought not to go this time, since the situation was getting worse and he didn't want to take a chance being involved if he was stopped by Sa'iqa.

"Send someone else with the American. Someone you can trust to take him there, but not one of us. Loyal Palestinians should stay away from those Syrian bastards who disguise themselves as fedayeen."

Assured that Hassan had such a driver he could count on, Ibrahim had given further instructions: "It is important that the car drive along the main avenue in front of the Sabra camp. The roadblock with our people there will recognize it and phone on to our people at the Museum so he'll be recognized there. Now, give me the description of your car and the name of the driver." He'd worked it all out very carefully this time, including the pledge of the two young commandos that they would not talk if anything went wrong, a long-established PFLP rule.

Outside, the two commandos placed the box in their jeep, backing around to turn into the street just as the heavy shelling from the Kata'ib stronghold near the port began to shake the earth around them. Driving a short block, they screeched to a halt as a blast tore a hole in the street. The younger one grabbed the box and scurried for cover as a shell exploded in the street ahead.

They darted into a deserted building. Unexpectedly, they saw two young girls peering at them from an inside door. They pushed inside. A middle-aged man and his wife sat at a wooden table, the litter of a sparse dinner before them. The man, a camp functionary paid by the UN, had assisted the Front over the years. He ordered the wife to make tea and offered what remained of their dinner. The frightened girls stood in the corner until their mother brought them to help at the cupboard.

Used to the endless barrage, the man was glad to have the commandos. "I'm Abdul-Majid, in charge of rations for the camp. You have duty tonight, eh?"

The older feda'i handled all conversation. "No, a meeting. We'll be glad to get away from this accursed place."

"I agree. They will kill us all." Abdul-Majid dreaded the order that would surely come for him to move back into the camp's underground shelters and tunnels honeycombing the hillside. Daily he saw the worsening conditions, the dwindling food and water, the pileup of refuse and sewage. The leaders insisted that everyone should move underground. Abdul Majid's family would soon have to comply. Heavy firing blasted their ears as the Front's heavy guns answered the barrage. "You should have your meetings in a safer place. Did you go to the command bunker?"

"No, just near here. To see Ibrahim Hussein for an assignment." Everyone knew that name. Bitter, cold, ruthless. All the adjectives that were supposed to describe an effective resistance leader somehow demeaned the sour-dispositioned Ibrahim. All knew him, few liked him, many feared him.

None more than the tired wan figure that lay resting on one of the three cots in the tiny bedroom behind a curtained doorway. Muna had persuaded her brother to let her move out of the underground hospital. She'd spent two months there in the company of two Palestinian nursing students and an indomitable Dutch woman who'd moved into the camp to tend the wounded. Constantly sick from the awful stench and the food, her hesitant work as a nurse was of no use, so Muna had taken over two classes of the school which met whenever the shooting stopped. She saw little of Munir since he'd become the Front spokesman. When she did, they usually quarreled. So it had been hard to ask his help. He had quickly arranged for her to sleep at the home of Abdul-Majid, the good-natured if inefficient warehouseman. There was no privacy and the little girls were always into her few possessions, but there was fresh air at night for which she would ever be grateful.

Now to hear Ibrahim's name in the next room quickened her interest. She moved her head to hear the conversation. "….a chance to fight the real enemy, the Americans. He's apparently an important one, trying to get away tomorrow morning."

"You mean from the American Embassy?"

"No, but he's been here for many years doing his spying. Ibrahim says his son also works for the CIA."

"Will you bring him here?"

"No, we will not bring him anywhere. We will stop his car and then let him go. He will go many places, eh, Walid?"

The younger one laughed at the joke. "Yes, maybe some of him will come this far."

Muna shivered at the talk. Then the words sank into her brain. She recalled Ibrahim's angry inquisition about Rich and his father. Stifling the gasp that rose from her throat, she half rose from the bed, alert to hear the muffled conversation.

"Does Ibrahim decide these things alone?" Abdul-Majid was a peaceful man and the daily killing and being killed was beginning to make him question things he had formerly accepted. Also, he knew the PFLP had a policy to leave Americans alone.

"Of course not, he's the responsible for special services."

"Special services," Abdul-Majid repeated the harmless sounding words. "How will you find this American?"

"We know what we know. We thank you for the safety of your house and for the tea. It is a scheduled matter and we must keep our schedule. We sleep at Sabra. I hope they're spared the cursed Kata'ib rockets tonight. We must be on our post by seven or we'll miss the assignment." He drained the tea and they left. Then, cursing, the older rushed back in to take the wooden box from the corner where the youngest girl had been playing with its lock.

Muna lay back, tense, her mind in turmoil. She must do something, but what information had they given? Three nights before, it had been easy to find out with a telephone call where the American living in Manara had been taken. The Front's agent at PLO headquarters had reported that the "tip" had been acted on and the man was in custody at the Fatah post in Raouche. The two security commandos at the school willingly accompanied her when she told them it was a mistake and her brother had asked her to intervene. Apparently, Munir hadn't yet heard what she'd done.

She sat on the edge of her bed. The girls would come in soon. What could she do? How to get away? Would Abdul-Majid help? He'd been questioning the Front's actions lately. But he was basically a weak man. No, he shouldn't be involved in this. He had family and they'd been kind to her. A plan vaguely taking shape, she lay back down in order to feign waking up when the girls entered for bed. The commando-type shirt and oversized pants were too heavy for the June night and she moved her foot to open wider the inward-swinging window. The pointing of her stretched foot brought a brief memory of ballet. In idle hours she'd choreographed in her mind a ballet to the beautiful music of "Raja'oun", the Palestinian symphony. We Shall Return. The title mocked everything she was doing. Richard was right. All their efforts, their increasingly futile efforts, were not advancing the Palestinians' return by one inch.

Muna had trained herself in a yoga-like withdrawal that numbed her to the misery and filth around her. But her rejection of the wrongs, the exploitation and the cruelty had grown more insistent, more open. The only way she could live with herself was in opposition to the small daily evils. Beloved by those who came in contact with her and revered by those in the camp who heard of her tender-fierce insistence on humane treatment for the camp's brutalized population, Muna was more of an asset to her cold-mannered brother's career than either he or she realized.

Knowing she must settle on a plan that would warn Rich's father, she reviewed the information she had. He was apparently leaving some time around seven in the morning. He'd be driving somewhere near Sabra. Did this mean he was going to the airport or to cross over at the Museum? Of course not the airport, it was closed. But how could they know he'd pass Sabra on the way to the Museum? It was considerably out of the way. They must know the driver who's taking him. Of course, it was the system she'd heard described before. You require a certain course or checkpoint so they can be "cleared" or "assisted." But what was it they'd said about waving him through the checkpoint, and then he would be killed? Would they shoot him? No, there was that grisly laughter about "some of him." It would be an explosion of some kind.

What could she do? There was no telephone she could use tonight, unless she left the area. Did she still have the Draper's number? Yes. What could she tell Abdul-Majid? Better to make it appear that there was nothing new or unusual. Her mind racing, she remembered where she'd seen Fawzia's aging Mercedes parked, it's side now riddled with machine-gun punctures where Munir had been fired on as he returned to camp last week. She was glad he'd brought the car back to the camp for safekeeping. He didn't know she had a key.

A stream of light entered the room as the six-year-old pulled back the curtain, calling out in her strange raspy voice, "She's sleeping." Muna turned, opening her eyes with a blink and her mouth with a yawn to support the child's declaration. Then she rose, coming out into the dimly lit and cluttered room where the heavy form of Abdul-Majid's wife was bent over a crude stone sink.

"Is it late? I must have slept for hours, and I only wanted to lie down a moment. Here, let me help you." She carried things from the table to put away in the shelves above. The ten-year-old girl dutifully helped her mother and was complimented by her father. He delighted in the child's pale smile but worried about what would be her future in this God-forsaken existence.

"I should have asked you to waken me. I must leave on a mission for Abu Fadhil. A message." She made it sound routine.

"But who will be with you? You can't go out in this? Some man should go. I will go. Is it far?"

"No, it is really simple and I have to drive." She knew that Abdul-Majid didn't drive. "It is near my aunt's house. If there is any problem I'll go there. Please don't worry. I'll bring some food if I can." That would make the departure more acceptable. Abdul-Majid liked to eat and the amount and quality of food was daily more disappointing. She went into the room where the young child had already fallen asleep on her unmade bed. She checked the canvas ammo bag she had, incongruously, bought in London as the "in" kind of purse. Her special pass was there. Then, to hide her figure, she donned the loose-fitting fatigue jacket and wrapped the red and white kaffiyah carefully around her head, tucking her long hair back and into the jacket. Giving a hug to the worshipful smaller girl, she looked into her tired eyes and promised, "I'll bring you something nice from my aunt's."

Outside, flashing lights from guns implanted along the side hill confirmed that everyone was spending the night underground. Nearby houses and buildings had been pulverized. Some nights the firing engulfed Abdul-Majid's building as well but tonight was relatively quiet. She edged down the street, turned the corner and unlocked the Mercedes with its memories of beautiful days. Shifting into neutral, she let the heavy car roll silently down the hill to the main street, using only the parking lights. At the end of the street, she started the motor and approached the camp-manned road block cautiously, extending the plastic-covered pass which always received special consideration…unless there had been new orders given. The sleepy commando, who'd seen her drive out of the side-street, checked the name and asked if she was a girl. She'd learned the cool contemptuous stare that must accompany her answer.

"I'm a feda'i." She was waved through. From there it was fairly simple. The situation hadn't changed since her failed mission of three nights before. Two more times she showed her pass before chugging up the steep hill where the aging house stood ghostlike in the pale moonlight.

Knocking, she called softly: "Um Ali. Um Ali! It's Muna. Um Ali!" Waiting, she heard the scuffing of sandals and chirping of the old woman. Stooping to be engulfed in the weak embrace of this precious woman, Muna found tears wetting her cheeks as she remembered the frailty of her own mother's last embraces. Pulling the metal door closed to lock it, Um Ali pushed her ahead up the veranda stairs and into the familiar over-furnished rooms. As she lighted a gas-flame for tea, she eyed the delicate features of this boy-clad creature she'd seen grow from a baby.

"You must bathe. Don't they have soap and water, girl?"

"Sometimes. Do I smell?"

"Of course you smell. I will heat the water." She prepared a small pot with tea leaves. "The American came three days ago."

Her heart jumped. "Richard?"

"The father, not the boy. I gave him the letter. He wanted to see you. He left his card, with writing on it."

Seeing the number on the card, she moved to the ornate hall shelf with its French-style telephone and sat on the gold damask Louis XIV chair. Her attire presented a ludicrous picture as she demurely crossed her legs, dialing the number. It didn't ring.

"You must not call at this hour. He will be asleep." Um Ali brought the steaming cup of tea, sugar and milk added as she knew Muna's British habits required. Ignoring the advice, Muna dialed again. No response. Again, letting each rotation click off its number before beginning the next. Beirut's telephone system was tired, weak, beset with massive circulation problems. Badly repaired damage from bombs and shells had hardened its arteries and weakened the overall system. Sipping the delicious restorative tea, she concentrated on the phone, dialing over and over. Once, she obtained what she thought was a ringing sound, but a busy signal cut in. Maybe there was a chance. She continued, Um Ali sitting near, her hair awry and night-dress pulled askew. She looked like some Picasso sketch in the fractured light. "Um Ali, did you give....?"

"Yes, my sweet child. He has the letter. I didn't forget. And you don't forget, do you? I told you that you wouldn't forget him. Not that one. He is strong. Straight. You should go to him. Go to America. Get out of this hell. I will tell Munir."

Not answering, she thought of what she'd written to Richard, telling him, yes, she knew she loved him. He deserved to know her feelings. Her frantic repetition of the dialing sequence was bringing no response. One more time. A ringing. Yes, it seemed to be ringing. A click. His voice, so like Rich's.

"Hello, Hello. Who is it?"

"Mr. Draper, you don't know me. You should not...."

"Hello, who is it, who do you want?"

"Mr. Draper, don't you hear me?" There was static and a busy signal overrode the words. "Mr. Draper, don't go tomorrow. Don't go in the taxi." No response, then again, his voice.

"Hello, who is this? What do you want?"

"It's Muna. Muna Atallah. I know your son. You must not go anywhere tomorrow." She spoke over the beeping which distorted his response, hoping that he heard her as she heard him.

"Hello, Hello, I can't hear you. Hello." He hung up.

She tried again, the desperation in her eyes telling the old woman that something was wrong. Failing to get any response, she hung up, pacing despondently in the memory-laden house. Finally she succumbed to the bath in water Um Ali had heated in the kitchen and poured into the large claw-footed tub. She was still unable to relax. The delicious tepid water fought her effort to work out some plan to contact this man she had to warn.

Could she make it through to his house? Not at night. She'd be stopped and questioned and wouldn't be able to explain why she had to visit him. She would try to phone again in the morning. And if not, she would drive to his apartment. Um Ali brought her soft beautiful nightgown and she lay in the luxury of its silky texture and the cool clean-smelling sheets of the comfort-giving bed. Sleep enveloped her worries. The tenseness that had marked her expression for months gave way to the placid beauty that had greeted Rich's eye fifteen months ago.

# # # # # # # # # #

Jolted awake by some awful premonition, she looked at the watch on the table. Six-thirty. W'Allah, she hadn't told Um Ali she had to be awakened. Jumping out of bed, she hurried into the bathroom for her clothes, calling for the old woman's help. "Um Ali. I must hurry. Please try that number on the telephone. It is very urgent. Please, now." She quickly dressed in the smelly rough clothes again as Um Ali clumsily dialed over and over, then gave up to prepare breakfast. "No, I don't have time. I must go now. Um Ali, that number, keep trying. If you get Mr. Draper, tell him he must not go now. It's very important, Um Ali."

"But he won't understand me. He's a foreigner."

"He understands. Just tell him. Oh, well, then say this: 'Must not go today'. Do you have that? 'Must not go today.'"

"Must go day." The old woman, still sleepy, was confused.

"Not go…must not go today. Alright?"

"Not go…must go today."

Muna grabbed her things, hurried out to the garden and opened the gate to where the Mercedes was parked. Not daring to back down the steep hill, she nervously maneuvered to turn the big car. Finally on the road, she noticed the silence. No gunfire. Stopped twice, she presented her Front pass, explaining she was a courier taking a message to PLO headquarters. She rounded the Bliss Street corner just as a white Ford taxi passed, heading down Manara street with David Draper in the back seat.

# # # # # # # # # #

Packing his toothbrush into his travel-battered suitcase, David tried to reconstruct the calls that had wakened him. Five times he'd picked up before he'd heard the distant voice. It sounded like long distance. Was it Lora? No, he'd have recognized her voice. He couldn't make out anything. He thought he heard the words "go tomorrow". But it was garbled. He closed his bulging bag and hefted it. He'd have to pay excess baggage in Cyprus.

Going to the kitchen, he quickly peeled an orange, its dry sections signaling the end of the citrus season for another year. Opening his last bottle of water, he drank and munched on the remaining fig cookies. Checking the apartment, he lowered the shutters which separated the balconies from the main rooms. He hoped Ramzi could find someone to live in and guard the place. The telephone rang, with an interrupted ringing that sounded like the testing of a repairman. Picking up the receiver, Dave hoped it wouldn't be a repetition of the harrowing series of calls last night. It was time to go down for the taxi. There was static on the line as he repeated "Hello" and held the instrument away from his ear. Nothing. He hung up and it rang again. Exasperated, he tried Arabic. "Marhaba. Na'am. Min biddak?" Nothing again but the mixture of sounds and silences that made one hang on, only to become more impatient. On the fourth such ring, David heard in response to his second "Hello" a voice, again far away…but not the same as last night. An accented voice, high and weak, almost eerie. "….ot….must go. Must go…today." The connection broke before he could get any more. He tried to make sense out of the words. Who felt he must go? The phone didn't ring again but the single honk from the street told him that Hassan had arrived. Getting his things and puzzling another moment in front of the now-mute instrument, he locked the apartment and struggled down the stairway with his load.

"Marhaba, Hassan."

"I not Hassan. Hassan no come today. I take you."

"You know the area, where I want to go?" No response.

Trying Arabic, he was given a full explanation. Hassan had made arrangements. Special permission from the Palestinians. Good, that's apparently what you need. "Are you Palestinian?"

"No. Lebnani. Jisr al Qadi." He named his village. "You pay now." Dave understood. There'd be a quick parting at the crossover point. He wanted to make sure of his fare. He handed him fifty pounds. The man shook his head. "Hundred pounds."

"Hassan agreed to fifty with the Pan American office."

"Hundred. Very dangerous."

He extracted another fifty from his wallet. He supposed it was only the beginning of the fleecing he'd see today. He'd heard estimates of as much as three hundred dollars to get deck passage on a boat out of Jounieh for the two-hour trip to Cyprus. He settled into the back, the plastic-covered seat already warm against his perspiring legs. He was breaking his own rule. Radio Taxi had felt it was too dangerous for the trip and he was going anyway with a driver he knew nothing about. Admitting that he felt none of the assurance and confidence he'd always felt before, he sighed, only wanting to get away from these constant problems. As they gathered speed he noted a Mercedes coming up the road from Bliss Street with a commando driving, the red and white kaffiyah failing to hide the obvious youth of the smooth-faced driver. They're bringing in all the young ones, he thought.

His gray-haired driver was a demon behind the wheel. The taxi spurted ahead, darted through the crossing, around a mountainous pile of smoking garbage and sped along the deserted thoroughfare. At Sadat Street, he suddenly turned to the right and headed up the back way to connect with Corniche al Mazraa, the "Farm Road" that was now a major suburban artery. The way his taxi was weaving through parked cars and debris, dodging the potholes and litter in the streets, Dave's concern shifted to whether he would make it to the Museum, let alone through to the other side.

#########

The sluggish Mercedes was no match for a car which the taxi-driver probably fine-tuned each week. Muna guessed that the taxi had taken Sadat street. She drove as fast as she dared, but traffic intervened. She had lost them. She knew where he would be stopped but that would be too late. She floored the gas-pedal. Everything she'd done this year had gone wrong and now she couldn't even do this right. She'd allowed herself to be used in deceiving Richard and then hadn't had the courage to accept that she loved him. She'd let Munir's selfish demands pull her into activity with which she had never completely agreed and then, deciding that she would only work at healing wounds, she'd failed as a nurse. Now she was teaching doctrines of the struggle which she hated to the young minds in her charge.

She had easily recognized Richard's father, whom she hadn't seen since the party. An older Richard, she thought. He should have left with his family. Why was he taking these crazy chances? Could Ibrahim be right? But the thought somehow seemed to reflect on Rich. No, it's another of the many innocent killings of this senseless war…and only she could do something about it. The taxi suddenly appeared again. She gained on it. How could she live if she let Rich's father be killed? She would succeed in this, no matter what. Her determination became confidence. Her control of the old car became more relaxed and skillful.

They were approaching the Sabra camp with its canopy of umbrella pines below the luminescent sky. The driver had managed a route that was thus far devoid of roadblocks. Would he try to avoid the check that was supposed to provide him clearance? Seeing the traffic circle ahead she realized the two commando underlings would be on the road leading off to the right. She increased her speed. The road was partially blocked by the rusty oil drums used in militia checkpoints. She felt calm.

As they circled the roundabout, she saw that her hopes the driver might go straight on through were not to be. Suddenly, the urgency and danger of her mission filled her heart. Foot to the floorboard, she tried to pull alongside the taxi. The driver looked back, alarmed at this Mercedes that had dogged him all the way and now sure that the driver was trying to push him off the road. Was that a gun in the driver's hand? Ducking down, he sent the taxi jolting forward with all the speed he had, hoping to make the safety of the roadblock ahead where Hassan said they'd clear him through. Rich, too, noted it was the same car he'd seen rounding the corner at the apartment. Noting his driver was crouching down, he also ducked below the back window.

Realizing she had frightened the taxi-man, Muna dropped back a little and honked, hoping he'd stop. The taxi was now slowing ahead at the roadblock. She must stop it. If she were there, they wouldn't carry out this madness. She sped ahead, planning to run the roadblock and then stop immediately in front of the taxi.

The older commando had recognized David's taxi first and left the younger one to detain the driver until he had placed the rubber trip-wire tube across the single open lane twenty meters ahead. The bomb had been concealed under a cardboard carton. Counting on the roadblock to divert the driver's attention, he quickly unrolled the tube and hastened back to join his companion and get a good look at the American spy. Receiving an eye-signal, the young feda'i waved the driver on, then whirled around as the speeding Mercedes swerved around the taxi.

Muna careened around the oil drums placed to close the second lane, barely missing a woman walking along the camp wall, then turned directly in the taxi's path, braking hard.

##########

The screeching jolt of the Mercedes' sudden appearance in front brought the old man's foot down hard on the brake, jolting David up from the seat. He had a clear view as the skidding car slowed ahead. The blast seemed to come from the roadside building. Dave's memory of this moment would always be in slow motion. The Mercedes was hit low from the side, lifted and blown across the road, its door crushed in and the whole side riddled with shrapnel. Flames shot out of the opened trunk and then exploded, enveloping the car. "Oh, God. Oh, My God!" Not hearing the heavy rattle of falling rubble on the taxi, he stared at the horrible scene. Dave's thought processes moved ahead of his subconscious as he yelled "Let's get out of here."

Unharmed and now alert, the driver did as he was told, knocking oil drums out of his way and circling onto the opposite sidewalk to speed back toward the circle. Looking back at the heavy black smoke, Dave noticed the two commandos waving their guns, one shouting and gesticulating after them. A shot pierced the rear windshield and the material above the driver's head. David's jaw was stinging and he reached to find blood from a slight skin wound below the left ear. The old driver, muttering some prayer or curse, headed back the way they had come.

They didn't speak all the way back to the apartment, Dave too shocked and drained, the old man angry at this foreigner who'd caused him to take such chances. He should ask for more money. But he didn't, remaining in his seat as Dave unloaded his luggage. No one was around to see his return and Dave was glad he didn't have to talk yet. Dragging himself and his bags up the stairs, he left it all in a pile in the foyer and entered the shuttered living room. Stepping to the only window from which he could see out, he stood shakily, seeking the calm of the restless sea washing the coastal rocks below. The heavy masking tape crossed out the view, denying him it's mind-soothing comfort. He opened the shutter, walked out on the open veranda and leaned on its railing. The peaceful sunlit shoreline settled his thoughts, but the awful scene played again and again in his mind. How senseless that some young Palestinian should be killed that way. His mind saw again the force of the blast which had blown the car through the high wall of the camp. Had anyone else been hurt…or killed? What would he now do? The surging sea had no answers for him.

Chapter 15

> "Only when you drink from the river of silence shall you indeed sing. And when you have reached the mountain top, then you shall begin to climb. And when the earth shall claim your limbs, then shall you truly dance."
>
> Khalil Gibran, "The Prophet"

His eyes fixed on the slow-sighing sea as it surged against the shoreline below, David pulled his mind back into focus. Each option his mind explored led to a closed door. He was confused, vacillating, unsure. Breathing deeply of the fresh sea breeze, he walked inside. The questions went with him. Was the young commando in the Mercedes trying to shoot him?…or somehow to warn him? Was the bomb intended for him? Had the telephone calls been warnings? Was the PFLP behind this? Was it Muna trying to interfere in his arrest the other night? Why would she try to help him? Who was the driver of that Mercedes?

David considered talking with Mack Pauley. But what did he have to tell the Embassy? Vague suspicions. He imagined the kind of grilling he'd get from the haughty security officer. He was becoming paranoid in this paranoid city. Only one certainty emerged from his thinking: he must leave. Moving his gear from the foyer where he'd dropped it, he went downstairs to see Allen. But no one answered his knock. Back in the dingy apartment, he wanted to clear his mind. Picking up the copy of Durrell's "Bitter Lemons" that he'd half-finished, he settled into the high-backed veranda chair. The pungent evocations of Greek Cyprus would be relaxing. But his mind was on the Sabra Camp bombing. Durrell's imagery couldn't replace the questions.

The lamp on his desk turned on. Electricity on. He tuned the radio to the Arabic news from Israel, the careful pronunciation easier to understand. Gemayel and Chamoun had rejected the Arab League's offer to send troops. Heavy fighting was reported in the Mudairej area. He remembered the town. Druze friends had taken him to the area for a visit with the mystical Druze leader Kamal Jumblatt two years before.

He turned the dial, settling on the hypnotic cadences of Egyptian singer Um Kulthum. Her emotion-filled words, repeated over and over for the sound more than the meaning, moaned like the sea. Leaning back, he closed his eyes. The throaty voice put him in a trance, devoid of thought, filled only with feeling. The radio went dead. He looked at his watch. It was ten forty-five. Why wasn't he out checking on a way to Damascus? What was he waiting for? It was the same feeling he'd had sitting and waiting the night the Fatah commandos had knocked on his door. Stirring himself, he braved a cold shower. He'd lost the day anyway. Only in the early morning would one find a taxi willing to try the route to Damascus. But he'd go make the rounds.

At eleven-thirty David left the building, stopped to tell Abu Ahmed and Mr. Issawi he'd been turned back because of fighting and had decided to take the Damascus route. Stepping into the hot midday sun, he walked down the narrow empty street. He didn't see the white VW parked by the lighthouse and didn't hear it behind him until he reached the end of the street. When it stopped beside him and the husky commando's pointed gun invited him into the back seat, he pulled away. But the Kalashnikov in his ribs persuaded him. When they pushed him down into the cramped rear seat his reaction was resignation rather than resistance. His tall frame scrunched into the small space, he didn't try to question his captors. Drained of emotion by the explosion, he realized it had also drained him of resolve. He needed to see Lora and the kids, regain his perspective.

#########

It was a cemetery. As they drove through the open iron gates, the neglected beauty of the place drew his attention.

An empty doorless gatehouse confirmed that the cemetery, too, was abandoned in this city of the dead. Why care for a cemetery when the whole of Beirut had become a burial ground? Headstones, small aboveground vaults, even a sarcophagus copied after the Roman ones in Tyre dotted the area with its uncut grass, untended shrubs and flowers intermixed with weeds among the stones. They drove along a road which circled up to the rock-walled terraced borders.

The VW stopped and the driver motioned Dave to get out.

Unbending his tall frame, he stretched and took in the scene. Hushed in the noon brightness, the peaceful view was marked by two cypress trees that stood like sky-reaching sentinels along the rock retaining wall. A third was cut down, a splintery gash indicating it had been felled by a stray shell.Nearby, a pile of freshly-dug earth with the digger leaning on his crude shovel. He wore a commando kaffiyah across the shoulders of his sweat-stained shirt. David looked at the shallow grave, never dug more than a meter deep in this part of the world. His mind froze, his eyes stared. Was this his grave? Was this some new efficient twist to the horrors of the Beirut war, shooting the victims into their graves, as the Germans had done?

Behind him, a Land Rover ground up the curving road, halted and its passenger emerged. He recognized the stern visage of Abu Fadhil, the now-familiar spokesman of the Rejection Front. Was he really Muna's brother? The slender flint-eyed young man in black pants and uniform jacket approached him and, strangely, offered his hand. Dave took it, not speaking. The younger man's grasp was firm. He didn't release David's hand. The eyes softened, an expression so unexpected that Dave's pulse quickened.

"You knew her, Mr. Draper, didn't you?" His speech was impeccably British.

"Who are...?" What did he mean? "Your....your sister? Yes, I know her, but not well. I tried to see her a few days ago. My son Rich, you've met him. He wanted me to...." Dave stopped, aware of something wrong. Abu Fadhil had said "knew", the past tense. His gaze took in the activity of two muscular commandos at the Land Rover. They were pulling a wooden box, a casket, from it. Arranging a Palestinian flag along its length, they lifted it and placed it alongside the open grave. A rush of confused emotion filled him as he gripped Munir's still-clasping hand.

"You didn't know? You didn't see her? In my aunt's Mercedes?" Munir searched the stricken face before him and watched it crumble into disbelief, realization, remembrance and, finally an overpowering grief as David pulled away from the grasped hand and staggered to the support of the low stone wall.

"Oh, My God! She was......Oh, why? Why this? Why did she try...why for me?" Shaken, trembling, angry, self-accusing. All these, but more than these. Despair. Desperate. Was there no way to undo this tragedy, to bring that lovely young woman back to the life she had so briefly tasted? Why her for him, who had lived a full life? Eyes filled with tears, he tried to stifle the great throbbing sorrow and pain. An arm encircled his shoulder for a moment and he looked into Munir's eyes, now also moist with tears.

"The camp commander knew my aunt's Mercedes and brought her to me. I couldn't have identified her otherwise. She is gone. It doesn't matter how, not now. We live very close to the edge. I know now. How much she loved your son, how little she was with us these last months. It's more my fault than...." He turned to face the grave and its waiting body. His voice broke. "She is more a martyr than any of the others. She gave without believing."

David turned to look at the unfinished wood coffin, such a common sight in Beirut streets with its covering of flag or drape. He shuddered to imagine what terribly torn and burned remains lay inside, remembering the delicate beauty of the dark-haired twin of the man beside him now.

"We must bury her. The camp is under siege and I must get back to my work." He signaled the men. Carefully as they could, they lowered the rough wooden box until it rested on the bottom. David watched, his eyes unwillingly riveted to the scene as they released the fastenings that held the crude cover and removed it as is the custom. The body, even smaller than he'd remembered, was wrapped in white cloth, revealing some of the plastic they had used to contain this physical wreckage.

The grave-digger handed his shovel to Munir, standing at the head of the grave, face set in a grim expression. Only his tear-flooded eyes showed emotion. His voice was clear and firm. "B'isim Allah, al Rahman al Rahim." The Moslem benediction and dedication: In the name of God, the munificent and merciful. He filled the shovel, then let the dark earth slip slowly off the edge. Two more shovels he emptied along the length of the white-shrouded figure, then handed it to the commando who'd dug the grave. Thinking Dave to be one who should also participate, the man handed the shovel to him. Looking first at Munir, who gravely nodded his assent, David scattered a shovelful onto the open coffin; then, thinking of Rich, he spread a second one before handing the shovel which was wielded quickly and efficiently as the commando filled and topped the grave. Munir signalled his driver in the Land Rover, who started the engine.

"Mr. Draper. You should not blame yourself for what has happened. Muna did what she thought she should do. But to me you are part of the enemy. Even if the accusations against you are not true, you are still an American, part of the conspiracy to deny us our homeland. You have no reason to trust me any more than the others, even the ones who tried to kill you this morning. We don't know who did this, but I will learn who is responsible. It was not authorized. But, please, I tell you now to leave Lebanon. Quickly. Today if possible. Tomorrow at least. I don't know how and I don't want you to tell me. Don't tell anyone else your plans, how you are going or by which route. If you can't leave then go and stay at your Embassy. They can surely get you out. The men will take you back to your apartment. They are sworn to secrecy." His eyes had returned to the cold, impersonal stare David had seen on TV. No handshake. He turned and climbed into the vehicle which turned and sped down the grass-lined road.

Unaccountably not ready to leave this sorrowful, yet peaceful place, David indicated to the two commandos "five minutes" and walked to where he'd seen late-blooming daisies in a clump near the terraced border of the cemetery. Picking several multi-stemmed plants, he arranged them together and placed them on the girl's grave. Standing, he felt moved to pray. Rich had told him the girl was more Christian than Moslem. Standing with his back to the two waiting commandos, he whispered the words that expressed his desolation, his sympathy, his petition for God's blessing of Muna's now-freed spirit and a dedication of the grave.

Now strangely relaxed for the first time since the accident, his thoughts turned to Rich. How could he tell him of this? The intense sun whitened the view as they drove down the winding path to the gate. No words were spoken. They dropped him off at the same corner where they'd so convincingly invited him into the VW.

#########

At the Front's office an agitated Ibrahim rushed to meet Munir as he climbed down from the Land Rover. They had disagreed on almost everything of late. Munir strode past Ibrahim. "Muna, is she alright? I heard that she…"

"Muna is dead. Blown up next to our roadblock at Sabra."

"No. No, she is not. W'Allah, she's at the hospital. My men, I mean those at the roadblock, they took her to the hospital. She will be all right. W'Allah, she must be all right. It's so terrible, my friend."

"Are you positive?" Munir was unbelieving. "Abu Jamil brought the body personally. They took it from the car. Who have I just buried?" Munir seized Ibrahim's shoulder roughly. "How do you know about this, Ibrahim?"

"I know. They swear it is her. But she is hurt bad."

"I must go to her. What hospital?"

"AUB. I will go with you. My brother, I am so sorry."

The contorted expression on Ibrahim's face revealed more than shock and sorrow. Were Ibrahim and his boys behind this attempt to kill the American? He stood stiffly while his close friend embraced him with a flood of condolences. They climbed into the waiting jeep with its following escort. Munir couldn't speak. Ibrahim had wanted to marry Muna, had tried for a year to enlist Munir's support for such a union. He must have loved her, if he was capable of love. Now look what he had done. "I am going to find out what really happened, Ibrahim. The camp people reported that the roadblock guard placed a device in the street. Whose order was it? Whose device? Someone laid a trap for the American, Draper. Is it you, Ibrahim, have you been making your own decisions? Was it your bomb that killed Muna?"

"Please, my brother, she is not dead. You will see."

Munir's charge hardened Ibrahim's face. Munir repeated his query, reaching to grip Ibrahim's forearm.

"No." But there was hesitation in Ibrahim's voice. "No. I am bound by the same discipline as you. Why was Muna there? Why did she follow this American?"

"I didn't say she was following the American. How do you know this? How did she learn about the device?"

"I...I one of the men at the roadblock. He told me she was foll...."

Munir cut him off. "He reported back to you. How Muna was blasted to pieces? Riddled with shrapnel? Burned?" Ibrahim had done it, this patriot who'd been his friend, his teacher, who had recruited him into the secret action arm of the group, who'd insisted that Muna be brought in too, whose rhetoric had finally peeled away to reveal only Marx and Guevara, not Palestine.

They rode the rest of the way in silence, Munir's mind divided between a prayer that Muna was alright and a growing fear of what the movement was costing. What was Palestine? His father said Palestine was only land and people; no institutions of its own, no culture, no philosophy, very little history. Was that the only objective? The land? How many more people have to be sacrificed for the land?

Reaching the hospital, he worked his way through the PLO checkpoints that now controlled access and rushed to the admitting desk. A nurse told him Muna was stabilized but in a coma. He turned to Ibrahim, who stood expectantly, defensively waiting for more questions, questions which no longer had room in Munir's tired mind. "I don't want you with me, Ibrahim. Go find out what you can do to repair this awful mistake. Find out who the poor woman was that I buried this morning."

Striding quickly down the long hospital corridor, he was shocked to find things so unkempt, so dirty. AUB's medical facility had been the pride of the Middle East. Now it was like some frontline facility, filled with patients on gurneys waiting for triage to decide which could be treated and which left to die. Commandos with kalashnikovs slung over the shoulder stalked the hallways, sometimes pulling doctors away from operations and forcing them to attend those the gunmen decided they should help. But necessary supplies of oxygen and medicines could only be provided by these same commandos.

The chaos was controlled as well as could be by the few dedicated doctors and nurses who stayed on, working long hours under unsanitary conditions, bullied and badgered but sometimes rewarded when they saved someone from imminent death.

They had placed her in one of the VIP rooms that had formerly housed only wealthy patrons and foreign dignitaries. Now drab and dirty, it still provided sun and relative comfort. She was alone, her left eye closed, the right covered with a bandage that covered the entire side of her face and neck. Her right shoulder was partly bare and the arm was splotched with dozens of black-stitched surgical wounds where shrapnel had been dug out. The arm itself lay twisted and strangely inert as if disconnected.

"We're waiting for power so we can X-ray the arm. Major nerve damage." The doctor was unshaven, his hair uncombed and his once-white coat smeared with blood. "I'm Doctor Faisal. I brought her from the hallway. Your men couldn't tell me who she was but someone from your headquarters identified her as Abu Fadhil's sister. Are you Abu Fadhil? I think I've seen you on TV." He bent over the barely breathing form, adjusting the needle which fed the vein of her left arm.

"Yes. My sister. Terrible. Will she recover alright?"

"She'll recover. But what is 'alright'? I doubt we'll get her left arm back into use. Especially with our limited means here. She's on oxygen because I'm almost sure her right lung lobe was pentrated. Her hip was dislocated, probably by the force which blasted her out of the car. But I've fixed that already. Some shrapnel in her upper leg. This type of bomb is filled with metal shavings. That's what has ruined her face. We don't yet know about the eye. It was good that the blast pushed her out of the car. If she'd been against something solid, she'd be dead."

Munir listened with an awful dread deep inside him as the doctor recited the list of medical problems. His beautiful Muna. Disfigured? She couldn't stand that. Could he? Oh, God, what had he done to her?

"We'll be digging for shrapnel several times over the next six months. These kind of wounds you have to close early. We take out what we can find and let them heal. Then we have to reopen them. There are usually deeper fragments." The doctor attempted a smile of encouragement and then left Munir. The sun's rays now shone directly on Muna's left profile. He moved to block it as her eye opened wide. Her left hand, restrained by the I.V., tried to feel her face and brushed over the thick bandage covering her right side. Then she tried to move her right arm and finally, with a grimace, tried to lift it with the left. Her eye then fell on her brother.

"Munir. Oh, Munir."

He bent down, resting his cheek against hers. "Muna. What have I done to you?"

She stiffened. "Was it your order to kill Mr. Draper?"

"Oh, no. Absolutely no. Never. I suspect it was Ibrahim, though. I should have realized. He's gone crazy. Irrational."

"Is Mr. Draper alright? Has he left Lebanon?"

"Yes. He will go today, I'm sure. I told him to. Oh, Muna, I thought you were dead. He believes you're dead, too. He has your letter to Richard."

"Oh, no. I shouldn't have written it. Now…" She looked down at her body, then out the window. "Munir, promise me. You must not tell him about me. I don't want Richard to know….to think I am still alive." Her voice trailed off to a whisper. "I don't think I really am anymore." A tear formed in her eye.

Tears welled in both of his, irrigating the despair he felt. What could he do to repair, to restore her life?

# # # # # # # # # #

In the apartment David went directly to his briefcase and extracted the blue envelope with Rich's name written in the graceful script. He had an overpowering urge to open the letter and learn more about this girl. Rich would certainly understand. But no, the letter was not for him. It was private. They'd always rigorously protected the rights of their children. Even when very young they were afforded the privacy of possessions, of correspondence. He looked again at the symmetrical "Richard", replaced the letter in his briefcase, and lay down.

"Greater love hath no man…." How did one repay the debt of life itself? He tried to trace in his mind the thinking of this intense and mysterious young woman, so delicate and refined in appearance. She had apparently risked her life in undercover work for the resistance a number of times. Then to have chosen to interpose herself between him and the bomb she knew was meant for him. Had she expected death? Now he knew that she'd loved Rich very much. As much as he suspected Rich must still love her.

Rising from the bed, he knew it was important that Richard know this. But to know it after this awful death? An overwhelming sorrow swelled in him again and he walked aimlessly through the apartment, tear-filmed eyes staring through the familiar walls. As his mind eased and cleared, repairing itself for the rational thinking and planning that was now an immediate priority, he recognized that there was something new recorded there. A debt. An obligation that, in some way, must be met. Accepting this brought a balance that enabled him to begin making his new plan.

He would not ask the Embassy for help. They couldn't really do anything except possibly let him stay there and this he didn't want to do. He could envision the security officer's stern "I told you so" lecture. The Embassy had officially warned that all Americans should leave seven months ago. He'd heard rumors that the British were organizing an evacuation caravan to Damascus. Maybe he should call Mack. The phone was dead. He'd have to walk.

There was no shelling or firing. The rumble of distant explosions, probably at Tal Zaatar where Munir was, seemed far away. With a new caution, David walked quickly along the street close to the walls and buildings, keeping a wary glance to the side and rear. Leaving Bliss Street for the lower parallel one that was less likely to have foraging patrols of gunmen, he descended narrow uneven steps between two buildings and entered the gate of the small Druze village so incongruously located among the hillside apartments, followed the dirt path past homes with small gardens, chickens and clutter, and exited on the side-street bordering the now-closed American School.

He reached the Embassy after a short walk down the war-scarred Corniche and asked to talk to the Consul by telephone from the lobby. Tired, he leaned on the Marine's high desk, waiting for Pauley to finish another call. The tension, the indecision, the awful sadness of the morning weighed him down. He hoped he'd attended his last burial in Beirut.

"I'm glad you're here, Dave. Why don't you come on up?"

"No, you're busy and I don't have time. I tried to phone but couldn't get a line outside that worked. Just wanted to ask if you've heard of anyone going out tomorrow....through Damascus?"

"I thought you were going today, through the crossing?"

"No, tomorrow. I want to get to Damascus. Have you heard of anyone going on the mountain roads? The British?"

"I've heard that rumor, too. No, they say no, not for the present. Their info is that most roads are either closed or mined now. Why don't you wait for a few days?"

"Maybe, but put me down as gone tomorrow unless you hear from me again. And, Mack, don't talk about my plans to leave, eh?"

There was a pause. "Well, no of course, Dave. But what do you mean? It doesn't get out of this office."

"I just mean let's keep it between me and you until after a day or two. Why don't you just keep our card on your desk?"

"Okay, but when you get to Damascus, call the Embassy and ask them to let me know you got there. Will you do that?"

"I will definitely do that. In fact I might take them all out to dinner to celebrate, the way I'm beginning to feel. Take care, Mack. Keep away from your windows." He hung up. Mack's assistant had earlier received a call saying Mr. Draper had been kidnapped. No sense in worrying him any more than he seemed already, Mack thought. He'd detected a new strain in David's voice. He'll be sensible. How can you advise anyone about anything these days, the consul worried.

Trudging back up to Bliss Street, David wished he'd gone the other way. The tank and barbed-wire blockade at the polic station was now manned by a mixed collection of Palestinian and Murabitoun warriors and the place was filled with comings and goings, cars scurrying in and out, loud discussions spilling over into the street. Was PFLP now in the Hamra area along with Fatah? Too close to turn around, he edged through the tangle of arrogant youngsters whose weapons pointed in every direction, passed his office and on to the apartment, unlocking the new iron door at the building entrance and relocking it from inside.

On the second floor landing, he was met by Allen holding a glass in one hand and a sandwich in the other. "Dave, come on in here. I've been wondering what in hell happened to you. First you're leaving and then you're back here and then the grocery boy tells Abu Ahmed that some men took you off in a Volkswagon. Have you finally got a first-person story I can use tonight?"

"No, Allen. I did start out this morning but the taxi-driver wouldn't take me through. Said there was trouble ahead and turned around. You don't argue with them, you know."

"…and what about the Volks?"

"Oh, just some students I know. Giving me a ride." That was a pun that Allen wouldn't recognize, for once. He didn't really want to talk. He didn't want to share the awful morning. A review of the situation might bring new doubts and fears to the surface and divert him from his determination to leave.

"So what are your plans now?"

"Well, I'm probably going to give the Damascus road a try tomorrow. But Allen, don't talk about it to your people, okay?"

"What do you mean, 'my people'? You think I have a militia?"

Dave grinned. "Well, don't you? The NBC faction, to produce those action films when the real stuff is too far away.?" It was tired humor and he was fed up with war wit. "I simply want you not to mention it to people, the drivers and the like. If I go I want to sneak out, see? I'm leaving a whole passle of unpaid bills."

"Check. Okay. Well. Listen, there's been a lot of mining of roads the last few days. Also, heavy fighting at Mudairej. I just got a full briefing on it. The Syrians have pounded hell out of Sofar and now they're moving down to Mudairej. So don't go that way. Remember the name, Mudairej. Its the only battle going on right now. Well, I don't want to waste one of my emotional farewell speeches if you're not going, so I'll see you, huh?" Dave grinned a casual goodbye, went on up and found a can of fruit to eat with some crackers. He was losing some of that waist bulge. Lora should be pleased. Keep this up and he'd look like a real war victim. Trying the phone, he was amazed to hear it working and dialed Radio Taxi. Salman's brother agreed to drive him to the CocaCola circle at seven a.m. He felt good. Settling down on the sofa, he could now concentrate on "Bitter Lemons" while the late afternoon sun provided light. Then, checking his luggage, he brushed his teeth in the darkening bathroom and crawled into bed, relaxed and certain in some way that he'd make it out tomorrow. He was asleep before the field gun below the apartment began it's window-rattling fire.

##########

Across the city, where another night's bombardment was reducing the above-ground remains of the Tel al Zaatar camp to rubble, Munir had been checking to make sure that Ibrahim had complied with his order to move into the bunker and supervise the move of communications equipment below ground. That would, hopefully, prevent his making any more plots like this morning's disaster. The image of the grief-stricken American in the cemetery reappeared in Munir's mind and he found himself thinking of his own father. Deep sadness encompassed him and he tried to find some work, some problem to solve so he wouldn't have to deal with the day's doubts. The questions now prying into his mind were bordering on treason.

Chapter 16

"How shall I go in peace without sorrow? Nay, not without a wound in the spirit shall I leave this city. Long were the days of pain I have spent within its walls, and long were the nights of aloneness; and who can depart from his pain and his aloneness without regret?"

Khalil Gibran, "The Prophet"

After six years in Beirut, David still didn't know why the busy crossroads was called the Coca Cola circle. It was not a circle and there was no bottling plant. A disruptive construction for a giant overpass to connect with a freeway was now stalled in its tenth year of construction. Its unfinished stanchions and long-neglected excavations added to the desolation of the area. Unloading from the taxi, David waited at the deserted curb. He had come too early, said the shopkeeper, opening his tiny foodstall. David bought orange juice, bread and yoghurt. The Syrian taxis had stopped their regular runs, but someone might come.

After a half-hour a vintage-gray Mercedes drove up. Bent, rusted and sluggish, it spewed black fumes and steam hissed under the hood. It was using more oil and water than gasoline. But when the driver announced he was going to Damascus, David was his immediate customer. An atrocious price was suggested, whittled somewhat and finally paid as David stowed his luggage in a trunk littered with tools, tin cans and two spare tires.

The driver, Walid, was an earnest but harried young man who'd been forced to bring a group of Murabitoun fighters from the north to join the militia in Beirut. He'd been trying to get back to his family in Tripoli for two weeks. With the coast road now closed by the Christian forces, he decided the only way was south and west to Damascus, then north through Syria and west to Tripoli. Allen had recommended a long southern detour to avoid the fighting but Walid assured David they could turn up to the mountains at Choueifat, only a few kilometers south of Beirut. If he was right, it would be a simpler and faster trip. Not caring any more, David settled back, enjoying the scenery.

The taxi climbed steadily in the foothills and David looked back on the rock-encrusted green of the furrowed landscape to the morning-lit sea…blue, serene, eternal. The confidence of last night was still with him this morning. Awake, refreshed and encouraged he knew he'd make it. How was not important. But Walid wasn't right. They were turned back and told to try at Bechamoun. Advancing up that small, twisting road, they passed through Souq al Gharb, meeting heavy war damage and lots of gunmen but no roadblock. A Palestinian soldier stopped them. They had just finished planting mines ahead. He had no advice except "further south". David suggested they again consider going all the way down the coast before turning to connect with the mountain road. After stopping twice to fill the radiator, David was concerned as much about the car's ability to last the day as he was about any dangers. They returned to the beach road. At Khalde a stalled taxi-driver told Walid to try the village road to Kfar Matta. Not knowing the area, Walid drove twelve kilometers to find that this road joined the one they'd been on before.

After returning to the coast again, Walid insisted they could take the scenic road through a canyon leading to Deir al Qamar, "House of the Moon" and on past Lebanon's Mount Vernon, the beautiful old palace of Beit-al-Din. David settled back again, taking in the fresh clear air and the beautiful country setting, letting his mind absorb the calm of this enchanted valley with its spiritual distance from Beirut.

The roadblock before Deir al Qamar required a time-consuming search of the car and of David's suitcases. The town itself, home of

Lebanon's former President Camille Chamoun who was such a roadblock himself, was tense and unfriendly. Walid's queries for gasoline were stared down by several before one old man told him the town had no petrol and waved him on. They drove past the turn-off to Beit-al-Din. David thought of the present-day irony of its history. The Emir Fakr-al-Din, Lebanon's first modern ruler, had made trouble with neighboring tribes and also with Damascus. His plea for British help was answered with a diplomatically phrased put-down which said, in effect, that the Emir had made his bed and could now sleep in it. Ironic. The whole world was saying that to Lebanon this spring. At a small village named Kafr Nabrakhe, Druze military guarded the crossroads. An old man dressed in the traditional black baggy pants threatened to shoot when Walid challenged his order to go back. What about the road to the Barouk Cedars off to the right? No, neither road. Walid appealed to the other troops languishing in a nearby tent. They told him they'd have to go to Sidon for petrol and the mountain road was closed by the fighting. But Walid persisted. They turned south to Mazraat Chouf. Making good time, they sped on through Moukhtara, home of Kamal Jumblatt, where the Drapers had been invited to meet this fiery old aesthete who now led the Moslem-Palestinian-Druze coalition. An hour later, stopping again to quench the monumental thirst of the radiator, they viewed across the ravine the majestic Barouk Cedars against the rolling landscape, a view almost worth the long morning's journey.

Ahead, another roadblock with men wearing the familiar black trousers and vest, their heads covered by a white cloth wrapped turban-style around a fez. The young men must be at the front. This post was guarded by two old men and three young boys. They were friendly and wanted to talk. "Go on through, but the road is closed. No petrol at Ain Zhalta, maybe some in Nabaa Safa. Our brave Druze sons are stopping the Syrian tanks."

"Where are the Palestinian fighters?" Dave asked.

"Oh, they're staying safe back in the city."

This was mountain Lebanon. Each group is its own nation. Filling the radiator from a drum of water, they drove on, Walid assuring Dave that the "empty" gas guage was broken. The road climbed and the old taxi slowed to a crawl as if unwilling to use what was surely its last liter of gasoline. Proceeding through Ain Zhalta they were stopped again by a single sentry. Walid asked to go on to Nabaa Safa to buy petrol. "How much gold do you have?" was the joking reply. What a hell of a time and place to run out of gas. The miserly Mercedes plodded onward. Its long years in the area had given it the characteristics of a camel.

They rounded a curve to find the road blocked and uniformed men hurrying, shouting. Sharply barked orders overrode the revving engines of trucks quickly being unloaded. A bearded soldier waved cars back so trucks could be brought into the petrol station that was apparently headquarters. Waiting for the traffic to clear, Walid moved slowly forward, his head out the side to ask about the road. His attention diverted by the frantic scurrying around him, the soldier didn't see them. When he turned to find the old taxi with its foreign passenger nudging him from the rear, he gaped in surprise and then exploded in anger. Dave regretted not knowing more Arabic swearwords. Clearly the most colorful were being hurled their way. Absolutely not, no possibility of going through. Heavy fighting up ahead, didn't they know there was a war on? The road was only for the military and will you two sons of dogs get this ancient junkheap out of the way? Harsher words. There was no arguing. They backed up and parked by a restaurant with a man-made waterfall bordering its veranda.

After measuring the few centimeters of petrol in the tank Walid thought there was enough to get through to Sofar. David walked down the street and came back with two orange sodas. They drank, silent and frustrated. Dave decided to try again. Approaching the bustling military post, he asked who was in charge. He was led to the same young man that had turned them back. He glared at David. "Is it possible to talk with the responsible officer?" David's slow precise use of Arabic surprised the man.

"I'm the responsible."

He'd blown it. I'd be a hell of a diplomat, he thought. The bearded face glowered at him. "It's important that I get to Damascus today. Can't you please let us go through?"

"Impossible. Dangerous. The road's closed. Anyway, the Syrians would turn you back. Go back to the city. Next week we will have Sofar again."

"I'll take responsibility. The Syrians will let us go to Sofar. Fighting has stopped, hasn't it? I don't hear firing."

"Yes, its stopped for now, but only God knows when it will start. You are crazy to be here. This is a war."

"Please. It's important. Let us through and we'll be out of the way." David was insistent. The soldier wanted to be rid of this English or American idiot. He shrugged his shoulders. Dave hurried down the street to bring the taxi.

They drove up again, other soldiers holding them until Dave called and got the attention of the "responsible", who loosed a torrent of curses and waved them through. They were forced off the road twice by the heavy-loaded trucks hogging the narrow highway. After several kilometers, Walid screeched to a stop. A hill of dirt blocked the highway. Above, on the mountain, a bulldozer was pushing great cuts of the mountain onto the road. Gun-carrying men were directing a truck coming through at the side and waved the taxi to a stop. Didn't they see the road was closed? Walid pointed to the truck skirting the boulder-strewn edge, but the soldier was adamant. "That's the last one. Then we close it."

David got out. If he moved one large rock, the low-slung Mercedes could get through. "Your captain gave permission." He spoke harshly. "How do you think we were allowed to come through to here?" The bulldozer operator was shouting. They wanted to finish the job and go back on the truck. David motioned Walid forward, rolling the rock to the side. Walid drove carefully around the ten-foot-high blockage placed to stop the Syrian tanks. They drove through a village. No sign of life. Untended sheep slowed them as they rounded the curve was Mudairej. The town had been battered. The heavy shelling had blown the fine old stone houses to bits. Shops along the road were exploded open and burned. They drove around abandoned jeeps and cars. Not a person anywhere. A cow crossed the road. They sped on through, each uttering his own type of prayer for the petrol to last.

The road out of Mudairej leads through open farmland and then turns sharply up the mountain to the left. Walid suddenly applied brakes. Up ahead was the largest piece of equipment either had ever seen, a Syrian tank parked square in the middle of the road, the muzzle of its enormous gun pointed directly at them. Two more of these Soviet-supplied behemoths were parked at the side of the road, crews working on one of them.

A neatly-uniformed Syrian officer, bearing the insignia of a Captain, came to meet them, asking Walid how he'd gotten through. After hearing they wanted to go to Damascus, he politely expressed his regret. It was not possible. The road was closed. Asking for identification, he was pleased to see David's passport. "Americans are still in Beirut? You're a journalist?" Giving a brief accounting of himself, Dave questioned him about the road, explaining they were almost out of gasoline. "You can get gasoline in Sofar. But you will have to stay there or go back down to some other city, perhaps Bhamdoun. The border is closed and will probably not open for several days." He took Walid's identity card and Dave's passport with him to his tent, used a field telephone to report on them and then smilingly directed them on through, warning them to watch for additional tanks. Before leaving, Walid told him of the bulldozed tank barrier. He smiled. "When we're ready, that won't stop us."

Seeing the efficient, well-disciplined way in which these confident Syrians handled their military duties impressed David. This was the first time in Lebanon he had observed what could be considered professional military behavior and operations. Like his Lebanese friends, he'd hated to see the Syrians come. Now he felt good. Maybe they could stop the fighting and killing.

The resort town of Sofar, perched high on the mountain, had been defended against the Syrian advance for a week. Now scarred by the ravages of battle, its main street was lined with wreckage. Sure that the taxi would not make it otherwise, Walid cut the motor and they coasted slowly down the incline into the town. The summer home of the Prime Minister up the steep incline opposite had taken a direct hit through the roof. Most shops were damaged. An armored car had rammed into a grocery.

Walid coaxed the engine alive again and, after a protesting cough, the Mercedes whirred as if it smelled the petrol station ahead. The brightly-painted building was a shambles of twisted and broken glass, its enameled-metal walls bent and the roof blasted off. The pumps, however, had been spared and the Syrians had brought tank-truckloads of gas. The harried-looking proprietor had been pumping gas for the lighter Syrian Army vehicles all day. He told a delighted Walid how little he'd have to pay for the liquid that now brought such high prices in Beirut. Several cars and a taxi were parked at the side of the station, anxious people standing around them. David approached a well-dressed man, finding out that he was from Sidon and was taking his family to Damascus. "Just wait. Two or three hours. They'll let the road open."

David sat under a pine tree near the gate to a large old house with a gaping hole in its side. Coming from the house, a young man wearing an AUB T-shirt greeted him. Recognizing Dave from a visit to the Institute office, he invited him inside. Walid would keep watch on the road situation. A medical student whose family owned the petrol station and several other nearby business buildings, Omar wanted to get back to Beirut to begin his internship at the hospital.

David was shown the damage the heavy shell had done to a beautifully furnished living room. What's the proper response to the pitiable but proud way in which people displayed their war damage, their badge of suffering? Omar was optimistic, thankful that his family wasn't harmed. In the adjoining sitting-room he introduced his mother, a sister and sister-in-law. The mother was directing a very young servant-girl in the placing of a luncheon spread before their guest, the best meal David had had in months. Freshly-baked thin mountain bread had been folded and placed on a large plate surrounded by small dishes of all the cold "mezzeh" the Lebanese do so well. It was soon clear to the hosts that requiring David to answer questions was interfering with a very hungry man's lunch. Omar took over the conversation, reviewing the battle they'd lived through the past week. The mother went with the servant to take a tray of food to Walid.

His hunger satisfied, Dave thanked his hosts, deeply touched by this reminder of Lebanese hospitality just as he was leaving. Outside, they learned from Walid that it was now less certain there would be a convoy. It was four o'clock. His young host proposed that they go down the road a half-mile where Syrian headquarters had been established. Maybe they could find out. Happy for a chance to stretch his legs and breathe in the bracing mountain air, David set the pace as they headed down the road to a large stone house in a walled compound, occupied by the Syrian command. Vehicles and soldiers filled the garden. Seven more of the gigantic Russian tanks were lined up neatly at right angles to the highway. Neither Dave nor the taller AUB student could reach the top of their treads.

As they passed the front of a gutted building, Dave noted the large English sign on the balcony advertising dental services. "Cavities Filled." Next to the sign was a "cavity" in the building large enough to drive a Volkswagon through. Their laughter at this irony caught the attention of the Syrian sentry. Omar asked to speak to the "responsible". The sentry called inside and a sergeant came. The Colonel was gone but they could see the duty officer. A young lieutenant greeted them. If there would be a convoy it would be before five. If not, then there wouldn't. He asked for David's passport, saying nothing as he flipped the pages filled with Arab visas and cachets. That was it. He was confident, efficient and clearly felt he had more important work.

Although assured he could spend the night with Omar's family, David was relieved to see Walid waving to them. The convoy was forming. Saying a quick "Ma's Salameh" and thanks, Dave climbed into the refueled taxi and they sped off. Thirty or so cars had collected and were being checked and searched by a team of carbine-carrying soldiers. Five o'clock approached and passed. At five-thirty the last of the large tank-carrying truck-trailers from Syria was waved through and the convoy started, led by a sergeant on a motorcycle.

At the border a half-hour away, the Lebanese posts were unmanned, immigration and customs offices empty. A mile further, at the Syrian control point the convoy was disbanded. Tired, they suffered through the usual visa-purchasing and other formalities before re-entering the Mercedes for the hour's ride into Damascus. A rapidly setting sun still lit the sky but lights were needed for the mountain-shadowed road.

##########

Damascus had no evening flights to the West and Air-France's downtown office indicated there was also nothing the next day. Amman had a daily British Airways flight. At the taxi compound David found a Syrian driver willing, for a higher price because of the late hour, to drive the four hours to Amman. Saying good-bye to Walid with an extra hundred lira, he piled into the back seat, hoping he could sleep. The pot-holed Syrian highway and the garrulous driver were determined that he should stay awake so, when they stopped for gas, he changed to the front seat where the jolts seemed less punishing. The driver wanted to talk. About, what else, U.S. Middle East policy. At two the taxi delivered him to the Institute's office. Using his key, he dragged his bags inside. The guestroom, opening off an inside office, was clean and neat and he found sheets in a drawer. The next morning he found that he'd used three of them.

In spite of his exhaustion, he awoke at seven just before the handyman, Mansour, arrived to begin his cleaning. Sending him for Ka'ak, Amman's delicious sesame bread, he breakfasted on that and some yoghurt. At eight, the energetic director of the Institute office arrived. Surprised, Kamil thought David was already in the U.S. Skimming over details of the weeks since he'd left Amman, Dave didn't share all his adventures. They already seemed unreal. British Airways was fully booked, having connected with a large travel group in Bahrain. Swissair was leaving at eleven. Kamil set all other tasks aside and drove Dave to the airline office. He bought a ticket to Geneva, London, and Washington. The connection in Geneva was close, but he'd make it. Gathering up his things, he thanked Kamil for again solving all his problems.

Cables were sent to the Institute office in Washington and to his family. Mail he'd brought with him would be sorted and mailed or delivered. He called the U.S. Embassy and they agreed to send a message to the U.S. Consul in Beirut as he'd promised Mack. He turned over to Kamil his complicated notes for telephone calls to the Amman relatives of friends still in Beirut.

They drove to the airport, said good-bye, and Dave began the debilitating process of baggage search and check-in. He finally entered the Departure lounge and settled on the low-backed seats designed, apparently, for no one taller than King Hussein. The flight arrived on time. After the hassle of another security check, a wait in the bus and another at the plane, he boarded and sank into a window seat near the front. The smiling hostess served a light snack and he delved into the somber sentences of an Economist article on the Lebanese war.

##########

Gradually aware that someone was watching him, he looked up into the half-mocking smile of an old friend, Heinz Lanser, an oil executive whose children had been school-friends of the Draper children in Baghdad. A lasting friendship had developed which both had nurtured with visits and letters over the years. Heinz was now Managing Director of the national oil company in Oman. Every visit Dave made to that fascinating country included an evening or a day with Heinz and his family, enjoying the energy and resourcefulness with which they pursued a range of personal pastimes. Expert on everything from sea-life along the coast to cave-drawings, archaeological sites and Islamic settlements, he was an indefatigable digger into the life, culture and history of everyplace he lived.

At the same time he was deeply involved in good works and championed the missionary societies that worked in the area, supporting their work and assisting their fund-raising. None of this seemed to take time from company responsibilities, which had increased steadily until he was now the CEO.

"David, I had no idea you were out of Beirut. I just talked yesterday with a Red Cross representative who met you last month. He thought your office would remain open."

Rising and climbing out into the aisle over the feet of his neighbor, David shook hands warmly with the larger man, glad to see a good friend. "No, home to spend some time with the family. There's not much we can do in Beirut now."

Heinz's large green-hued eyes with their heavy brows pierced his friend's glance, searching for some elusive clue that he sensed was telling him David was more than just tired. "You look good for a war-victim. How is it now? Is it safe in Manara?"

"Relatively safe, yes, but much worse now. The city is, it's a very sick place, Heiny." Then brightening so that his friend wouldn't think him as emotional about Beirut as he was, he smiled, "and its very boring. The curfew routine is just that. Boring."

"I want to hear about it. I have a special reason now. Look, come up and sit with me here." He led Dave through the partition to first-class, Heinz glancing at the steward who nodded his assent. Tired but now relaxed, David recounted the events of the past month, adding anecdotes and observations he knew Heinz would appreciate. "Lora will be glad you're out of there. Are you going directly to Utah?"

"No, I have to stop in Washington at the office. Rich is there, too, working." The thought of seeing Rich so soon brought to mind the burden of what he had to tell his son, so he didn't hear Heinz's next words at first.

"Would you consider going back to Beirut to work with the ICRC? International Committee of Red Cross. You've seen them, surely. They've had a team in Beirut for a long time. They need more staff. I'm taking a couple of months to go in and help. Hoped you'd be there. Was planning to seek your advice."

"Of course I know of the Red Cross. They're doing good work. I thought it was permanent staff, though." David's mind was reaching for defenses, for rationalizations with which he could explain why this opportunity was not for him.

"No, they use volunteers for short periods in emergencies. They need help in Lebanon, particularly people like you, Dave, who know the country, the language, how to get things done. Lots of negotiations, you know, to get supplies through, reach the wounded and people cut off by the fighting. Uses lots of man-hours. They need people who can take responsibility. Not sure what I can do, but I'd be out of the Gulf this summer anyway. The company practically runs itself now. Would the Institute release you?" The answer, if he wanted, was yes. But would the family? "You know the situation better than I, Dave. There are two Palestinian camps under virtual siege. One is something-Pasha, let's see, Jisr al Pasha, the Pasha's Bridge. The other...."

"Tal Zaatar." The words brought an immediate memory of Munir Atallah at the cemetery, so pressured, so resigned. The reports about life at Tal Zaatar were already a part of the darkest lore of the war. How that fragile girl had lived and worked there he had wondered. Thinking of her, his mind cleared. "Yes. If ICRC wants me, I'll try to go back." Was this the way he could pay the debt? Would it assuage the guilt we have when we know others have sacrificed for us? Or was it simply that he knew he was needed?

Heinz stopped talking, sensing that David was deep in thought. But he would return. Good, it would make the job more enjoyable to be working with his friend. It was agreed. David would stop in Geneva to see the ICRC people. Heinz was going to Beirut July first. David thought he could be there by July fifteenth. He put out of his mind how he would tell Lora about this. He returned to his own seat, saying he had work to do on a memo for the Institute's Board. In reality, he needed to re-think this change of plans.

# # # # # # # # #

In Geneva, things went smoothly, quickly. Heinz, back in his native country, rented a car and they drove directly to Red Cross headquarters. The efficient if over-formal way in which appointments were handled and arrangements made impressed Dave. Filling out the long forms and records took over an hour. He was sobered by the request for instructions "in case of death" and by the disclaimers one had to sign. Heinz insured him his insurance was valid on such an assignment. He signed on for at least two months, as Heinz had done. When they offered expense money, he declined, indicating that his travel was provided by the Institute and that he was sure his salary would also be paid for the period. Heinz, knowing the meagerness of Institute salaries and perks, insisted that ICRC agree to accept vouchers for any additional expense. Grateful that his friend insisted on this, Dave knew Heinz did not ask such an arrangement for himself.

They drove to Swissair and David made the necessary changes that would allow an early morning departure. Heinz wanted Dave to motor with him to the Lanser's chalet-home near Zurich, meet the family and spend the night, promising to bring him back for the flight. But it was clearly too long a trip and, persuaded of this, Heinz drove to a small hotel he knew. At a favorite restaurant nearby, Heinz asked David to tell him more about Beirut but his guest, enjoying the delicious veal in a mushroom sauce that only the Swiss can create, wanted to forget Lebanon for a while. He asked Heinz to review his own news and give him a view of the oil situation in the sheikhdoms and of the OPEC pricing dilemma. They parted at eight-thirty. David bought a TIME for news of the U.S. election, but was asleep by nine-thirty.

Chapter 17

"Let not the waves of the sea separate us now."
                                    Khalil Gibran, "The Prophet"

Arriving in Washington at three p.m., David was slowed only by the customs' official wanting to know "how it was in Beirut." Finally at the phone, he called Richard's number at Justice. The dial tone ringing in his ears, he still didn't know what to say. Unconsciously, he fingered the letter from Muna in his coat pocket. The deep-south accent of the secretary informed him "Mr. Draper is busy. Who is it that wishes to speak with him?" So like Rich to instruct a secretary with that approach. "This is his father." The rapidity of his coming on the line indicated Rich was at the next desk, and not so busy.

"Dad! Where are you? I expected to get a cable. I wanted to meet you at the airport. How are you? I'm glad you're out. Did you hear the news? Dad, did you get to see Muna? Mother asked you to check, remember? Did you find her? Is she okay?"

"Wait a minute, Rich. Let's see. You probably want the last answer first. I…I have a letter from Muna. She wrote it some time ago. I…well, we'll talk. When do you get off work?"

"I'll leave now. I already told my boss I had to meet you. I can be at Dulles in, well, takes an hour, I guess. Do you want to wait for me? Taxis are impossible, about twenty dollars now. I'll only charge you ten!"

"I'll wait for you. At 4:30 I'll be at the parking lot exit. Know where that is? Where you used to pick me up, remember?"

"Sure, I'll find you. Do you know where she is, Dad? Is she in Tal Zaatar? The news says its cut off, under siege."

"I'm sure she's safe now, Rich." He paused, trying to postpone further discussion of Muna. "Rich, you asked if I'd heard the news. What news?"

"The American Ambassador was killed. Murdered, trying to cross over to see President Sarkis. He had the Embassy counselor with him, a man named Waring. Do you know them?"

"I didn't know the Ambassador. He'd just arrived, Rich. Bob Waring, yes I know him. He wasn't killed, was he?"

"Yes, Dad. Both of them and the Lebanese driver." That deep, pit-of-the-stomach revulsion and shock returned. So many, many times. When would it end? David's silence transmitted the extent of his feeling to Rich, who spoke softly, "Dad, I'll see you. Four-thirty."

Grateful for more time to plan how he could break the news about Muna to Rich, David found a bench outside the customs area, deserted until the next international arrival. He'd always believed it wrong to withhold bad news from people. The letter might give him higher hopes, only to have them destroyed. At any rate, the letter was his. It had to be delivered. Rich could cope. He thumbed through TIME, not sure what he was reading.

The small green Fiat pulled up and Rich's long form unfolded out of the side like a slow motion jack-in-the-box. A strong handshake pulled them together in a long embrace. Rich fitted the luggage into the cramped space of the little car. Finished, he looked at his father expectantly. Shouldn't he tell him before he reads the letter? David delivered the letter to his outreached hands. "You'll have to move the car out of the lane, Rich."

"I know, but can we park somewhere while I read the letter?"

"Of course." He'd hoped Rich would wait. It didn't matter. There was no place or time that would make it easier for either of them. Pulling in at the end of a long row of parked cars, Rich cut the motor. Opening the envelope, he took out two pages filled with small neat writing. "It's my first letter from her." David watched a 747 glide past the swept-wing roof of the graceful airport building. An occasional mumble or sigh accompanied the rapid digestion of the letter's contents. Finishing, his son turned with a gleaming smile."She's mine, Dad. She's willing to…she'll marry me. I'm sure of it. She realizes now how senseless everything is out there. Tal Zaatar. She tells about what they're doing, the suffering. I wish you'd opened the letter. You might have been able to get her out. She's in the camp."

"She's not in the camp, Rich. Not any longer."

"You saw her? Where is she? Has she left Beirut?"

How do you tell a death? How do you decide when another person is ready to hear that someone they love is gone? How do you phrase such unacceptable news? Does it matter how? "Muna is dead, Rich." Looking straight ahead out of the grimy windshield to see another silvery plane gliding in to land, he felt as much as he saw the sagging down of this erect young man who sometimes seemed a stranger. There was no other response. David's words had said it all and the son knew his father well enough to know there was no question. The matters of how, when, where were not relevant in this moment of overcoming pain. Only the why was relevant and would always remain relevant to Dave. Tears filling his own eyes, David turned to place his arm across the boy's shoulder. "She was killed, blown up in a car, Rich. She was trying to warn me. What she did saved my life. I…I don't know why. I don't know why the bomb was there for me. I don't know why she did what she did. I think she knew. She sacrificed herself. I believe she knew."

Rich stared straight ahead, the awful words of his father penetrating one by one, painful probes that deepened the anguish. Even the unacceptable thought of choice between her life and his father's intruded for a split-second, the most painful probe of all. As a boy, he'd had dreams that he and his father were in a war for Palestine, but they'd been fighting against Americans. Once he'd dreamed that his father had been killed in this war and he had to bury him. Rich's eyes turned to his father and he saw how moved the older man was. Then, remembering Muna's hopeful and love-filled phrases, he wept, putting his head down on the steering wheel, accepting David's handkerchief to wipe away the tears. Tears that overflowed his heart and mind to flush out the brine of bitterness, the salt of sadness. He straightened and started the engine. They headed for the airport exit.

Composing himself as best he could, David recounted the essentials of his visit to Fawzia's house, his near-contact with Muna when she tried to warn him and to intervene with Fatah, and finally the story of his ill-fated attempt to cross over at the Museum area. Rich listened, guiding the car along the expressway that cuts through the lush green of Virginia. His mind was only marginally dealing with the narrative that Dave was unfolding. Staring at the road, he saw images of Muna in a dozen different attitudes and expressions. Time, the healer, had stopped for Rich. The wound was still open. He was still trying to accept her death, not prepared to think of present or future.

Arriving at the Beltway, Washington's merry-go-round speedway that had transferred traffic congestion from the city to its suburbs, Rich drove on under the eight-laned highway packed with slow-moving traffic. He was less tense now, Dave noted, but there was still not a word from him. They crossed the Potomac at Memorial Bridge, Rich remembering the family's custom. They'd lived in Washington between overseas stints, and always when they returned to the city they had gone as soon as possible to visit the Lincoln Memorial. David didn't really know why or how it had become the habit it had, but he knew that if there was any emotion to his patriotism, that sorrowing face of Lincoln brought it out more than the flag.

Rich found a vacant parking space along the monument's traffic circle and they walked rapidly up the long flight of steps, looking up at the brooding statue as they climbed. Inside, they stood quietly for no more than a minute, then turned to go. "If Lebanon could only have a Lincoln now." Dave's comment was more to himself than to his son. They descended slowly and at the bottom, David turned to see again the wise, patient Lincoln.

At the hotel, after parking, checking in and going to the room, Rich finally spoke. "Do you want to read the letter, Dad?" David took the envelope from his son. Rich sat in an armchair, his long legs stretched out, head back. He closed his eyes as if the act of doing so might also close his thoughts.

David switched on the lamp, sat in the other chair and addressed himself almost reluctantly to the fine lines of script. "Dear Richard, and I now know how dear to me you really are. More than any time earlier, I realized it when you called to me on the beach just before New Year. It was such a delicious shock to hear your voice. I had to fight myself not to turn. At least to look at you once again. I ran because I was still confused, still afraid. I'm not any more. I now see that you are right, though it's not important whether you are or not, because I know that I can't continue an existence that doesn't hold the promise of seeing you again, or of being with you. You told me that first night that your priority was love. Your priority is now my priority. I could just say that you are my priority. But it's more than that. Here in the camp, I've changed my work. I refuse to have anything to do with the war. My work now is only to help those who need help and I'm teaching the brave lovable small children. I had a great fight with Ibrahim. He now realizes that I care for you and it has brought out all the worst in him. I don't see Munir very much. He's very busy. I don't want to know any of his business, anyway."

"I can't describe the conditions here in Tal Zaatar. Every day it becomes more horrible for the poor children who don't understand the stupidity and destruction around them. I used to be able to get out to find and bring in supplies or to take messages. Now, with my teaching, there is no reason to leave and I miss the visits I could make to the house and Um Ali, where I could be clean and civilized for a few hours. But it will end soon. It must. The camp has only a little food left and the water supply is bad. Maybe now that the Syrians are coming in, they will help us to move out. Each day we bury more people and so many of them are small children. There is no room for more graves. I would not like to be buried the way they do it here."

"But I have hope that something will happen to release me from my responsibility here. If it doesn't, as soon as I can be free, I will write again, from somewhere. I know my father would approve of what I've decided. Munir will understand someday. I love him but he's wrong. I now know this. He's not an anarchist like Ibrahim. He's honest. He doesn't hate like the others. That's why I've never been a good Feda'i. I was never able to hate. Oh, Rich, I wish I could be with you for just an hour, to see your eyes, your smile, to feel you close. Then I could endure all this. If you could only write me. I will stay until it's over and then if you still want to, we will build our own life."

"It was wonderful to spend an afternoon with your Mother. Did she tell you? She was so loving. I want to know her better. I'm as well as its possible to be here in Tal Zaatar. I feel like I'm lifted by your love and carried above the awful experience that surrounds me here. Someday we'll be together, Insha'allah. If God wills. 'Your name is in my heart.' I love you, Muna."

David handed the letter to Rich, his emotions drained and a great disappointing bitterness at the thought of what ruin war visits on the young, who are least prepared to handle it. Asking Rich to join him for dinner, he knew the answer. Rich's eyes and shaking head explained that he wasn't ready for any more contact. "I'll call you tomorrow at the office, Dad."

"Of course. I understand. I'm calling your mother tonight. I'll tell her. Not everything, yet. She should know about Muna." He also had to tell Lora about returning for the Red Cross, a worry interrupted by Rich's long parting embrace. "Son, I may be going back to Beirut next month. For the Red Cross." Rich was silent. Unvoiced questions. He sighed and left his father alone.

Dave picked up the telephone to call Lora. How could he tell her about his close calls and Muna's death and then tell her he wanted to return? He couldn't. Not now. He'd call her tomorrow. He dropped onto the comfortable bed. It was 2:30 a.m. in Beirut. Just two hours before the day's battle would begin.

# # # # # # # # # #

The Institute's head office was an old but solid brick and stone rowhouse just off Massachusetts Avenue in an area occupied mostly by Embassies. Arriving a little after ten, Dave was greeted warmly by the chiefly female staff. Even those who only knew him by correspondence had been concerned about his safety. Their questions were all the same. He gave brief answers to complement the quick embraces and handshakes that slowly propelled him up the stairs to the office of the Institute's president, Tom Winston, a man Dave usually disagreed with.

"Well, you finally decided to get out of that hell-hole. I'm relieved you made it alright and the Board will certainly be. I've been getting calls almost every day." Tom always looked haggard to Dave, who knew his health wasn't good. Today, even his usually-energetic fussing with his pipe was without energy and there was an unhealthy pallor about his face. The continuing budget problems of the Institute gave Tom a never-ending series of crises. Dave was glad he'd chosen the least expensive way of handling the family's evacuation and his own. "Do you feel up to a staff meeting after lunch? Everyone's anxious to hear about Beirut and I don't want to hold you too long from seeing the family and starting your vacation." Observing Dave's nodded assent, he went on. "Any problems, Dave? Anything I should know? Assume you closed the office for the duration?"

"Sort of. Mothballed it. Ramzi will open every Tuesday morning for student mail and translations."

"You know, Dave, most of us don't understand why you stuck it out so long. Is it worth it to keep things going?"

"Well, obviously I thought so. There were others who stayed too, Tom. AUB was open, even the American school." He detected criticism in Winston's comment. Was he somehow suspect because he'd stayed. "You never instructed me to leave."

"I know. I felt that you're closest to the situation and your judgement should prevail."

"Then we're in agreement. At least on this. You asked if there was anything you should know about. I've been asked to spend a couple of months with the International Committee of the Red Cross. I'd like to do it, unless you have something pressing. There's not much doing in summer anyway and I'd be on leave."

"The Red Cross? Where, in Geneva?"

"In Beirut."

"My God, Dave! You've just come out! What's with you and that God-forsaken city? Have you told Lora about this?"

"I want to do it, Tom. They need people who know Beirut, the Lebanese, the Palestinians. It's bad, Tom. The Kata'ib are trying to starve out the camp areas. Lora will understand. Do you?"

"No, I don't understand, but I've known you long enough to give up trying to understand you in these kinds of things. Someone else could handle this assignment. Why does it have to be you?"

"Because I was asked. How could I say no?"

"How long?"

"Two months. July 15 to September 15."

"Okay, you give one month of leave, we'll give one month of assigned duty, seconding you to the Red Cross. Is that alright?"

"Yes, Tom, thanks."

"No, wait a minute, we'll consider the whole period as a work assignment, so the insurance will be sure to hold. Now, I've included you in the lunch date I have with Ambassador Mansouri. Says he knew you when he was on UN assignment in New York. Now, tell me how you got out." Dave recited the events he would have to repeat at lunch and again at the staff meeting. The Chinese curse, "May you live in interesting times" should add "and have to tell everyone about them."

The lunch with Tom and his old friend from Egypt was pleasant but the conversation confirmed that neither the Arab countries nor the U.S. was seriously concerned about Lebanon. Dave decided not to share fully what had happened. Thus, the arrest by Al Fatah became a simple questioning. The explosion which had killed Muna became a bombing he'd seen trying to cross to East Beirut.

At the Institute meeting later, the staff's questions were revealingly naive. Expecting anyone working with the Institute would be informed and sophisticated on the Middle East, he found himself trying to review the complicated confessional system of Lebanon's once-upon-a-time government. Economic and social elements in the dispute were largely ignored by the press and David had to explain why U.S. policy on the Palestinians was central to the problem. The discussion finally ended.

##########

Walking down Massachusetts Avenue in the orderly beauty of a Washington not yet hot and humid. David wanted a good prime rib dinner, the kind of beef you can only get in the States. But he must call Lora. Entering his room, he went directly to the phone.

"David. I've waited by the phone all day. Richard didn't say what hotel. I expec….Oh, Dave, I'm so glad you're out of Beirut." Anger, hurt and love all mixed together.

"Lora, forgive me. I should have called you yesterday or this morning. Rich called. I should have realized. How did he sound?" and then, "How are you and the kids, Lora?"

"We're fine here, David. Rich and I talked for an hour. I want the whole story, of course. He told me about your crazy idea of going back. Dave, we have to discuss this."

"I'm sorry, Lora darling. How can I expect you to accept this? But you should have heard it first from me. I goofed." It was his old apology-word, but it didn't work now. He'd broken his own rule: Tell Lora important news before you tell the kids.

Her voice was strained. "When will we see you?"

"Tomorrow. Should be there by three or four. The office is getting the ticket. I'll call. I love you, Lora."

"Do you?" He could almost hear her tears. "Bye, David." She hung up. Lora always stopped talking when she cried. He knew that. He wanted to comfort her, reassure her. He slumped on the bed, then got up and rummaged in yesterday's jacket for the envelope with Rich's number. Phoning, he was relieved when Rich agreed to join him. A long shower would feel good. But the picture of Lora, weeping without him there, stayed in his mind.

There was an overnight change in his son. A new hardness in his eyes, a firmness of his jaw, a patience in conversation. These observable evidences would be permanent. The emotional shock of last night had redefined, maybe strengthened Richard. It was too early to see if it would also harden him. "You talked with your mother last night?"

"Yes, I had to talk with her. She's so wise, Dad. Her words, just hearing her voice, it helped. A lot. I guess I can accept this. I'll have to. You called after I did?"

"No, I put it off. Didn't call 'till this evening."

"Oh, oh. Guess I goofed. She was shocked about your Red Cross stint." They both gave full attention to their salads. The steaks were perfect and eating helped him put aside his problems, but Rich only picked at his food.

########

Rich took a long lunch hour and drove him to National Airport, bringing up the ICRC job in Beirut several times. But David didn't want to discuss it until he'd squared this with Lora. Rich's last words at the departure gate were asking whether her he might be able to find out more about Muna and her brother.

The flight west droned on forever. He slept part of the way, his long frame wedged uncomfortably against the window. Finally, they landed at Salt Lake airport. It was good to be home.The three of them were waiting, Lora in a summery pink shirtwaist dress. Wide smiles lighted their faces as he walked through the arrival gate. He kissed them and held Lora close. It was so good to feel the form of this loving creature who'd shared so much with him. How could he leave her again so soon? Should he pull out of the ICRC job? But he knew he wouldn't.

"Dad, did you really get taken hostage?" Rob was going to pester him for all the details. Danny was satisfied just to be close with her Dad's arm around her. Questions, incomplete answers while they hassled for baggage. They piled into the roomy '72 Chevy and headed through the city and south to the university town where they'd kept a house through the years.

Salt Lake City with its wide, well-ordered streets was like a tonic to David. He was always moved by this peopled valley of his pioneer ancestors, its temple spires and mountains. Only one other city provided the same feeling of inner peace and spirituality. Jerusalem, with its landscape of rolling hills, churches, mosques; its mixture of the gnarled old with the symmetrical new.

The house was large but somewhat cramped. Three student guests were still there with the family. A classmate of Robbie's "refugeeing" in the States until his family could return to Beirut, shared his small room. Attending summer school were a Lebanese student friend and a grad student that had rented a room from Rich when he'd lived there before going to Berkley. It was a busy household and David delved deep into the family chores, his mind finally won away from the war routine of the past year.Discussion of the ICRC job brought tension and he tried to steer clear of it. It was clear that Lora didn't want him to go. It was also clear that she wouldn't make it difficult, if he insisted. Of course it changed the plans she'd made. Her disappointment was always there, but she kept it mostly within.

Soon, he began to get requests for press interviews, TV talk shows, and lectures before university and church groups. So they found themselves driving to Salt Lake City or spending evenings in TV studios or lecture halls. One news "cut-in" turned out to be a two and a half-minute interview in which he would explain the "crisis in Lebanon." The woman interviewer hardly knew where Lebanon was and was shocked to learn that many Palestinians were Christian. The predominant questions were always whether the Arabs were going to be difficult about selling their oil to the energy wasting Americans, and whether poor surrounded Israel, which had already captured four times the original territory assigned to it, would be "driven into the sea" by the bloodthirsty Arabs.

In an hour's interview on a regional network show, Dave was able to provide some rational explanation of the Lebanese war and to say some of the things that he felt Americans needed to know. He explained why only the U.S. can make peace in the Middle East. He detailed why there must be a Palestinian state, how this would, in effect, solve the main political problems that have beset the area for a quarter-century, even those of Israel itself.

"What of Israel's right to secure defensible boundaries?"

"Israel's present boundaries including the occupied territory are defensible only because of the massive U.S. help it can obtain immediately when threatened. There are no 'defensible' borders with modern push-button warfare. Secure borders for Israel seem to be borders that provide Israel with maximum protection and the Arabs with maximum exposure. What of secure borders for Jordan, for Syria, for Egypt, for Lebanon? No Arab army has ever crossed Israel's original boundaries, but Israel routinely violates the borders of Lebanon."

"Will the Arabs use the oil embargo again?"

"Of course, if they want to support the Palestinians. All the world except the U.S. and South Africa support Palestinian rights to the land taken in the '67 war."

"Yes, but an embargo will make everyone angry at the Arabs. Besides, they need the money. And we need oil."

"Not true. They don't need the money. In fact, its a shameful giveaway of the natural resources of countries like Saudi Arabia, Kuwait, the Gulf, where that's all they have. The oil is worth much more to them in the ground. Here in the States, we are using forty percent of world oil production, more than our share. To me, an embargo is the moral kind of warfare, much preferable to what I've seen in Lebanon."

"Do you think the next administration will be able to bring peace to the Middle East?"

"No, candidates are ignoring facts in favor of rhetoric. Israel must become a responsible, peace-supporting member of the world community and a law-abiding state in the Middle East." As he finished the interview, Dave thought it was just as well he was leaving soon. If he kept on this way much longer, he'd be thrown out of this country that so tested his patriotism. Long ago, he'd parted with "my country, right or wrong." If he couldn't love its foreign policy, maybe he should be leaving again.

#########

The three weeks passed quickly. He'd had some good family times but had missed not having Rich with them. They grow up and away so very fast. His best moments were alone with Lora, driving someplace or cleaning up in the kitchen after a meal. They'd played tennis, swam, hiked Timpanogos mountain which seemed much steeper than when they'd climbed thirty years before as students. Vacations were always hard for David. After the second week he began to get restless, to feel useless. There were things in the house and yard that needed doing. If he stayed longer he'd start pressuring the family on these vacation-spoiling jobs.

Each day he was thinking more and more about Beirut. The foreign news coverage wasn't very good in Utah. They watched the two evacuations by sea arranged after the Ambassador's murder. Noting the PLO help, they saw familiar faces and friends on TV. The Kata'ib continued the shelling of Tal Zaatar and seized the nearby Jisr al Pasha camp, killing many and expelling the rest. As a result of the Arab League's June meeting in Cairo, a few Saudi and Sudanese troops had been sent in. Christian forces were shelling the airport and had destroyed one of MEA's planes. The Moslems opened a new front in the northern mountain villages in order to draw off some of the forces besieging Tal Zaatar.

David spent hours phoning State Department friends and contacts, urging that Lebanese be granted refugee status. But the Christian enclave and its developing separatist government was pressuring the U.S. and Europe not to take such a step. They didn't want to reduce their ranks through further emigration. Meanwhile, over a thousand Lebanese students in the U.S. were unable to receive money from families or sponsors. Other thousands had fled the war-torn country without funds. There was no assistance for these new refugees, an unfairness hard to explain in view of the American aid granted for Hungarians, Cubans and Vietnamese. However, the U.S. was providing medicines and supplies through AUB Hospital and this was much appreciated.

Dave said goodbye to Dannie and Rob at the house. They had other plans for the day and he preferred it that way, feeling the need to be alone with Lora. His flight wasn't until three and they drove up to the city in mid-morning. Parking at the venerable Hotel Utah, where Dave had splurged on the bridal suite those many years ago, they strolled through flower-filled grounds of the adjoining Temple Square. Oblivious to the tourists, they sat on an out-of-the-way bench, viewing the granite temple with its six-spired design.

Twenty five years before they'd entered that building to find happiness with each other. The promises they'd made had mostly been kept, Dave thought. Lora, too, was remembering the beauty of the ceremony. He saw her as she'd been then, breathlessly eager, excitable, reaching out to others, not very worldly. He drew her close to his side and bent down to kiss her. They sat in silence, each with thoughts that delivered the same voiced concerns:

"Do you think Rich…?"

"I can't help but think of Rich…" Smiling at this evidence they were thinking alike again, David continued. "I worry how he'll finally adjust. It tore my heart to see him. I guess it tears even more when I realize how she died."

"You think about it a lot, don't you?"

"Yes. Yes, it's there all the time. You know the Arab concept, Lora. Whoever saves your life becomes responsible for you, has the right to tell you what you should do with yourself?"

"Is it Muna that tells you to go back to Beirut?"

"No, no, of course not. Maybe it was Heiny. Maybe it's fate. If I hadn't met him on the plane. If I'd been on the British Airways flight. I've become an Arab. I'm a fatalist." He laughed and changed the subject.

Something had changed him. Something new in his mind, his thinking, that she was not a part of. Lora had lain awake nights trying to figure this out, to find some way that would persuade him to stay with the family, to ask for another assignment from the Institute. He acted as if the ICRC assignment were inevitable or decreed, as if it were a role only he could play. It left her unable to talk about it and filled with foreboding. She'd had a medical checkup just before he'd arrived including a cervical biopsy. After hearing his plans, she'd almost wished there was cancer so she could make him stay. Now, he was leaving and there was so much to say, so much she'd wanted them to do together.

The meal was pleasant, but both made it almost a business lunch, reviewing family finances and decisions that had hung fire to the last day. They drove to the airport in an uneasy silence and Dave's sixth sense told him she was crying before it was confirmed in sight or sound.

It was a difficult farewell, filled with the inanities that people reach for in desperation to stave off emotional collapse. Somehow they made it to the gate. When the plane was called, he crushed her to him for a long embrace and left, not wanting to look back. It was good he didn't.

Finally composing herself, she walked out of the airport and drove the big empty car down the freeway. It came to her mind at the same time that it did his in the plane that there had been no mention of his return or what they would do in the fall.

Chapter 18

> "And you, vast sea, sleeping mother, who alone are peace and freedom to the river and the stream, Only another winding will this stream make, Only another murmur in this glade, And then I shall come to you, A boundless drop to a boundless ocean."
>
> Khalil Gibran, "The Prophet"

Wearing the useful armband that the ICRC had provided, David walked along the Ras Beirut streets that held so many pleasant memories. Reporting his return to the Consulate, he saw that new staff had been brought in, young singles unencumbered by family. He knew no one in the Embassy. Leaving, he strolled the Corniche. The sea sighed and groaned as it rinsed and tasted and then regurgitated the city's waste back upon its uncared-for shore.

Beirut was dying. Great open wounds lay untended. Supurating sores of oozing garbage were ineffectually cauterized by burning. Their sour smoke odor now dominated streets that had once offered delightful smells of food, spice and blossoms. A broken city. Broken windows. Broken buildings. And broken persons, their damaged bodies now seen on the streets in increasing numbers.

There was less new garbage, though. Less food to throw away. Even less of the endless flow of paper the modern city uses to wrap its food before and after its journey through the digestive tract. As the toilet tissue ran out, so did the other niceties. As in all wars, the time of crudeness had set in.

Beirut lay suffering under a crossfire of adolescent gang-killings that politicians were insisting was a civil war, fought for democracy and justice. A few brave efforts at some kind of social action had been started by desperate residents who realized that the people had to be heard from, but the fear that filled the city prevented their administration of first-aid to the barely-breathing metropolis. Soon, last-aid would be insufficient.

The trip back was uneventful. He'd overnighted in London and swam for an hour in the Airport hotel's pool to work the jet lag out of his system. The flight to Damascus seemed endless, but on arrival he'd been lucky to connect with the intrepid AUB driver, Omar Fa'our, who was at the airport to pick up surgical supplies for the Hospital. Fa'our offered the only way to get back in, unless he waited for the ICRC to lay on special transport.

A neat, energetic man of tremendous resourcefulness, Fa'our was one of the unsung heroes of the war as he made daily trips to Damascus after the airport closure. Alert to day-by-day changes in the battle lines, acquainted with local commanders and able to gauge the path of safety in the maze of uncoordinated fighting, he ferried critically needed medicines, equipment and personnel over the dangerous and constantly changing routes to Beirut.

With one other passenger, a Lebanese nurse, the three hour trip provided an up-to-date evaluation that was probably more accurate than he would get from the ICRC or the Embassy. Waved through most road-blocks as soon as the familiar AUB station-wagon was identified, they made good time in spite of the detour around the static front-line that now separated the Syrians from the Palestinian and Druze fighters. Fa'our dropped him off at the Coral Beach Hotel just after the sun had dipped under the Mediterranean haze. Introducing himself at the desk, he was grateful to hear Heiny's booming shout from across the lobby.

"David, you're a day early. I had just been assuring them you'd be here tomorrow. Come and meet the group." The introductions were friendly, but Dave's lack of French was a problem with several. On the whole, it seemed like a competent and companionable group, diverse in age and background but that would make it interesting.

Although he'd planned to live in the apartment, he understood the complicated security and transportation arrangements that required he live with the team. The room was comfortable and he already enjoyed the prospect of being that close to the sea. Taking a quick shower—they even had hot water—he went down to dinner with the group in an empty dining room. Their long table had heavy candles that looked ready for use. But electricity lasted through the main course. When it fizzled out, they lit the candles while the chief of the mission briefed Dave on the tasks before them.

He would be on the team working with Tal Zaatar, which meant almost daily trips there as well as some involvement in meetings with the Phalangist and Chamounist forces that were now so intent on wiping out this last stronghold of the Rejection Front. Heinz was assigned to supply and relief liaison with PLO. He would also be involved with Dave's team, arranging for convoys of food, water and medical supplies when they could get through.

After dinner, David and Heinz stepped out on the veranda overlooking the small cove that provided the hotel's beach area. "Are you seeing a man called Abu Fadhil at Tal Zaatar?"

"Yes, I remember him. He's in charge of liaison with ICRC. They won't let us inside the camp to assess the real needs. The Front is paranoid about letting any of their military secrets be discovered by the Red Cross. The Phalangists apparently think we might send in a team that would stay there and make their shelling of the camp less acceptable to the world."

"Aren't they a little late to worry about what the world thinks?" Dave was wondering what Munir would say when they met.

"The Kata'ib's determined, Dave. They won't stop until they've wiped the camp off the face of the map. They've just about done it now. Most of it's underground. From what we hear of those rabbit-warrens they must be living hell."

"Do they stop the bombardment when you bring in supplies?"

"They always agree to. Trouble is, the guns from the camp start up and that gives them the excuse. You've got to be watchful every minute."

"Don't the Palestinians want the help?"

"Yes, but they want us to give it to them outside the camp. They take it in. We have to get in and see what the medical situation is. Someone's going to have to decide soon to start bringing people out of there. At least the women and children."

"Surely they can see that. I know Abu Fadhil. I'm sure that he would want to get them out."

"I think you're wrong, Dave. The leaders are resisting the idea totally. We've heard they've killed people trying to get out. They see it as their last stand, their Masada, if you will."

"But there are plenty of other Palestinian camps, here in West Beirut and in the South."

"They're not Rejection Front, not PFLP. This is their last piece of real estate. The PLO, Arafat's men, control the other areas. PLO influence at Tal Zaatar is only nominal. The Front men are tough. They don't obey the PLO, they use it."

"...and they're willing to sacrifice all those poor people? Dear God, Heinz, when will it stop?"

"You know when. When they get their own country. Not really until then. You and I have known that for twenty years. Do you see any change in the U.S. attitude?"

"Not really. They're busy guzzling gas, oblivious to the problems over here. As long as the Arabs sell us their oil, the U.S. won't take them seriously. I'm discouraged. From that standpoint I didn't mind leaving, but it was a hard goodbye with Lora." She was always just under the surface of his thinking. They went to their rooms, Dave with the instruction to sleep in if he wanted. There was no trip to the camp tomorrow and the others were involved in a trip to the South for which it was too late to obtain his clearance. Going to bed, he realized he'd have to have more clothes from the apartment and made a mental list of the things he'd do tomorrow. Distant guns pounding Tal Zaatar hardly entered his consciousness as he dropped off to sleep.

#########

David's first trip to Tal Zaatar three days later was a shock. It had been at least two years since he had been in the Dikwaneh and Sin al Fil industrial areas across Beirut's usually dry "River." That part of the city constituted Beirut's "other side of the tracks". The varied communities there were mostly poor, minorities and day-laborers. The camp occupied a high promontory commanding access across the valley to the apartments and businesses of Ashrafiyeh, predominantly Christian and now the rightist stronghold. Tal Zaatar had been a bustling refugee town within the mainly Christian area of the city. Now its thirty thousand Palestinians supported radical Moslem factions. The Rejection Front had taken control and the camp was heavily fortified. Tel Zaatar boasted its own ammunition factory.

The purpose of the trip was simply to consult with the camp's leadership on what might be done to alleviate the suffering. The ICRC was no longer able to get assurances from the Kata'ib that such meetings could be held safely so they'd stopped clearing them. Heinz had cautioned that the rightists would watch the meetings and try to capture or kill the Rejection Front leaders. Thus, they never knew in advance where meetings would be held and who would represent the PFLP. Today the discussion was to be held in a warehouse in Sin al Fil, hidden behind a large block of buildings that protected it from the direct fire of the Kata'ib guns. As they approached, the vehicles and armed men in the street signified the Palestinian delegation was already there.

His neighbor in Manara had always said "War is easy, with binoculars." Now, involved close up, Dave could almost smell the tension that held the whole area in its grip. They parked their brightly marked vehicle and were directed through a sliding door to a dark corner. A table of sorts, with chairs and boxes for seats. In the dim light, David couldn't discern the features of the battle-dressed men. Then, as one turned, he recognized the haggard face of Abu Fadhil, Munir. Deep glistening eyes glared at Dave, checked to see the Red Cross armband and then came forward.

"I see, Mr. LeSueur, that you have a new member in your team." He shook hands with the team leader and then with Dave. His expression was friendly, his tone communicating concern as he spoke, "I thought you'd left our war, Mr. Draper, last month."

"I left. The day after we last met, Mr. Atallah." David was still seeking for some clue to this steely-eyed young man. Could he after all have been involved in the plan to kidnap or kill him? The eye-contact now, as in the cemetery, told him no, as did the firm handshake.

"Mr. Draper was pressed into service through another of our volunteers, a long-time friend. We're glad to have him. We needed someone who knows Beirut and understands some of the complexities." Gabriel LeSueur was a soft-spoken Frenchman who'd studied at Princeton and spoke English almost without accent. He was uneasy about the security arrangements and wondered how long the meeting could last without increasing the risks to both sides. "Abu Fadhil, I suggest that we get started as quickly as possible. We have two vans of pharmaceuticals but no food today. If your men will help our drivers transfer these cartons, you may wish to send those things immediately. We need to discuss, to know what you have decided to do about evacuation." They moved to the makeshift table. David, seated across from Abu Fadhil, noted the Kalashnikov, an incongruous accessory to the articulate words.

Abu Fadhil momentarily rested his head on elbow-propped hands. "I'm afraid I can't be helpful on that, Mr. LeSueur. Our people have decided to stay, siege or no siege."

"But we hear reports of actual starvation. Can you subject the women and children to such conditions?" David didn't enter the discussion. It was better if he listened and learned first. "We are prepared to arrange a truce to bring out wounded, women and children. Surely this is the humane thing to do." LeSueur bent forward over the table, his face tense and sympathetic.

Abu Fadhil's face was flushed, his gaze averted. "You've heard our position before, gentlemen. I don't want to be repetitive. Believe me, the people, even the women and children…and, yes, the wounded too, they are even stronger in their determination. Daily, we receive visits from them, urging us to hold fast. They know they have no place to go, anyway." David was startled to hear the last and his quick glance sideways brought Abu Fadhil's eyes to meet his own for a moment, telling him that David knew this last was not true. There were plenty of places where the ICRC, or even PLO, could safely move them.

"Let me explain the last. Most of those who live in Tal Zaatar have been uprooted twice. Some, more. We see this hellish piece of land as ours and we're determined not to give it up to yet another enemy. In the words of an Arab proverb, what makes us swallow the bitter pill is that which is more bitter."

"But surely there are some who don't feel that way. Will you allow those who want to come out to do so? And the wounded, the ones who need surgery? Again, I ask officially, won't you allow our medical team to enter the camp?"

"I'm sorry. This is a war, gentlemen. I obey the decisions of my commanders. I am told that there is to be no evacuation, no one is to come in. I will tell them of our talks, your requests and the assurances you have given me. We are grateful for the International Committee's efforts. Sometimes I think you are the only ones we can trust." He paused, hoping there would be no further discussion of getting people out. He had tried for weeks to persuade the leaders to evacuate wounded, at least.

Munir had memorized the rhetoric, and he did believe that this was another Black September, that they were fighting for their very existence. It was his eyes that were weakening his resolve. He could be strong if he were blind. The need to evacuate was everywhere he looked. Not just faces. They were the worst, but the cracks and seeping sewage in tunnels and bunkers, the filthy hospital area with its flies and rats, the school now closed. His eyes were betraying him. They were now his enemy.

And what he didn't see attacked his mind through the inward eyes of memory. Muna. Muna and all she'd meant of beauty, of goodness and happiness in his life. Now seeing this American the bitter memory of the bombing returned in force. The stupid bombing. Ibrahim's paranoid suspicions and ruthlessness. The vision of how frightening she looked with the bandages removed, the ugly scarring which still distorted her face, the limp arm hanging at her side as she tried to help Um Ali in the garden. And now, how could he keep her secret from this man who cared? And from Richard, who'd surely loved her?

He roused himself. The team had been discussing something but were now looking quizzically at him. "Please forgive me. We don't get much sleep these days. Now, gentlemen, may we discuss food?...and water? Our other sources are unable to get through. We need flour, badly. We need the other basics too, of course."

"We should have brought some supplies today, but our stocks are low. Tomorrow we will bring flour, tomorrow or day after."

"If I send a car with you today, can you give us some flour?"

"It's that bad already? I think, Abu Fadhil, you ought to press the subject of evacuation. No, I don't believe you should send a car with us. Some of your own people, the PLO, made trouble with us over the last time. They insist that we not take any of your people with us anywhere. We will send back one van, the medical van, with flour and a case or two of oil. You can meet it at the regular place. What time is best?"

"For us, just after sunset. But for you, earlier, eh?"

"No. We've had full assurances and good cooperation along the route we now use." He looked at Dave and the latter knew that this would be one of his first assignments. "The shipment will be 'more medical supplies,' you understand?" He had never told Abu Fadhil that they'd been warned by the Kata'ib that only medical supplies would be allowed through, but surely the quick-minded young man had grasped it.

They discussed the water problem for a half-hour. All the city mains in the area had been ruptured and most closed off. Every effort to bring in a continuing line that would make the precious liquid available in the camp area had been frustrated. A sixteen-year-old boy had been killed trying to connect a hose to one broken pipe. The last project had been simply to connect up an interminable line of garden hoses, reaching a half kilometer through the battle area. LeSueur had predicted some shell would sever the hose, exposed on the surface as it was. Instead it had been dismantled and most lengths stolen during the first night, leaving the critically-needed water to run into the rocky ground just short of the camp area. Tank trucks had been used but were constantly sniped at, most of their cargo spilling out of the bullet-holes before delivery. "We'll ask PLO. They have tank trucks. Maybe we can make runs at nighttime. But we'll send cases of plastic-bagged water with the food today."

LeSueur arose. A list was produced of food and medical supplies for the camp's two overworked doctors. David wondered if PFLP leader George Habash, an AUB-trained doctor, was now in the camp, if he ever used his medical skills in helping the refugees. His thought was interrupted as LeSueur handed him the list, saying that it ought to be checked against what was delivered today. A commando guard moved into the street to check the area.

A loud explosion shook the building, rattling its sheet-metal siding with a sound-magnifying cacophany. They pulled back inside. Another. Apparently close to where they'd parked the prominently-marked vans. It was ICRC's practice to park their vehicles in areas open to view from all sides in the belief that they were safest when their Red Cross markings were clearly visible. It put them in visual range of the Kata'ib's long-range sniping guns, but that was a necessary risk. This shelling seemed to be directed at the clearly-marked vehicles. Another burst. Then silence. Then the zings of long-range sniping shots.

"I think they're trying to tell us something, Abu Fadhil," LeSueur grinned. "Trouble is, I'm just not sure exactly what. Do they want us to leave or do they want us to stay?" Another fusillade of shots. "We'd better not go. Don't you agree?"

"Yes. I'll have some of our men go back. Maybe they can arrange some diversion, draw their fire." He gave orders and four commandos moved cautiously into the street, edging along the side of the building to get to the next street.

"This building is safe. We might as well be comfortable for a few minutes." The slender Palestinian slumped back to the line of seat-high boxes and sat, leaning his back against the stacked crates of ceramic tile that filled the end of the warehouse. "Mr. Draper, why don't you sit here with me?" He wanted to talk to this American who was again involved in his life. There was still a flicker of suspicion remaining in his mind that Ibrahim had been right. Ibrahim, who'd loved Muna more passionately even than Munir had known. For a week he'd punished himself for her accident and then was killed at the exposed gun position on the hill. Munir suspected he'd sought death. It was better to die when he did. He had become inhuman, irrational, bitter that Muna loved the American. Ibrahim, his friend and comrade. His enemy. He must forget him, forget that he was ever this Munir. He was Abu Fadhil. He returned David's gaze. "Did you see your family then?"

"Yes, I spent three weeks with them. They're in Utah now."

"...and Richard? How is he? You saw him?"

"Yes, of course, he's working in Washington for the summer." Dave noticed the other's quick attention to this news.

"In Washington? For what agency?"

"For the Justice Department. It's a summer internship. Students are hired in jobs that complement their academic studies. He's working in a research section, a division where his bosses are women. Afraid Rich is not ready for Women's Liberation. Maybe too many years in the Middle East." David was unaware of the Front's investigation of Rich in the U.S.

"Women's Liberation will have to wait for national liberation in most countries." The Palestinian dismissed the subject. He also dismissed as stupid and unworthy the suspicion that had re-entered his mind about Richard working in Washington. He was sick of suspicion and wanted to have one relationship where it didn't intrude. "And Richard? How did he…? Um Ali told me you took a letter from Muna. How did he…?" He couldn't finish.

David was silent, recalling again the tortuous trauma of that afternoon at Dulles Airport. "How did he take the news of her death?" He turned, looking again in those deep-black eyes with their shared memories of the graveside. "I'll never know. He loved her, deeply, this I do know. If I could have helped him I wouldn't have left. But there's nothing anyone can do."

"Yes, that I am learning." But there was something Munir could do. Richard should know. How could he keep his promise?

"It will heal. He let me read her letter. She ended quoting that Feirouz song 'Your Name is in my Heart.' I think Muna's name will always be in his heart."

"The letter. Did she, was she bitter?"

"Not bitter, no. Disillusioned, freed from the rhetoric of the revolution or whatever you call it. She wrote that she'd decided to leave. Which made it even more difficult for Rich to accept her death."

Munir knew it, although she hadn't told him directly. Why hadn't he gotten her out? His jaw closed tightly as he fought his feelings. "You're a pacifist, aren't you, Mr. Draper?"

"No. What made you think that?"

"You're a Mormon. Aren't Mormons pacifist?"

"No. You don't know much of Mormon history. We were a persecuted people too, you know, driven out of our land. I think you have us confused with the Quakers, the Society of Friends? My ancestors in Utah at one time fought the U.S. Army for their rights. The Mormons sent a battalion to fight against Mexico. But, I personally believe war is ineffective. The most inefficient means of aggression ever invented. Maybe it's justified in defense of your land or to regain your land as you are trying to do. But I don't see any part of the war here in Lebanon as justified, for any party, including Palestinians."

"What other course do we have?"

"You, as Palestinians? None here. The Arabs, of course, have the oil and the economic pressures they can exert."

"They're afraid of America, afraid you'll occupy the wells."

"Well, it's the strongest weapon they have and much preferable to war. If the Arabs had countered the establishment of Jewish settlements on the West Bank with an oil embargo, Israel would have been made to back down. No one, not even the U.S. zionists, are that much in favor of the settlements. Yet every new Israeli settlement advances the take-over they seek. One thing Lebanon seems to be proving is that none of the Arabs are willing to support the Palestinians. I think your liberation movement is dead." Surprised at his own vehemence, David was sure he'd gone too far, offended the young idealist. "Understand, I'm speaking as an old man tired of all the hypocrisy I've seen. Forgive me."

Forgive him? Munir was taken aback at the depth of feeling of this American. "What should we do, then, now that the Syrians are here to do what Hussein did in Jordan?"

"It's an opportunity. The best one you've had since '67. Passive resistance, that's the only weapon left to you. The whole world wants the problem settled."

"What do you mean, passive resistance? Not fighting when the Israelis attack across the border? Lebanon's been doing that for years. We're tired of being the anvil and many Lebanese agree with us. They want to be the hammer for a change."

"Well, I don't think there will be any Arab wars to get your land back. To get their own land, possibly, like the '73 Sinai War. But not to regain Palestine."

"What do you mean, Mr. Draper, by passive resistance? You mean in the West Bank and Gaza, of course."

"Yes, but not just that. If all the Palestinians in Israel would go on strike it would paralyze Israel. Remember Ghandi. If you'd never agreed to work or cooperate in any way after '67, you would have become an intolerable burden, an insoluble problem for Israel. You could make passive use of your masses of refugees. For instance, the Lebanese border. Why not move the Palestinians in Lebanon to the border area and announce to the world that they are going to walk across the border to their land, unarmed, led by their imams and priests? You could ask sympathetic foreigners and notable figures who've taken a stand for Palestine to march with you, at the head of the group. I know many Americans who'd join such a march, many who would pay their way here to join it."

Munir was silent, thoughtful. David sighed. "Forgive me, Abu Fadhil. These are just the muttering of a malcontent. I grow impatient with history as I get older. Nothing is simple, there are no quick or easy answers. But, seeing what's happening here, I don't believe you can win your land back from outside."

Munir nodded, still silent. What could he say? All the American had said was true, though he had conveniently left out the U.S. role in manipulating the Arab governments who were now dismembering the resistance. "Your government will always support Israel, whether it's war or this passive resistance you speak of."

"The U.S. and Israel itself will find it more difficult to oppose passive action than any violence you can organize. But you're right, the U.S. won't allow Israel to be defeated. I'm not for the destruction of the original Israel either."

"What is the original Israel, the Nile to the Euphrates?"

"No, the UN-defined state or maybe the '49 boundaries, but certainly not the '67 conquest. You're not the first country to lose land to others better equipped or better supported. What makes your case is that after '67 you were deprived of all your land. This is the international crime that is not acceptable. The world realizes it owes you a state but don't expect it to be the right size and dimensions." He stopped, realizing how preachy he must sound to this young revolutionary. "I'll get down off my soapbox. Sorry. Haven't talked this way in years."

They stood and shook hands, David wondering why since there was no indication of departure yet. The firing had continued at a reduced but constant rate and the team was still concerned.

Abu Fadhil yawned and stretched. "I enjoyed our discussion, Mr. Draper. Oh, one thing: Better not to use my name with the others. Munir Atallah doesn't belong to me now. We have a rule that we must use our, what you say, nich-names?" David corrected his pronunciation of nickname and agreed to call him Abu Fadhil.

They surveyed the scene from the warehouse door again and talked with the commando guard outside. The consensus was that this would be the best time to go. David would ride with the second van and bring the food to Sin al Fil, where they would meet the PFLP jeeps. Again, Munir shook his hand. "I'm glad you're here, Mr. Draper." Looking at the others, he commented, "You now have a small United Nations."

"Yes, but we get along better," LeSueur said as he turned away and led his group along the building to the vehicles.

# # # # # # # # #

Two weeks passed and a dozen attempts were made to get supplies into Tal Zaatar. Only five such transfers were made, though. Each operation had to be carefully planned, discussed and negotiated with PLO. That facilitated the crossing to the Eastern area but the real problem, of course, was the twenty-four hour shelling by the siege forces of

Kata'ib. They were determined to destroy this stubborn outpost so close to their center.

David participated in two of the meetings with Kata'ib leaders. Reasonable men, their heartlessness hidden away somewhere out of view, they spoke the sweet words of logic that military men have always used to justify their killing. "But it is simple. At the first guarantee of their surrender, we will stop the shelling. We will help them evacuate." Who was worse, those who persisted in the brutal barrage or the ones who kept the women, children and even wounded in the fighting area? A token hundred and fifty Arab League troops had arrived in Beirut and taken position at the Museum cross-over point. Egypt now joined Saudi Arabia, Kuwait, Jordan and the Gulf States in support of Syria's decision to help the Christian forces and abandon the PLO. Maybe it was the only way to save Lebanon.

David wondered how much of this was the work of Kissinger and how much might simply be the result of the Palestinians' own mistakes. Did Munir realize that his extremists and Marxists had frightened the conservative anti-communist Arab regimes? Tal Zaatar refugees should have been moved years earlier. Now, it had become a symbol of the Palestinian liberation movement itself. "I almost hope they can hold out." Heinz told David.

"Madness. War is a communicable disease. Maybe you've caught it, Heiny." Dave had been depressed for days. The ICRC mail hadn't brought him anything from Lora yet. He tried to keep his nightly few paragraphs to her optimistic and cheerful, never mailing his running narrative until he'd added some kind of upbeat comment. But he never wrote of the future, of when he'd return, or of their moving to Cairo as he'd proposed last spring. He realized this when he read a letter from Rich: "Dad, will you be coming home in September? I need to have a long talk with you. I think I'll change my specialty. Not sure yet." With only a year to finish, why was he changing now? Would this mean another year of tuition? The letter didn't say much, didn't mention Muna, ended with, "Do you go to Tal Zaatar?"

David visited the apartment to meet the PLO captain that Ramzi had managed to install as a tenant there. Conversation with him convinced David that the young man was the best possible protection they could have, not only for their apartment but also for the building and, indeed, the whole neighborhood. The man had already foiled an attempt to steal two of the cars left by departed tenants. The neighbors seemed grateful for his presence. He seemed to enjoy the apartment but thought Dave should move in. A graduate of AUB, he also reflected the Palestinian despair. Friends invited David for lunch. Before even finishing the meal they began the morbid listing of deaths and injuries known to the guests. The etiquette of war, listening to fellow inmates in the asylum. After one such lunch, he stopped for a haircut at the shop of his first Beirut friend, a young Moslem he'd dubbed the "Mayor of Manara" because he always knew the neighborhood's affairs. Now, he was philosophic about the puzzling twists and turns which alternately revealed and then hid Syrian intentions in Lebanon. Seeing the Syrians turn against the PLO, the Moslems now felt they had been cynically used to provide the Palestinians a base in Lebanon. They resented the Palestinians now almost as much as did the Christian rightists.

The barber was an exception, loyal to the pro-Palestinian Arabist position that had marked the Moslem-Druze grouping. Yet, his principal comment could have been made by a conservative Maronite: "We were given our independence in 1943, Mr. Draper. We didn't have to fight for it. We didn't deserve it. Now we Lebanese are fighting for our independence. We're a nation, not a pawn to be moved around by the other Arabs or a servant or a whore to be bought and paid for." Walking away from the earnest handshake of this friend, David marveled. How pleasant and analytical the Lebanese can be, while their country is being destroyed by its neighbors and friends.

On August second, an early morning meeting was scheduled to persuade camp officials to allow evacuation. David rode through the city in the small car with its giant red crosses, a supply van following. The heat and the humidity oppressed him. He'd lain awake much of the night, listening to the soft lapping of waves and thinking of Lora and the children, knowing they didn't understand why he had returned. As he transited the hulk of this once-vibrant pleasant city, he now questioned himself. Why, really, had he come? Was it the debt to Muna? No, he knew himself better than that. He wasn't anywhere near that noble. Something else, some force, almost, had drawn him back.

The city was barely functioning. Oft-savored scenes had now become savaged. All of the random elements that had produced pleasant, luxurious urban living were now relegated to their material origin, unworking, ungiving. There was still some beauty for the eyes, but whose eye would see beauty now? Several times in the war Dave had experienced an eerie feeling that he was seeing the future, that the future siege of the haves by the have-nots that was predicted by Britain's historian-author C.P. Snow had begun in Beirut. He could imagine New York in this condition.

They arrived at the meeting-site. Munir looked pale and drawn. He was obviously ill, his breathing in short continuous intakes as he managed to smile a greeting. All energy seemed to have been drained from his lithe frame. His eyes were sunk deep and now shone like two fiery diamonds in dark-rimmed sockets. His clothing was undeniably filthy. The commandos had come out to the warehouse under cover of darkness and waited three hours before the arrival of the ICRC team, which parked the single van and car in the open area. Five team-members scurried out to the shelter of the nearest buildings and along the hundred yards to the warehouse door. LeSueur had other business.

Dave, as head of the group, grasped Munir's hand vigorously, noting the weak grip of the feverish young man. "You don't look well, Abu Fadhil."

"It's just a summer cold. I'm better off than most. Even my men here, there is something with all of them. I hope you've brought the surgical drugs."

"I think we have everything. The syrettes, the myacins, plenty of alcohol…"

"Alcohol? We don't need so much alcohol. We can use salt water to wash the wounds. We need the things on the list, the list we sent…" He was shouting, argumentative, not himself.

"We'll get the things out now and you can see. I believe."

"Never mind, the others can do that. We have to talk, over here." Used to command in the camp, he didn't realize the authoritative tone he was using with David. They sat, facing across one end of the table. "We want to send out our wounded. How soon can you arrange it?"

Though it had been inevitable and he'd expected it any day, David was surprised and responded with a rush of planning and detail unleashed in his mind by the good news. Tomorrow morning, certainly. What about this afternoon? No, there wasn't time to arrange proper liaison with the Kata'ib and maybe not to get enough ambulances. How many wounded? How many stretcher cases? Abu Fadhil had no notes, only vague figures in his head. David wondered if he really knew—if anyone knew—how many near-dead people would crawl out of those buildings and caves and bunkers. He decided they'd bring additional ambulances just in case.

"What about the others? Will they be allowed to leave?"

Abu Fadhil's eyes bore into him, sparks of anger the only remaining energy in his sick body. "Allowed? Of course they will be allowed. They have always been allowed to leave. Do you think our leaders want these people to suffer? You asked me to make arrangements so we could get the wounded out, those in need of surgery. That's what I have arranged. They are ready. I only hope the Kata'ib will hold their fire." He sank back, then added. "Of course some of our women will accompany their wounded. Will there be a place for them?"

"There will be a place for anyone who wants to come out. We will make trips all day if necessary. We can get about twenty ambulances, twenty-two I believe is the number we have that we can call on. It's fortunate that Dr. Jacobson is with us today. He arrived only yesterday. Maybe he can ask you some questions to get a more specific idea of what we will need." Dave turned over his place to the Doctor, moving to where he could make notes.

The meeting hadn't gone well. It must look to the others like his relationship with Front leaders was antagonistic. He'd thought the young Atallah had liked, even trusted, him. Maybe it was his sickness. Anyway, much to be done. The battle was finally drawing to its tragic end. He wondered how many were really left in this burial-place that was Tal Zaatar. Recalling the bitter taste of zaatar when sprinkled on the moist inside of the hollow brown bread, he thought the translation of Tal Zaatar for him would always be "Hill of Bitterness."Dr. Jacobson patiently probed for the information they needed on the condition and classification of the wounded, whether they would be brought on stretchers, how many would need immediate therapy, whether there were heart cases, how many infants, and the information they'd been seeking for so long on communicable diseases. Having gotten all the information that Abu Fadhil could give him, the physician felt they could organize the evacuation. They agreed on where ICRC would bring the ambulances, a large open parking lot on the edge of the camp.

Determined to part with Munir on better terms and worried about his condition, David asked the Doctor to examine him.

"I'm all right, Mr. Draper. I haven't been able to rid myself of this bothersome cold." There was coolness in his voice, an attempt to pull the cloak of dignity around what he knew to be his increasing vulnerability with this American. Each time they met his mind saw Muna and Richard together.

The Doctor guided him back down into the chair and was taking pulse, looking at his darkened eyeballs. He turned to David. "I've suggested he ought to be among those evacuated. There must be some serious infection."

"That, of course, Doctor, is out of the question. You will see tomorrow what we mean by our sick and our wounded. I am the picture of health by comparison." The Doctor took a syringe from his bag and Dave was glad that Munir acceded to the administration of an injection, accomplished in privacy behind a big crate.

They prepared to leave. The Doctor went to make sure his notes accompanying the medicines would be given to the camp nurse. Thus Abu Fadhil and David were left inside the cavernous and musty warehouse, each wanting to ease the tension he felt in the other.

"Forgive my rudeness, Mr. Draper. My father used to say that Arabs are either gentlemen or barbarians, that other people can be in between but Arabs go direct from one extreme to the other."

"I didn't hear rudeness. Tiredness, sickness. You aren't well. I'm a bear to live with when I'm ill. I'm so relieved and pleased at today's news that nothing else matters. Can you be sure your people won't open fire if we get a Kata'ib promise? This will be the first time we've been inside your area."

"Yes, of course. I'd hoped it could be this afternoon."

"I'm afraid it couldn't possibly be laid on that quickly. Is it that bad? Are there some who won't make it?"

"Yes, there are some, but that's not new. Who knows who will make it through the day? We had five killed outright last night, all in one small dugout. What the Kata'ib would call a lucky hit. As you know, we're not able to give much in return."

"Does this mean it will soon end?"

"No, we have ammunition and we'll hold here. Maybe Syria will come to it's senses. Maybe Kata'ib will stop. We hear rumors. As you know, the radio doesn't tell us much."

"Nothing encouraging, anyway. Something will work out.

Lebanon can't take much more of this." In saying it, he wondered if Munir felt he was slighting the Palestinians. But, after all, this is Lebanon, with its own people and problems. Even in Tal Zaatar Lebanese were being killed. "I'm afraid I was very pessimistic in the long talk we had. I hope I was wrong."

"You're very much like my father, Mr. Draper, you know. He always apologized for being pessimistic. But Muna called him an optimist. He believed the U.S. would settle our problem, make Israel give up the West Bank. Before we started to quarrel, we had long talks. His thinking was much like yours."

"You haven't encouraged me. I have sons and I know how little a father's thinking impresses them." He smiled, wanting to lighten the mood of this exchange which was becoming so somber.

"No, no I want to encourage you. You are 'Abu Richard.' Your son is much more like you than you realize. And I am much more like my father than I ever thought before." The last was added in an aside as the young man peered out at the bright sun beyond the doorway. "He wanted me to become an architect. To build things. Look at this, this Beirut. Is it the work of architects? Destroyers, we are all destroyers."

The Doctor signaled he was ready. Dave regretted having to end the conversation. He might not even see the young Atallah again. He was so ill. And, of course, he could be killed any day. They shook hands, eyes meeting for a moment. Impulsively, David placed his arm on Munir's shoulder in the way he had so often with Rich and Rob. The response was also impulsive. Munir clasped the older man to him in a close embrace, remembering the last time he'd felt his own father's gray head close by his.

Shouldn't he break his promise and tell him about Muna? He should know she had not been killed. When the evacuation was finished he must get out to Fawzia's and talk with Muna again. Richard should know. Muna must understand. He followed this father who had so affected him out to the street and walked with him in the shadow of the warehouse. The cars were parked across a wide space intended for a future traffic circle. He watched the straight figure of David striding across to the open-doored vehicle. "Ma'a Salameh".

"Fi amaan Illah." David used the Iraqi phrase for parting, "In the Safety of God", expressing his concern for the young man. He reached the car and looked back as he heard Munir's voice.

"Ma'a Salameh, Abu Richard." Munir waved again.

There were three shots. The first hit the top of the sedan. The second hit David in the left temple, caving in the turned face as his waving hand fell and his lifeless body wedged against the open car door, then slowly slid to the pavement. Munir's eyes saw it all as the tall American crumpled to the ground. But his mind also saw the battered form of Muna. "W'Allah! Laa! Oh, no!" His cry filled the silence of the street.

Chapter 19

"The stream had reached the sea. Once more the great mother holds her son against her breast."

Khalil Gibran "The Prophet"

The sprawling city lay quiet below, barely breathing in the August heat. The Red Cross plane flew low, circling the business area. Rich gazed intently, recognizing the gaunt blackened shells of the once-proud hotels and the destroyed center city. The sun's bright rays sterilized the streets but his mind turned to the human tragedies hidden in those miles of rubble. How many others were spending this day as he would, tending to the dead?

He'd persuaded his mother not to come. Quickly leaving his Washington summer job, he'd come directly, grateful for ICRC's cable that he could come in with their supply plane from Cyprus. Rich was numbed by his father's death. Even reading David's letter that arrived just as he was leaving had failed to bring his grieving to the surface. It intrigued him to find out his father was dealing with Munir on almost a daily basis. Did Munir know of the shooting that killed his father? Was he or the Front involved? His lawyer's mind toyed with the thought and dismissed it. What did it matter, whose bullet? So many down there, wielding their weapons, were guilty of manslaughter. But those who gave the orders were the murderers.

The early August evacuation of wounded from Tal Zaatar had taken place on schedule. The family watched the TV coverage carefully, hoping for a glimpse of their father. There was only a brief mention of the killing of an ICRC volunteer the day before. They didn't know this was their father's U.S. obituary, "name withheld awaiting notification of next of kin." Rich had gotten Lora's call at work. After more calls, he realized he'd have to take over the arrangements with ICRC. But he'd wanted to be with his Mother. He should have flown out to Utah. She needed him more than he was needed in Beirut for these mundane details, closing the life of a father he'd never really understood. But someone had to come.

They hadn't been able to decide what to do about the body. The second cable gave a hint of problems and indicated embalming was unavailable. Apparently someone was required to claim the remains. It took almost a week to arrange his trip but he was assured the body could be stored. Stored. That word confirmed to Rich the impersonal nature of his task. He knew how his Dad had felt about such things. Not important where or how one is buried, the "remains" being only that, a physical shell to be discarded. Rich shared the belief of his parents in the eternal life of man's individual spirit.

As the plane glided in over the airport, he wondered if that spirit-man was now aware of the family's great paralyzing grief, or of his son's presence in Beirut. Was he somehow monitoring this last attention to the physical David Draper?

At breakfast in Cyprus, he'd read the details of the fall of Tal Zaatar. Fifty-two days they'd held out under virtual siege. Twelve thousand had fled the camp as Kata'ib forces raked the area in a final killing rampage. Had Munir also given his life in this useless battle? The thought added even more depression to his day. He couldn't remember Munir without also seeing Muna.

The plane rolled to a stop on the deserted tarmac and he saw vans and trucks with their large red and white markings. Several men waited as he descended the fold-down ramp with the suitcase he'd stowed behind his seat. He recognized the bushy-eyebrowed face of Heinz Lanser immediately, though he'd been only thirteen when he'd seen him last. Hearing the germanic accent, he recalled mimicking him after family visits in Baghdad.

"Richard. I am so sorry." What could Lanser say? What could Richard say in answering? Mr. LeSueur, who was apparently head of the team, handled it best with his gentle but formal expression of condolences. Lanser was gruff but emotional, insisting on a clumsy bear hug. This close friend was having a difficult time with David's death. Driving back to the hotel, Richard listened as the older man bared his anguish. "Richard, he'd just gotten out of Beirut. We met on the plane. I suggested he come and help us. No, Richard, I persuaded him. If we hadn't met on the plane that day…I should have realized…"

Richard cut him off. "My father would have come anyway. He had other reasons. We know this now. I should have known before. He had to try to help." Then, to ease the older man's distraught mind, Rich outlined the details of Muna's death and of David's certainty that she had died trying to save his life. "But it was more even than that, I think. Dad was devastated by what was happening here. For the Lebanese and what it meant for the Palestinians, too. His last letter to me said he didn't want to continue in the area. He thought his long involvement in the Arab world should come to an end."

Lanser was shaken by what Rich had told him but still not able to relinquish the blame he felt. "He should have taken a year or two in the States and instead I pulled him back…to this."

"Dad was never any good away from the Middle East. After a few weeks, he always wanted to be back. We don't know why this had to happen. Maybe his time had come. He seemed to sense it. Mother believes that. She told me she'd always felt their involvement in the area would end in some awful incident." They rode on in silence.

The team was housed in the Coral Beach, formerly Beirut's nicest resort hotel. Rich indicated he would use his father's room. It had been left as it was, his things untouched. Opening the door, he saw the unfinished letter first. Written in David's rapid scrawl, there were only two entries, ending with "I have a strong feeling that tomorrow will provide the breakthrough and the evacuation can begin. I've had great satisfaction these past weeks, Lora. I know you find me hard to understand. I do love you. Always remember that." Rich sat on the bed, the paper trembling in his hand.

They drove to AUB Hospital and were led along an unswept basement hallway to that depressing area that forces man to look at his ultimate future. The strong chemical odor of the morgue was mixed with an acrid people smell. Even underground the heat invaded the ruined city.

The family name in Arabic was about all Rich had learned of the written language, and he recognized it, labeling the steel tray which the white-coated attendant pulled out. Impersonal and tired-looking, the man swiftly drew back the covering. This was not his father. What kind of single bullet can so completely destroy a face? No part nor feature recalled the memory of his father. Lanser took him by the arm and moved Rich to look from the other side. There, the side of the face was whole, the visage a part of what Rich's memory could conjure. The hospital attendant covered the grisly flesh and hair so gruesomely intermixed. "We will see if a Doctor can…"

"No. Nothing needs to be done. I'm the only one of the family…" He turned to Lanser, "Can we bury him here…in Beirut?" Rich was now certain. He'd discussed the possibility with Lora in their last phone call. Now he knew his mother shouldn't see this body, even repaired. It seemed indecent, like looking at a sleeping man's nakedness. They walked up the stairs. Rich stopped at the surgical desk to ask if he could see their family friend, a surgical nurse, but she had been evacuated.

Heinz Lanser had hoped the Drapers would make this simpler decision. Complicated arrangements would prolong their grief. Burial here was better. Strange that the cemetery should be one David had himself located. A week after his arrival, the committee had been approached by the Netherlands Embassy, asking where they might bury a national who'd been killed in shelling of his apartment. The British-American cemetery, used for other expatriates as well, was located in a battle area. David knew of another and took them there. Heinz had gone along, curious as to how David knew the place, but David wouldn't talk about it.

Suggesting that they stop at the American Embassy, Heinz was surprised that Rich didn't want to involve them. "But they'll have to know, to register the burial, won't they?" Heinz wanted the Embassy to know Rich was in Beirut. He worried that this young man might decide to roam around the city.

"The death, yes. But that's already been reported to them, hasn't it? I called State Department in Washington to find out who was here, hoping that one of Dad's friends might be. They're all new, people who don't know Dad. No reason to go now. I'll tell them where the grave is."

"I can do that for you. But, Richard, don't go anywhere without letting us know. Your father told me you're a loner and like to explore. Beirut's dangerous now. You don't want to get picked up like you were that time by the Kata'ib."

"Yeah, they thought I was spying for the PLO. Don't worry, I'm not planning any visits." There was no place in Beirut he wanted to go now, anyway.

Back at the hotel, Heinz dispatched the driver to make arrangements at the cemetery and have someone prepare the grave. He had a meeting to set up a new delivery system to provide food for Tal Zaatar refugees who had flooded into West Beirut. Relieved that Richard was handling himself well, he left Rich to the personal things that had to be done.

It took only a half-hour to pack the clothes and things into the large suitcase, leaving room for things from the apartment. He selected some clean things, clothes he should be buried in. There was probably a suit at the apartment, but a suit and tie didn't fit with that battered face. An open white shirt. Finished, he went out on the room's veranda and sat for awhile watching the swells and ripples of the calm sea. He remembered that Mediterranean smell, soft and pulsating, somehow more seductive than the Pacific shore. Occasional shots pierced the quiet, an integral part of this new Beirut, like traffic noises, no longer distracting.

He thought of Munir. Heinz had told him of the close working relationship David had developed with Munir and how disturbed the Front leader had been when the Kata'ib sniper had killed him. Any thought of Munir always turned his mind to Muna. Should he now talk with her brother, this "Abu Fadhil"? His father had never mentioned if they'd discussed her death. Questions. Problems. Beirut had nothing else to offer.

Deciding to eat something, he went downstairs to a table by the empty pool, alone with his thoughts. Finishing a sandwich, Rich asked the driver to take him to the apartment in Manara. The man checked with Mr. LeSueur, who came over and handed Rich a Red Cross armband. "Use this if you have to. We're not sure about the Manara area anymore."

The arrival of the Red Cross Land Rover excited some interest and Rich recognized faces for which he had no names. He'd hoped to talk with Fuad, but the Hakims were now in Jordan. All their foreign friends were gone. The Issawi family was still in Beirut, but there was no one on their balcony overlooking the street. He wondered if they had heard the news of the death. Abu Ahmed came out as he was opening the building door with the set of keys he'd found on the hotel-room dresser. He knew. His wife also appeared in their doorway looking stricken, almost afraid, with her small children clutched around her. So the neighbors knew as well. As they appeared to greet him, he tried to respond but the language barrier was even greater than the emotional barrier.

Abu Ahmad accompanied him upstairs. Rich understood from his words that the PLO captain caring for the apartment was usually gone during the day. He made Abu Ahmed understand that he was not taking much, that the Institute would keep the flat, that they wanted the Palestinian there. He wished he were alone. Sensing this, Abu Ahmad repeated the litany of condolences and left.

Still framing the seascape with the treetops and the ornate balconies of the pink house in the foreground, the living-room window was now broken. Shreds of glass hung to the heavy tape that had criss-crossed it. The veranda windows were also blasted in and piles of glass crunched under his feet. The canvas veranda curtains hung in shreds like the sails of some derelict schooner. Colorful but unmatched sheets covered most of the furniture and dust stirred in the breeze flowing through the rooms. It was momentarily pleasant to be back in these familiar surroundings. The porch settee where he and Muna had talked so long had been brought in out of the weather. In the dining room he pictured Muna reflected in the mirrors of the white-painted armoire.

He lifted the Isfahan prayer-rug down from the wall, hoping it would fold into his father's bag. He removed "The Dervishes" painting from its frame and rolled it inside the carpet. In the master bedroom he opened David's closet and chose a pair of near-white trousers. Then he filled a large envelope with the family's most recent snapshots from a box-file where Lora kept them by the year. How do you decide what your Mother wants to remind her of, or help her forget, your father? She'd eventually have to come, or maybe the Institute could simply ship everything. There wasn't that much. His family had never been collectors, savers. Anyway, nothing could be shipped now. The port had been closed for over a year. Maybe the apartment would be bombed. Let the war have this too. It had taken everything else. He left.

Outside, waiting for him were the elder Issawis with their doctor-son, and the lighthouse-keeper, whom he'd known principally for the beauty of his daughters, now married, who'd taken Rich's eye on his first summer visit in '72. He shook hands, accepted their genuine grief and placed it alongside his own so they could circle it with their ritual of sympathy. Should he tell them of the burial? No, it wasn't right to expect them to take any chances leaving the area. There had been enough tragedy in the neighborhood. With the militant Tal Zaatar refugees now milling through the area, serious incidents were already being reported.

Back at the Coral Beach, he rearranged the packing and fitted in the things he'd brought from the apartment, laying aside the light clothing he'd take to the morgue to cover that naked alien body. He talked at dinner with Heinz and with some of the others, trying to forget the next morning's burial, wanting to interest himself in the quiet but dangerous work of these impressive men, wanting to understand his father's last days.

Finally leaving the others, he and Heinz Lanser walked out along the small artificial beach breakwater where a half moon lit the sea. Shell flashes from the East could be seen prior to each dull thud, punctuating the endless narrative of urban war. They didn't say much, talked mainly of their two families. Lanser took hold of Rich's shoulders. "Promise me, Richard, that you'll bring your mother and Robert and Dannielle to visit us in Switzerland next summer. I'm going to send tickets for you. You promise?"

Rich promised, thanking the older man. Next year. Where would the family be? Thoughts swam through his mind. Finances, insurance. Was there a will? Where would they live? Would his mother have to work? Should he quit law school? How were Dannie and Rob going to handle this? They said goodnight, Lanser leaving first. Rich stayed, leaning on the balcony rail, trying to postpone the worries now flooding his mind. Unable, he went to the room, undressed and lay on the bed, lulled by the soft wash of the Mediterranean against the rocks and sands of the troubled Beirut shore. Slowly, he drifted into sleep.

Chapter 20

"You have sung to me in my aloneness, and I of your longings have built a tower in the sky. But now our sleep has fled and our dream is over, and it is no longer dawn."

Khalil Gibran.

The cemetery was quiet now. The picking and shoveling that had grated his nerves as he waited for the burial party was done. The grave was now finished and the fresh mound of earth five meters away was crowned by the old caretaker who'd dug it, cursing at the war that had deprived him even of his gravedigger. A couple of scraggly birds picked at the fresh-dug soil and then skittered along the stone wall of the cemetery's edge. The steep slope above produced a few daisies and a profusion of green shrubs and weeds. Two of the three tall cypress trees had been hit, one recently with its upper half now broken and touching the foot of the newly dug grave. He remembered only one had been cut down before, on that awful day when he'd been so sure he was burying his beloved sister.

The death of the American had moved and changed Munir deeply. Perhaps as much as had the death of his own parents. He'd relived the shooting dozens of times. Running into the street to give the help that was too late, he had almost lost control of himself. The sight of that life-shattering blast was now his most vivid memory of the war. He'd seen much worse. Maybe it was the fever, his weakened condition. The days following had been a nightmare. Determined to stay on in the camp, he'd prepared for death. Every night. Every morning. Deafening high-explosive barrages that had even made conversation impossible.

On the twelfth, they'd insisted he leave with other leaders through an escape tunnel as the camp fell. Munir no longer cared, was sure they'd be killed or captured anyway. Now, safe outside the camp, he could be with Muna, try to help her reconstruct her life.

Tal Zaatar was finished. How much of the movement was finished with it? Was he himself finished? Had Draper been right that the liberation movement was mortally wounded in Lebanon? He'd almost decided to miss yesterday's meeting with the ICRC. Seeing the Swiss volunteer, known as the "Oil capitalist" among Palestinians, he'd been relieved to hear that Richard was here to bury his father. Admitting the illogical Moslem abhorrence of delaying a burial, he'd nevertheless supposed they'd take the body back to America. But Lanser said Rich would bury him in Beirut and described where. How had Richard known this cemetery?

Going directly from the ICRC meeting back to Fawzia's house he spent the rest of the day with Muna. She looked better and had arranged a head scarf that covered the scars of her face. She smiled at him, the first time since the bombing. He waited hours before he could summon the strength to tell her of Draper's death.

She gasped, her twisted face stricken with grief. "My poor Richard!" was her only response.

"I'm going to the cemetery. He'll be buried in Beirut. Tomorrow morning. Come with me. Um Ali says you've never gone out except to the hospital. Just ride with me. I need you there. Draper had become my close friend." He didn't mention Richard.

"Oh, no, Munir." She drew the scarf across her face.

"You'll stay in the car. No one will even know who it is."

He insisted and, finally, she had agreed, making him park down the hill. "Munir, is this where that poor girl is buried?"

"Yes, Muna. I'll never be rid of the memory of that day." He didn't want this connection. He wanted her to think good thoughts. Today she would see Richard. He must decide what to do. What would Richard say to him? Should he have come at all? No, he had to be there. There was no choice but to come, to honor this man, this friend. Richard would know of their Tal Zaatar meetings. But he knew his real reason was Muna. And Richard. Draper would want him to try.

He walked back down the hill, not wanting to be seen here, possibly identified in this enemy area of the city. There would be many others coming, from the Embassy, the ICRC group, the Drapers' friends. He'd brought roses but they were quickly wilting, their scent diluting the strong earth smell wafting from the grave. He looked again at Muna, worrying, and then moved closer up the hill.

The Red Cross Land Rover arrived alone. Only a suit-clad Lanser and the driver accompanied Rich, who wore the same kind of tan pants and blue shirt his father always wore. The others would come soon. He moved across to greet them at the gravesite, shaking hands wordlessly with Rich, whose fierce look told him how taken aback he was at Munir's presence. An uncomfortable silence was broken when Rich went back with Lanser to carry the unfinished wood coffin. Munir silently moved to help, the caretaker fussing alongside. They placed the box on ropes laid beside the grave.

There was no flag, Munir noticed. Something should cover the coffin. Draper had served with the American navy in the World War. Why was there not an American flag? Going quickly down the hill to his vehicle, he removed the Palestine flag that they always carried, the same one they'd used here before when he'd thought he was burying his sister. Muna looked at him questioningly from the back seat. She couldn't see Richard. He should tell her. But he didn't, taking the flag back up the hill. Looking first at Rich for a reaction, he quickly spread the Palestinian flag over the box, Lanser helping to straighten it. Where were the others to pay respect to this man? But there was no one else.

Rich bowed his head, Lanser and Munir and the driver stood around the grave. Emotion shaking and interrupting the words, the tall young man said a prayer of dedication over his father's grave. The words were strange to Munir; simple, straightforward, dignified and ending "in the name of Jesus Christ, Amen." He finished, head bowed for a minute longer. Looking up, Munir murmured "B'isim Illah", so instinctively he hardly realized he'd said it. So many burials in this city.

Positioned around the grave, the old man supervising, the four lifted the casket, lowering it by rope into the meter-deep hole. The caretaker lifted the flag and Muunir folded it and handed it to Rich. Then, Lanser brought his Bible from the car and read the twenty-third psalm. The words brought back mental pictures of his youth in Jerusalem. Attending a mission school, Munir had memorized this passage. It was alright for the priests to teach Moslems from the Old Testament so while his friends had learned the Beatitudes he had mastered the beautiful lines of the psalm. The accented stentorian voice, reminded him of Father Leonardo, the Franciscan who'd headed the school.

"...and I will dwell in the house of the Lord forever. Amen."

########

The caretaker carefully descended into the grave and removed the lid of the wood coffin with his hammer. Rich knew the custom, but for a moment he debated whether the coffin shouldn't be left covered. Deciding his father would want it, he helped lift the cover from the grave. Anything that would hasten the destruction of this unmeaningful remnant. The white cloth shrouding the body he had so tenderly dressed that morning was a hospital sheet. The circular insignia in its center was folded under so that two words of the hospital's logo showed: "American" and "Beirut."

Climbing out, the caretaker handed the shovel to Richard. Hesitating, he looked down at the white-covered body. Then he sank the shovel deep into the mound and slowly spread the earth along the length of the shroud. A second shovel. Then two others. He wasn't sure of the custom but supposed he was representing his mother and Dannie and Rob. Then he handed it to Heinz Lanser and finally to Munir.

Whispering "B'ism Illah al Rahman al Rahim," Munir, eyes glistening, sprinkled a shovelful and then another. Giving the shovel to the caretaker, they moved away, standing to watch the bent figure finish the work. The driver finally relieved the panting old man. It was finished.

Rich picked some daisies leaning defeatedly in the hot sun. Kneeling to place a spray of them on the fresh mound, he looked up to see that Munir had brought three roses. Were they from another grave? Observations clicked slowly in his brain. Then his pulse quickened. Was Muna's grave nearby?

Overcome again by that gripping sorrow that tries to dull the pain, Rich rose and looked into Munir's dark eyes for the answer. His query brought only anguish in the brother's stare. Slowly, Rich looked at other nearby graves. He tried to picture Muna's face in death. Grateful that he couldn't, he let his mind recall his first sight of her as she stood framed in the doorway of the apartment. He turned again to Munir, his voice only a whisper: "Is she…? Where…"

Munir avoided his gaze. "No, Richard." Then in a softer personal tone "Will you leave today?"

"Yes, at two. The Red Cross plane to Cyprus." He sighed. This twin brother brought her so painfully to his mind. "What about you, Munir? What will you do now? I wondered where you…" He didn't know what to say about the fall of Tal Zaatar.

"Oh, we have much to do. We're trying to get our people resettled, to keep them fed. The…the war goes on." Then, to change the subject, mainly, "I'm back at Aunt Fawzia's. Um Ali is still there and she feeds us and fusses. You've met her. I don't think she realizes any more what's really going on."

"How much longer, Munir? How will it all end? Is there anything left to fight for?…or against?"

"You'll have to ask Hafez al Assad. Apparently the Americans think Syria can solve everything." When you can't handle a personal dilemma, talk politics.

"Didn't someone have to come in?"

"Yes, but not to take sides. Now we know the purpose of the war. A bit more sophisticated than the Jordanian solution but it had to be. This, after all, was to be the final solution."

"You mean 'final solution' of the Palestine problem?"

"That's what your father thought. He said the resistance was now dead. He said it would be buried here."

"He used to call himself the Institute's 'house pessimist.'"

"You think he was right?" Munir's face was strained. "No, he isn't right. Our people are stronger than he knows...than he knew." The declaration was unconvincing. Looking back to the new grave, Munir spoke in low tones. "He was a strange man. I couldn't think of him as an American."

"I know. Sometimes I felt the same way. I think even he wondered sometimes where his loyalties lay. Maybe expatriates who live for long periods away from their own country should become citizens of the world. Dad always felt uncomfortable and alien discussing things back in the U.S. He had a different view, an almost foreign perspective. I feel the same way, even after being in the States again. In my classes, my responses come from things I've learned out here and I know others are thinking from a different perspective. I've spent most of my life here, probably gone to school in the Middle East as much as you have."

"Maybe you should become a Lebanese citizen."

"No. No, thank you. If the Palestinians have been betrayed here, then think how the Lebanese must feel. They've been used, badly. All this slaughter, destruction of their whole country. Dad thought Palestinians could only win their land back from the West Bank. He used to talk of Ghandi's tactics."

"I know, we had long talks. Talks which will always be...." Munir's voice faltered, "...important to me. Maybe he is right. Maybe we can do more from inside. An Intifadha."

Rich didn't understand the Arabic word. Was this Abu Fadhil becoming a pacifist? "Well, I'm for the individual, for the most individual freedom possible. Until you find someone you love. Then you share your freedom. That's what Muna meant to me. You didn't know how much. She is still with me and always will be. All the 'causes', including yours, interfere with the individual, use people, destroy love…destroyed my love."

They faced each other and Munir offered his hand, holding it as if he wanted Rich to stay. "What will you do now, Rich? You finish law this year, don't you?"

"I'd just written Dad and asked for a long talk. I'm not sure what I want to do with my life. Are you, Munir?"

The strained face looked away. Munir looked much older than Rich remembered from that tennis date. Defeat and bitterness had replaced the cold proud gaze. "I promised my father I would become an important architect. I must build something. Sometime. Somewhere. I'll work it out someday." Munir's other hand grasped Rich's shoulder. "Well, Richard, you must go. Give my condolences to your family. Allah yahalik. You know what that means?"

"Yes, God help you too. And Palestine. Ma'a Salameh" Munir still held his hand. Now he gripped it hard and looked into his eyes. "Richard, come with me to the car."

Rich was startled by the change in Munir's voice, the emotion in his eyes. They'd said goodbye. This was a strange request. They walked down the hill past the remaining cypress sentinel that had witnessed so much burial in Beirut.

Chapter 21

> "Love gives naught but itself and takes naught but from itself."
> Khalil Gibran

Munir led the way, cutting across the small rise that still hid the car. Skirting around scattered graves hidden now by scraggly untended growth, he suddenly stopped.

Turning, he collided with Rich who reached out to hold his arm. "I was going to tell your father the day he. I'm sorry, Richard. She wouldn't….She can't…"

"She?" Rich interrupted Munir's strange flow of emotion. A feeling deep inside seized him, propelling his thoughts. "She?", he questioned, his hand gripping the muscled arm.

"Muna. She didn't die. She is badly wounded, scarred. She insists you should not know. Made me swear to it. I can't keep this any longer, Richard, but you may not want to see her." His eyes focused ahead to the parked car.

Rich released his hold and stumbled up the rise, tripping on a buried headstone. "She's here. She's here?"

Munir nodded. "In the car. But she's…."

Rich was striding ahead down the slope where the small car was parked. There was no one in the front seat. A quick motion on the other side. The rear door opened and a figure covered with a blue scarf scrambled to escape back down the road. Rich's long-gaited run brought him to her side. He reached for her right arm. A cry of pain sounded under the scarf as he realized the arm was lifeless, soft and dangling. Releasing it, he still needed to hold her. His hand grasped her around the waist.

"Muna. Oh, Muna! You're alive. You're here. Why didn't you let me know?" There was no answer. Her left hand held the sheer scarf tightly at her neck. He bent his head close, seeing vaguely the memory of her face. Clasping her close, he whispered his pleas, his love.

The nearness, the familiar beloved smell erased his long months of mourning. She was murmuring something. "Oh, Munir, why have you brought him back to me. You promised. I can't show him my face. I can't even bear to see it myself." The words were muffled by the scarf and Rich tried to remove it. But she grasped it desperately, turning her right side away.

"I love you, Muna. Not just your face...or your arms. I won't leave without you. Not this time."

"Muna, he loves you. Richard is...I couldn't let him go on thinking..." Munir stroked her scarf-covered hair and tried to loosen her grip of the silky cloth. "It's only her right side, Richard. And her right arm. The AUB doctor says it can be repaired."

Rich released his hold, stepping back. "I can't leave without you, Muna. I've left my father here. I won't leave you. I love you. Remember what I told you about love, the most important thing in my life?"

Turning to face him, her body stiffening, she spoke in the cool commanding voice she'd used when telling him they must part. "I can't stand showing myself to you, Rich. But if it will help you to understand why I can't go with you, I will. It's not just you that would see me this way. All the others in your life. I can't bear being so ugly, someone people can't look at, someone they pity." With her good left hand she swept the scarf clear of her head and turned her head so the scars and lacerations of the right side, the deformed earlobe, the damaged nose and the scar tissue partially covering her eyebrow. All shared the brutal revealing spotlight of the midday sun.

Rich's shock was deep within but his expression didn't change. To remember a person so classically beautiful and then see the awful destruction of that beauty by man's violence was to stare into hell itself. Rich reached and took her into his arms, holding her close with his face against her unblemished cheek. Then he moved to embrace the scarred half of her face. She tried to shrink from him but he persisted.

Finally, she relaxed. He knew the roughness of his cheek against the still-tender surgical scars must be painful but she had to know he loved all of that face. "You're beautiful, Muna. You'll always be beautiful. This doesn't matter. We'll work this out together."

They stood, embracing, he not wanting to let go and Muna thinking "If I could go through life in this embrace no one would see my awful face." She broke away. "Someday when all the surgery is finished…"

Munir reached to embrace her. "Yes, when we…"

Rich interrupted, "But you can't have the surgery here. We'll go to the States. They do wonders, Muna."

"You're leaving today, Rich. But I must find a way to get her away from this Beirut madness."

"Oh, no. I can change my departure. We will go together. Can you get papers for her? Her medical records? Lanser will help us get to Cyprus, I'm sure." He released Muna but still held her left hand. "I'll come with you to get her things."

"But you have to return with the ICRC, don't you? I'll bring her to you tomorrow", Munir promised.

"No, Munir. I'm going with you. I won't be separated again. I'll sleep at your aunt's if necessary. We can leave tomorrow."

Muna again draped the scarf over her head as he helped her into the small car. They drove in silence to the Red Cross Land Rover and Rich explained the situation to Lanser.

"We'll have to get Liaison working on this." Then, aside to Richard, "Are you sure you want this to happen so soon?"

"I'm certain, Heinz. We're all certain."

The gruff older man didn't fully understand but could see the emotion of both Rich and Munir. It was something he could do for David. "We'll do it. You're a lot like your father, Rich."

#########

Munir gunned the motor down the hill and out of the cemetery, finding the unguarded alternate streets that would take them to Fawzia's home. He was thinking of his father and of Richard's. Both would be happy about this.

The End

Epilogue

JERUSALEM December, 1982

The city spread before him, an intricate tapestry of man's struggles for his God. The morning chill relaxed its hold as warm fingers of sun found and caressed the heaven-reaching minarets and cypress trees that accented the history-worn hills. Munir's gaze sought the undisturbed rock of the landscape, ignoring the incongruous modern towers that now scarred the horizon. The soul-waking voice from the Haram al Sharif below had called forth its cadence for the day and then given way to comforting echoes from the city's other mosques. Now the bells of the churches would receive the day and announce its benefits, its beckonings. At this hour, Jerusalem was Muslim and Christian and one could forget the successes of the Zionist takeover.

He stood with feet apart, relaxed and feeling the warmth, the pulsing peace of his homeland. The gold-tinted morning melted melancholy and offered optimism. Munir took of it gladly, if only for the moment, breathing deeply of the cold pure air and silence, benisons that would soon give way to the day's traffic and turmoil. The strange aura of Jerusalem he'd remembered from youth was still there, an upreaching mystery of light and hope. Perhaps Father Leonardo, his boyhood teacher, was right: Christ had left his halo over Jerusalem.

"Al Quds", meaning "The Holy". Munir whispered the Arabic name of the city with reverence. They had tried to modernize, but the strength of its pastoral landscape prevailed. The Jordanian-built hotel outside of which he now waited to begin the day's work had barely disturbed the placid profile of the Mount of Olives. Even the stark fortress-like apartment blocks that the Israelis had built on the city heights could not disturb the symmetry and order of this placid landscape. Could any architect, builder or government destroy the soul-stirring quality of Jerusalem? Those who had built the inarticulate monstrosities of the Byzantine occupation didn't change the spirit of the city and today's rulers couldn't.

He began the simple tasks he'd been assigned, nurturing the hotel garden, pruning the roses but often looking up to feast on the panoramic view that spread out from the old city immediately below. It was a new experience, this work. Digging his hands into the earth of Palestine seemed to sustain and strengthen him, to heal the wounds of the years in Lebanon. He worked to the edge of the terraced garden, overlooking the wide highway curving up to the entrance past rocky Jewish cemeteries now restored after years of Arab neglect and desecration. His father would have been pleased to see these graveyards tended and respected again. The sun reflected on the bright gold of the Dome of the Rock and revealed the richly-colored tiles of this Mosque of Omar which crowned the old city.

The layers that history had built there made it difficult to picture the tragic figure of Abraham leading his fine young son, Ishmael—not Isaac as the Jews believed—up the escarpment to the sacrificial rock. Or to imagine Jesus, in sudden anger, upsetting the stalls of the merchants and moneychangers in the great temple. Or to picture Mohammad answering God's call as he raced the white steed Buraq into the heavens from the rock. But Munir could envision the young warrior-caliph Omar as he joined his soldiers in the back-breaking work of clearing rubble and garbage from the Holy site and building the Al Aqsa Mosque, Islam's earliest shrine.

Why couldn't all this history, this religion, bind men together on that stark plateau of the revered city, instead of setting them at each other's throats? His father had said that if a man could understand the history of Jerusalem he could know God. "And if you know God, you will know and understand yourself, my son." Was this why he had returned after sixteen years to the place that had shaped him and then so completely claimed him? Since his parents' death in 1971 after their unhappy exile in Karameh, Amman and finally London, Munir's every waking hour had been devoted to and controlled by the resistance. Now, finally, he was free of their imposed dogma.

Sixty-seven had seen the captivity, the enslavement of Palestine and the world had allowed it. But it had also given life to the resistance movement. The six-day war had conceived the external Palestine liberation effort and now Israel's entry into Lebanon's civil war was killing it. Liberation was now controlled by Arab regimes with agendas of their own. Some new initiative, some germ of Palestinan rebirth must be found. But where? There were no longer any answers to be found in Lebanon, in Syria, in Jordan or Egypt. Tal Zaatar, Sabra, Shatila, tragedies that would haunt Palestinians forever, had convinced Munir there had to be a better way. Tel Zaatar's merciless siege, starvation and slaughter was worse than Sabra or Shatilla for Munir because he'd been one of the "responsibles"; why hadn't he stopped the killing, insisted on surrender?

The memories murmured constantly in his mind. The empty, haunting eyes of the children; especially the ragged puny little girls trying to bring some playtime pleasure into the camp's daily horror. The heroic, ignorant mothers who were so easily talked into supporting the suffering and sacrificing their young for the stubbornness of the leaders.

An awful self-indictment had daily gathered more evidence of his own responsibility and guilt. The years had passed somehow but the scabs of healing daily work were always picked away by the night's remembering and reviewing.

And always at night his mind relived the awful unnecessary plight of his sister, Muna, scarred and crippled in the bomb-trap set by his comrade, Ibrahim. Another wound that would not heal. At least she was safe now in the States. She and Rich had sent pictures showing the almost perfect reconstruction of her face. Even the arm had been restored. They wanted him to settle in California.

Abu Khalil, the Front leader had told him when Muna left Beirut that he was now "The perfect Feda'i, no loved ones to hold you back and hatred in your every fiber". Hatred was there, alright. But not the angry spite that had once motivated his militance against the Zionist occupiers. He knew now the deeper hatred brought by betrayal. The conniving and self-serving Arab leaders who pursued their own interests behind the screen of rhetoric and negotiations. The PLO politicians who pretended a power they no longer possessed. The Front leaders, more disunited than ever, with their underhanded dealings and unproductive terrorist missions that accomplished nothing except the sacrifice of more lives. The millions in tribute paid by the Gulf states to buy patriotic prestige and political safety.

But more than all of this was his distrust of the American government. He couldn't possibly go to America, not even for a visit. Without American backing, Israel would have had to settle their differences, live with their Arab neighbors and allow self-determination for Palestinians. His hopes had soared after the Sadat initiative and Carter's Egypt-Israel accords. When Begin immediately broke the agreement, building dozens of new settlements and Carter didn't act to stop them, he'd realized the U.S. couldn't be counted on.

Now, with the actor-President willing to support Israel's massive invasion of Lebanon he had stopped hoping. Lebanon had taught all of them that liberation of the West Bank and Gaza couldn't be accomplished from outside. The Liberation movement was buried in the Beirut rubble and now, even the PLO weaklings were forced out of Lebanon. There was no longer a border for the Front to use.

So the only answer had been to return to his Palestine.

He'd come to find solutions, at least for himself if not for his people. Six months of planning for a new identity and a faked death to deceive the Front had brought him over the border and through the initial

Israeli screening. Knowing full well what the Mossad would do with a high-profile Rejection Front leader if they discovered him, he had to plan each day with intricate discipline, governed by fear.

Munir had learned to isolate his fear, this trauma that lies deep in every man's mind, ready to cut off access to the nerves and muscles, even to the reasoning process. His resistance experience had taught him fear could be controlled, dominated, even used. It was now the regulator, the signal system which had governed his every action as a Feda'i. His reasoning came out of this higher power system, which activated the hook-up to his decisions. Thus he had full confidence in this land filled with enemies. Discovered, he would face torture and execution. Knowledge of this had priority in every action of every day.

He continued his digging, as if he could somehow dig answers out of this unyielding Mount of Olives. The trowel hit rock, the almost barren rock that is everywhere in Palestine. The earth might now be Israel's but the rock was Palestine. Unyielding, unfruitful but also unsubmissive, unconquerable.

Standing to view again the sacred city, Munir's eyes took in the gravestones below and he vowed that he would be buried in Palestine. The peace of Jerusalem as it awakened to the new day gave promise. Deep within his consciousness, answers were forming. One word filled his mind: INTIFADHA. The shivering. The shaking off of the intolerable weight suffocating his Palestine. He would be patient but they must win this time.